The Lion of Blacklaw Tower

Highlander: The Legends, Volume 2

Rebecca Ruger

Published by Rebecca Ruger, 2022.

This is a work of fiction. Names, character, places, and incidents are either a product of the author's imagination are used fictitiously, and any resemblance to actual persons, living or dead, events, or locales is entirely coincidental. Some creative license may have been taken with exact dates and locations to better serve the plot and pacing of the novel.

ISBN: 9798362905170
The Lion of Blacklaw Tower
All Rights Reserved.
Copyright © 2022 Rebecca Ruger
Written by Rebecca Ruger

All rights reserved. No part of this publication may be reproduced,
distributed or transmitted in any form or by any means,
or stored in a database or retrieval system,
without the prior written permission of the publisher.
Disclaimer: The material in this book is for mature audiences only
and may contain graphic content.
It is intended only for those aged 18 and older.

Chapter One

Lanark, Scotland
Spring, 1307

"And where would you be going?"

Ava Guthrie startled and spun around, the hood with which she'd strategically covered her head falling off one side. Relief came quickly when she spied her friend, Innes, standing in the shadows of the closes between two buildings.

She righted the hood, pulling it tighter around her face, concealing the wealth of dark brown hair within as she dashed into the shadows with Innes.

"Never you mind that," she whispered at him in response to his query, their eyes the only glittering thing in this alley at midnight. "And what are you up to, lurking nae better than any bluidy English, leering and sneering all the day long?"

"Never you mind that," he shot back, one dark brow lifted in challenge, to see if she would bark at him for using the same reply she had. "Ava, you might cover yer hair but there's naught to be done about the way you move. Nae right-minded man—English or nae—would mistake you for a lad, despite yer slight figure. Pulling the skirts tight against you dinna make them breeches, you ken. If you are seen, and without papers to give you reason, 'twill nae be—"

"Then it would behoove me nae to be seen," she returned pertly, "and that means going alone. One is more easily overlooked than two." She darted from the wall and across Wellgate

Lane and gritted her teeth when she heard movement behind her, knowing Innes had followed her anyway. When she'd taken cover once more and Innes had come swiftly, slamming his back against the wall beside her, she turned a scowl upon him.

"And let you have all the fun?" he asked quietly.

"What I thieve is my own," she warned. "I will nae share." As it was, whatever prize she might pilfer tonight was already promised to another.

"Stingy, you are, and dinna I ken it."

"Innes Seàrlas, go on with you, ere you get me caught out past curfew."

"'Tis naught but your constant chirping'll get you caught now."

Ava rolled her eyes and hissed at him, "Is nae Caitir expecting you? Or is that big belly of hers you made nae to your liking?"

Ava was well-accustomed to Innes' arrogant smirks and his sometimes quick anger. He showed the latter just now, the former erased right quick with Ava's question.

"I had nae anything to do with that, as well you ken," he insisted hotly.

Innes Seàrlas was a compact, tightly wound man, not much taller than Ava, and wiry in the sense that his muscles forever seemed coiled, ready to burst into action. His dark hair was not thin but was dispassionately straight and fell so often onto his forehead or into his eyes that a regular characteristic of his was to tip his head forward before swinging it back to throw all the hair off his face. He did this a hundred times a day at least.

"I ken nae anything," Ava said to him, barely above a whisper, "but that for weeks and weeks you were sweet on her and then—"

Innes pulled himself away from the wall to put his face close to Ava's. "If it's jealous you are, Ava, you ken there's nae reason to be. Say the word, and I'll be—"

Ava cut off Innes' teasing, not heard only for the first time now, with a hand over his mouth when she picked up on sloppy, lumbering footfalls heading their way. *Sweet St. Andrew*, she cursed inwardly. *What more this night!*

Just as Innes went completely still, realizing the noise as well, Ava peered around the corner of Eduard Dwelly's townhouse, having only a second to spare to recognize the coming nighttime prowler by his lumbering gait. She stretched out her arm to haul him into the shadows with her and Innes.

Hamish yipped a little start of fright at the same time Innes grumbled, "Bluidy hades, Hamish!"

"What? I was only—"

Ava and Innes shushed him at once. Everything about the lad was big—his body, his head, his heart, and his voice. Whispering was simply not something he was capable of.

And then, in typical Hamish fashion, he smiled down at Ava and Innes. "Hey, what are you two doing oot and aboot?"

Still not a whisper, but improved, the level of sound.

Before Innes could answer, Ava did, softly but firmly. "I am about my own business and it's nae any of yours. Or his." To Innes, she suggested, "You might better see him returned, rather than wasting your time following me."

Innes scowled anew. As a regular practice, he was usually the one who gave orders within the loosely connected and sometimes familial band of homeless persons who dwelled inside Lanark and occasionally worked or laid their pallets side by side when necessity demanded. But there were no steadfast rules in their world, roles could easily be upended, all of them under the thumb of the English for years now. So when Ava took off, out from the shadows to cross another dimly lit lane, Innes neither protested nor followed. Like Ava, he had a soft spot for Hamish, who was purely too innocent in a simple sort of way to not find himself in trouble if left to his own devices. Innes would not abandon him now. She'd hear tomorrow what he was about tonight. And likely they both would have some idea what she was about.

She could fend for herself, and had been for years now, since the English had come and the women weavers, with whom she'd found work—paid for in meals and the occasional odd garment thrown her way, and a place to lay her head in the same part of the house as Dottie Og kept her hens, and her mean goat, and that lone sow until the English had confiscated the pig—had cited the tightening of the English belt around them as a means to shoo her away; they hadn't anymore the means to provide for her.

Somewhere near, perhaps only a street away, the low growl of a dog sounded, though not close enough to worry Ava. The snarl erupted into a full and angry bark, which might well assist Ava if any of the guard went toward that sound to investigate, while Ava steered away from it.

She made her way past the parish kirk and toward the northernmost vennel, this narrow lane the darkest of any inside the walled town. The granary sat at the end of the lane and all the communal grains, which at one time had served the town itself but now belonged to the English and were doled out thinly, were kept there in that round wooden barn. More than a year ago, Innes and Ava and another, simply known as Bean and who had since moved on from Lanark, had tunneled out a good portion of the ground beneath the timber building, large enough only for one person to slither through, and small enough to easily be concealed by pine boughs and other brush.

It was rather a regular practice of Ava's to pilfer a bit of grain from this store several times a week. More often than not, the proceeds went directly to Evir Bullock, who had six bairns to feed and none to help, her husband having been strung up at Gallow Hill more than a year ago after a drunken brawl with an equally inebriated English guardsman. Ava never took more than what might be concealed inside her threadbare cloak or easily tossed away if she should ever be caught, never enough that its loss might be noted from the supply source. In return for her generosity, Ava knew she could depend on a few bannocks come her way at least once or twice during the week. And almost a month ago, when Innes had left three plump hares at Evir's door one morning, Ava and Innes had been invited to sup that night with the Bullock brood. 'Twas the first time in years either Innes or Ava had taken a meal indoors, upon a bench, the fare served upon wooden trenchers.

As ever, Ava encountered no trouble gaining entry to the barn full of grain. By now, after dozens of occasions of this exact thievery, she knew that the English bailiff who oversaw the shed during the day either didn't know or didn't care about proper storage, that he never rotated the crop yield so that the oldest grains were always used first. Thus, despite the near complete darkness inside the slanted roof storage shed, Ava easily made her way straight from the burrowed hole at the west side of the building to the freshest stores near the doors at the east side. Quickly and quietly, she filled the worn jute pouch she'd retrieved from Evir's windowsill two days ago with threshed grain from a full drum barrel closest to the door.

Never more than a minute would pass from the time she entered the silo until she slid out between the tunneled earth and the bottom of the wall with booty in hand, and she always went head first upon her exit so that she wasn't surprised by any wandering guard. Tonight, however, her one minute was well used as she found herself stuck, wedged in that tight space. She must have unearthed and collapsed a bit of ground when she'd entered, filling the hole a bit, as her narrow hips now did not easily glide through the suddenly narrower opening.

"God's bones," she cursed, tossing the jute pouch ahead of her so that she could leverage both hands against the frosty ground and wiggle herself as needed to escape. It took quite some doing to squirm free of the space and then the hem of her léine was caught, snagged on the jagged underside of the wooden siding, eliciting another exasperated expletive from Ava before she was able to extricate herself completely.

Perspiring now with anxiety for too much time wasted, despite the crisp chill in the night air, Ava finally got to her feet and retrieved the pouch of grain, only then to be confronted by not one but two of the town's night watch, lucky Englishmen who only happened to be at this exact moment walking the perimeter of the walled burgh.

She froze, hoping they could not make her out from twenty feet away, as she was garbed sedately and stood with her back to the darkened side of the granary. She supposed she oughtn't consider her luck so unfortunate on the whole; this would be in fact the first time she'd ever been discovered at the granary after dozens and dozens of expeditions.

So nae, they did not overlook her, but came straightaway to her, one of them calling out, "Here now, what's this?"

Ava focused first on the speaker but finding him younger and smaller—mayhap greener—she guessed that any hope of escape might well lie with the second man, older, perhaps more proficient at sniffing out lawlessness, presently showing more suspicion than the younger man's mere surprise. Thus, she turned her smile onto him as the men came within three feet of her.

However, before she might have spewed forth some hastily imagined tale, giving her presence here and now some profound defense, which might see her duly chastised but only sent on her way, the older of the two soldier's frown of suspicion lightened with some impreciseness, before it evolved into a debauched leer that raised gooseflesh on Ava's neck.

"Got ourselves a thief in the night," he said.

Instinct screamed at her to run, but mayhap instinct played itself plainly across her face, on which the man focused with a great and deliberate menace, so that he acted swiftly to prevent her from fleeing, closing the distance between them and taking up her arm in a bruising grip.

"And I know just what to do with a thief such as this," said the soldier. "Ill-regard for the rule of law will be quickly forgotten when I get between your legs."

Ava blanched, realizing a fright such as she'd not known in a long, long time, which was then multiplied by disgust as the man dragged her up against him and ran his tongue over her face. He might have been aiming for her mouth, but Ava jerked her face away at the last second so that his tongue scoured her cheek, up to her temple, wet and beyond distasteful for the stench of his breath. She struggled in his grasp, wanting to free her arm, though escape seemed unlikely, his hold being so inflexible. Oh, how she wished she'd not rejected Innes' company.

"Good swiving is what you need, luv," he rasped at her, grinding his pelvis against her in an unseemly but unmistakable fashion. "A taste of my prick'll cure you of bad habits."

Ava fought against him with greater vigor now, unconcerned that she might be charged, in addition to thievery, with a crime against the Crown, as any assault on one of its soldiers was named—and punishable by hanging.

The younger man only stood idly by, actually taking a step out of the way as the more seasoned and despicable soldier wrestled to control Ava's flailing arms and kicking legs.

Screaming would not help, she knew, would only bring more of his kind, those Englishmen eager to demonstrate their power over the defenseless. More than anything, Ava did not want to be raped; greater than that, though, she did not want to be violated by many.

At the exact moment she was able to rake her fingers across the man's face, she saw a third man enter her periphery. A whimper escaped now, her chances of avoiding the hell sure to come dwindling—until the newcomer laid low the young soldier with a whack to the side of his head, using the blunt end of the hilt of his sword, which dropped the lad instantly.

The man attacking her, enraged by her scratching, which broke skin in lines across his face, was startled as he straightened and growled at her. He, too, caught sight of the third man and then his fallen comrade. In one swift move, he thrust Ava away from him and swung around to confront the newcomer, drawing his thin English blade.

Ava was pushed to the ground, collapsing in a wobbly heap, barely managing to put her hands down to prevent herself from landing face first. She lifted her frightened gaze to the action in front of her. A man she'd never seen before, though whose size and extraordinary presence should have warranted much attention despite the rough peasant garb, now squared off against the one who'd meant to attack her.

Ava scrambled backwards at the same time she realized the never-before-seen peasant had brought a wee dagger to a sword fight. The Englishman who would have violated her smirked his pleasure at this reckoning. To Ava's amazement, the unknown peasant smirked in return, his façade more chilling for how lazily sure he was of himself. There was almost a curl to his lip, seeming to enjoy the fact that the Englishman believed himself in possession of the upper hand.

Mayhap the soldier perceived the arrogance of that smirk as well and thought he might better call for assistance, which he did, though his shout was cut short by the peasant's lunging at him.

Ah, here was a true fighter, a warrior, nae only some inept and mouthy abuser of women. The peasant moved with sure grace; this not his first fight at close range.

Ava was only briefly distracted by an anxious, "Psst!" come from somewhere close. She found Innes standing in the gray shadows of the back of another building not twenty feet away, waving at her to make haste and get away. She could not though, being so entranced by the actions of the stranger in the peasant garb who handled his long, silver-hilted dagger with such casual ease. In the bleak gloom of the midnight hour, he stood a full head taller and much broader than the vile soldier and yet danced around him with a grace only a well-trained, well-used warrior should possess.

They dodged and parried and danced around each other until Ava began to believe her shadowy savior only toyed with the English guard.

Mayhap the Englishman was not without his own combat resources—or maybe desperation imbued a man to call upon assets he'd not ever before made use of. But surely he must have realized, same as Ava had, that the peasant looked decidedly—alarmingly—at ease with that dagger, in the way he tossed it so effortlessly from hand to hand when the guard had slashed at him with his sword.

When they finally came to serious blows, the fight was swift. The Englishman, possibly believing he had not another choice, despite the much longer blade in his hand, simply launched himself at the imposing peasant, didn't even bother to lead with his thin sword. There was no tussle, though, since the man had essentially run into the stranger's blade, embedding it into his own heart it seemed.

The peasant man cursed, not without vigor though it came as a hiss, "Bluidy bollocks!" He retrieved his dagger from the man's chest, holding up both his hands and the bloody knife at the same height as his face as if to say he was guilty of no crime. The wounded man stared, his eyes shimmering in the shadows, mayhap filling with tears, before his legs buckled and he crumpled slowly to the ground.

Aghast and stricken with horror at this unexpected and foul turn, Ava blinked several times and then squeaked out a cry when the peasant turned toward her.

What she feared now, she could not say, but it propelled her to her feet. And she hadn't realized that she'd dropped the pouch of grain until now, when the man approached her and bent to collect it, presenting it to Ava, standing within reach. Mechanically, she reached out her hand for the stolen goods. Blindly her fingers found the rough jute of the sack, her gaze transfixed by the shadowy figure who stood in front of her.

An odd tingle of consciousness rose in her, not as hairs standing on end at her nape to warn her of malevolence, but as a breath-stopping sensation of awareness of another.

He stood tall and straight, possibly as much as a foot taller than her, crowned in short wavy hair as dark as hers and owning shoulders wider than two of her.

Their hands were still connected by the cinched pouch as Ava considered him, her face tilted upward as he stood so close. He just stared, that was all, his compelling dark gaze seeming to take in the whole of her face with a frank and raking glance, to which she responded by blushing furiously. And though she was sure 'twas too dark to see the embarrassing stain across her cheeks, a slow smile spread across his hard features, softening him to near beauty.

His lips, raised just now in suspicious humor, were neither too thin nor too thick, settled neatly upon a perfectly set line of white teeth shown by his untimely smile; his chin and jaw were chiseled well, square and covered in many days growth of stubble. He was, on the whole, quite pleasing to regard, 'twas only that his manner left so much to be mistrusted, Ava thought—killing people and then grinning so...provocatively at her! Who was this man?

She inhaled sharply, well aware that she was becoming undone by his smile, which did not leer at all as the dead Englishman's had but seemed to profess some pleasure to have unsettled her.

Greatly flustered now, she tugged gently at the pouch, which was released to her possession. The man who had just killed for her remained as he was, smiling still at her, definitely finding amusement in her disturbed state.

Disturbed indeed! Enough so that the coming of others—more English guards—escaped her notice until it was too late, until a flash of movement to his right widened her eyes. Everything happened so fast. In shock, Ava covered her mouth and swallowed her yip of fright as the man was brought to his knees by a blow to his head.

A hand grabbed at her arm, turning her head as three soldiers pounced upon the fallen peasant.

Innes had come, was tugging desperately at her arm and wearing a stern look as he dragged her off into the night.

Chapter Two

"Three days of hell I've been through," Ava ground out at Innes, "and cease, will you nae, telling me to quit my haivering! A man is about to hang—for me! For my petty crimes, and for what I've done!"

"'Twas nae you who stabbed your knife through the guard's heart," Innes reasoned—not for the first time, and to little effect.

"Innes, please," Ava begged, covering her forehead with one hand. "Just help me think. What should I do?"

Innes shrugged, rightfully much less affected than Ava was, and slumped into the pew in front of her in the nave at St. Kentigern's church, where they sometimes met and sought the counsel of the young and patriotic Father Valentine Turing.

Father Val was not to be found, but that was not unusual as he was often busy throughout the town and indeed, the entire parish. The soft spoken priest might very well at this moment be consulting the prisoner, hearing his last confession.

Innes turned in front of her, laying his arm along the back of the pew. "Ava," he said, his tone suggesting more concern for her plight than he'd previously demonstrated, "you canna break the man out from the prison at the castle. Likewise, once the cart begins to move toward Gallow Hill, 'tis nothing to be done. Aye, it's shameful—but that's nae on you. You dinna ask the man to interfere. You dinna...."

Ava closed her eyes in despair and tuned him out, having heard these arguments before. Innes couldn't understand. Only vaguely did she acknowledge that given a swap of circumstances, she too might employ such generic reason to make him appreciate the choice had not been his, to lessen the resounding guilt that would no doubt gnaw at him same as it did at her right now.

But she could not only bow her head and submit to this as the outcome, that a man whose name she did not even know, whose smile had curled her toes so deliciously, would hang in a few hours' time, having gallantly saved her from what surely would have been a vicious assault. 'Twas nae right. Nae just!

Indignation and that heavy mantle of a guilty conscience propelled Ava sharply to her feet, cutting off Innes.

"Naught will be achieved sitting in the kirk," she advised. Certainly since she hadn't been praying.

Innes stood as well, stepping out into the aisle with Ava. "*Jesu*, but what are you planning now?"

Her eyes watered but she did not allow tears to fall though helplessness overwhelmed her. "I have nae idea. But Innes, whatever I do—stay away from it. I can nae have harm brought to another in my stead. Whatever will be—"

Ava paused and both she and Innes turned toward the west as a shaft of gray light appeared in the narthex. The unmistakable figure of Hamish appeared there in the entryway, softly closing the thick wooden door behind him. As ever, the pale, round face of the overgrown lad was lightened by a simple smile when he spied his friends.

"Ken I'd find you here," said Hamish, his grin easy. He lumbered forward, his big upper body moving generously left and then right with every step. "But we should go now. They're crowding already, on High Street and Gallow Hill." He frowned suddenly, his thick forehead drooping down over his narrow eyes, looking from Ava's watery eyes to Innes' grim countenance. "Dinna...dinna we want to be close, to see the hanging?"

Ava sighed and shook her head. Poor Hamish, ever without a clue. Simply born that way—or as Dottie Og had alleged more than once, dropped too many times upon his head as a bairn—he beat whatever drum the town marched to, adopting whatever opinions were put to him, whether they be foul or good. Occasionally, this might find the big oaf of a lad seemingly in concert with their English overlords, merely parroting what edicts and views were heralded by the governing body and then taken up and repeated by residents too fearful to gainsay them. Thankfully, Hamish was usually and simply corrected by a few choice words from Ava, for whom he held dear a quiet devotion.

"Nae, Hamish, we dinna want this man to hang," she told him. "He rescued me from...certain disaster and his hanging should nae be celebrated."

Hamish's big round shoulders sagged dramatically, and he lowered his gaze to the huge, fleshy hand at his side, from which dangled a dirty scrap of linen, the corners bunched inside his fist, the end of it obviously weighted down with something hefty.

"Have you rocks in there?" Innes asked.

Hamish nodded.

"Meant to hurl at the prisoner?"

Another nod, while he kept his gaze downcast. "I ken he was bad."

Carelessly, filled with so much agitation, Ava muttered, "Better they find their mark with the English today, Hamish." She faced Innes again, considering the blue eyes he turned her way. "Keep him in hand. And dinna mind what I am about."

With that, she turned and left the church, touching Hamish's arm affectionately as she passed.

Innes called after her, his tone annoyed, "You dinna ken yourself what you are about! Dinna be foolish on account of a stranger to you and all of Lanark!"

Outside, greeted by a gray and turbulent dawn sky, Ava flipped her hood once more over her head and made her way along the dirt road toward the better packed ground of High Street, blending in there with dozens and dozens of curiosity-seekers, cruel people she decided uncharitably, roused from their beds with glad hearts, eager to take part in the melee and general enthusiasm of a hanging.

She wanted to hate these people, ducking out of their houses so early, abandoning the day's labor to bear witness to the hanging of a noble man. But then she'd lived so many years among them that she understood, at least partly, that much of their supposed glee was only relief that trouble and peril had found a home in someone else—even better a stranger. 'Twas hard enough to live inside a town occupied by petty and vindictive foreigners, that they had little tolerance for criminals coming to make more trouble inside their domain. The townspeople's tolerance of murderers apparently spanned across the national divide, these people pretending a great affront that one of their besiegers had been killed. They didn't know, though, what he had done—either offender or savior—and thus she couldn't hate them for cleaving to whatever the bully English spewed as their current cause, the townsfolk being removed themselves as the bully's target.

Of course, she assumed her savior noble based on his actions, knew nothing of his birthright or heritage. He'd been dressed as plainly as she, in coarse wool and wearing for a while a face-darkening hood, until that had been whipped off his head as he'd faced an enemy. Only belatedly, when she'd been well-free from the tragedy near the granary, did she recall how fine were his deerskin brogues. They were not worn and threadbare, were not patched willy-nilly, repaired so often to contain only ghosts of their original forms. Aye, that had not registered with her immediately, Ava herself having been so invested in her shock at his rescue and then in her first awestruck impression of him, a warrior true, of great height and breadth with dark hair made golden by midnight's bare light and eyes that glittered with savage intensity for that one brief moment when she'd met them.

And then his smile....

Oh, but he should not die. Nae for her!

The sheriff's court of yesterday had been a closed affair, and though word traveled about town usually as swiftly as would a sparrow from limb to limb, nothing had been passed along but conjecture, the details of the court—and the prisoner's identity—kept hidden from the denizens of Lanark. And though Ava had several times gone to the kirk seeking Father Val, expecting him to have been in attendance, she had not encountered him once.

The sheriff himself, Walter de Burghdon, though not unknown to the townspeople, was a figure seen but rarely. While his soldiers garrisoned in the castle at the edge of town, he'd taken possession of a fine home just outside of town, beyond the River Clyde. What Ava had known—that a prisoner was in hand—the townspeople did not, not until the arrival of Sheriff de Burghdon on his fancy stallion, when speculation became the day's work. Conjecture was soon rewarded, when late in the morning, the sheriff had departed the walled town. Shortly after that four men, carpenters all, made haste to Gallow Hill. There, they'd made rapid repairs to the platform, which had suffered considerable damage three weeks past when the town's communally owned bull, Lachie, had escaped his pen and wreaked havoc for many hours. Before he was wrangled, that requiring seven different ropes held by almost a dozen men, he'd caused much destruction—to homes, wattle fences, market stalls, and lastly to one of the thick posts supporting the platform of the gallows. When he'd rammed his thick, curvy horn into that vertical beam, the timber platform had collapsed, slowly at first, only listing precariously until the bull's attention had been captured elsewhere and the front corner of the platform had fallen, all connected planks dropping one after another to the ground, a cloud of dry dirt dust risen to add an exclamation to that demolition.

But aye, though the carpenters had been told nothing, little was left to question save for the identity of the criminal charged and his crime, the latter of which neither Ava nor Innes had shared with any.

Within fifteen minutes of her reaching the square in front of the recently repaired gallows, the presence of the armed garrison already heavily seen and felt, the crowd was large, suggesting the town proper might well be abandoned completely. Entrepreneurial sorts sold eggs and milk and butter; a group of rowdy lads harangued and harassed any who stood too close or happened by, their disdain not exclusive to any one gender, age, or occupation; a group of the town's most prominent womenfolk, glorified more so in their own minds, stood with chins raised and lips thinned, judgment having been passed by now; dogs barked and bairns wailed, while the din of the throng remained mostly sedate, riled still with questions and not yet with contempt aimed particularly at the man about to be hanged. That would come when he did.

Another long quarter of an hour was suffered through, Ava still having no idea what she might do—if anything—or if she were brave enough for what seemed the only recourse available to her. Actually, there might be two possible options available to her to see the wrong righted, so that no man was made to pay for her sins. Her palm was sweaty now, for having clamped her small knife so ferociously for the last half an hour; she didn't know what might be done with her small dirk, nor even if she had the courage to use it, but she felt closer to having some response to injustice with the wooden hilt in her hand. Otherwise, the only other solution she could imagine would be to announce her presence and her identity as the thief in question. She would be compelled to lie and say she herself had killed the English guard. Ava didn't suppose for one second she wouldn't struggle to put out that mistruth; it was the consequence, the imagining of the bailiff unwinding a noose from around the magnificent peasant's neck and looping the heavy cord around her own that infused her with terror.

A last ditch effort, she decided, if no other reasonable idea appeared to her before that should come to pass.

The gray of dawn had dispersed by now, but the later hour showed still an overcast sky, the sun refusing to shine upon so heinous a spectacle. And Ava knew exactly when the prisoner was first presented to the assembled mob though little could she see over all the wool-clad shoulders and heads squeezed so close around her. The sedate crowd erupted into jeers and calls, which reached its fever pitch almost instantly before settling into the familiar raucous, enlivened din of any other angry mob. Ava would never understand why they regularly seemed to enjoy a hanging.

She stood on tiptoe, to no avail, and then was only shown snippets of the procession by bouncing off her feet into the air. The sheriff led the parade, seated as he'd been previously upon that great white stallion. Father Valentine was there as well, on his swaybacked packhorse beside the sheriff, his façade washed to serenity, administered by prayer, Ava imagined. Beyond that rode two more soldiers of the garrison upon fine English coursers and then walked the hulking figure of the black-clad bailiff, his shoulders so wide as appearing to need a different propulsion than his lengthy flanks, the top half of his body moving opposite the bottom while he kept one hand of fingers curled around one bar of the cage alongside which he walked. His mammoth silhouette concealed that of the prisoner for some time that Ava was left to bore holes into the bailiff's pock-ridden face, devoid of any covering to hide his ghastly identity, almost as if he dared someone one day to bring a reckoning to him by showing his face so freely. Beyond the wagon drawn cell, another dozen soldiers walked and would likely take up positions close to the gallows as the crowd was already hemmed in by at least another two score and ten of the castle guards.

And then she saw him, the prisoner.

Upon the flatbed of the drawn wagon, in a cage of metal bars, upon his knees with his hands tied behind his back, the man knelt erect, seemingly unaffected by the poorly sprung cart, not toppled onto his face or smashed against the side rails for the uneven march.

Ava held her breath, putting her hand onto the shoulder of the man in front of her as she hopped again and again off her feet. Little was gleaned, too much distance between she and the man who had saved her life and now would pay with his. She thought only that he appeared to be searching for someone. He did not swivel his head quickly or frantically, but he did turn his gaze about the crowd, and somehow Ava was not compelled to believe he only did so to cast into an iron memory the faces of those wishing death upon him, intending to revisit them one day in hell.

And all the while the crowd jeered at him, called him names, and hurled insults with as much vehemence as they did wilted and rotten produce. Someone lobbed a dead chicken into the air, but it failed to reach its mark by several yards.

Frustrated by the distance between herself and him, and further unnerved by seconds ticking away when she had yet to formulate a plan to save him, Ava pushed between the gawking and heckling onlookers, meaning to get closer to the gallows. She heard her name hollered above the din, and though she recognized Innes' voice she ignored it. He could not help her now, and she didn't want either him or Hamish to be in any way associated with her.

Moving through the unyielding crowd proved more strenuous than imagined and Ava had not gone far when the level of noise increased significantly. A quick lift of her face showed the back of the man walking up the wooden steps to the platform. She paused, arrested by the shape and size of him. The coarse woolen mantle and hood he'd worn the other night were gone, showing a man garbed only in breeches, boots, and a creamy linen tunic. None of this was remarkable in any way, but for the way in which he moved, more easily discernable for the dearth of garments. Even with his hands tied behind his back, he was able to walk with a catlike grace that belied comprehension, and quite honestly, was startling for its arrogance. A man bound to die should not be able to walk so proudly, his head held so high. He just should not.

The distraction was fleeting, though, and Ava began again to wrestle for a better standing within the crowd. She'd barely gained any more ground by the time the sheriff unrolled a wide but short scroll and began to read aloud, lifting his voice so that the nasally sound might carry well as the crime and punishment were declared. He was but a sentence or two within the reading when the very casual mention of the criminal's name drew a belated but then collective gasp from the people closest to the gallows.

***

John Craig stared out through the rusty bars of his cage at the crowd gathering, looking for a pair of eyes slanted as a cat's.

The king was wrong. Robert Bruce had recently advised that John should wed, that he needed to have *someone on whose image you might call to give you both peace and purpose.*

Bah.

Magnus was wrong as well. A woman did not make a man whole or make the war machine he'd become more human.

Women—and the idea of that fabled love that so many were eager to attach to those fair creatures—were naught but trouble. Made a man weak. *Jesu,* look what the quiet lass, Lara, had done to his ever sensible, always sound cousin, Magnus.

John had only departed Lismore a fortnight ago. At the king's summons, come by way of a messenger from the Douglas knight, Sir James, John had been tasked with aiding Douglas in his overtaking of Lanark. Robert Bruce wanted the castle walls torn down and the castle laid to waste, useless then to any ambitious enemy. John and a few of his most trusted men had been the first to enter Lanark two nights ago, simply to scrutinize the town and its defenses. John had done so dressed as a peasant, while keeping in the back of his mind that this place was where William Wallace had first made his name, having killed the sheriff here a decade ago.

He considered his own predicament now. Not quite the same celebrated victory as Wallace in this place, not at all the beginning of a fabled career as one of Scotland's true-hearted warriors. Aye, John's name was already well-known, but he was just now not quite the lion roaring. Nae, he'd go out with a snap of his neck, or worse—and God forbid—a slow and agonizing death, twitching and kicking while the crowd cheered. They were never pleased with a quick death, bloodthirsty bastards.

Having once listened to his king espouse the necessity of a strong and good woman at a man's side to temper the fierce edge of the warrior within, having watched Magnus lay his world and his heart at the feet of Lara—who had never quite warmed up to John, though he knew not why—John now believed more than ever what he'd held as truth for years: women were trouble.

This then, indeed, was the ultimate irony, he supposed. But at least he would die being vindicated by the truth as he knew it: women weakened men, were no good but as breeders and keepers of more men. He'd never met one—whom he had not plied with coin—with whom he'd want to spend any fair amount of time. He didn't know a woman learned in the art of war, who had a head for strategy and swordplay or any other useful occupation or intention. Mayhap excepting Beathag, the old battle-ax; a finer brewer—noble occupation, that—he'd never met. But och, he'd taste no more the brisk, honey mead she made so faithfully for Blacklaw's people.

Instead, he'd hang now and for some lass he'd never met—and for what? A fist-size pouch worth of grain and eyes slanted as a cat's? First time in his life he'd had his head turned by a woman who wasn't selling something, herself or other wares, and this was his reward, an ignoble death.

He sighed and considered the cage in which he rode as the shouts and jeers seeped into his consciousness, overwhelming his self-loathing. He supposed he should be thankful he was not drawn by his feet at the tail of some swaybacked nag; that humiliation was generally reserved for those who acted in greater concert against the English authority, the crown specifically, whereas John was only charged with murder of a lowly English guardsmen. Charged and sentenced without a trial, by the by. Not that it wasn't true. He'd killed that salivating man, would do so again, having freed the cat-eyed woman from his evil clutches and cruel intentions.

The crowd, all Scots save for the heavy presence of the English soldiers, riled John's sour mood even further, for their unabashed delight to see one of their own hang. Fickle, they were, those townspeople under the English thumb. They'd jeer him today and cheer on Sir James Douglas on the morrow, if he made good his pledge to sack the town and free them of the tyranny of the English rule. A different tune they'd be whistling then.

The cart in which he was caged began to move. Apparently the scaffolding they'd erected was too far from the garrison where he'd been imprisoned for him to have simply been marched through the streets on foot. John eagerly scanned every face as he was driven through the sea of people, looking for her, while his jaw ached for how tightly clenched it was, reviling his own idiocy.

Still, he needed to see her. And he'd be right pissed if the shadows of midnight had played her false. He needed her to be glorious and bold, nae foolhardy and helpless. If he were going to die for her, and he was, he needed to know she was worthy of his death. *Jesu*, but do not show him some insipid, lifeless thing who in the light of day was naught but a troll, the slant of her eyes her only redeeming feature.

She was more than that, he knew. He'd been unable to expel her from his mind at any time over the last thirty-six hours. He'd only stumbled upon her, or her upon him, as he'd been hidden between two buildings half past midnight on that day. Her furtiveness then, keeping to the shadows, darting with purpose through the darkened streets had been what first garnered his attention. As his own movements had been the same, he'd been instantly intrigued by the slyness and caution of the figure. Truth be told, he might have only watched the figure dart by, might have hoped that person's schemes, whatever they had been, would draw attention from his own. But as he stood unseen at the stone wall of the apothecary's shop, he'd watched the hooded figure scurry across the torchlit street, moving from one shadowy corner to the next relief of darkness. He'd known straight away 'twas a woman, the figure slight and the movements too lithesome to be that of a man. He'd first been intrigued by the hood falling away from her head, just before she'd disappeared from the dim light, revealing a long and riotous mass of hair, onto which the light of the city's torches had cast a golden glow, albeit briefly before she'd been rendered into shadows as she'd gained the side of the house. When next she moved, the hood had covered her hair again. Before intention had made itself known completely, John's feet had moved, cautiously following her. He'd moved when she had and stopped when she'd stopped, always only one position behind her, from street to street and house to house, from shadow to shadow. When she'd reached the granary at the edge of town and had—fantastically—burrowed between the bottom of the timber wall and earth beneath it, surely a well of space having been previously carved, John had smirked at her daring.

She might not have been caught but that despite her slight frame, she seemed to have gotten stuck upon her exit. A foul and most unladylike curse had been hissed into the night as she fought with whatever held her back, the upper half of her body free but her hips and legs stuck in the slim opening. Her poor luck had continued. Though she'd eventually managed to free herself, wiggling her slender hips aggressively to do so, she'd emerged fully from the building just as two of the English guards had been making their nightly pass, coming round the side of the granary just as she'd gotten to her feet, plucking from the ground the pouch she'd tossed there when she'd been forced to spend time extricating herself.

"Here now, what's this?" Asked the younger of the two English soldiers, rapidly closing in on her.

John, standing directly across from her, with the soldiers' backs to him, had spied over one's shoulder the smile that had lightened her face—so bewitching it had opened John's mouth with wonder, he recalled furiously now—meant to distract them no doubt, but which had done its job too well that any suspicion of criminal activity had been supplanted by reprehensible thoughts. One of those men had caught her hand, jerking her swiftly and forcefully against his body, putting out vulgar words, so that no mistake could have been made of his purpose.

In his mind, John only skimmed over his involvement, his coming and dispatching the two men, one laid out by a thrust from the butt end of his sword while the other, the one who had touched her, had required actual killing for the wee resistance he'd managed. He skipped over that to get to the part in his recall when he'd stood before her, and she'd lifted those catlike eyes to his. Their color was unknown—would now remain so, he presumed—but aye, all of her face was breath-catching.

So aye, 'twas her fault that he was now about to hang. Not because she'd stolen threshed grain for whatever reason—hunger was usually the case—but for owning eyes such as hers that he'd been so distracted as to have not heard or recognized the presence and arrival of three more guardsmen, one who'd visited upon him the same brutality that he'd marked the first soldier with, a blow to the head that had rendered him senseless and immobile.

The last thing he remembered was the widening of her magnificent eyes. Slim fingers had leapt to and covered provocatively shaped lips—that, just before she'd turned and had made her escape as he'd fallen to the ground.

But had memory served him correctly? Was she as comely as he recalled? Ethereal for the way her skin was so flawless and pale, with eyes too large for her face and lips so pouty and sculpted so sensually?

Another aggrieved sigh was expelled as he told himself it didn't matter now.

The prison cart stopped at the base of the gallows, atop which a lone thick rope swayed and waved, moved by a frivolous wind. John said no prayer but for a quickly broken neck as he was led—shoved and prodded—up the wooden steps, his hands bound behind his back. The shouts and screeches of the cruel mob disturbed him not at all. He'd heard worse. A well-met battle produced sounds that put this bloodthirsty caterwauling to shame.

He was actually eager to assume his position under the noose; he would have a clear view of the leering crowd, might well be presented with his best and last chance to see those eyes again. He stood tall and proud, his chin elevated. Next to him, the black-clad bailiff waited on the sheriff. Sadly, while his crime and sentence were read out for all to hear, the sheriff's voice resounding, carrying easily and then quieting the crowd a wee bit, John could not find her.

He did, however, find Eachann, his captain, who had come with him inside the city two nights ago, dressed as John had been as a downtrodden peasant. He stood quietly within the grumbling crowd. Eachann, in his bold and indomitable way, inclined his head solemnly at his laird. John was not sure if he should be advised of a plan to rescue him or if Eachann was only giving a faint and grave fare thee well. This, too, did not matter.

The mob of spectators, walled into the shape of a sloppy circle by the presence of dozens of silver-helmed English soldiers, listened attentively to the charges laid against him, delivered in Longshank's English, much of which some of them possibly could not understand. But for his name, given proudly at the time of the brief court session and called out loudly now, which drew a gasp from many. The gasping went on for several seconds, first directly in front of him and then further back in the crowd. Soon, whispers were heard announcing his other moniker, *the Lion of Blacklaw Tower*, and now a hush was generated, the crowd going still, becoming morose. The hanging of an unknown, a common criminal, albeit a murderer, was cause for celebration; the execution of one of the foremost knights of his age, in service to the true king of Scotland, gave them pause. They might well suffer the English sheriffdom of their city but not any true Scot had given up completely on hope, that freedom would one day be theirs.

Even the sheriff, proclaiming his crimes and sentence, halted his diatribe, read from a prepared scroll, frowned and scanned the crowd, unnerved by their sudden unease. He cleared his throat and continued, enunciating the words *murderer* and *reckoning*. He paused again, this time as the crowd began to whisper more feverishly, all eyes focused on a hooded figure moving through the mass of bodies, the only person walking.

John fixed his gaze on the figure just as the sheriff did. His breath caught once more; he knew it was her.

Clearly, he did not expect any rescue from her, wanted only a glimpse of her, just one more in the light of day.

She moved as if urged by angel's wings, her walk elegant, nearly serene for how graceful were her movements. When she was within twenty feet of the gallows, she lifted her hands and pushed back the coarse beige hood from her hair and face.

Several more gasps spilled forth, so startling was her beauty. As soon as she dropped her hood, she raised her gaze to John. He smiled despite his rage, he could not help himself, as relief flooded him. She was greater and more vibrant than what his memory or the shadows of the night had perceived.

Well worth it, he thought, even as a larger roar of anger churned inside him for what his fate would be.

Chapter Three

John Craig, he was named. How very ordinary a name for so extraordinary a man.

"John Craig!" was whispered again and again, heads turned to deliver this information to those who did not stand close enough to have heard it said first. Almost immediately another name was attached to that very common one: "The Lion of Blacklaw Tower!" was hissed with nearly as much reverence as "Murderer!" had been uttered with such contempt before his identity had been revealed.

And while the crowd was now distracted to stillness with the identity of the man—unknown to Ava, for all the clamorous ballyhoo it had generated all around her—she continued to make her way to the fore. The shouting of the crowd had dissolved into a wary murmuring—whoever was the man, John Craig, suddenly his execution seemed to sit unwell with these people—and at some point Ava's continued movement began to draw attention.

And though she still had no plan to bring about the man's rescue, she understood one thing about herself and the basic premise of creating a diversion. For reasons not entirely known to her, her appearance was often accounted as striking—*disarming*, Father Val had once said; *dangerous to behold*, Innes had teased her; *born of a witch, to be sure*, Dottie Og had charged. Perhaps a disruption might serve the man well. He *had* been searching the faces of the crowd. Were there planted here in this mob those who might essentially see to his rescue if only they could be provided a disturbance?

When she suspected many gazes followed her progress through the crowd, which seemed now to part in advance of her coming, Ava slowly lowered the hood from her hair and showed her face left and right, eliciting as many gasps as had the revelation of the about-to-be-hanged man's name, before lifting her eyes to those who stood atop the scaffolding.

She met straight-on the intense brown eyes of the man called John Craig. Aye, he'd been an impressive shape and savior at midnight, the shadows revealing more of his actions than his person, even when he'd so briefly stood close to her. But now in daylight, albeit under a mean gray sky, he was remarkable. He towered above her, and not only because of his lofty position upon the scaffolding, but for how proud and formidable he managed to appear despite his predicament, which included presently a thick noose around his neck.

Rendered breathless at the sight of him, she was then stunned to see a slow and appreciative smile curve his sensual lips. And while she didn't understand his smile—what was wrong with this man that he would find something either amusing or appealing at this particular ominous moment in his life?—she turned her gaze onto the staggered sheriff.

And mayhap Walter de Burghdon concurred with Father Val, or Innes, or Dottie Og's assessment of her appearance, so stricken was his response, himself still, his mouth open, staring at her as if he doubted she could be real.

"One last kiss, my lord," she begged of the sheriff before he recovered himself. "Before my love is forever wrenched from this life."

The sheriff, while initially as stunned and wordless as any at her appearance, cleared his throat and thought to shoo her away, waving the scroll in her direction, his scowl returned as he recalled his present circumstance. The crowd would have none of it, and began immediately to shout out their anger, with furious calls for mercy. Stones and eggs and other rubbish were lobbed at the sheriff, who cowered and used the scroll to deflect the projectiles. The bailiff stepped forward to the edge of the platform with some attempt at menace, while the soldiers on the ground tightened their circle, some drawing swords. The hatchet-faced bailiff was immediately pegged with so sizeable a rock, Ava was sure it had come from Hamish's stash.

Her heart raced with fright and dread and other debilitating things, and Ava knew she had to act now, before courage deserted her fully. Before the sheriff had given permission, she approached the steps, blocked by a guard there, his hand held in front of her face until the sheriff called out impatiently, "One moment! 'Tis all you will have!"

Ava climbed the wooden steps, which creaked loudly in the growing silence. The knife, still clasped in her sweat-moistened hand, was unseen inside the cloak she wore. She looked at the steps and then at the planks of the platform when she gained that area, and then at the trapdoor of wood that made an outline around John Craig's feet.

And then she stood before him and lifted her gaze slowly upward, over those fine brogues and wool breeches that were not at all threadbare and a tunic that was mayhap a wee snug but was held together by quality seams of thick thread and covered shoulders impossibly broad.

By the time she raised her gaze to his face, her heart was in her throat, her stomach lodged somewhere in her chest.

Oh, but he was simply too beautiful to die.

Thick auburn hair was his crown, disheveled and drooping onto his forehead; a face of rugged beauty despite the bruises near his temple and under one eye, was weathered and loved even by spring's discriminating sun and covered in many days' stubble; his eyes were certainly brown but flecked with gold, striking for their intense perusal. Ah, but the smile he'd worn had turned now, devolved into a sneer of unmistakable contempt, his gorgeous full lips actually curled with disfavor.

Ava's heart lurched and dropped, believing instantly that his genuine and justified disdain would haunt her until her own dying breath.

Right now, she had only a rough idea of a strategy developed, one unlikely to find success, the thought of which gathered tears once more in her eyes. She knew she needed to offer at least something of her guilt-ridden conscience. "I'm sorry," she told him in a broken voice. "That you will lose your life for mine." She could think of nothing else to say and so straightened her spine, rose onto her toes, and pressed her lips to his at the same time she circled her arms around his lean waist.

She did not consider it a kiss, as she was instead bent on cutting away the ropes that bound his hands with her knife. She could not save him, but he looked exactly like the sort who would know how to save himself if the conditions could be made right.

But a kiss it was, or it became one, under the masterful persuasion of John Craig's mouth.

Later—much later, when the capacity to process the machinations of the mind returned to her—Ava would think it odd how thoughts raced through her head, and in what order. She thought first the kiss was only a necessity, a distraction made by her. She'd not counted on heat and intensity, on the subtle pressure of his firm mouth. She hadn't given any thought to a response, hadn't imagined that her heart would slam into her ribs, or that her eyes would close so softly and naturally, or that it might occur to her—at this most inopportune time—that this was the first kiss she'd ever known. He molded his mouth against hers and caressed his tongue along her lips, and her breath hitched in her throat and her lips parted, and her hands nearly forgot what they were about behind his back as she slanted her face and experimented with her first kiss and all the riot of emotions it caused inside her, all under the watchful attention of hundreds of suddenly quiet people.

Quiet, until the sheriff stuttered his displeasure, and the bailiff growled his meanness, and stomped to Ava's side, trying to wrench her away. Her eyes snapped open, only inches from the Lion's face, his brown eyes reflecting both a severity and a delight. Breathless with renewed awareness and fright, knowing she would be wrestled away by the strong bailiff, Ava made sure the knife was tucked into John Craig's hands just before she was finally yanked away from him and sent sprawling onto the platform.

The noose tightened dangerously on John Craig's neck as he lunged forward at the bailiff, his surging wrath obvious.

"Get on with it, then!" The sheriff called out desperately as the crowd cried out their disapproval of the mistreatment of Ava.

On her knees, Ava cast a glance out over the crowd, moving slowly forward, loud and angry again. Her eyes widened when she saw Hamish burst from the mass of indistinct faces and forms to charge the gallows, tucking in at the last second, putting his shoulder into the foremost wooden beam, the newly replaced one, crashing into the stage in the same fashion as Lachie the bull had.

Chaos erupted in full and then prevailed for several seconds. The bailiff was thrown off the stage with Hamish's initial thrust. The sheriff fell to his belly, ten feet away, clinging to the corner support lest he be tossed down as well.

The platform lurched and sagged on that far side, first swiftly as Hamish crashed into it and then slowly, as if it objected to the insult of the battering and then resisted its fate, shattering and falling, in response to the continued pressure of Hamish's shoulder against the beam. Ava began to slide toward the edge, her feet scrambling on the rough wood to keep from being tossed into the air and into the mob once the structure collapsed completely. She pivoted on her bottom, looking for something to hold, at the same time realizing John Craig's predicament was not any better, but far worse. Once the platform disappeared beneath his feet, there would be nothing to keep him from dropping and swinging. With renewed fervor, she tried to get to her feet, to get to him, since his hands were not yet free. He was the only thing onto which she might cling to gain her feet and she did, grabbing at first his calves and then his thighs to right herself, using him as her tether on the precariously tilted stage. Without a word, while he worked yet on those ropes behind his back, Ava crawled up his body and fought with the tightened noose around his neck, trying to remove it. She met his intense brown eyes again, but nothing was discerned even as they stared so forcefully at each other, both fixated on their chores, she on removing the noose, he on freeing his hands.

The crowd, always eager to be incited to anarchy, pressed forward more, their cries unintelligible but angry. They recognized the loss of control and would be eager to get in some licks before the English gained control of the situation again. They pelted any and all English persons, soldiers and administrators, with heavier missiles, rocks and hard bread and whatever they could find. Someone swung a short wooden plank overhead, presumably bringing it down onto someone else, the weapon disappearing as it was brought down, out of sight in the crowd. The noise was deafening.

And then, just as Ava finally wrestled the rope up and away, John Craig flexed his big arms and ropes snapped at his back and went flying, and he was free.

The stage tilted more. John Craig grabbed Ava's hand and raced for the landing at the top of the steps, leaping at the last second as the platform disappeared completely beneath them, pulling Ava through the air with him. He crashed into the railing and Ava into him, but they did not stop. He flew down the stairs, wielding Ava's pitiful dagger in one hand and clutching her hand in the other.

At the bottom of the steps and while the whole burgh seemed to be embroiled in one massive melee, John Craig sought no fight. He only tried to force and forge his way through the crowd, side-stepping English soldiers beating down townsfolk and sometimes the other way around.

"Ava!"

The fretful shouting of her name gave her pause.

"Innes!" She called back, tugging at her hand.

"Keep moving," John Craig urged, barely turning around, not allowing her to seek out either Innes or Hamish.

But they did not, or could not keep moving, confronted just then at the rear of the mob by an eager English soldier.

To Ava's amazement, John Craig—who was clearly so much more than merely a weary wayfarer—managed to disarm the man with naught but her dagger and then stab him mercifully only in the shoulder to subdue him, this achieved essentially one-handed, never letting go of Ava's hand.

Ava cried out then, when someone slammed into her back. She was immediately pulled out of harm's way, John Craig spinning himself and her so that their positions were exchanged.

Another cry burst from Ava, finding Innes about to be confronted with the knife in Craig's hand. "Nae!" She wept, near hysterical, clutching at his raised arm. "He's for me."

Lowering the knife, he nodded curtly and clipped, "We have to move."

***

John scanned the crowd for his captain, Eachann, having spotted him earlier as he'd been led through the mob in that cage on the cart. He found him dispatching an English soldier, a fleshy thwapping sound elicited when the butt end of Eachann's sword met neatly with the man's face, just under the nose guard of his helm.

He hollered Eachann's name so that his captain would know his direction, and then made straight away for the gates of the town, hoping to God that most of the English men-at-arms had attended the hanging and were now embroiled in that riot with the mob. He held onto her wrist, ignoring the man who trailed behind her, who'd called her Ava, until she resisted more as he led her, nearly weeping for another.

"Hamish!" she cried. "We need to find Hamish!"

John halted and turned, moving the knife he brandished out of the way as she almost crashed into him for his quick stop.

At his angry frown, she explained, "Hamish, who busted the gallows."

Jesu. He did not have time to wait!

The man who'd joined them pointed at John with some authority and said firmly, "Go to the west gate, nae the main one. Ava will lead you." To Ava, he vowed, "I will get the lad and meet you there."

The young man turned and fled, returning to the wild throng. In the next second, Eachann burst from another section of the crowd, grunting and growling as if a lion himself.

"This way!" John called. "Eachann!" He didn't wait for his captain to catch up but began moving again, wanting to get gone since now that they were detached from the crowd they were very noticeable standing out in the open of the street.

Once more he pulled the lass behind him, not needing direction toward the west gate, having perused it himself days ago.

His brain was on fire, his improbable rescue and assumed freedom not yet won. But oh, what somersaulted in his head had little to do with crime and punishment. He'd just had confirmation of thoughts that had both teased him and plagued him over the last thirty six hours: she was magnificent. She had green-eyes—striking, incomparable green eyes. And despite the lingering animosity toward her, for being the cause of his near-death, her unsophisticated kiss had been eye-opening and heart-pounding, and might be the sole reason he would not, could not, let go of her hand.

Whoever she was, whatever her story or her life inside Lanark, that would now be a closed chapter in her book. He wasn't leaving without her.

By the time they reached that westernmost gate, Eachann was directly behind them.

"I'll take him," Eachann said, about the lone soldier guarding this avenue.

The lad ahead of them clearly had never met a fight, looked ready only to wet himself, cowering and shriveling before John and the lass sailed by him, leaving him to Eachann as directed. John released her hand only at the last minute, to hoist himself up onto the wall, the gate being closed at ground level. He reached down for her, hauling her up next to him, sparing a glance to see Eachann handily dispatch that unqualified foe. In the distance and headed toward them were the men she'd claimed were *for her*, one big and one not, sprinting in their direction, the shorter one waving impatiently, telling John to persist, as if he thought John had paused, waiting on them.

John leapt down outside the wall, his feet landing on uneven earth, and turned to collect her. She was already seated on the edge of the wall and pushed off with a yip that was cut off when she landed in his arms. Just as Eachann gained the wall, John grabbed at her wrist again. Running was their only option; it wouldn't be long before the English regained control inside and mounted units were sent to recover the escaped prisoner and the collaborators.

His long strides carried them swiftly over the heath-strewn landscape outside the wall. John sent several glances over his shoulder, pleased to find Eachann managing to keep pace with them, and her friends following in the distance, but no English as of yet.

They could not stop until they were in the clear, which would not be found in this wide open meadow. Vaguely, he judged they'd run almost half a mile before they were happily swallowed up by the trees of a wooded vale. Even then, John did not lessen his speed, not until even greater distance was put between him and the prospect of a noose again secured around his neck.

When finally he paused, he was sure plenty of distance separated them from any pursuit. For now. Chest heaving, he drew in and turned, waiting on those who followed. The lass, possibly less accustomed than he to such speed and for such a distance, panted more desperately and sank to her knees.

John Craig did not release her hand even as she wilted completely, collapsing to the ground, her skirts briefly billowing about her. Only when she was settled, appearing as if she would slump no more, would not fall flat onto her back, did he let go. He straightened and settled his hands onto his hips, considering the other baggage for which he was now responsible, as they came behind Eachann.

The large lad, who matched John's great height but outweighed him by at least three or four stone, though possibly had not yet known twenty springs, garnered quite a bit of consideration. John wondered first if he would expire on the spot for the energy he'd just spent, and then, with some annoyance, if the oaf might slow them down. As it was, and while the lad breathed with difficulty, he did not appear troubled by his inability to catch his breath but kept his narrow brown eyes gently upon the cat-eyed woman.

The other man, barely that, perhaps not more than a score and two or three years, was more fit, did not struggle greatly to breathe, though he was clearly winded. He also did not struggle with any ambition to keep his gaze off the young woman. 'Twas not like the big oaf, the way this one watched her with such dedication. It seemed he only waited for her to meet his gaze that some communication might be shared. Feeling eyes upon him, that young man turned his unfriendly gaze upon John and a wee staring contest ensued until the man blinked and his mouth pinched before he returned his attention to the lass.

And suddenly John Craig wanted to know who these people were, and more importantly, what kinship if any they shared. And this was not only in acknowledgment of the returned favor granted to him, his achieved rescue in response to what he'd done for the woman two nights past.

"Who are you?" He asked forthwith, his gaze still on the young man whose blue eyes were trained on her.

But it was she who answered, drawing John's equally fervent regard. She lifted one hand off the ground and waved it haphazardly first toward the big man and then the other man before dropping it back to the ground. "'Tis Hamish and this is Innes Seàrlas, and I am Ava."

When John only stared at her, for how little this revealed to him, she added, "Hamish dinna ken a surname. If once he might have claimed one, it has since been forgotten."

"And you are...kin?" John wanted to know. Was there only one surname to know?

Ava—aye, the name suited her perfectly, being a delicate sound to match so beguiling a face, though by now he'd witnessed firsthand enough of her deeds to understand she was not at all delicate—answered again.

"We are nae related, but for circumstance," she said. "Fringe people, without true kin or homes."

Eachann hitched up his breeches and stepped forward to insert himself into the conversation. "Sure and then you'll nae be missing anyone or any place. And all the better, is it nae, laird, since we've got to keep moving?"

John nodded, knowing this was true. Of Eachann, he asked after his army. "Where are they?"

Eachann, more than ten years John's senior, though he looked much older, winced a bit before admitting, "They are nae close, I'll tell you that. And dinna be killing the messenger but Sir James was...called away, I guess he was, and—"

"Called away?" John repeated, suddenly seething. His army along with Sir James' were both expected to take back Lanark. "While I was sitting in a prison, bound to hang?"

Eachann flapped his hands a bit, asking for calm it seemed. "Aye, but nae like that, called off to any worthless purpose, and nae before I assured him that you would want that he attend the more serious matter—a summons from the Bruce himself—and that we—the Craigs—could well see to your rescue."

"Is this a jape?" John clipped, truly astonished as he so rarely was. "The Craig army would see to...? And then only you contrived to get inside the town?"

"Well now, as to that, aye, we had some trouble. Seems they tighten the gates same as they would have the noose, when a hanging's about to happen."

"So what was your plan? If she had nae—"

"Sure and that dinna matter now, am I right?"

"Bluidy hell, you had nae plan," John accused.

"Nae, I had nae goddamn plan," Eachann raged. "And how could I? 'Twas you who said to keep it slim inside, leave the army outside. 'Twas you who said you'd manage yourself the investigation of their defenses there, dinna want the scouts about the work that should have been theirs. And I had nae word from you, had nae idea of your circumstance until I saw you just this morn, in that cage and then under that noose. And aye, the army is exactly where you left them, where you wanted them sitting—your plan, three miles gone, so they would nae draw notice, raise any suspicion." Ruffled by John's thinly veiled accusation of ineptitude, Eachann frowned at John, and reminded him of their fortunate, present situation. "And it still dinna matter, lad," he ground out, his own displeasure presented, "as you are standing right here in front of me and nae with any mark around your neck. So might we bristle at another time, laird, and keep moving at this time?"

Whatever John might have responded to this travesty was put off when the big lad, Hamish, said without a hint of urgency, "Here they come."

John and Eachann spun around, facing the lad, who stared over their heads, back toward Lanark.

John scowled, nearly ready to dismiss the lad's observation, as nothing was heard or felt, the area around them absent any sound save the distant rushing of the falls at the river. A moment later, he felt it, the ground trembling ever-so-slightly beneath his feet.

He looked down at Ava, who was staring at her hand, her fingers splayed flat on the hard earth, but vibrating almost imperceptibly. When she raised her fascinating green eyes to him, John once more reached for her hand, pulling her to her feet.

"Let's go," he said, knowing further south was their best option.

"To the caves," suggested Ava just as the five of them began to move, giving John pause.

"Aye," agreed the man, Innes, "the English will nae ken to look there."

While he didn't like the idea of being trapped—a cave suggested a one-entry cavern where they might easily be confined—he bowed to their presumed superior knowledge of the local terrain. Certainly, they could not outrun men on horseback. "Lead the way," he said to Innes.

Innes stepped in front of the party of five and ran swiftly and efficiently, did not squirrel needlessly left and right but made a straight path through the brush and trees. John tugged Ava along directly behind them, keeping a firm grip on her hand, unwilling to lose contact with her, but not he thought because he owed her his life. Eachann followed close and John assumed he kept a good eye on the lad, Hamish. At one point, Eachann called out in a panting voice, "Lift those legs, lad. Aye, keep coming along."

They made straight for the River Clyde, which was rocky and not particularly deep in the area to which Innes brought them. The river just here was sunken, the bank being brief and shrouded in more trees and a great disorder of twiggy brush, and presented as a short cliff, falling straight down to the waterway as they ran along it. The ground, though, was hard and dry and gave them no trouble.

Innes went down onto his bottom, his legs dangling over the cliff bank and then scooched forward until he could hop down onto a lower promontory of rock and then another and another until he stood directly beside the rushing water. John followed next, one hand on the earth used to steady himself as he hopped down, turning at that first shelf of rock to collect Ava. She ignored the hand and employed the same tactic Innes had, scooching forward on her butt, until her feet were close to the ground below and she propelled herself off the ledge and landed next to John. Without looking at him, seeming to know the way better than he, she followed Innes.

John was pleased to have the noise of the water tumbling over half submerged rocks to disguise any sounds this party made but did not appreciate that he could now not hear the advance, if any, of the English. But he pressed on, following Innes and Ava as they made their way along the river, stepping carefully about the narrow ground here, sometimes having to keep their backs flat against the wall of the cliff to keep from toppling into the water. Walking sideways at one point himself, his palms against the flaking shale, John glanced back to mark the progress of Eachann and Hamish. His captain kept steady pace with him. Somehow John was not overly shocked to see the lad, too wide and large to navigate the slim ledge, simply walking through the river itself, nearly waist deep but seemingly unperturbed by the cold water that crashed into him as he lumbered upriver.

"I've got 'im," Eachann assured John.

After negotiating almost fifty feet along the unstable precipice, Innes disappeared, ducking left into the cliffside, where John assumed the cave must be. When John reached the nearly circular opening, he swept aside some overhanging foliage and followed Ava inside, disappointed that the cavity was not deeper. The depression inside was not any greater than the width of the opening, about ten feet. And aye, it was wretchedly dark within but even the slightest of torches struck near the mouth would easily show five persons hidden within.

Innes and Ava had squatted against the far interior against the left wall, while John positioned himself opposite them, his back to the right wall, making space for Eachann and Hamish. Those two came only seconds after John, Eachann standing near the opening, blocking what little light there was, encouraging Hamish to exert more energy to climb up from the river.

"Up you go, big boy," he said. "C'mon now, last bit of puffing 'fore you can settle."

Hamish came head and chest first, clambering with his hands while Eachann tried to pull him up. As Eachann bent over him, John took note of the heavy tassel of brush hanging over the top and most of the right side of the opening, a wee satisfied now that the depression might be well concealed, certainly to those not knowing to look for it or standing directly above it.

When Hamish finally entered the cave proper, he did not squat on his haunches as the other men did and did not sit with his knees drawn up to his chest as Ava did, but chose to stand, his head and neck curved forward with the line of the low ceiling.

All were quiet, almost as if they expected in mere seconds to hear the pounding of hooves and shouts of the English militia searching for them.

Escape was not yet accomplished to a final satisfaction, and he was without an effective weapon, had naught but the lass' too small blade, and so John was yet on edge, not quite ready to celebrate victory. He did not care for any harrowing situation in which he could not control and cared even less for what reliance he must put in these men—Innes, Hamish, and even Eachann after his earlier inexplicable behavior—to fight now in his stead should the need arise.

While silence reigned both within and outside the cave, John allowed himself to again be arrested by the face and figure of Ava Guthrie, an endeavor made difficult by the lack of light. Little detail was seen of anyone but for the whites of eyes or teeth if any showed them. Ava remained mostly still, but did turn her face about a wee bit, and every once in a while a spare shaft of light from outside the cave found a home upon her pale skin or the generous curve of her lips, and once as she bowed her head slightly, upon the fringe of lashes protecting her eyes.

He did not consider himself a ridiculous person, and it wasn't only once that he'd been accused of having little use for women—there might be some truth to that indictment, but then there were also tales in his history that warranted his inability or unwillingness to find value in any female—but damn if he hadn't believed for a few seconds that he might die a happy man, Ava Guthrie's kiss the last thing he'd have known.

Now that's some ridiculousness, he told himself. An unsophisticated kiss from a stranger? To bring a smile to his cold heart? Nae, it should nae be so. He would not let it be so.

Jaw clamped, he quit his ardent study of her and turned his attention to the opening of the cave, where nothing moved for nearly a quarter of an hour.

They were eventually made aware of people searching for them, but there were no shouts, and there was no thundering of horses overhead. Some came but not too many and mayhap they only walked their steeds along the clifftop, directly above this cave, searching the river glen for the escaped convict and his cohorts. Bits of loose stone and dirt dropped from the ceiling. John casually brushed at the debris that landed in the hair at his forehead while watching Ava screw up her face, closing her eyes tight as her position seemed to bear the brunt of the gritty assault. Innes gallantly lifted one hand above her face, offering what little defense he could. When a larger clump of earth fell from the cave's ceiling onto the side of her head, Ava turned and buried her face against the crook of Innes' shoulder. The man hastily pulled her into his embrace, using his left hand now as a shield over her.

John fixed a hard glare onto the slim fingers curled into the young man's tunic, his jaw tightening so hard his teeth ached.

When the searchers left the area and no other pursuit appeared to be close, Eachann straightened to his full height, his crooked gait indicating some pain realized for having squatted so long. John stood next, wanting out of this hole in the earth, and went to the mouth of the cave, peering out past the hanging vines and across the river, finding it quiet and vacant.

Chapter Four

When all around them remained quiet for more than a quarter hour, the party of five left the concealment of the river caves and climbed upward, away from the banks of the Clyde and onto vast open land, over which the man named Eachann said they would have to sprint.

"Canna be dawdling out in the open," he reasoned, "and only be as those foolish red deer, idling like they're nae targets."

And run they did, not an easy feat, not again. Though the meadow was covered only in sleeping heather and creeping thistle, the pace set by John Craig's lengthy strides was grueling, and the cold air burned her lungs before they'd covered half the distance across the open field. She flung a glance over her shoulder, measuring Hamish's progress. Unsurprisingly, he lagged far behind, but a sharp call from Eachann to keep going didn't allow for Ava to slow and run astride with poor Hamish.

For a long time the tree line ahead of them, at which they ran, never seemed to get closer. By the time they finally dashed past the first of the towering pines, Ava was sure her entire chest was ready to explode, and had she breath enough, she'd have cried out her glee when finally they stopped again.

John Craig, in the lead, stood panting, his hands on his hips, winded but not greatly so. The man, Eachann, showed a face that looked as Ava felt; his lips were parted, his teeth bared, his brow knitted with distress while he walked in slow circles, his face tilted upward, trying to catch his breath.

Her wobbly legs felt as if they were made of pudding and for the second time that day, she happily collapsed onto the cold hard ground. She dropped her hands and concealed her own physical anguish by bowing her face toward the ground.

"Far enough," she rasped, when she was able to speak. "We dinna need...you go on."

Innes came next, having slowed his pace as soon as he saw they'd stopped. He stood close to Ava. Hamish came then, putting his hands to his knees while he fought to catch his breath.

After a moment, Ava raised her face to John Craig, where he stood not ten feet from her. "We are nae longer indebted," she presumed. "We will be fine from here." They might have to keep themselves hidden for a few days, she and Innes and Hamish, but the furor inside Lanark would die down and they would surely be able to return.

John Craig stared down at her curiously, as someone who just begins to understand that they know something that not everyone has comprehended.

"Go on? Lass, nae without you," he said. "You can nae stay here. Nae any of you."

"Aye, we can," she insisted. "We'll stay gone for a day or two," Ava said when he continued to stare at her with his wild brown eyes. "We can..." she let this trail off, still breathless, her stomach twisting disagreeably inside her, imbued with some sense of what he was about to say next, which only was just beginning to dawn on her.

"You can nae go back," John Craig repeated.

"You are, all of you," said Eachann, turning to include the breathless Innes and the alarmingly red-faced Hamish in his speech, "outlaws now. Warrants will be sworn for your capture, for the aid you've given to the Lion of Blacklaw Tower."

Ava looked at John Craig, who returned her gaze solemnly but not without a hint of impatient scorn. "You can never go back. You most of all, your face ogled by every person inside that wall—"

"We live there," Innes interjected curtly, moving in front of Ava, blocking her view of John Craig. "She just saved your bluidy life, mate, but it's nae for you to say where she—any of us—may go or nae."

John Craig let out a derisive bark of laughter, a sound ugly enough that Ava was glad to have no clear view of his face. "Aye, by all means, hie back to Lanark and see if you dinna have any luck keeping your neck out of a noose."

"'Twas only removed from yours because of her!" Innes challenged.

Ava thought the argument weak.

John Craig did as well, and shot back in a clipped tone, "'Twas only put there in the first place because of her!"

Flippantly, Innes advised, "Nae one told you to kill anyone, mate."

"You would have let her be mauled?" John Craig challenged with a snarl of disgust.

Just as both men lunged forward, the scraggly man named Eachann leapt between them, pushing at their chests.

Ava jumped to her feet.

"Bluidy eejits!" Eachann charged. "Stand down, both of you. Stand down, I say."

He gave a good shove in each direction, which effectively moved Innes back a few paces but did not budge John Craig, who glared fiercely at Innes, his lip curled.

Eachann turned his back to his own man and faced Innes, Ava, and Hamish.

"Dinna be daft about it. It is what it is, and you canna go back," he snapped. "We'll see you somewhere safe, then do as you please. But right now, you're with us," he went on and then pointed a finger at Innes and raised his voice again, "and you'll goddamn do as I say and quit your bleating, if living satisfies you better than nae."

Duly chastened, Ava nodded glumly while Hamish intoned, "Aye, sir."

Innes stood in front of her and thus she could not see his expression, but it must have been conciliatory in some manner that Eachann nodded stiffly and announced, "And we still have to keep moving."

Ava sent her gaze past Innes and Eachann to where John Craig stood, a bit unnerved to find his brown eyes not on Innes but trained glaringly on her, his lips still twisted, his displeasure not diminished. If he had stripped her naked, she couldn't have felt more *seen*, more exposed. He managed to convey a wealth of expression in his heated glare. A shiver coursed through her at the contempt etched on his handsome features. But he only unnerved her in that regard and with his ferocious anger for a moment before he turned and strode angrily away, deeper into the forest.

They walked on for another hour, eventually leaving the forest and forging a trail now along another waterway. They walked single file along the rocky shore of this river under a canopy of woody branches, oak and elm and hazel. The sun never did show itself and the chill in the air, unnoticed before the tedious and mostly silent march, poked and prodded at Ava so that she held her hand at the front of her neck, clasping the open front of her cloak together.

Occasionally, Ava let her regard fall heavily on John Craig, on his dark head and broad shoulders, but mostly was pleased to keep herself out of his immediate vicinity. He unnerved her, and in ways she didn't understand. Aye, he was an angry man, but given his circumstances, 'twas to be expected. But there was something else about him that filled her with a dark disquiet. It might have been the way he stared at her, so thoroughly as if he would comprehend all her secrets at once by way of his piercing regard. It might have been the gaze itself. She'd never met brown eyes that had given her pause. Blue eyes or green eyes might be arresting or mesmerizing—even Dottie Og's father's cloudy blue eyes, with their milky centers, were rather fascinating—but she'd never met a pair of brown eyes that were not ordinary, not until she'd met John Craig. It was the way he used them, she understood. John Craig did not simply glance at a person, he looked *into* them, she'd decided. Or, she'd concluded this based on how she'd been made to feel as the recipient of his steadfast gaze, all the ones that came after his initial and thorough regard: thoroughly inspected and found wanting.

Sadly, it was not a reaction she had never met before.

As a person who lived on the fringe of society, almost satisfyingly when alternatives were considered, Ava had met all sorts of scorn, was faced often with unwarranted rejection and equally unjustified condescension.

Innes and Hamish had been subjected to the same, or mayhap worse since they were male and thus people were also inclined to fear them, for what trouble they might be expected to bring. They lived hand to mouth, all of them and any other displaced person, eking out their existence day by day. There was a certain underlying freedom to any person condemned by poverty and a lack of means to walk the streets and sleep sometimes out in the open. There was freedom from those ties that bind, and from a long day's labor as known by any cottage-dwelling and land-rigging soul, and freedom from the constraints of society—the homeless were universally and generally derided, but then they were somehow granted freedom from adhering to the town's strict moral codes.

But then with freedom also came a dearth—of connections, of a true home, of the want to attach emotions to people. She hadn't always been homeless, and the choice to be so had been hers, alone and with forethought. At the time, more than six years ago now, she'd left the home of her father and his family, choosing instead a life on the streets. She hadn't expected that it would be easy—it was not—but then life inside the large keep to which she'd been born as the illegitimate daughter of Baron Cowie, William de Vaux, the one he'd made with a lowly scullery maid who'd not survived the birthing, had been nothing short of a living hell. 'Twas no secret who she was, the evidence irrefutable she'd been told more than once, her green eyes having only ever been seen on the timid maid, Jonet, whose disturbing beauty had led to her demise. And as much as her mother had been purportedly—to hear the servants tell it— revered for her strange beauty, her bastard daughter had enjoyed no such esteem. The baron's wife and his legal offspring, three daughters and two sons, had made certain of that. Instead, she'd been the butt of every jape, the object of daily scorn, the recipient of cruel pranks, made to labor as had her mother but tainted by the stigma of illegitimacy, subjected regularly to whippings and more than once caged in a cell in the dungeon for some imagined slight against them. Her father had done nothing to alleviate the misfortune of her birth.

Aye, she understood—with Father Valentine's help—what she'd been about in Lanark, why she'd carved out the role she had, seeking kinship with other displaced persons, making herself invaluable to some, robbing from the haves to give to the have-nots to earn favor, all in an attempt to find what she'd been denied all her life—those frightfully nebulous things that every person craved, kin and love and acceptance. In a life too often soaked in bitterness, she craved sweetness. After living so many years without emotion to protect herself, she yearned and fought for every sentiment now, wanting to feel for other people. And she'd fashioned a nice little life for herself there in Lanark, good despite the presence of the English.

And all that work for naught now, all those relationships lost. Exiled again, she was, and needing a fresh start somewhere else.

While cataloguing her own losses presently, it dawned on her what ruin she'd unwittingly visited upon both Innes and Hamish. Her heart beat hard and fast inside her chest, and she slowed her pace, waiting for Innes to catch up with her. Hamish was directly beyond him, bringing up the rear. When Innes came abreast of her, she fell into step beside him.

She checked herself before she'd uttered what had been at the fore in her mind, that if he'd heeded her demand that he leave her to her own business, he and Hamish would not now be in a similar disagreeable circumstance. It was not right to lay blame at his feet.

"Innes, I dinna ken what else to say but that I am sorry," she said to him, her voice small. "I feel as if I've robbed you of a fairly decent life there in Lanark."

Innes shook his head, apparently dismissing her concern. "I dinna take orders from any, nae even you, Ava. 'Twas my choice to lend aid to your—but *Jesu*, what was that? I ken you would nae want to see a man sway at the end of a rope for you, but, *Jesu*, why did you kiss him?" He slanted a heavy frown at her.

Ava shrugged, having no answer yet though she'd asked herself the same thing many times by now. "I-I had nae...I dinna ken what else to do. But I ken I needed to be close to him, to free his hands, and get the knife to him."

Innes snorted some disdain. "A simpler embrace might have seen it done," he charged. "Thirty ways to get him the blade without having to lay your lips on him. *Jesu*, Ava, but afterward—your cheeks, your eyes! Dinna tell me you found nae pleasure—"

"Innes!" She gasped with outrage. "'Twas a melee by then. I was shocked and frightened and—"

"Aye, tell yourself that," he said with some heat.

Disregarding his misplaced anger over that specific aspect of her crimes of the day, Ava returned to her original intent. Indignant now, she said, "I only meant to apologize for your present situation, which is now as dreadful as my own, but one I ken you did nae seek." She looked sideways at him, searching for acceptance of her remorse, finding only a bare and tight nod, Innes' jaw fastened firmly now.

Ava allowed him to march on ahead of her, fearful that the friendship she'd shared with Innes for half a decade was now, as was all of her life, in peril. She did not pretend she didn't understand his annoyance, hadn't pretended at all over the last few years that she didn't know of Innes' tender regard for her, which was entirely different than Hamish's innocent affection for her.

Hamish soon walked alongside her. Ava turned her face up to him. "Are you angry with me as well, Hamish?"

Without hesitation, the big lad observed, "Nae much to churn over, Ava. We are, the three of us, still together. Dinna matter where we do that."

Ava sighed again, little appeased, and trudged on, the day not getting any better.

And mayhap Innes' anger—or resentment, whatever the true case was—only simmered and then boiled over as they marched along. A few minutes later he called out to John Craig and his man at the front of the line, his voice sharp, "And where *are* we going? Walking to where? Have you an army nearby or do you nae?"

"Aye, we do," said that man, Eachann, over his shoulder.

Eachann looked at first glance as if he could demonstrate an agreeable proficiency in many a scene, be it inside a brothel or battle or at a laird's table. His beard and full head of hair were untidy, but his garb was pristine; he was not so overly muscled that anyone would assume straightaway that soldiering was his life; his blue eyes were deep set, lending him an air of contemplation; he was both crusty and decisive in any action but then showed so much patience, having not yet turned to upbraid Innes for his impertinence.

"And are we nae headed that way?" he called back now. "But if one more person asks me where the bluidy Craig army is, as God as my witness I'll nae be accountable for my response."

Hamish chuckled at this, but Innes was riled yet, mayhap looking for a fight. He did that sometimes.

"'Tis questionable though, you have to agree," Innes called out. "Have us running like stags through an open field for nearly a full mile and now we've walked almost another one. Did you leave your army, sir, at home?"

The older man still didn't turn around to address Innes properly, but threw back in a snarly tone, "Nae one forced *you* out of those gates, lad."

John Craig said something, but it must have been addressed only to his man, being unintelligible to those that followed.

Innes jogged a bit to catch up with the two men in the lead, his ire prickled.

"Innes!" Ava called out, meaning to caution him.

"Nae," he said, smacking John Craig on his shoulder to get his attention. "I want an answer," he said when John Craig turned around. "Do you have an army or are we only pretending you do?"

John Craig finally stopped walking, and thus the entire party did.

With some disloyalty to her longtime friend, Ava wondered if Innes was just now regretting his outburst. John Craig turned around and walked a few steps back to Innes, looming over the shorter man same as he had towered over Ava when they'd stood close. This time, Eachann made no attempt to step between the two men and reduce the friction. To his credit though, Innes did not shrink or back away. Indeed, he lengthened his spine, standing as tall as he was able, not an easy feat, Ava guessed, in the face of the quietly dangerous roar of the Lion.

Without raising his voice—without needing to, to advance his own ire—John Craig clipped out, "Wide open country here. I'll nae lose any sleep if you choose somewhere else to be in it. In the meantime, neither Eachann nor I are answerable to you. It's been said my army awaits us. What you choose to believe is your business."

A good dozen feet behind Innes, Ava was rooted to the ground, with enough self-awareness to keep her eyes from widening. She had guessed he did anger well, possibly often. He was no less beautiful for the fury shown in his scowl, only more savage, his mahogany eyes somehow achieving a sparkling menace though no sun shone to light that fire.

Inexplicably, Innes would not let it go.

"What are the chances," Innes asked, tilting his head in that cocky way of his, "of more English finding us 'fore we happen upon this phantom army?"

"You are free to go where you please," John Craig said brusquely. "In fact, I might insist now that you do."

"Aye, but you've rather diminished our choices, being that our names will now be scribbled next to yours, as outlaws—you said so yourself."

"Nae one asked you to interfere—"

"I could nae bluidy leave her to her own decision-making!" Innes interjected, swinging an arm wildly and indiscriminately behind him toward Ava. "Obviously, something defective has taken hold, to make her behave as she did."

"Again, you are free to go where you will," said John Craig, with greater calm. "If it's with us, then quit the bellyaching. If it's nae with us, I suggest this moment now as a fine time and place to part company."

"You sure you want that, Craig?" Innes challenged, tossing his head to move the hair off his forehead. "Parting company, you'll see only the back of her, and all signs point to that being fairly distant from any honest wish. She goes with me, you ken?"

John Craig chose to ignore that provocation, did not even spare a glance to *her*. "You take issue with our route, and when you are given leave to make your own, you take issue with that. Which will it be, lad? I've better things to do than to stand around listening to your haivering."

Innes snorted. "You're right. And off we go." He turned and walked back to Ava. "Dinna need his high-handedness. C'mon, Ava. Hamish, let's go."

Mouth open, Ava stared at Innes' back as he kept on past both her and a gawking Hamish, before giving her regard to John Craig. She found his seething brown eyes upon her now, while he stood with his hands on his hips. For her part, she was not so much indecisive as she was stunned. What had just happened? Why was she thrust into the center of it?

And why did her feet refuse at the moment to move?

John Craig wasn't anything to her. She didn't know him, little more than the color of his eyes and the power of his kiss, but...did she want to? Know him?

Nae, that was not why she hesitated, she assured herself. Only someone ignorant in all the ways in which the world was ugly would not comprehend that their chances of safety were far more favorable in his company than away from it.

"Ava!" Innes snapped at her when she hadn't moved.

One last look at John Craig, and she offered the slightest of apologies in the vague and not fully realized wince she sent his way before turning and following Innes and Hamish.

She heard behind her the Lion's harshly uttered, "Bluidy fools!"

Instant regret was not something that Ava had occasion to deal with so often in her life. Regret, aye, but usually it was of the late-arriving kind. Many a bold and quick decision she'd made over the years, life-changing ones, and never had doubt so immediately gnawed at her from the inside out as it did right now. And how absurd, she thought, that her chin should quiver at this moment.

Innes had paused, turned to wait for her and Hamish to catch up.

He attempted to paint a kinder picture than what reality was likely to show them.

"We're better off," was his first lie. As he moved on again when Hamish and Ava came abreast of him, he said, "We can choose our own destination. Straight to Edinburgh, that's what we ought to do. Lots more available to people like us. Chances are we'll come across a few familiar faces," Innes said. "They'll set us up nice, first few nights. We'll find our way, make our place soon enough."

Ava wasn't listening.

Even as she told herself to stop turning her head for one last glimpse of him, that opportunity gone after she'd walked but a few hundred feet along the twisting riverside, she kept looking back.

At some point she was forced to admit to herself that she half-expected—hoped, if she were honest—to find him giving chase, come to make her stay. For a brief moment, she touched the pads of her fingertips to her lips, reflecting finally upon his kiss, the only one she'd ever known.

How ridiculous, she thought, to imagine a virtual stranger should mourn her departure and wish to make her stay.

Her own father, when she'd announced her intention to depart forever from Redhall House, had nodded and said 'twas for the best. He'd gruffly granted her leave to take the clothes she'd made that were her own and the shoes she'd worn, for which she'd once bartered a delicately carved hair comb made of bone that had been her mother's, though the baron had sternly warned her not to try his long-suffering tolerance by taking anything that was not her own. His reaction had come as no surprise to her; the baron had never wanted anything to do with her, had dismissed her as easily as he'd ignored her presence for fifteen years.

After a while, and with the aid of that unfortunate recollection of her sire, Ava stopped turning around, stopped hoping John Craig would have wanted to know her.

Chapter Five

It was no longer a quiet and furtive march about the upland areas of Lanarkshire, intent only on evading pursuit and capture. John Craig stalked along in a straight line as if he hunted war itself, regardless of beinn or glen or any other water they encountered after they'd angled away from the River Clyde. His hands remained fisted at his sides for nigh on an hour and his expression never wavered from grisly.

In a fortuitous manner, John and Eachann did eventually find the Craig army, or rather Eachann was sighted by the Craig scouts when he'd chosen to stand at the crest of a beinn and relieve himself, at the same time being able to survey all the glen before him.

"Put yer wee spindle away, old goat," was hollered from below, the caller unseen, the chortling that followed boisterous.

"Bluidy halfwits," Eachann grumbled, his own mood soured by that of his laird over the last hour.

John and Eachann then made their way to the foot of the hill and into the trees where were concealed the forty-seven men of the Craig army. As had been the case for almost a year, John lamented the diminished number, mourning those lost at Methven and Dalrigh in service to the king last summer and autumn. He greeted them warmly and only briefly outlined how he'd been detained inside Lanark, making mention of his capture and near hanging but not of Ava Guthrie and her part in his escape.

"*Jesu*," gasped Henry Hackett, "fighting for your life inside those walls while we're idling away the days out here, wrestling over who gets the choicest bits of the hares and squirrels snared." He shook his head with some disgust.

John dismissed this readily enough. He was, on any given day, ready to give his life to the cause of freedom—or, apparently to a green-eyed enchantress in dire straits. In truth, rarely did he greet a new year expecting to still be alive at year's end, for how brutal and desperate were some of the battles he'd seen. Thus, still breathing with all his parts intact was not anything he would take for granted.

"And where has Sir James gone?" John asked after the Douglas knight, with whom he'd expected to lay siege to Lanark.

"Sure and he'd received word from our king," said Duncan, a Craig lieutenant, "and how old was that news, nae one can say. Given leave to draw down to Douglasdale, he was, for the purpose of bringing over to the patriot's side any or all of the ancient vassals of his family." Duncan, lanky and long of face, of an age with John, and wearing his long hair gathered into a band at the nape of his neck, shrugged and presumed, "Though I ken secretly, he was more eager to right some particular wrongs he and his name have sustained at the hands of the English, Clifford specially."

Robert Clifford, who'd been given the Douglas lands by a vindictive swipe of ink from the English king. Aye, Sir James would not want to miss an opportunity to turn those tables.

"Something critical afoot," said another man, Finn, nodding his head to underline his statement. "Could tell by the Douglas' eyes as he listened to that harried messenger. Something big brewing."

John exchanged a questioning glance with Eachann. If this was true, that would be the first any had heard from Robert

Bruce in months, not since last autumn. Of late, it wasn't even supposed he was on the mainland.

Another lieutenant, Uthrid, whose face—certainly in profile—was dominated by a long and pointed nose, and who wore pale skin under a shock of bright blonde hair, asked of John, "And now what's for us? We canna make nae mark on Lanark without the Douglas and his men-at-arms."

No, they could not. Having been within Lanark's wall, John knew there were simply too many Englishmen for he and his men alone to stand a chance of retaking the town.

"Double the posting to the south there," he instructed. "We were chased for a while by some of Lanark's garrison. They ken who I am, might nae give up so easily." He glanced overhead, toward the still-gray sky, locating the sun's position by a bare brightened spot, judging at to be mid-afternoon. "We'll keep here for the day and make for Lismore Abbey on the morrow." He gave his regard to Eachann again, who'd stood next to him since they'd come, half-expecting some dissent for this plan since they'd only left Lismore Abbey a few weeks ago.

Instead, Eachann nodded and scratched a bit at the hair at his temple. "Aye, better chance of getting news there than out here. Magnus will have been made aware of the king's status and whereabouts. He'll have a better idea where we should or might be deployed next."

With that settled, John took himself off from the throng of soldiers, leaving Eachann to tell the whole story of his capture and near-death, the cause of it all, if he saw fit to do so. John didn't care. He was familiar with the area from days ago when he and Sir James had settled their armies here and knew that the Mouse Water was close. He went to the horse line, pleased to find his big bay destrier among the string of steeds, saddlebags and belongings intact. Bemoaning the loss of his own sword and dagger, he appropriated one of each from the supply wagon, from the few spare arms left to his army after more than a year away from Blacklaw Tower. Securing those in his belt, he next collected a change of clothes and made for the river, where, despite the cold, he stripped down until he was completely bare and had himself a speedy bath in the icy water.

When he was done, he dried himself with the tunic he'd worn earlier and dressed swiftly though he had no worry that the cold would seep so far into his bones; his still-simmering anger and churning thoughts would heat him up but quick.

He knew it would be near impossible to ignore any thought of Ava Guthrie, and so he let them play out until they might exhaust themselves. Flashes of her striking green eyes were impaled in his memory. The feel of her inexpert but tantalizing kiss likely would haunt him for days or weeks to come.

By now he'd decided that she and the angry man, Innes, might be more than only friends, if anything should have been gleaned from the way the man barked at her to follow, and how she'd responded by meekly doing so.

She was then, spoken for, and thus none of his concern. Her welfare and safety were not his problem.

Still, more than once he wondered why he'd let her walk away from him.

The question inside him was curious, but only because he thought he should be asking of himself, *Jesu, but did you want her to stay?*

No, he most certainly did not, he assured himself. Aside from not wanting to be saddled with three common people untrained and therefore useless in most regards, there was the matter of her character to consider. Her efforts to save his neck notwithstanding, he knew her to be a thief of the night who apparently kissed persons unknown to her, simply to alleviate her own guilt and all while entangled with another, Innes.

Aye, that reckoning was harsh, but it suited well his want to smite her and her clumsy but still wholly unforgettable kiss from his mind.

Thirty minutes later, freshly bathed, feeling more human than he had in three days, John was only returned to the general assembly of his milling army for a quarter hour when they were all alarmed by the unmistakable blast of an English cavalry horn. Akin to the blare of the trumpet that sounded off the nobility's idle fox hunt, signifying prey being hunted, the noise was strident and entirely too close.

Immediately, he thought of Ava. Outside this small forest of trees in which they sat, the land was sparsely populated, useless as arable farming land, and too rocky to serve as prime pastureland. Thus, it should be expected that few people were about being of concern to the English, enough to sound their horn. Since they'd parted ways little more than an hour ago, John feared that surely the cavalry horn was blown in pursuit of Ava and Innes and the giant lad, Hamish.

"God's bones," Eachann griped, standing from the fallen log upon which he'd made a seat only moments ago. He cast a heavy scowl toward the noise before turning and pinning John with an exasperated glare. "They got 'em running, my guess."

John, already on his feet at the first sound of that horn, nodded, and said to his suddenly attentive men, "To arms, men."

"Make haste, lads," Eachann ordered as the Craig soldiers moved at once toward their horses. "If they're chasing these three we met, the very ones who set free your laird, there's a big hulking lad who'll nae be able to outrun yer mam let alone a mounted sassenach."

Within five minutes of the first blare of that horn, John Craig and his small army were racing headlong out from the trees and up the braeside. Atop the peak where Eachann had relieved himself earlier, John examined the forward glen and the hills beyond, though nothing was ascertained in the form of any movement. Wasting no time there, he spurred the bay destrier down the far side of the beinn and up the next hill, now able to overlook the River Clyde from a distance of a quarter mile, seeing a section of it far upriver from where they parted company with Ava and the others earlier.

Eagle-eyed Henry Hatchett was the first to spot movement.

"There!" He said, pointing further upstream than the open area where John had focused his gaze.

'Twas only movement and little more than that, the distance showing naught but three dark shapes coming out of the trees that concealed parts of the river, running haphazardly. He recognized them immediately as Ava, Innes, and Hamish, given the outstretched arms of the slightest figure, which was exactly how Ava had fled from Lanark this morning, running wildly with her arms lifted and flailing at shoulder height, as if she were only concerned with maintaining balance. He recognized also the figure of Hamish, being so much bigger than the other two and trailing them by many lengths, his gait not equal to Ava's, or Innes in the lead.

"Hyah!" John bit out harshly, urging the horse into swift speed down this smaller hill.

His army followed, the noise of their coming thunderous upon the cold, hard ground. Eachann incited the Craig men-at-arms to battle, his roar of, "Have at 'em, lads!" called out as soon as the English were seen, coming from the river, giving chase to those three people.

A quick scan of that English unit showed mayhap twenty mounted men—a score of dead men they would be, before another quarter hour had passed, John presumed.

He kept his gaze focused on Ava, more convinced of her identity the closer he got to her.

There was nothing between him and her but a field of winter-brown heath and golden bracken. With a furious knee to the destrier's flanks, John persuaded him to stretch out his legs, judging the distance between him and Ava, and then between the English and Ava. Just as he thought he might indeed reach her first, Hamish stumbled and fell, and Ava turned and ran back to him.

"Nae!" John ground out between clenched teeth. "Christ, Ava. Run."

She did not but reduced her own chances of escaping the English by stopping to help Hamish to his feet, allowing the enemy to gain on her. Innes ran independently, never once looking back to mark the progress—or lack thereof—of either Hamish or Ava. He might have noticed the Craig army coming, might have discerned the numerous plaids worn by at least half his army and deemed them a haven, shifting his trajectory to run straight toward them.

John curled his lip and urged his steed into swifter flight, his gaze steadfast upon Ava. Her hood had flown off her head, the prize of her silken mahogany hair revealed. Hamish was on his feet again and they were once more running for their lives, and John knew exactly when she realized the presence of another army. Hanging onto Hamish's arm, she pointed at the Craigs, and like Innes, they sprinted now straight at them.

And when they were close enough that faces and expressions could be made out, John fastened his battle gaze onto Ava's perfect green eyes, alight with fright. In the space of a second, she recognized him and her run faltered, she sagging with relief.

She knows I will save her. That had been the first thought to cross the plane of her reasoning when she spied him, John fathomed. Her expression told of this, eyes shining, lips parting, a grateful smile wobbling. She'd pinned all her hopes on him same as any maid might pin her colored ribbon onto the most worthy knight of the tournament. There was some inspiration in that, some damnable pride that came with the faith she'd just shown to him.

Only seconds after John drew his sword, he heard the hiss of metal scraping against metal over and over again as his men did the same. When he was twenty feet out from Innes in the lead, he shouted for them to fall to the ground, out of harm's way. "Down! Down!"

They obeyed instantly, all three of them, dropping like stones to the ground.

But damn! Just as John's horse flew past the cowering Innes, the English came abreast of Ava and Hamish. Thankfully, the enemy knew the fight could not be avoided, knew that clashing swords must precede any taking of prisoners or harassing of peasants. To Hamish's credit, when he and Ava plunged to the ground, the big lad had gathered her under his bulky form.

At the head of his army, John's sword was the first to meet with an English blade. As with any mounted engagement, his hip and shoulder were thrust first into movement, before he projected that motion into his arm, swinging his hand from left to right, which first parried the enemy's blow only seconds before the follow-through of John's swing, his force being greater, saw his double-edge blade swipe across the thin mail at the man's neck. John had learned a hard lesson inside his first mounted and racing melee, having used a thrusting motion which had seen his sword lodged successfully in the enemy's chest, but which had subsequently been what had unseated John, as his inflexible grip on his stuck sword had yanked him backward and off the horse's end.

He wasted no time on this man's true demise, but kneed the destrier onto the next opponent, angling himself in the saddle to present a slimmer target, holding his sword above his head as if he would strike straight down but then swinging that same left to right pattern that had felled more English than John could ever count. And on it went, the entire forces of the Craigs and the English engaged wholly, with clangs and grunts and cries to give voice to the brutality of the unexpected skirmish. And yet, there had never been any question as to the outcome of the scrum, the English being outnumbered by more than two to one.

When it was done and the field of winter heather was littered with bodies and blood, and English coursers, some now seated by dead men, meandered aimlessly about the perimeter of the fighting arena, John reined in, panting, and sought out Ava with ferocious eyes, his battle mien yet intact.

Hamish was just lifting himself off of her, rolling and flopping onto his back.

Ava sat up at the same time she lowered the hands that had covered her head. She drooped onto her bottom, her shoulders settling low, and glanced around at the remains of the fray.

John breathed easier, but only for a split second before he realized a ribbon of blood making its way from her temple downward, along her hair line. He walked his steed over to her, sparing a moment to glance at Hamish, with his arms flung wide while he stared at the sky, seemingly unharmed.

When he was close and she lifted her green eyes to him, John inclined his head at her. "You are hurt." He pointed a finger at her temple.

A wee breathless still, she shook her head at the same time she touched her fingers to the blood. "'Tis nothing," she said, "just us crashing hard to the earth when Hamish was kicked by a passing steed."

Innes arrived then, expressing concern for Ava now that was curiously lacking when they were all running for their lives, he several lengths ahead of her. He landed hard on his knees next to her, his hands gentle upon her as he inspected the wound at her forehead.

Ava tried to brush away his hands and attention.

John turned his destrier about, needing to assess the damage to his own army. He went first to where a small crowd of Craigs had gathered, dismounting as he reached them. He shouldered his way to the fore, finding Geoffrey Kerr on the ground, on his back, his midsection covered in enough blood to give little hope of life.

John cursed volubly and went to his haunches, checking for a pulse, not surprised when he found none. Standing again, he called for the lone wagon traveling with the Craigs to be brought up and scanned the field for any other wounded men, knowing some relief when no other fatality was found, though several others showed grisly injuries.

Eachann appeared at his side, his swiftly donned helm now propped against his hip, his chest still heaving with his exertions. "We canna linger," he said to John. "Who's to say there are nae more of them, lurking or coming? We best make ourselves scarce."

"Aye," agreed John. "To the forest then, the larger one beyond where we loitered earlier."

"And what of them?" Eachann wondered, pointing his dull metal helmet toward Ava and Innes, and Hamish still sprawled on the ground.

"They'll have to come with us," John determined, incapable it seemed of unclenching his teeth. "And stay with us as they should have earlier, until we can deposit them somewhere safe." At his captain's nod of understanding, John walked over to the trio, planting his boots in the periphery of both Ava and Innes, drawing their attention. "You ken now, do you nae, you are safer with us?"

Ava nodded almost immediately, her façade yet bloodless for the fright she'd just known. The pissant, Innes, gave his response more slowly, his nod being accompanied by what look an awful lot like a sneer, which made John really want to smack the flat of his blood-soaked sword against the side of Innes' head.

It needed a huge measure of restraint, but John did not raise a hand against him. However, he didn't mind giving him a taste of his dark mood. "We'll see if I canna do a wee better job of keeping her from nearly getting killed again."

Innes lunged to his feet but apparently had no other plan than that, only snarled his dislike of John's mockery while he made fists with his hands at his side. Ava stood as well, touching Innes' arm with some familiarity that seemed to calm the man while it simultaneously irked John.

"Innes, please," she said. "Let us be thankful for their intervention."

Dismissing the both of them, his mood unaccountably curdled yet more, John nodded toward Hamish. "Is he going to be able to ride? Or shite, can he even get up?"

"Aye, I will. I can," Hamish answered for himself, finally sitting up, wincing as he did so.

John cast a scowl over all three of them, snapping unfairly at Ava, "And cover up that hair, ere we find ourselves run to ground because of it."

***

She wanted nothing more than to crumble and sob, for how awful the entire day had been—and apparently was going to continue to be.

They rode silently, this much larger party, following a river she could not name, which was sometimes naught but a trickling stream, before they turned away from it, marching quietly north over hill and glen. And while Ava felt remarkably safer for the company of the Craig army, she wasn't entirely sure how she felt about their present circumstance, their destination unknown, and at the whim of the Lion of Blacklaw Tower. Mayhap she would have only been appreciative of her assumed safety and not anything else but for the fact that John Craig had all but made it known he did not desire their company.

The Lion of Blacklaw Tower.

And now she knew. What all that frenzied whispering had been about when first his name was announced to the crowd gathered for his hanging. Legitimately earned, his moniker, Ava had realized.

John Craig was savage in battle. She could rightly attest to that, having witnessed his prowess of two nights ago and his bid for freedom this morning and then not more than half an hour ago, what brutality she'd viewed between her fingers as she'd cowered on the ground like a frightened and frozen hare. And thank God he and his army had come, or God knows what would have become of she and Hamish and Innes. Brutal and merciless had its uses, she guessed, served the warrior well.

Ava and Innes rode upon one of the purloined English horses. Hamish had likewise been given a horse, fortunately a docile gray mare, since he had about as much experience riding as did Ava. Destitute persons rarely had occasion or opportunity to ride a horse.

She rode behind Innes, her arms wrapped around his waist, her hood dutifully pulled close around her head. After the first few hours, she laid her cheek against Innes' back, unable to keep her eyes open any more.

"I'm sorry, Innes," she said, "I dinna ken why I'm so tired, the sun nae even gone down yet."

"Aye and will we all nae sleep like the dead this night?" Innes supposed, patting her hand around his middle. "We've nae ever ken a day like this."

She was wakened by Innes when they stopped, close to sunset the now-clear sky told, showing the sun resting atop a distant range of mountains to the west.

The traveling army had entered a thin wood before Ava had dozed, and she thought they might only be deeper inside that same forest, the trees tall, effectively breaking the wind, and the ground strewn generously with moss and bracken and lifeless pine straw.

"Where are we?" Ava asked.

Innes shrugged. "North is all I ken."

Having never traveled as such before, they only followed what others did, dismounting when the soldiers began to do so. Innes walked the borrowed steed over to where the horse line was being formed, further ahead than where a group was already milling about. Ava waited, her arms crossed over her chest inside her cloak, telling herself not to look immediately for John Craig, as her eyes seemed to want to do. When she caught sight of him, she told herself it was unavoidable, his presence so impressive, he the leader of these men giving out quiet orders, assigning a perimeter guard and sending off hunters of game and foragers of kindling. One fire, he instructed, but only if they could amass enough dry tinder, presumably to avoid a smoky blaze.

Ava stood thirty or forty feet away, at one end of this makeshift campsite, wondering if she, or even Innes or Hamish, would be given some chore or instruction. They were not. John Craig clipped out a few more commands to his own men, and without sparing even half a glance in her direction, took himself off, away from the clearing and into the woods.

Honestly, with his departure came a bit of relief. While she recognized it for what it was, she did not analyze the why behind it. Innes and Hamish joined her and the three of them were approached by the Craig Captain, Eachann.

"There'll be bread and ale, what little we've to share. Mayhap some game, if the hunters ken success. You can make your beds hereabouts," he said, waving his hand in their general vicinity. "Water is that way," he said, pointing specifically east through the pines, "but dinna stray beyond that or be gone too long. We're done for the day, nae chasing anyone through the forest should you get lost."

Ava and Innes nodded. Hamish was distracted with a spot on his tunic, where it fell to his waist, some brown gooey stain that he scrubbed his fingers over, bringing his hand to his nose to sniff out its identity, and which made him screw up his face with a clear distaste.

"I'll um, I need to take care of something," she said when Eachann had left them, her cheeks pinkened, never recalling a time when she'd had to announce her personal needs. Neither Innes nor Hamish seemed to find anything odd about her statement and Ava marched into the trees, heading toward the stream Eachann had pointed out.

Before searching out the stream, she sought out privacy to see to her needs, not easily found with so few low hanging branches or taller brush in this forest. When she was done, she found the creek, the water being not more than fifty yards from the camp. It was small and shallow, the water clear, and Ava knelt beside it, washing her hands and her face, scrubbing a bit at the dried blood at her temple. She rinsed out her mouth as well and drank greedily, so parched from having had nothing to eat or drink all day long. The water was icy cold but refreshing.

She stayed there, not in any hurry to get back to camp. And she didn't fear the distance between her and Innes and Hamish, since she spied several Craig soldiers further upstream or about the forest so that there always seemed to be some person within shouting distance at least.

In the same way the small flickering flames of a fire might mesmerize a person, the clear glossy surface of the water called to her now, reflecting the trunks and foliage across the small ravine. Ava sat then, contemplating with a late-coming dread and disbelief the events of the day.

She was sorry that her tenure inside Lanark had come to an end and wondered if ever it would be safe for her to return there, for Innes or Hamish as well. She knew guilt, had wrestled mostly with that all day long, for having been the cause of her friends' current displacement. Just now though, she wallowed in a wee spot of self-pity, for how unhinged, unsafe, and unstable her life was just now. She'd made a fairly decent life for herself inside Lanark. Though she'd been homeless and regularly hungry, it was familiar, and she'd learned that the worst of circumstances were usually short-lived. She may not eat today, but certainly she would tomorrow, had more often than not proven true. She knew the town well, like the inside of her hand; knew where to lay traps for hares; and what time the almoner would appear with charity; knew where warm and dry straw could be found as a bed; and the basic timing of the English sentinels' walks.

The unknown terrified her, having to start anew. And while she supposed she should be grateful to not be alone in this predicament, Innes and Hamish's equally dire future only brought the guilt to the fore and after only a few minutes, Ava found herself crying at the water's edge, rather distraught at the trouble she'd brought to herself and them.

Sitting with her legs crossed, observing no one close enough now to see or hear her cry, she let her face fall in her hands for a moment, giving herself over to desolation as she rarely did.

Oh, if she could take it all back—the stealing of the grain, the worry over a stranger who'd saved her from the assault, her absurd scheme to see him freed, all of it. All because her stupid skirt had gotten stuck on the underside of the granary wall. How ridiculous! Her life upended over those few seconds it took to free the blasted skirt!

Someone clearing their throat jerked Ava's face up and around. To her mortification, she found John Craig approaching the stream, come from just behind her. Of the fifty people with which she now traveled, this was absolutely the *last* person she would have wanted to see her cry. She wiped nervously at her eyes and nose, ducking her face away from him, until she faced the creek again, adopting instead an *oh, what the hell* attitude. What did anything matter now?

"I...I am simply nae accustomed to so much chaos," she defended her tears, which he'd have to be either deaf or blind to have overlooked. "Nae all at once." And she sat perfectly still, hoping he was only passing by.

The chaos only continued though, as he went to his haunches beside her, splashing water on his face, snapping his wrist roughly to remove water from his fingers when his face was washed.

Remaining on his haunches, he angled toward her, the toe of his boot pivoting on the ground.

"And yet you bring chaos," he observed, not without a trace of irritability.

But it was only a trace, and before she dissected his statement, Ava considered that his tone was contrived to sound less contemptuous. She wondered if he had to persuade himself to not sound so angry as he mostly had in her company since she'd known him.

"Climbed right up those gallows steps," he went on, "dragging your fate along with you."

She had, hadn't she? But—"Would you nae have done the same, if a person was bound to die for you?" When he only shook his head, preferring not to answer, though Ava didn't believe she needed that supposition confirmed, she recalled idly, "I was horribly frightened, but I could nae...I couldn't let you die for me. I could nae have lived with that." She chanced a glance up at him, supposing it must take people eons to grow accustomed to the fierce intensity of his dark-eyed regard. Did they ever?

"So I am left to point out that mayhap in the future you will leave the thieving to those who can," he said. "Why dinna your man, Innes, take that role?"

"Oh, bother," she cut him off, simmering over the way he'd said that—*to those who can*. Bah. "The grain was meant for Evir, a woman who lost her husband and who struggles to feed her bairns." *Oh, God*. What would become of Evir and her brood now? Ava bit her lip, disheartened by yet something more to fret over.

After a moment of silence, she eyed John Craig again.

He studied her yet more, mayhap hadn't taken his hard glare from her while she'd just worried over Evir's fate, and then he lifted himself from his haunches to stand straight, but he did not bid her a good night or simply take his leave.

She was conscious of the fact that the kiss seemed to hang between them, a little terrifying in some manner, almost gigantic in its importance—but which neither one of them had mentioned so far.

He cleared his throat and sounded partly aggrieved when he said, "Come. You should nae be out now by yourself, in the gloaming."

With no reason to either gainsay him or remain as she was, Ava stood and brushed off the rump of her skirts and walked ahead of him away from the creek. She'd not taken more than half a dozen steps before he attacked her from behind, covering her mouth with his hand, his other arm wrapped tight about her chest as he dragged her backward, away from what had served as her path, into the trees.

It didn't dawn on her to scream, but she did instantly struggle in his grasp, scratching at the warm flesh of the hand that covered her mouth as panic seized her.

"Hush!" He hissed firmly but quietly at her ear. "Riders."

Ava went still in his grasp, her eyes wide over his hand, her chest heaving against his arm.

Near her ear, he made a bird call, something vaguely familiar to her, or at least put out with enough competence to sound as a real bird might. She noticed then no other sound immediately, neither birds nor critters. But then she realized what he had heard, a cloaked rustling noise, the slightest clinking of metal, a horse's harness jangling. All the Craig mounts had been queued at the opposite end of the camp, and this sound was coming from across the creek, up the incline of that bank and from within those dark trees there.

John Craig maneuvered them around the stout trunk of a pine, his hand finally falling away from her mouth.

"Down," he whispered with less urgency at her ear. "On your belly."

Trusting him implicitly, Ava complied immediately, dropping to the ground for what seemed the millionth time today. Her hands fell into a pile of leaves and damp forest foulness, eliciting a grimace. She did not startle at all when John landed half on top of her, one arm and one leg thrown over the back of her, possibly to disguise the light fawn color of her mantle. His right elbow settled into the earth and the leaves beside her shoulder, and he kept his head low as he surveyed the trees and shadows beyond the stream.

The quiet moving of a horse, mayhap more than one, was heard again.

John gave another low bird whistle, his head turned momentarily back toward the camp to make the sound carry in that direction. Within seconds, an answering call was heard. The camp had thus been made aware of these possible intruders.

"Fire," Ava whispered to John in the quietest voice she could manage, concerned about that being spotted.

"They hadn't lit it yet," he told her, his voice lower still.

They stayed like that, silent and frozen on the ground, for many long minutes.

And all the thoughts that swirled in her head hadn't anything to do with the riders picking their way almost too quietly through the trees within twenty yards of them.

As if she couldn't help herself, as if no peril threatened her, she closed her eyes and concentrated on him.

He was big and hard and so taut with alertness just now that a great comfort was known for being under his wing.

She was neither obtuse nor blind. She'd seen people touch, embrace in warmth and love, had witnessed even simpler though still caring contact. She'd rarely known it for herself. She'd not ever been in a man's arms, if in fact she were now.

She hadn't known she craved it. Hadn't known anything about such awareness, not until John Craig.

Chapter Six

The fronds of a fern hindered much of his view, but John did not adjust himself to see better. Whoever picked their way with such quiet carefulness over there would come into view eventually, or they would go away. He could see very well the spot just near the stream, at the bank where he'd only moments ago found Ava—crying no less. He would be able to see if any man or animal crossed there and was bound to come upon them.

Hushed voices reached him, the words indecipherable, but the quietness of what was spoken advised they might suspect others were in the area. This also confirmed that there was more than one person.

As the creek ran east to west, so too did the stealthy riders move, staying on the far side of the narrow water.

By now an agonizing three or four minutes might have passed, so slow was their pace.

Ava began to shiver, either from the cold of the ground seeping up into her or from foreboding, John could not say. He used his right arm to draw her further under him, shifting smoothly and noiselessly until his body covered more of hers.

"Shh," he whispered against her hair, his face pressed against the side of her head, while he kept his gaze trained across the shallow creek. He felt her nod in response. Her trembling continued, albeit with less intensity.

Thankfully, the interlopers continued on, though still with a sluggish pace that another several minutes passed before John felt it was safe to move. Even then, he only took himself off Ava, but stayed low on the ground and at her side, shoulder to shoulder with her.

Much better, though, putting space between her body and his. *Jesu*, but that was awkwardly enticing. Mayhap because he already knew her kiss was sweet and beguiling did the feel of her body beneath his—and he sprawled so intimately on top of her—produce such mayhem in him.

"Hold for a few more minutes," he whispered, his voice husky, sparing a glance at her, finding her eyes closed.

When he could no longer hear any noise that might belong to any trespasser, John slowly rose to his feet. He scanned the area a wee bit before helping Ava to rise. Her hand was like ice. John's fingers stiffened before he let go of her hand. He would have no business trying to warm her small, cold hands. He fisted his own, then wiped his hand on the side of his breeches, as if that might somehow remove all traces of contact with her, or the memory of it.

Two lads, Henry and Iain, crept up to him, daggers in hand.

Jaw tight once more, John inclined his head, giving them leave to follow those riders, to see what might be learned about who they were and what they were about.

"English?" Ava asked, still employing a whisper.

John only allowed, "Could be."

"My God, they're everywhere," she complained, her thin brows dropping over her green eyes.

"Aye, Longshanks has flooded the lowlands with them," he explained gruffly, "wants our king apprehended and tried for treason. 'Twas said the Prince of Wales showed himself on this side of the border, about his father's war, the old war dog too ill to fight his own crusade of injustice." With that said, he lifted his hand, indicating she should precede him back to camp. He needed to get away from her. Needed to swiftly and with great vigor dispel from his mind any sense or recollection of how small and soft she'd felt in his embrace.

Christ, but she was dangerous.

Just then, Innes' voice was heard, calling out in a whispered hiss for Ava—until Eachann's voice followed, chirping at the man to hush. Ava, apparently more clever than either Innes or Eachann, waited until she was in sight of the camp before she answered.

"I'm here, Innes." Still, she kept her sweet voice low.

Innes, having been facing Eachann, mayhap giving him some argument for shushing him, swiveled quickly at the sound of her voice. After sparing only a fleeting glance at him, her eyes hooded now, unfathomable, Ava went to where the anxious and controlling Innes was.

John spotted Hamish sitting cross-legged on the ground near where a fire might be made, though it would have to wait until Henry and Iain returned. John scowled anew at this, wondering if the lad had only stayed perched there when everyone else had taken cover at the alarm he'd sounded of riders in the area; that was where Hamish had been sitting earlier, when John had left the camp, gone to the stream.

He needed to get rid of these three, he decided. And quick.

Innes was a hothead, possibly dangerously so. Hamish was simply too absentminded and inattentive to not cause trouble to someone in some way, eventually. And Ava....

Ava was her own brand of danger, practiced unintentionally he was sure, but perilous all the same. For simply being female—he'd never met a soldier who would be pleased to have a women among a moving army; bad luck they were, everyone agreed—for the way she looked and the distraction she presented, being so bluidy striking that there wasn't one among the Craigs who'd not looked twice, or ogled her outright and at length, himself included.

It didn't seem to matter to him that she was, he had to assume, Innes' woman. They were not wed, he knew; she'd given different surnames, hadn't announced Innes as her husband when she first introduced them. She'd jumped when Innes called and had laid her hand on him with a vexing ease, seemed capable of calming the man's foul temper, hinting at some closeness. Such a relationship might likewise be assumed by the unmistakable hostility Innes had displayed toward John, the meaning behind it easily ascribed to a man being sore about his woman kissing another, no matter what good intentions were behind it. But Ava Guthrie belonging to Innes Seàrlas...? All the more reason to see her—all of them—gone. Being fascinated by another man's woman was bad business, no matter how mesmerizing the woman or how unworthy the man in question.

John understood that he'd only been lucky thus far, had escaped what fate should have been his for having been so effortlessly preoccupied with her. But luck was a fickle creature, never staying so long in one place.

Aye, they needed to part company.

At that moment, his mind chose to play for him the scene of her running at him today, when those English had been chasing her. He didn't need to close his eyes to recall the look in hers, the way she'd met and held his gaze, not any other's. Likely, that moving image would be embedded in his brain for some time to come. Presently, with the recollection, came the same unaccountable reaction: his heart sped up, his stomach twisted in anguish, a damnably peculiar reaction to a virtual stranger in peril, spellbinding kiss notwithstanding.

Assuming that so long as Ava remained in any close proximity, he would wear this scowl and know this inner tumult, John removed himself again from their campsite, meaning to get on a bit of hunting himself, needing to ease all the fury and frustration that had been his constant companions since he'd first laid eyes on Ava Guthrie.

***

She woke in the same spot and position she'd assumed when she'd fallen asleep, on her side and nestled between Hamish and Innes on the ground, with little to offer her warmth save for the heat of their bodies.

She stared at the gray sky overhead, dawn not yet risen fully, while the hollowness of her stomach made itself known. And she wondered what the day might bring, as she did almost every morning. Hope was not something she'd made good friends with, but she'd adopted a habit of believing that each new day offered fresh opportunities for betterment, an improvement of her circumstances. Sometimes this centered solely on what she might eat that day, or who might be in need of aid that she could possibly give. That was all she had, and not much else, to sustain her every day, survival being always an overwhelming priority.

Her present circumstance might well suggest that survival was at greater risk, and yet she did not feel burdened by worry over this. She was ensconced with the army of the Lion of Blacklaw Tower; survival seemed not only likely but probable. Nae,

Ava's concern this morn could be summed up fairly easily: what now?

To her left lay Hamish, his footprint upon the earth in this spot between a sturdy hazel tree and a towering pine being almost the same as the amount of space Ava and Innes together consumed. He rolled onto his back, yawning without sound, though his mouth remained wide open and shifting for many seconds.

"Nae quite as comfortable as the straw in Dottie Og's pen," Ava commented quietly to him, referring to a place they'd sometimes made their beds.

Showing no surprise to find her awake as well, Hamish only remarked, with his customary volume, "I dinna like her place. Nae right hand side to rise. Unlucky, that."

Ava grinned briefly, aware of Hamish's predilection with the need to always rise from his right side, which at Dottie Og's place, where space was severely limited, had been nearly impossible to do, forcing them to rise from the left, considered a bad omen for the day.

"Do you ken our misfortunes stem from that, Hamish?" She asked, with only half a mind to seriousness. "From rising one too many times on the left?"

Without hesitation, and with a wee solemnity, Hamish stated, "All our misfortunes began at our births."

Before she had time to mull over this sad but probable truth, Innes turned over on her right side.

"Bollocks, Hamish," he groused almost instantly, "you'd wake the dead, I vow."

Not giving Hamish time to respond to the allegation, which might have only been louder in defense of the charge leveled against him, Ava asked Innes, "Where will today bring us?"

Innes made a face, which Ava judged as sudden disgruntlement, likely having little yet to do with being wakened by Hamish.

"At the mercy of the lion," he said.

"Getting on some place called Lismore Abbey, I heard them say," Hamish informed them.

"Further north," Innes alleged, "by the way they spoke of it. We'll ken better when we're there, what town might be close to serve us best."

Aye, they would fare better inside a larger burgh or city, where they could meld into crowds or the shadows of dwellings or buildings, where their occasionally criminal activities would be conspicuous.

"Sure and that all depends on what the English are about," Innes said, sitting up and rolling his neck as if to relieve a crick. "And will we nae be pleased to never see another one of their hackit pusses again?"

Ever literal, Hamish challenged, "I canna see nae half of them, always with their helms on."

"You just take it from me then, Hamish," Innes said, "toads they are, all of them. Murdering toads."

"North is guid then, is it nae?" Ava asked, rolling to her feet. "The further away the better."

She ducked off into the trees and found a private place to see to her needs but did not go to the same stream where she'd washed her face last evening, not wanting to chance running into John Craig again. Though she hadn't detected any wakeful movement from the Craig camp itself, she was taking no chances.

Her recently discovered but incredibly inconvenient want to be in his arms was not something that had any chance of becoming reality, was only a tantalizing yet frivolous dream, one that had no place in her presently upended life. Aside from the very obvious class distinction between them—he a laird, his legend known far and wide, and she a peasant, known only by Innes and Hamish and mayhap a few people inside Lanark who would likely forget her very name before the month was out—there was also the other truth to consider, which he'd made no effort to hide, that he would be quite happy to have never met her, or see her again once they parted ways.

Within the hour, Ava was mounted once again behind Innes, not at all looking forward to a long day in the saddle. She'd not ever ridden for more than a mile or so, and those times had been rare, but yesterday's lengthy gallop atop a horse had made her wonder seriously why people didn't walk more places. Muscles in her legs, ones she hadn't known existed before last night, had introduced themselves with screaming enthusiasm. She didn't expect that today would be any different, that her achy muscles would have so quickly adapted and overcome. Actually, she expected greater resentment from her body tonight, for the bruising pace that was set early and maintained most of the day.

The trek was made mostly in silence, communication all but impossible unless one only wanted to spend the day shouting over the thundering of galloping horses. Ava hadn't anything so important to say that it couldn't wait until they stopped, thus Innes and she exchanged but a handful of words all morning.

And none of the Craig soldiers rode so close that she felt compelled to make conversation with any of them.

Shortly after noon, they stopped at the base of a tall and inhospitably steep mountain, watering horses at the thin stream that twined in the beinn's shadow. Ava dismounted as some of the Craig men had, leaving Innes to the care of the courser, eager to stretch her aching legs. It took some doing to walk with a normal gait and give no hint of how raw the insides of her thighs were. Most every inch of her body would have been quite pleased if Innes and Hamish wished to part company with the Craigs here and abandon their furious pace. Surely they were well beyond the reach of the English by now. *Most* of her body, anyway; her keen eyes could not seem to avoid seeking out the impressive figure of John Craig; her brain wondered if she'd been thrown back into his path for any particular reason, wondering if she should be so bold as to imagine Fate had a hand in their reunion.

And then, for all the times her eyes did seek and find John Craig, she wasn't oblivious to how many of those times she'd been met with a returned stare. She hadn't any idea what it might mean, being that his visage on those occasions displayed no more charity toward her or even a slightly diminished scowl than it had at any other time. Still and always, he was severe in expression any time she found his regard upon her.

Her constant awareness of him, though, did mean that she was not startled as he approached her now—wary indeed, but not unnerved by surprise. He had dismounted and was simply walking his huge destrier about, his strong hands loose on the reins, mayhap not so much seeking her out as simply striding in her direction.

And yet he paused when he was within half a dozen feet of her. Ava bit her lip and met what looked to be a shrewd-eyed scrutiny.

"You might better be served by riding side-saddle," he observed.

"Oh," she remarked without an ounce of cleverness. "I had... I dinna ken that is a guid idea. Already, I feel as if I am only one hard bounce away from falling off the rump."

His brows drew down and his head tilted in such a way that ava next expected an eye roll, though that never fully materialized.

"Ride in front of your man," he said. "You'll be chafed bloody otherwise."

Ava's eyes grew large but only for a second before she reined in her reaction. She was not of a mind to discuss with this fearsome warrior the delicate condition of her inner thighs.

"I will—"

"She's fine," interrupted Innes, returned now and still holding the reins of the horse they'd shared, "and dinna need coddling, do you, Ava?"

Caught between the sweet temptation of a more comfortable ride and the need to take the same position as her friend, she forced a tight smile and chose the latter, "I am fine, thank you." She removed her gaze from John Craig then, and thus was not privy to his reaction before he ambled away in the next second and Ava was given leave to breathe normally again.

"If you were smaller," Innes said, a grumble in his tone, "that might be feasible, but nae way I can manage the horse around you."

She nodded, accepting this as sound reasoning, knowing full well the other side of the coin was closer to the truth, that he was not large enough to make it work.

They moved on after only a quarter hour, Ava once more seated astride behind Innes, and employed the same grueling pace as they had in the morning.

It was late afternoon when they came upon an isolated group of cottages, at least two of which were built into the side of a hillock. They did not circumvent the small settlement but rode straight at it. Ava counted six houses, if that be what the long thatched structures were. There was one huge, two story barn and several other smaller lean-tos and outbuildings, but that was all, with naught but a mountain behind them in the north, and a vast loch to the south over which was situated the most curious structure, a round, thatched roof dwelling that sat on scraped-raw timber pillars but showed a small islet at its base. A causeway of stone and timber led from the solid earth out to that islet and its round cottage.

"How remarkable." Ava mused, her eyes darting to take in everything at once, at this tiny hamlet entombed in this glen, with no fortress or stronghold in sight to project any defense of whoever might live here.

***

John was pleased to see plumes of smoke rising from all the dwellings of Eynon Kenith's settlement. Long had it been since he'd made himself known here, but pleased he would be to reacquaint himself with these fine people.

"All is well, then," Eachann said at his side, possibly knowing the same relief that John had.

The very remoteness of their homesteads both protected and endangered them, John had always thought. Eynon Kenith was more than three times John's age—had been a contemporary of his father, in whose company John had first been introduced to him and this location—and had moved heaven and earth, several times, to keep his family safe.

This then, might be their longest stay at any place, having removed from their home country, Wales, and then a generation ago, having been forced from England when Edward I had made war with Wales and Eynon's position inside England had become untenable.

When they were within shouting distance of the closely situated dwellings, John called forward his standard bearer and only he and young Gille-Caluim rode ahead, the latter unfurling the Craig banner and hoisting it above his head, the bottom of the heavy pike on which it was affixed tucked into a leather cup attached near the pommel of his saddle.

They came slowly from those dwellings as John and Gille-Caluim neared and all that was quiet in this valley erupted into joyful chaos, as much as thirty or so people could make, when John's crest had been identified.

He felt more often a greater man here, so gladly welcomed, laddies and lasses rushing his destrier, smiles bright upon these pale faces. He acknowledged them with his own smile before lifting his gaze to Eynon Kenith, who'd come to stand and wait at the head of the walkway leading out to his renovated crannog. Dismounting not far from there, he left the destrier in the care of the Kenith lads and allowed his smile to open fully as he stepped into Eynon's fond embrace.

John could never think of him as an old man, not when he stood so tall and erect, his bearing born of strength and tenacity, having less to do with bravado. But old he was, white-haired and bearded, his blue eyes sinking further into his face as the years went on. The arms that enfolded him and the hands that clapped on his back were not weak, enfeebled by years, but robust, forged by a constant of hard labor and hard fights.

"Great honor, this is," Eynon said as they parted, his English vastly improved from when first they'd met when John had been but a lad.

"Aye, and pleased I am to find you and yours well and safe," John told him. He shifted his gaze and gave a courteous bow to Eynon's wife, Morvel, her face old though the eyes that crinkled warmly at John were very young.

"You do not ever change, John mac Cormaic," said Morvel, dipping her chin to her chest as a bow. "So proud and strong yet, and so honorable to take the time to call on us."

Eynon, known for years for his inability to be too serious for too long, cocked his head and peered beyond John. "Someone chasing you?"

John grinned again. "Nae this time. Or nae still." He made a show of laying his hand over his bare neck, his thumb over the left side and four fingers on the right. Pretending to grimace, he intoned, "Was close though."

Eynon clapped his hands together. "Grand, and you've tales to tell, yea?"

Knowing it was expected, that Eynon loved news but mostly of the entertaining, life-intact kind, John nodded and Eynon lifted his hands, broadly waving forward the remainder of John's party, which simultaneously called forth his own kin, the less intrepid ones, who spilled out from behind thatched huts, as if they'd only waited Eynon's permission.

He was welcomed by Eynon and Morvel's eight children, most older than John as well, wed and having flocks of their own, and all those children, third and fourth generation Welsh Keniths living here in the fastnesses of the Highlands.

In his life, he'd traveled far and wide, had visited noble houses and both Scottish courts and English ones before the war, had been to France and once had spent a fortnight at the grand fortress at Dunnottar, a pair of years before Wallace captured it. At no time and in no place had he ever known so warm a welcome as he invariably received from these people. Never had he been treated as less than beloved kin himself—he and his men—and not once had he ever imagined his coming either untimely or undesirable. Truth be told, if they had not settled an area that was so remote, and if war had not kept him busy for so many years now, he'd have made a point to come round more often, so valuable was their friendship.

The Craigs came happily, horses charging down the hill, those old enough or long enough with John able to recall their last rousing visit to this area more than three years ago. The Keniths were equally engaged, having few reasons outside of admired visitors to know such joy, both parties thinking on the evening ahead.

Morvel interrupted her husband's speech, reminding John of the names of his children's children who gathered again around him, names he would likely not remember come the morn.

"A woman travels with you," she said, her gaze cast beyond John to the coming Craigs.

John swiveled his head, catching sight of Ava, her hair flying loose and remarkably so behind her as they descended.

"Aye," he said with a sigh, explaining her presence with a crooked grin aimed at Morvel. "Uh, aye, and she being part of the reason for my most-recent close call with the English."

"English?" Morvel gasped, her hand going to her chest while her mouth hung open.

"Nae, she is Scots—in blood and birth and boldness," he confirmed.

Morvel removed her stark gaze from Ava, even as Innes reined in and they dismounted, and settled her regard once more onto John. One thin brow lifted, and a grin overtook her. "Yea then, I'll want to hear this tale."

"I figured as much, my lady," he allowed.

In Wales, Eynon had been a wealthy nobleman and Morvel his aristocratic wife, a descendant of Bleddyn ap Cynfyn, once the king of the counties of Gwynedd and Powys. Here, they were naught but farmers, fisherman, and shepherds, but Morvel had lost little of her noble graciousness.

Eynon rolled his eyes. "Pray, lady wife, neither surmise nor contrive, when we still have so many daughters and their daughters with which to tempt him."

John grinned anew but the gleam in Morvel's eyes was not subdued.

"Too young he is for our daughters," she reasoned, "too old he is for their daughters."

She frowned then and stepped forward, unceremoniously reaching out to John's neck, moving the collar of his tunic out of the way, with the effrontery of a mother, inspecting the area where surely remained the redness from where the noose had cinched so tightly.

"Hmm," she said, lifting piercing, knowing blue eyes to John. "So much said just there."

"Read nothing into anything but my words, my lady," he advised, though his mood remained unchanged, still cheerier than any he'd known of late. "Which," he added, as an afterthought, "I'll nae give if I should expect you'll twist them to your own delight."

"I will do as I please, as well you know, John mac Cormaic, and off with you now. Go on, get the hunting in, lest we have naught to feast with but the fowl and fish."

This, too, was well-known to John. They would not rush the meal, providing only what they'd already prepared for their own families, but would make a feast of it, sharing generously of their whiskey and wine, and putting out a feast that would only be made whole by the addition of some larger game, which John and some of his men, and Eynon and his sons would pursue now.

And he might have escaped Morvel's machinating just then, but that she stopped him before Eynon would have taken him away.

"Bring her to me, if you please," she said. At John's hesitation, she challenged him. "You would leave the poor thing to the absent gallantries of your soldier men?"

He knew better than to argue with her, and he wished never to be the cause of Morvel's irritation. The feast she would oversee and provide would be well worth whatever plot was presently being engineered, whatever she imagined she might believe about the matter of Ava Guthrie.

With a sigh, he nodded and made his way toward his army and through the horses and men, to where Ava stood with Innes and Hamish.

"'Tis a fine family, of Welsh origins, with whom we've passed many a pleasurable night," he explained briefly to all three of them. "They will insist on providing a feast for our visit, and so we will hunt first—if you're so inclined," he thought to add, extending that invitation to Innes and Hamish. He met Ava's green eyes, no less startling now than on any other occasion he'd stared into them. And while nothing should be gleaned from her expression—he did not know her well enough to judge her thoughts by way of her countenance—something leapt in his chest for how anxiously but steadily she returned his gaze. "The lady wife of Eynon Kenith requests your company."

"Mine?" She questioned, thumping her forefinger onto her chest.

"Aye, possibly she dinna believe any Craig capable of either chivalry or consideration, by my understanding," he said dryly. "Feels you will be better served for in her company, and that of her daughters. Come," he said next, extending his hand.

Ava stepped forward and lifted her hand at the same time Innes spoke up, his frown as quick and dark as Ava's submission had been hesitating and anxious.

"You canna simply walk off with her," he argued, "and these people unknown to either—"

"Stand down, lad," John said curtly just as Ava laid her fingers in his palm. "I've just said these people are kent as friends to us. It is nae for us to refuse our hosts." More darkly, with a greater warning in his tone, he advised as well, "You are among the

Craigs now, and counted as one of us. Dinna make me regret bringing you here."

With that, he led Ava away from the pair and toward the causeway where Morvel waited. Eynon had moved, likely readying all that would be needed for the hunt, but Morvel was still surrounded by several of her daughters.

Almost immediately, and when they were still dozens of yards away, Ava wondered in a small voice, "But what am I to do with them? Or what do they want?"

"They want to ken you, and if I ken Morvel, she'll want to make these few hours both amusing and enjoyable for you. She is of a giving and solicitous nature, lives and loves to coddle."

"Oh," Ava said succinctly, and followed that with, "But you will—will you be with me?"

John turned and considered her, her sudden unease. "Never say you've been abandoned by the fortitude that sent you up the steps of the gallows."

"You must have realized by now that was a fleeting, hastily-designed, and wholly uncharacteristic side of me," she presumed.

"Lass, somehow I dinna suspect that is truth talking."

Chapter Seven

Ava stood before a woman who at one time must have been a great beauty, with clear blue eyes and nearly flawless skin. Only her hair truly gave away her advanced years, being wiry with gray strands, though it was swept neatly into a serviceable but not unattractive chignon. She wore a fine léine of brilliant red, the sleeveless gown revealing a kirtle of bright gold. The léine was joined at her chest with a metal pin shaped as a swan's head, while the bodice was embroidered with gold threads.

The woman looked her over, rather regal in her perusal, Ava judged, so much so that she momentarily wondered if she should be bowing or curtseying. The light blue of the woman's gaze sat last and longest on Ava and John's joined hands.

John released her hand then and introduced her. "My lady, may I present Ava Guthrie, late of Lanark. Ava, this is Morvel Kenith, and you are nae to believe one word she says about me."

Ava tore her gaze from Morvel Kenith to stare with some disbelieving wildness at John Craig. Was he...making light of something? Actually teasing? 'Twas hard to say, his expression as unfathomable as ever, his brown eyes engaged in some wordless exchange with the woman. Ava was astounded.

"Unless it's given as praise, no?" the woman presumed, arching a thin brow.

"Naturally," John returned, still sounding as if he might be engaging in a jape, but looking as he always did, severe and without humor but then also so very handsome.

"We are honored to receive you, my dear," the woman said next, addressing Ava.

"The honor is mine, my lady," Ava replied, smiling with a wee wonder for what might have just transpired.

She was subsequently introduced to the daughters of Morvel: Merderun, Gwerith, Elena, Mabilia, and Angharat—names she would not be able to recall in the next five minutes, she was sure. Each of the daughters were at least twice as old as Ava, all of them pale-skinned and dark-haired, but none of them showed so remarkable a beauty in their relative youth than their mother surely had at any age.

Then Morvel raised that one brow again at John Craig, who stood at Ava's side yet.

"That is all, John mac Cormaic," Morvel Kenith said dismissively, as her grinning daughters surrounded Ava and began to push and pull her toward the curiously round, thatched roof house. "She will fare well with us, never fear."

When Ava cast a glance over her shoulder, a wee unnerved by the way they'd so easily confiscated her, the ever-so-slight curving of John's marvelous lips put her somewhat at ease—which was remarkable, as she'd never seen him make such a face. If she didn't know better, she'd have thought he was thinking of smiling.

Morvel Kenith followed behind then, stepping into the path of Ava's gaze. "Go on, my dear. You'll see him soon enough, will have all night to be mooning over him."

"Mooning—?" Ava repeated, briefly struck mute by this. "Oh, gosh, nae. I just...."

"Everyone enthuses over John mac Cormaic, Ava Guthrie. Let us not begin our association with lies."

That accusatory challenge was swiftly forgotten as Ava stepped through the round house, the daughters of Morvel releasing her to walk on while Ava paused and gaped.

Plenty of buildings and houses and structures she'd walked into in her life—kirks and priories, tower houses and manor houses, crofts and hovels and inns, as well—but never had she seen anything like this one. It was as primitive as it was sumptuous.

She'd had to duck under the edges of a reed and bracken thatched roof to step inside and thus was surprised by the height and breadth of the interior. At the exact center of the round house sat a wide hearth, accessible from two sides, made of clay and stone and showing at least one enclosed section that might be an oven. Two large timbers, part of the structure of the building, rose up from beneath the floor and met with the roof; they flanked the hearth and from these another wooden pole was attached perpendicularly with rope made of wild flax, where hung two large kettles over the hot coal fire. The floor surrounding the immediate area of the hearth was covered in more clay, and beyond that, covering all the remainder of the floor of this house was a thick matting of bracken and rushes and hay, and in several sections, fur hides had been laid atop this.

A curved bench made of more timber had been fashioned into the interior wall, broken occasionally by doorways, one of which clearly led to an area where livestock were housed—Ava heard bleating and clucking coming from that opening. Curiously, another platform was fashioned overhead, circumnavigating the house where the thatch met the wall. Hay and more fur were seen overhanging some sections and Ava wondered if that entire raised area served as a loft for sleeping.

There were only two windows inside and both faced the loch water and not land, both shuttered now, though their light was not needed since several pine tapers, set into odd iron holders, burned as fir candles around the house. Another bench, this one free standing, sat in a semi-circle at the opposite side of the hearth, closer to the fire, its construction hidden now since all of it was covered in brightly colored wool blankets and more fur throws. Bundles of drying grasses, wheat and barley and others, hung from rafters overhead. A weaving loom sat against one part of the wall, half-filled with warp strings of vivid blue, and directly before Ava, just inside the door in front of the fire, apparently was the kitchen. A quern stone and a collection of pots and utensils, of wood and clay and bone, sat neatly there, where obviously all work was done whilst sitting on the floor.

"This is...this is amazing," she finally remarked, a wee stunned for how cozy and comfortable it looked, for all the bright colors found amid the gray and brown earthen works.

She was compelled to step forward by the advent of several young girls, all of them dark-haired and blue-eyed. They came giggling and squealing, rushing around Ava and scampering to different parts of the house.

"Come, come, my dear," invited Morvel. "We've much to do to prepare."

"Yes, of course," Ava said, "and what can I do?"

"Oh, but Mam," cried one of Morvel's daughters—Mabilia, Ava thought it was, "but look at her hair."

Mabilia had remained close to Ava as they'd entered and now lifted one long and snarly lock, confusing Ava as she stared so covetously at the tangled mess, which was not so different in color than her own.

"Mam, please let me attend her hair," Mabilia begged. "So long it's been since we've had any reason to fuss so."

Nervously, Ava ran her hand down the side of her hair, pulling it closer to her head, embarrassed for its condition. "Oh, no, please. My hair is...long has it been since it was washed properly. We had to hide inside this cave and all this dirt kept falling—"

"Then a washing is first, yes?" Mabilia asked, wide-eyed with enthusiasm.

"Oh, that's nae—" Ava began to demur, truly embarrassed now.

"Yes," interrupted Morvel, standing on the opposite side of the fire, a gleam of purpose in her blue eyes now. She clapped her hands, and two more daughters came toward Ava. "Let us treat our guest."

And then she said something in another language, presumably Welsh, which Ava of course did not understand, save for three words, *John mac Cormaic*, which was answered by the Kenith daughters in wide-eyes and ribald laughter, just before Ava was seized and dragged to the rear of the house.

***

It was more than two hours later by the time the hunting party had returned, processed and prepared the red stag that John had been given the honor of bringing down, and before they washed up and returned to the round house. The majority of his army had made themselves useful around the settlement in the meantime. He spied Henry and Iain, those two rarely separated, splitting wood with several of the Kenith grandchildren; Eachann, who'd cried off from the hunting, was just now one of the men steering one of the Kenith lock boats back to shore; also inside that long boat, Eynon's son, Hywel, proudly held up the crowded string of fish they'd caught; upon the braeside, a half dozen Craig soldiers helped the Kenith lads bring in the sheep for the night, moving them steadily down to the pens; John caught sight of Innes Seàrlas near one of the family's smaller houses, on the mainland, his arm leaned against the house, and with a dark-haired Kenith lass standing in his gaze, with her back to the wall and making eyes at the man. John scowled at this, for how quickly Innes seemed to have forgotten about Ava, and then for the greater ire it raised, thoughts of Innes Seàrlas behaving poorly.

He paused then, waiting until Eachann caught up with him and inclined his head in Innes' direction. "I dinna want any trouble. Put someone in charge of keeping him in line."

Eachann turned his frown onto Innes and decided, "Aye, I'll have him draw lots with the lads." He winked at John. "I'll tell Henry to make sure he draws the short stick."

John nodded, knowing the men would indeed draw lots to determine which would be charged with taking turns at watch and in which order they'd go. Though they might partake of the feast provided, the crannog was only large enough to house during the evening not more than a dozen guests, John would imagine. At the end of the night, he and his men would be expected to find their beds inside the large barn as they had on other occasions they'd visited.

He ducked and stepped inside the crannog now, his senses immediately inundated with the aroma of roasting fowl, and the oat-y scent of bread baking. The candles made of pine fought vigorously for attention, their scent being almost as strong as any other.

He stood just inside the door, reluctant to go further since Ava Guthrie sat directly in front of him, ensconced with Mabilia and Elena. Truth be told, he was rather arrested by the sight of her and wasn't sure his feet would obey any command to keep moving.

Ava in her worn léine and threadbare mantle, with her hair in its customary knot at her nape and her cheeks at any given time stained with dirt or blood was eye-catching enough. But this Ava, with her hair apparently freshly washed and arranged in long waves around her face and shoulders, much of it still damp, and with her pink-tinted cheeks, wearing a borrowed léine of a bold green that highlighted the magnificence of her almond-shaped eyes, was truly a marvel.

Mabilia was busy at her side, adding thin braids to the side of her head, while Ava sat crossed legged, using the quern and grindstone, running the stone up and back along the quern, grinding pepper would have been John's guess, as another scent assaulted his nostrils. He paid little heed to her chore, though, thought of nothing once Ava lifted her green eyes to him. The golden dimness of the interior of the crannog lent an emerald sheen to her eyes, and he would have wagered much if any bet was to be made about the pink in her cheeks rising to red at his coming.

He thought a smile might have been her greeting, as that seemed ready to come, her bonny face animated and showing what looked to be some pleasure that he'd returned. Whatever had been or was going to be her reaction was nipped in the bud. It took him a moment to realize that his scowl—fierce and nae pleased at all to find her so bluidy beautiful—had forestalled her response. She bit the inside of her cheek briefly before she lowered her eyes from him.

John sighed, his own ineptness irksome, his want to keep his distance more troubling when failure seemed more likely.

Morvel spoke up from further inside the crannog, and John jerked into motion, heading toward her.

"Do not be scaring that sweet child with so cruel a face, John mac Cormaic," Morvel said in her native tongue. "She has been watching the door for hours, awaiting your return."

Sensing the teasing in Morvel's crinkled blue eyes, John warned good-naturedly, "Pray do not spread false tales, couched in a language she cannot understand to refute," he said in his very rusty, never fully learned Welsh, which garnered a shameless smirk from Morvel and more vocal tittering from a few of her daughters.

"Always too clever, you were," she remarked and switched to English. "Here, John, move these kettles down to the warming stones. Eynon brings a spit impaled into some worthy beast, I presume."

He did as she asked and aye, soon enough, Eynon and Elena's husband, Ithel, entered with the dressed stag, the pole of the spit leveraged on their shoulders.

John stepped out of the way, taking a seat on the closer curved bench, trying not to send his gaze too often in Ava's direction. As she always did, Morvel managed everyone and everything, overseeing the roasting of the stag, directing her daughters about the cooking of other foods, telling people where to sit as they entered, calling for Eynon to produce the wine.

Ava stood on the other side of the fire, seen here and there around the turning and roasting deer. Mabilia untied the apron from Ava's back and Elena collected the quern and ground pepper from her. She was steered with a hand at her back around the fire just as Morvel commanded her gently to sit.

What happened next was simply another marvel, Morvel at her finest at maneuvering things to her liking. Ava went first to the far bench that lined the outside wall, possibly wanting to be either unnoticed or unobtrusive. Morvel would have none of it, squawking a bit in Welsh, waving her hand until Ava understood she was expected to sit at a place of honor at the area closer to the fire, for those guests would be served first. Morvel's eyes skinnied a bit when Ava took a seat several lengths away from John, offering him little more than a shy smile, likely in response for how she'd just been scolded into obedience in words she didn't understand. The bench began to fill as more of the Kenith family and John's officers came for the meal. Eynon, his work done for the day, sat directly beside John. Several people, adults and children, sat in the rushes and fur in front of this bench. Seeing this, and possibly not wanting to assume a position greater than she thought she deserved, Ava moved from the bench to the ground, squeezing between Mabilia and Angharat's daughter. This seemed to suit Mabilia just fine, as she whispered something to Ava that turned her sensuous lips upward in a rare smile. Lost for a moment in the glory of her easy smile, John couldn't say for sure how so much shifting occurred, save that Morvel had a hand in it, pretending to want to squeeze more people in, waving curtly at this one and then that one to move this way or that, until she smiled with unrestrained glee when it was to her liking, and Ava was now situated directly in front of John. She sat so close that he had to open his legs, putting a boot on either side of her. Her loose hair brushed against his knee or calf with each turn of her head.

They were not the only ones who sat as such. Mabilia's husband sat next to John while she, at his feet, turned and familiarly laid her arm over her husband's knee, asking how the fishing went. A younger lass was on her knees, facing her grandfather, her small hands laid on his thighs, while she spoke with great animation to him in Welsh, her speech too fast for John to understand though Eynon seemed tickled by whatever she was saying.

Ava turned her face around and up to John. "Is this all right? Am I crowding you?"

"Nae," he said and then was forced to clear his throat. "Nae, you're fine." He looked up, aware that his own face might now be flushed, and caught the end of Morvel's smirk, before she returned her attention to one of the kettles and its contents.

Eachann had been directed to a space at the end of the same bench on which John sat, and Hamish had come, was seated now to John's left, along the outer wall, making conversation with the Craig scout, Iain, who must have drawn one of the longer twigs. Innes was not in attendance but by the time the wine began to flow and almost every Kenith was accounted for within, the crannog was nearly bursting at the seams. It would clear out after the meal, he knew; the younger children would hie to the lofts to watch the goings-on from above.

Of course, it should not have been expected that enough flasks and cups would be available for every person, so that John was not surprised when Morvel announced that some would have to share. He was even less surprised, after witnessing some of the lady's machinations, that when Eynon pressed a carved horn into his hand, the old man nudged at him and pointed to Ava, advising he would share with her. John nodded, but held off taking a sip, knowing Eynon would want first to toast their gathering.

Eynon waited until his wife paused at her tasks at the hearth and lowered herself just at its side, until she sat on her knees. She accepted a delicate bone cup and gave a nod to her husband.

"Welcome to our beloved Craig friends," Eynon began. He did not stand, but lifted his metal chalice, holding it over his head all the while he spoke. "This is many years in the making, our reunion with John mac Cormaic and his fine army. Our hearts delight that God has kept him true and safe, and we will not fail to remember to pray for his continued safe-keeping, for he is the Lion of Blacklaw Tower and our freedom, chased for so many years across three countries, rests ably on his shoulders and those of his ilk." Eynon lifted the chalice even higher and proclaimed, "Welcome the Craigs!"

Shouts and cheers followed, both inside and through the open door, where many more Keniths and Craigs gathered. John drank of the wine in the horn and then passed it on to Ava, who sipped more delicately.

Next, Eynon said, "Been long enough, this meeting, that I feel obliged to relive once more the very first meeting between ours and theirs."

Any who'd sat just here several years ago when John had come last would surely recall the tale, but aye, there were plenty *ours and theirs* who might not ever have heard it. John nodded at Eynon, *aye, it is well*.

"There is something to be said," Eynon began solemnly, "for the fact that the very same devil who would steal freedom now has done so many times—too many times—before. Thus, we must go back to Wales a generation ago, when I myself was a young man." He raised his cup again, this time finding his wife. "And my bride was not yet mine. And so the English came, the constant of doom at their lead. Edward I and his troops did not find the taking of Wales any easier then than this attempt to take Scotland now. And lo, one of his fiercest knights was cut down, and thought to make his escape across the bridge of boats the English had constructed. But his wounds were grave, and his armor weighed him down and life began to ebb, until...?" he lifted his hand again, prompting his adult children and mayhap some of the grandchildren, any who knew the tale, to fill in the blank he'd left open.

"Until the indescribably beautiful Morvel of Anglesey fished him from the Menai Strait," several people finished.

"Ah, such learned children, you are," Eynon teased, and he led everyone in another round of drinking. "Sure and she did," he went on then, "and did not the warrior wake under her care, and"—he pointed now at Morvel—"you know he could not have helped himself, under her spell."

Morvel only feigned a self-consciousness for being so central to this tale, waving a dismissive hand as she lifted her chin.

"That was Cormaic Craig, for those not in the know, sire to our most-esteemed John Craig," Eynon continued. "We cannot be sure, of course, but we surmise that the elder Craig might have indeed feigned much of his torment by wounds, simply to remain in her company."

A wave of raucous laughter followed this, even from those who'd heard the story so many times by now.

"We drink to his strong heart," Eynon proposed.

This time, Ava held the horn and drank first before handing it to John.

"But then the fighting was not done and our heroine's very life was in danger and who should come to her aid—or rather, not wish to be parted from her—but the hero, Cormaic Craig, who whisked she and her family to England and out of harms' way."

John listened attentively, as much as he was able, nodding appropriately when so inclined, and sipping thoughtfully from the horn of wine. Mostly, though, his regard was captured by Ava, sitting at his feet, nearly between his legs. The constant exchanging of the shared wine, and her attention on Eynon's tale had made her shift on her bottom so that she sat sideways between his feet, offering John a perfect profile view, from which he was frequently unable to wrench his gaze.

"So honorable a man was he, that next he sought and found the captured freedom fighter—that would be me, children." Eynon said, eliciting more giggles and guffaws. "Even as he knew that her heart was otherwise engaged, he sought to make her happy. We drink to his chivalry."

And so they did. John noticed that Ava took smaller and smaller sips.

"Paid the ransom for this old man, then young," Eynon said, growing somber, as if he recalled now specifically and fondly that man, Cormaic Craig, "and asked nothing in return but that I keep our beloved Morvel safe. We drink to his selflessness."

John watched Ava stare at Eynon with a bit of awe and then transfer her gaze to Morvel. John moved his gaze there as well, a witness to the exchange between Eynon and his wife, the blessed harmony between them. Ava next turned her gaze up to John, her lips parted with wonder at the tale, he had to assume. "How beautiful," she said quietly.

Eynon cleared his throat, quiet for those last few seconds, stirred to wistfulness mayhap by the memories invoked. "Never has there been a more good and kind man," said Eynon, "who, once his strength was returned, could as easily have sliced off my head as reunited me with my love. We drink to our forever friend, though gone too long he is."

All hands were raised, whether they held a drink or nae, and the cheer that went up was as it ever was, loud and heartfelt, and instilled John with thankfulness and a sense of pride, to be that man's son, to claim that hero as his sire.

Chapter Eight

Food was served after Eynon had finished. The Kenith daughters stood and collected trays from their mother and first walked them around, offering sweet breads and cheese and what looked to be dried figs. Never having partaken of so generous and offering under so unusual a gathering, Ava only did what John did, as the platter was presented first to him. She selected a few tasty morsels and kept them in her hands, sampling first the semi-soft cheese, which was bold with flavor. 'Twas only the first course, she presumed, since the huge side of venison still roasted on the spit and the kettles were yet filled with their simmering stews.

"So we've done with tradition, the praise of our dear friend, Cormaic Craig," Eynon Kenith said when flasks and horns and cups had been generously refilled, "and never let that be laid to rest in my life. But here now, John mac Cormaic, there is some narrative, comes from Lanark so I hear about a length of rope strung round your neck and a compelling explanation for that charming discoloration about your face. And who will be telling that tale?"

"Dinna begin with *his* neck, that's for sure," Eachann called out, looking pointedly at Ava, his grin encouraging.

Ava froze as so many blue eyes settled with great expectation upon her. "Oh, I only ken the half of it, but I'm...I am nae guid at weaving stories." With purpose, hoping to remove so much attention from herself, she turned her face up to John.

"And they ken I would turn even the heartiest tale into a sleep-inducing yarn," John said.

"'Tis true!" Someone called out, and more laughter followed.

John shrugged, appearing so unbelievably lighthearted. Ava was transfixed, until her attention was drawn by Eachann, rising to his feet in her periphery.

"My lot in life," Eachann groused, yanking up his breeches as he stood. "Want something done right, got to do it myself."

A round of anticipatory applause rang out, and Eynon Kenith chuckled and leaned across John, patting Ava's shoulder. "You stop him, lass, soon as you hear anything that does not agree with the truth."

"So it begins with Sir James Douglas and our laird, John Craig, making plans to survey, quiet-like, the city of Lanark, planning to wrest it from those foul English hands. And we'll drink to their daring," he said, holding up his own leather-clad flask, "for everyday fighting to rid the land of those English." He took a long pull from whatever filled his flask. "And the laird stays for two days inside the walls of Lanark, dressed humbly and creeping stealthily. Being a character and figure of less consequence—and dinna I look more the part garbed in peasant togs?—I can come and go more freely. But here we are, folks, and one night the laird catches sight of a person, moving with greater stealth than he, and you ken, he never was one to keep to his own business. So he follows this figure and that brings him to the granary at the edge of the city and it's crawling onto midnight, and no one should be about. And we'll drink now because all this speaking has me parched." Laughter followed and many drank while Eachann did. He wiped the back of his hand across his mouth and continued, pointing the flask in his hand at Ava. "And it's this one, Ava Guthrie by name, that is that figure he's been following. What she was doing there, inside the granary, is her business alone."

All eyes turned to Ava, who bit her bottom lip, before being compelled to confess, "I was stealing,"—this presented as more of a question than a statement which caused a moment of perplexed silence before Eynon broke it, slapping his knee and guffawing.

"You? And that face? And such innocence? No, you were not."

Everybody started laughing and Ava turned astonished eyes to John, even as she opened her mouth to assure them that she had been. Almost imperceptibly, John moved his hand off his thigh onto her shoulder, so close to his leg, squeezing his fingers gently while he barely moved his head side to side.

"Och, and japing us now," Eachann proclaimed. "Still!" He insisted with another chortle. "A lass of remarkable pluck, is she nae!"

Eachann carried on and Ava mouthed to John, "Why not?" Why did he not want her to reveal the truth, her part in it?

"Why?" He mouthed back.

"But aye, she was accosted," Eachann said, "and not in a kindly fashion, you ken. So the son of Cormaic Craig did what his father would have done and dismissed the peril to his own person and his mission and arrived in time to be of service to her. But ladies and sirs, he is only one man, and were they nae many more"—he paused and sent a puzzled frown to John— "shall I give them numbers in the dozens, or should they ken 'twas only three that came at you? Aye, keep to the truth, then. So there it is, three English bad men pounce on him, and he's nabbed for the slaying of another—but did that one nae deserve it? And then three days he spent inside the gaol and I canna say what hell that must have been, but mayhap the laird would speak now in that regard...?"

"I will nae," John said succinctly, finally pulling his gaze from Ava. "Imagine for yourselves any hell that troubles you and multiply that several times." While they stared at him, awaiting further explanation, he inclined his head toward Eachann. "Carry on."

Eachann nodded and widened his eyes and mouth while he surveyed the rapt audience. "Let us drink to his valor, and never let it be said he is nae his father's son." He paused and sipped once more. "And this next part now, I can give it honestly, being witness to the remarkable event," he said next. "He's been at the secret court, judged guilty of murder, and a bloodthirsty crowd gathers round the gallows as they bring out the prisoner. The sheriff—like as nae still wondering how it all went awry—is reading the charges laid against him and this Ava Guthrie that you've met makes her entrance—grand it is and we'll drink to her beauty, for 'tis nae but truth to say a cross-eyed wench with more warts than teeth could nae have pulled it off."

Ava lowered her reddened face and felt John Craig's fingers squeeze her shoulders once more so that she was compelled to turn her face up to him. He offered her their shared cup. Ava shook her head, declining. Already, she felt the effects of too much wine, never in her life having been allowed more than a sip or two.

"Picture it, can you?" Eachann went on. "Three, maybe four hundred people gathered like fish in the net, jostling for a better view of the man about to hang. But all go still and quiet when she reveals herself, and what have you?" He leaned his face forward and enunciated the following, "She begs of the smitten sheriff, might she give her fare thee well? And you ken they dinna make 'em like we do here, bonny lasses"—Eachann paused and glanced around, most specifically at the Kenith women— "or apparently as they do in Wales," he added, which was greeted with plenty of cheers from men and women alike. "Before the sheriff can pick up his chin from the floor, she marches straight up those stairs. At this time, I dinna ken her, or why this stranger needs a farewell to the laird, so my eyes are as large as any when she approaches—"

"Kissed him, she did!"

Ava swung her head around to level the treacherous Hamish with a sturdy glare.

And while the round house full of people went silent save for what gasps followed, Eachann groused, "You're a guid lad, Hamish, but you're ruining the fine story I'm weaving here. But there you have it, folks. I dinna get it either at the time, but that's exactly what she did. The lass is locking lips with him in the front but sawing at ropes behind his back, though even I dinna ken the latter until all was done."

The crannog erupted in more gasps and whistles and cheers of delight.

Though mortified to have this told so bawdily and in front of these kind people, Ava felt no judgment in the collective response, only shock and admiration. Thus, she only pretended a great embarrassment, not half of it real, covering her cheeks with her hands as she ducked her head.

"Dinna be shy now, lass," Eachann called out. "You were nae then! So now drink to her absolute boldness, and recall you've been warned nae to accept what looks like innocence at face value."

Again those warm fingers at her shoulder, which had never left after first they were put there, pinched as a consoling action. She could have cried for how beautiful was his touch, even as it was made as part of his show, even as it was likely prompted by a wee inebriation. Before she knew what she was doing—later, she would likewise blame this on the consumption of too much wine so quickly—she bent her arm at the elbow and laid her fingers over his.

"Did what she intended it to do, though," Eachann said proudly. "A wee and clever distraction—"

"Tasty one, I'd wager," called out one of the Craig soldiers from the crowded doorway, which had the people in the room guffawing once more.

Someone whistled loudly while others banged on the floor and benches and walls with their hands or drinking vessels.

"Aye, we should assume that it was, and we should drink once more for that's a fine plot she conceived, eh?" Eachann said through his own merriment. "And then things get interesting, friends," he said next. "The big lad, that's Hamish," John said, pointing in his direction. "Used his shoulder and only that, burst upon the scene, taking out the legs of the scaffold. God is guid, you ken, and the hooded bailiff was the first to topple. And those two, still standing, somehow managed to unwind the noose and cut the ropes, all the while making cow eyes at each other."

Ava gasped anew at this, sure her cheeks could not flame any brighter red.

"Do I fib, lass?" Eachann asked, pointing across several people at her.

"You exaggerate, for certain," She said, so much joy inside her even as this was so unnerving. "I was simply evaluating him—closely, of course, seriously—making sure he was worthy of my time and effort."

"Aye," called Eachann in response, his bright eyes foretelling of a blast coming. "And he, like as nae, was about the same evaluating, with his tongue shoved so far down your throat."

More ribald laughter followed, the room erupting in chaos of glee.

Though she laughed, she could stand it no more. Without thinking she leaned further between John's legs and buried her head against his knee, her arms covering her face. She felt John's hand lay atop her hair, and brush downward, with a tantalizing familiarity, one from which she might never recover.

"Buck up, lass," Eachann urged. "You figure in each part, lass."

Ava lifted her face from John's thigh. "Aye, but throughout the rest of the story, with so much less...embarrassment." So much hope was attached to her words.

"Mayhap," Eachann teased. "And we'll skip over the next part, that's just us running and let's drink to our swiftness, for a slower man—or lass—would have been overtaken by those chasing us."

They drank again.

Elena went round with a tall pitcher and refilled several vessels, including John's. He took a sip and asked with a raised brow if she wanted more. Ava shook her head, feeling no awkwardness for how she sat, nestled fully between his knees, one arm still flung over his thigh. Even as John returned his attention to Eachann, who carried on with the telling, Ava was pleased to sit and watch John Craig. Never would she have suspected him capable of any cheerfulness, let alone to be able to drop his fierceness so much as to be smiling at whatever Eachann was saying now. The creases that made paths in the corners of his eyes, previously believed to have been created by his regular habit of scowling, were indented deeply now as he smiled at whatever Eachann was carrying on with.

Very interesting, she thought, and could not be bothered to remove her gaze when he turned his magnificent brown eyes upon her, possibly having felt her stare. She wasn't listening at all to Eachann now, even as another round of amusement filled the crannog, but maintained eye contact with John. The smile she showed him hadn't anything to do with Eachann's embellished story but was wholly a reaction to his easy smile. Somewhere inside, she sighed at the beauty of it.

She was brought back to reality when she heard her name on Eachann's lips.

"...and never did I see the laird's face so bloodless," Eachann was saying, "But that was him, when we realized those dastardly English had her on the run once more. Thought we were done with them—the English *and* Ava Guthrie and her friends—but nae yet. And mayhap Scotland would ken her freedom if we could somehow contrive to use this green-eyed lass as bait to every army of those devils, and we'll send John Craig in to defend her. Fought like the devil, he did, and a man would have to be blind, deaf, or dumb to nae ken why. And now drink to his sword, and may it ne'er be parted from his side."

Ava lifted her face, studying John's. He looked about as comfortable as she had for all these awkward revelations. He was smiling yet, but it was forced now, she believed; his jaw was tight, his cheek twitching as he stared down at her. He lifted the horn to his lips, breaking their shared gaze.

Ava felt wonderfully lighthearted, a wee lightheaded as well, and was sure she'd be quite pleased if this night never ended.

***

He was among friends—family truthfully—and here more than anywhere he could let down his guard. Aye, some of his soldiers made their way in and out, never too far from the fine food distributed, but mostly inside were the Keniths and thus he needn't be conscious of what he regularly was, setting an example to his men: to be ever vigilant; to let each decision and action be made upon honor; to be the defender of freedom and of those too weak to defend themselves; to never recoil before any enemy; to never lie and to be faithful always to any pledge given.

But this now, here with Eynon and Morvel and their family, was a rare opportunity for him to relax the constant vigil over his code of honor. And, as he'd learned more from Eynon than his own sire throughout the years, to give himself over occasionally to joy when the circumstances allowed.

Never more at any other time in any other place did merriment and cheer present itself as an option than it did when he visited the Kenith crannog. And on this night, far removed now from that rope-hanging end that had almost been his and with Ava settled so gorgeously at his feet—and now, with Eachann's heavily-ornamented tale finally finished—it was easy to grasp at joy.

The free-flowing wine didn't hurt. And much later, during the meal itself, when the venison had been carved and served, along with herring, cod, and pies filled with savory rabbit, the whiskey had come out, loosening that tight noose of duty and restraint yet more. John could have grasped at so much that he wouldn't normally allow or have the chance to embrace.

Still, he had never been one pleased to have attention thrust on him, was not a teller of tales or a maker of merriment. Instead he was gratified to sit in conversation with only a few at a time, eager to catch up with Eynon and Morvel, learning what these last few years had been to them, thankfully mostly kind despite the war that had ravaged so much of the land.

Ava stayed close for a long time, though sadly she did remove her arm from his leg when a pair of Kenith granddaughters bespoke her time and attention, drawing her into some surely entertaining but mangled conversation about what she *should* have done instead of kissing John mac Cormaic to see him freed.

Ava did not abandon her position until Gwerith and Wilim picked up their instruments, the *crwth*, a stringed lyre, and the *pibgorn*, a pipe horn utilizing a single reed housed in a carved body of bone. She was given no choice to resist, pulled and implored to her feet by those grandchildren of Morvel, and while Eynon encouraged her, advising, "Just in the way there, lass. Might as well dance."

Indeed, even John had to tuck his feet under the bench once the raucous dancing began, which saw anyone engaged moving around the perimeter walk of the crannog and sometimes spinning round the aisle created between this bench and the hearth. All those laddies and lasses who had spent so much time above in those lofts, watching and listening with eager eyes and ears, climbed down now to join in. Hamish was likewise urged to his feet and went skipping drunkenly by John at one point, wringing another grin from him.

Mostly though, he let his gaze unabashedly follow Ava, even as he knew he probably should not. She was entrancing enough, simply sitting and breathing, staring at a man with those bottomless green eyes. Ava dancing, her freshly washed hair bobbing about her slim back and shoulders, her bosom bouncing enticingly, her eyes shining with undiluted pleasure, laughter falling from her bewitching lips so easily one might think she did so every day, was another matter altogether. She was, in that instance, a brilliant temptation, one from which he simply was not strong enough to keep his gaze.

She danced for a long time, either unwilling to rest or unable to, for all that so many wanted to engage her. 'Twas only Wilim needing a break from the pibgorn that allowed Ava to return, to collapse onto the bench next to Morvel where she sat now. Her face was flushed bright, her smile unbroken, as she sat and caught her breath. When Morvel rose to serve yet another course, this one of both sweet and savory tarts and pies, Ava stood as well and offered to help.

More food was presented, more dancing followed. Things quieted to great satisfaction much later in the night when Eynon's daughter, Angharat—the quietest of all the Keniths—stood in front of her parents, just to the left of the red-coal fire, and sang an old Welsh hymn about a lover gone to war. Her voice was truly amazing, haunting for how much emotion she applied to the singing.

Gwerith thought so, too. Seated with her *crwth* in her lap, a leather strap connecting the instrument to her neck, she rolled her eyes and wondered, "And how am I to compete with that?"

But she tried, and her brother joined in on his pipe, eliciting another round of lively swaying and dancing.

Like all good things, the night too soon came to an end. Long ago, children had worn themselves out, had given in to sleep, some taking themselves back up to those lofts built into the high part of the wall. Others dropped in their mothers' arms or had already been taken by a parent to their own smaller, private crofts on the shores of the loch. One by one, people departed the crannog, meaning to find their own beds.

Not wanting to overstay his welcome, John rose to take his leave as well. The few remaining Craig soldiers followed suit and sleepy, sometimes drunken good nights were passed here and there.

He turned at one point and found Ava standing close, fidgeting a bit with her hands.

"I dinna ken where I should go," she said, answering the question in his eyes, "or where Hamish and Innes have made their beds."

Morvel appeared then, offering a thick fur blanket to Ava. "Take this out to the big barn, Ava. Plenty warmth to be found there."

Ava thanked her politely, her smile and words sincere, and left the crannog, trailing after a wobbly Eachann.

Morvel kissed both of John's cheeks and twined her arm in his, walking him to the door.

Just outside, she stopped, and they briefly watched as Ava scurried ahead, leaning her shoulder under Eachann's arm just as he began to tip precariously. Ava's soft giggle floated back to the watching pair.

"You know, John mac Cormaic," Morvel said quietly, "that it is not in my nature to leave any guest wanting, to send a young woman off to the barns with all the men. So many men."

John scowled, reminded of this fact, and thus her lack. "But you do this night."

Morvel showed a knowing grin, highlighted by moonlight. "She is safest now. With you. You have made your mark on her. Not any who watched you tonight would think she was untethered—do not interrupt me," she said when he opened his mouth to refute this. "She looks to you for all the answers, trusts you above all else, has risked her life for you. I know you believe your life allows no place for a woman. Possibly you fear that the lion cannot roar if he is tamed, made soft by love, but think how strong and resolute it made your father."

"I have always believed you a very wise woman, my lady," he said carefully, "but you are wrong in this instance. Ava Guthrie is nae—"

"Of course I am not wrong and do not lie to me, John mac Cormaic. I caution only this: give her nothing but whatever her blind trust in you deserves. Or give her everything. Let her be the one to change your mind. Do not play both sides or give half-truths and half-measures. That is not the man your father raised."

He could not help but narrow his eyes at her. "That's a hard blow, even for you, in your motherly fashion."

"But if you are all she has to safeguard her, then I must use every weapon to protect her from that darkness in you." She paused before adding emphatically, "This one is worthy of you, my love."

Having acknowledged sometime in the last hour that he was a wee inebriated himself, he could only counter this with the first thing that came to mind. "I dinna even ken her."

"But you want to," Morvel presumed. "And that would not be a terrible thing, John mac Cormaic."

He sighed, and then swiftly winced and said, "Sorry," waving his hand between them after he'd just blown his wine and whiskey breath into her face.

Morvel dismissed his concern with a kiss to his cheek.

"Did you love my father, even a little?" Drunkenness allowed him to finally ask after all these years.

Backing up to meet his gaze, she laid her hand on the cheek she'd kissed and told him, "Your father was as irresistible as you, my dear, it was difficult not to. But I loved my husband more and Cormaic understood that. And he honored it." She patted his cheek lightly. "Be wise, as was your father. Be not dishonorable."

John laid his hand over hers and nodded. "Guid night, my lady."

He went on then, jogging a bit to catch up with Ava and Eachann. He latched onto his captain's free arm just as Ava and Eachann cleared the timber walkway and helped maneuver him all the way out to the barn.

As Ava and Eachann continued inside the big open door, John paused to speak with Iain and Henry just outside the door, sitting on a tightly packed bale of hay, and was happily informed that a dozen Craig soldiers prowled in a wide swath around the Kenith homestead.

"And they'll come in another few hours," Henry said, "and I'll send out a dozen more."

Satisfied with this arrangement, John headed inside the barn, arriving just in time to see Eachann slip away from Ava's grasp, lowering himself to the ground.

"This'll do just fine, lass" the captain said, his words slurred a bit, as he went immediately onto his side in a soft pile of hay next to a sleeping and snoring Hamish.

Ava straightened away from him and glanced around. Most of the stalls were filled with horses and cows. Most of the open area of the aisle was filled with soldiers, who'd already made their beds. She lifted her eyes to John. "Should I just find a spot?" She wondered.

Little could he make of her expression, the barn being nearly as black as pitch away from the moonlight of the doorway, but heaps of uncertainty tainted her speech.

"Up the ladder," he said, nodding his head toward that barely seen apparatus in the front corner. "I dinna relish being trod upon many times overnight by any of these sots."

Ava carefully picked her way over several more bodies and flung the fur throw over her shoulder, then able to use two hands to ascend the steep steps. John followed and surveyed the eerie gloom of the loft, and then pulled his dagger from his belt to cut through the rope of one of the hay bales stored up here. He spread that out and arranged other compact bales around the pallet he'd created, their being just enough space for the two of them.

Ava gave a sparse "Thank you" and quickly settled on her back on the thick bed of straw.

John stretched out next to her. The darkness was pervasive that even a sideways glance at her showed little but that she'd flapped out the fur over her, kindly arranging half of it over John.

"Is your family like this?" Ava asked when she settled again on her back, her voice low in deference to all those who slept below them. "Is that why you are so at ease here?"

"Nae, my family is all but gone. Two sisters remain, both wed and moved on. Blacklaw Tower is essentially a monk's cave, with my mam and sisters gone."

"But were they...cheery," asked Ava, "as are these people?"

John snorted out a laugh. "They were nae. Of course my father was a warrior laird, dinna see much relevance in merriment, or mayhap could find nae cause. Neither was my mam the sort that laughed easily."

"That explains so much," Ava said through a yawn.

John chewed the inside of his cheek briefly, wondering if he dared inquire what she might mean. He was saved making a decision as she continued with her queries.

"Is that story Eynon told true? Did Morvel save your father and then, in turn, he saved her?"

"Aye. When he lived, we visited more often. That was before the war, though."

"They drink rather enthusiastically of the wine and whiskey," Ava remarked, and then yawned.

He chuckled at this. "I dinna ken but a few Welsh people aside from the Keniths," John said, "so I canna say that wine and whiskey flow so freely in any Welsh house, but it always has when I've come here."

"But where do they get it from?"

"They are nae only shepherds and farmers, but they trade extensively. Did you see the loch boats sitting at the shoreline? Aye, they use those, go up and down the loch, take the river all the way to Stirling, do plenty of trading. Eynon has a man there, in Stirling, takes his goods out to Leith, by my understanding."

"What do they trade?"

"Livestock on occasion, and presumably some of the woolens they weave here, but mostly fish. They harvest quite a bit of herring here, make that run to Stirling once a week." He turned his head and lowered his voice. "Dinna believe for one minute that Eynon dinna have a wooden chest buried somewhere close, filled to the brim with coins. English and Scots."

"Did they build this?" Ava asks. "That strange round house and all these other buildings."

"They revived it, mayhap," John allowed. "'Tis an ancient crannog. Everything else they built. We were here—my father and I—when this barn was built. I dinna ken I was more than five at the time."

"Did...did your mother ken about Morvel?"

"Are you nae exhausted, wanting only sleep?" He asked, more wishful than sure.

"I am verra sleepy, but this was all just so...fantastic, I don't want to close my eyes and have it all be done. And do not deflect," she said next, boldly. "Did your da hold onto his fondness for Morvel? Did your mam ken of it?"

John sighed. "Aye, my father held onto that fondness. He never betrayed my mam, I ken. But then he and Eynon also became verra fast friends, and that bond remained strong all his life."

"What was your mother like?"

"She was a great woman in her own right," he said. "Proud and strong." He pondered this briefly. Aye, she'd been those things, but she'd sometimes been petty and often cool, so that he couldn't recall warm and fond moments so much as the overall of her, that she was stalwart and brusque. Still, she had been a good mother and noble wife and chatelaine to Blacklaw.

"Are they safe here?" Ava asked next. "Out here in the middle of nowhere?"

"You ken half of the Highlands is in the middle of God's nowhere? But aye, for the most part, or for now. They pose no threat and are so far remote it is unlikely the English would even stumble upon them. The Crannog is fairly easy to defend from within unless they are besieged by larger numbers."

Another moment passed, Ava fiddling with the fur and moving her legs a wee bit on the straw.

John closed his eyes, hoping to court sleep now, hoping to God his brain did not become fixated on her proximity.

"You should partake more often," Ava said after a while, her voice sleepier yet. "Of the wine and whiskey, that is."

"How's that?" He asked without opening his eyes.

"You are so much more agreeable now," she answered. "More than ever."

"Hangings and running for my life make me contrary," he retorted promptly.

"But that was days ago now."

Groggily, John reminded her of all the things he'd been stripped of in those first few days: his sword, his horse, his army, his freedom. And before she might have assumed there would be more congeniality in the future, all these things returned to him, he set her straight. "This here, as sweet as it is, is merely distraction. War and fighting are what must be sought now, and thus a persona must be honed to deal well with that."

"So...you are angry, gearing up for war."

"I am always angry, lass."

"But..."

"What?"

"Never mind," she deferred.

"What?"

"You are much more handsome when you're nae. Angry, that is."

He was sleepy, nodding off. The last thing he said to her was, "Much *more*, she says. Must believe me handsome even when the rage does have a firm hold."

After a few seconds, in which time she might have believed he had finally fallen asleep, she whispered, "She does."

John ground his teeth and staunchly refused to dwell on those bewitching words.

He wasn't sure how much time had passed when next he had wakeful awareness. 'Twas still dark as coal all around.

He woke to find Ava close to him, as if she had sought out heat, on her side and facing him, with so much less space between them now.

Later he would blame it on the drink, which had indeed made him sleepy but hadn't addled him at all—though apparently, it had made him, in this instance, *agreeable*. Certainly he'd not been drunk or addled enough that he'd not heard her whispered confession, *She does*.

So then he decided, just before he did what he could not seem to stop himself from doing, that he would have to pretend on the morrow that too much drink made him do it. With that settled, he turned onto his side and pulled Ava into his arms, stretching the fur over both of them.

Ava murmured something unintelligible and settled quickly enough. John set his chin on the top of her head, inhaling the sweet scent of her hair.

Oh, that Morvel. She was sly, that one, to thrust so much upheaval to the fore of his mind. He'd been so happy repressing and ignoring every thought of Ava, every blessed thing that entranced him.

She was soft and small in his arms, deliciously so. Hadn't he imagined she would be?

He would not dishonor her, but he could hold her in his arms while they slept.

Chapter Nine

She was, in truth, very sorry to leave the Keniths. She glanced back several times as the Craig party departed, at the round house and all the other squat buildings and the people standing before them, more than once throwing up a wave of her hand.

Overriding this sorrow, however, was the hazy memory of a very provocative dream she'd had, one in which she'd been held in John Craig's arms all through the night. She specifically remembered thinking inside that dream, *I don't ever want to wake*, being so snug in his embrace, so blessedly secure, the smell of him—woodsmoke and leather and his own man scent—wafting gorgeously around her. Only a dream, she mused. When she woke this morning, John was standing in front of her, dusting straw from his person, straightening his belted plaid, telling her they would be offered a fine meal before they departed.

She'd been immediately sorry that the smile-inducing effects of the wine and whiskey had been lost in sleep and the overnight hours. He was returned to his regular aloof self, mayhap cooler than usual, staring down at her with stony eyes while his mouth was set in a hard line once more.

When she could no more make out any single figure of the waving people at the Kenith homestead, Ava settled as comfortably as she was able in the saddle, resigned to her present fate, another long and grueling day behind Innes atop this fine horse. Once more an annoyingly highspeed pace was set.

She realized a moment of guilt, having forgotten all about Innes last night.

She asked him where he'd been, how he'd passed the night.

"Put on watch," he grumbled with some heat, "assumed to be nae better than any of his soldiers. Dinna even get to eat naught but a trencher of the venison and some cheese."

Assumed to be nae better than any of his soldiers came off as particularly petulant, since so many might aspire to be so noble as any man taking up a sword in defense of freedom. Ava dropped the subject, sorry she'd brought it up in the first place.

Perhaps there was some benefit to be had for their swift ride; likely they'd not have reached their destination until well after dark if they'd traveled at a slower, more comfortable pace. As it was, the keep known as Lismore Abbey came into view just as the sun was setting, when the sky in the west was smeared with streaks of orange and purple.

"It's a proper fortress," Ava remarked, leaning left to see past Innes' shoulder, and unable to keep the awe from her voice.

"Just a resting place," Innes reminded her, "nae meant for us—or we for it."

The keep itself was at least as large as the castle at Lanark, the one the English had overtaken and where they garrisoned their men-at-arms. It boasted two forward rounded towers and was surrounded by a daunting wall of stone possibly three stories high. The gates to the impressive abbey were wide open, one of them and part of the pale stone wall reflected in the glistening loch that was situated just to the right of the fortress.

As they had maintained a position at the rear of the moving Craig army all day, by the time Innes, Ava, and Hamish caught up with the force, three Craig men, John included, had already dismounted and were now walking under the gatehouse, into the bailey while the bulk of the Craig army only milled about, none of them looking worse for wear for the grueling hours-long trek.

Innes brought the horse to a halt near the Craig men and dismounted with some stiffness and one quiet but aggrieved grunt, enough to suggest his aches and pains were similar to Ava's.

When she slid off the horse, she was forced to stand still for several minutes, her face contorted in a wince, while she waited for the feeling of continued motion to leave her thighs. She was jolted from her own sense of discomfort when Hamish stopped near her and Innes and his dismount was not only less graceful than even Ava's graceless alighting but was so sloppy that his foot was briefly caught in the stirrup, causing him to tumble to the ground. The huge destrier, God bless him, stayed perfectly still, was not spooked by Hamish's ineptness.

Ava covered her mouth with her hand, hiding the immediate grin that came, but then gave liberty to her laughter when Hamish himself began chortling, simultaneously wheezing, "God's teeth, but I hate riding."

She rushed to his side but could do little more than make motions as if she would help him to his feet, since she obviously couldn't lift him. She didn't mind teasing him, "You looked like a sack of grain, rather dumped off the saddle."

"Felt that way," Hamish said, having to go onto all fours to push himself to his feet. "Promise me now, Ava," he said, breathless and red of face, "we'll nae ever ride again."

"Nae if we can help it," she said, still smiling, brushing off Hamish's left side, which had landed first and now was dusted and coated with grass and dirt.

She straightened and turned, seeing that Innes was walking both horses over to where another horse line was being established. Her fingers made wrinkles in the front of her léine, wondering what now. It had been years since she'd come to a new place, ill at ease suddenly as this was no large burgh or city where no one could rightly say, you're nae wanted. But here they could; she wasn't certain what kind of welcome, if any, might be extended. Mayhap the laird of Lismore did not want any peasants without means to dwell in his demesne. 'Twas his right.

"I dinna ken we'd be brought here if it was expected we'd be rejected," Hamish said, as if he'd read her thoughts or had similar ones himself, "but gudesake, I hope they feed us ere they toss us oot."

Ava burst out laughing at this, her weariness and anxiety forgotten in the face of Hamish's constant concern for his frequently grumbling belly. Hamish only shrugged when she directed her mirth at him. God bless him, but he never made any apologies for his relentless appetite. And she was still wearing her large smile when she faced the walled keep again and now saw John Craig and Eachann and that third man returning.

When his gaze met hers, his scowl appeared to return, and Ava's smile faded.

While Eachann addressed the Craig men, John walked directly to where Ava stood with Hamish.

"There is room aplenty inside the hall to make your pallet," he said.

He looked at and spoke directly to Ava, who grappled with surprise at this unexpected boon, though she was compelled to refuse the generosity. She shook her head. "I will keep with Innes and Hamish."

The dark brown slashes of John Craig's brows angled low over his golden brown eyes. "The invitation is extended to the three of you, since you dinna have a tent."

Oh.

"Oh, um, I will see what Innes says—" she paused when his brows lowered yet more.

"*Jesu*, and why would he want that you should spend another night upon the icy ground?"

"He would nae, I am sure, but—"

"But nae anything," John Craig interrupted. "Dinna be daft. Take yourself inside. We've come too late for last meal, but they'll have some bread and cheese now, and a bit of ale."

Hamish moved immediately, incited to smile again at the mention of food.

John Craig now lifted a brow at Ava, either questioning her foot-shuffling or challenging any pretense that the offer of food and a dry bed place did not sound like heaven.

Ava nodded and John turned, following Hamish into the keep. She followed more leisurely, chewing her lip, her gaze on John Craig's broad back and wide shoulders.

"We are invited inside," she told Innes when he caught up to her, his frown asking the question.

He fell into step beside her, and they passed through the gates and crossed the wide yard, entering the hall in John Craig's wake, while Hamish had taken the lead. Ahead of them John Craig walked beyond where Hamish had paused just inside the door. Ava and Innes stopped where Hamish had, all three of them taking inventory of the cavernous hall.

The late hour meant that the hall was empty save for a few people, all male, milling around the head table. One of them stood and skirted round the table to meet John Craig. And here was a man as remarkable in height and breadth as was John Craig. He was crowned in nearly black hair and wore an expression just as fierce as any of the Lion's. Yet, while his expression did not ease or lift to great pleasure, he embraced John warmly it seemed, holding him for more than only a perfunctory moment. When they parted, they spoke quietly, neither including nor seeming to exclude those other few men in their immediate vicinity from their conversation.

Ava had to believe their presence—Innes and Hamish and hers—was mentioned or explained in greater detail. She could not tell, but saw the black-haired man glance in their direction, nodding subtly while John spoke to him. He seemed to direct his dark gaze specifically at Ava, but only for a second. Assuming this was the laird, Ava straightened her shoulders before he removed from her what had looked to be an assessing gaze.

He turned then, addressing one of the men at the high table, who promptly stood and strode straight toward the only other occupants of the great hall.

This man was neither so large as John Craig or that laird, and neither was his visage the sort to give one fits. He was merely an ordinary-looking man of average height, but who thankfully wore a pleasing expression, one that increased in depth as he neared.

"Guid tidings to you," he said with a broad smile before he stopped in front of them. "I am Lismore's steward, Sten. The Craig has made us aware of your circumstance," he said, aiming a mildly curious look at Ava, "and your present need for a light repast. Won't you sit," he invited, extending a hand to the nearest trestle table. "And I will see what can be arranged, and how quickly."

With that, and after a smiling nod and a clap of his hands, he took himself off, and Ava, Innes, and Hamish made themselves comfortable at the bench and table.

Exhausted, she wanted nothing more than to drop her arms and head onto the table, but a greater calling had her remaining upright, eyeing the back of John Craig as he spoke yet with the laird of Lismore. When they finished speaking and the laird turned one way and John Craig the other, Ava blinked and lowered her eyes, eyeing the dirty hands she laid upon the board, not wanting to be caught staring.

She worried needlessly, it seemed. John Craig did not approach them at all, but made straight for the door, and left the hall without a word to any of them.

Unaccountably disturbed by this, she stared at the door he closed behind him. A sigh was breathed, and her shoulders shrank now as she allowed the weariness to consume her, even as she bristled at his leavetaking as if he knew them not at all—knew her, she was specifically thinking, she acknowledged to herself after a moment.

She felt rather abandoned, a feeling which was as ridiculous as it was real.

Never before had she bemoaned her lot in life, living on the fringe of society and bound to stay there all her life. But inside her, at the moment, she wished she were someone else, someone worthy of more of John Craig's attention.

Removing her regard from that thick wooden door, Ava found Innes' gaze upon her, the sour mood that had been his all this day yet intact, or since revived, it appeared.

***

Walter de Burghdon's fingers shook as he scratched wildly at his temple, disheveling the thin hair there. Once more, he read the missive come just this morn, delivered by the king's own messenger, likely penned by the hand of the king's administrator, that weaselly clerk with his upturned nose and his beady bird eyes, whose name de Burghdon had no need to recall. In all likelihood, that clerk smirked the entire time, while recording Edward's words—these words in front of Walter now, not any of them pleasant.

Closing his eyes, the sheriff threw back his head and wrinkled his face in near agony, wanting more than anything right now to have back the boastful notice he'd sent off with such haste to the king a sennight ago. 'Twas his own fault, that he'd not wasted any time crowing about his astonishing feat, after learning the identity of the prisoner in Lanark. A fine feather in his cap it had been, to have apprehended the Lion of Blacklaw Tower himself, John Craig. And for a hanging offense no less! And how quick he'd been, in his ambitious glee, to get word to his king. Walter had sat right here at this table, his feet propped upon the smooth wood surface, dictating the letter to the castle's steward, his fingers steepled together, his delight unrivaled. All the while he'd uttered the words to be penned announcing his triumph—the big fish he'd snared in his net—he'd pictured himself returned to London, recalled in glory, gone from this godforsaken land of heathens.

As easily as we have bequeathed favor, so too can we take it away, read part of today's missive from the king.

Curious, was it not? Walter thought, chewing the inside of his cheek. The king's first response, when Craig was well in hand, had been succinct—*make haste to dispatch the rebel to his fate*—lacking even the barest praise.

THE LION OF BLACKLAW TOWER

Today's hastily conveyed missive—both the messenger and his steed had all but collapsed at the door for the speed of their flight from Carlisle—was an entire page essentially threatening great harm to de Burghdon's name and fortunes if the rebel Scottish knight should not be retaken.

We marvel greatly, the dreaded letter had begun, *that as of yet, three days hence, we have no affirmative on the action taken at Lanark. Is the blasted Lion hanged, as dead as directed, as we commanded upon receiving news of his capture?*

And now Walter had the unenviable task of communicating the news to the king that not only had the Lion escaped the noose crafted specifically for him but that since then, a score of English men-at-arms were cold and dead upon this savage land, felled by the very man they'd hunted. The *bequeathed favor* was in serious peril now.

The sheriffdom of Lanark, of course, was not the indulgence whose revoking Walter would bemoan; 'twas the price to be paid *for* the favor. No, the greater favor was a baronetcy in York and the four-hundred acres, with a purported £1000 a year—that had been the favor. The sheriffdom of Lanark saw only 100 marks per annum and brought little more than headaches and too much time separated from his family. But with the barony in York, his daughters would have advantageous marriages, his wife might be gifted fine jewelry now, his sons would inherit in his name. Seventeen years fighting the king's ignoble and bloody insatiable wars and finally—finally!—Walter had been rewarded.

All in jeopardy now.

How it had gone to rot so swiftly still stunned him. But never would he say to his king that a green-eyed lass, nearly unholy for how much she resembled Walter's own youngest daughter—enough so that he'd been stricken to ineptness with astonishment—had been allowed to maneuver herself into a position of willing accomplice, all right under his nose. And merely because it had taken him a full minute to convince himself that the striking peasant had not been his own sweetly innocent Margaret.

Walter de Burghdon could not be certain, but he had some suspicion that this Lion, this Scottish warrior, in particular drew so much more of Edward's ire than any other rebel north of the border. If he were a wagering man, Walter would have taken any bet that said the king only personally disdained John Craig for his assumption of a lion on his banner and crest. The lion, king of beasts, was indicative of nobility, valor, and honor, of which Edward was sure he possessed in greater fashion than any other mortal. How pleased he would be to smite out any who dared to dress their heraldry in a manner befitting only the king! Or so Walter believed. In any case, Edward wanted John Craig hanged, gone and forgotten, and Walter knew that he needed this to happen, for his own future to be secure.

And yet, with his own dereliction, and the subsequent loss of twenty lives in pursuit of the escapee, Walter was now shorthanded here at Lanark, and could ill afford to send another score of men after the Lion of Blacklaw Tower. In the same vein, he could not now easily request of the king that more archers or foot soldiers be sent to Lanark for just this purpose. He might be expected to make do with what fewer numbers were available to him, which made his stomach turn, his chances of success seeming slimmer by the day. And yet, if he failed again, if the Lion had truly slipped through his fingers and could not be apprehended again, Walter did not doubt for one minute that royal *favor* would indeed be withdrawn.

Being ever a man of resoluteness, even when the required actions drained all the blood from his face, Walter de Burghdon recalled the steward into his chamber, meaning to get this business settled.

He began to dictate his letter to the king, portraying to the scribe an air of confidence that he could only hope might be received as such by Edward. He portrayed John Craig's improbable escape as having been designed by persons of greater import than only that stunning green-eyed lass and the bull of a manchild who'd crashed the gallows to the ground. Not only did he *not* neglect to mention the ensuing massacre of twenty men from the garrison upon the hillside within five miles of Lanark, but he embellished the rout, suggesting the Craig army must have been close, must be plentiful and well-supplied, must indeed be stopped before they made designs on Lanark itself.

True, he had no choice, and the urgent missive was seeped for a time in humble pie, though it was generously garnished with more of the chest-thumping bravado he was sure would appeal to the king. He, Walter de Burghdon, would personally see to the apprehension of the criminal John Craig once more soldiers—and specifically archers—were sent to Lanark. Edward didn't like failures, didn't like whiners or those who made excuses; he cherished action above all else. Thus all the bad news had been delivered as more reviling of the scourge Scots, and Walter's stated plans for redemption had seethed with both righteous indignation and back-clapping self-praise, reminding the king how he'd earned this position in the first place.

Groveling would earn him no favor, but it would possibly grant him time to do what must be done to keep the favor previously assigned to him. And do what he must, he would. He had everything to lose.

***

It had been many years since she'd dined in the great hall of a fine house. She supposed she might have felt more uncomfortable if not for the presence of Innes and Hamish, which meant that she was not alone in her circumstance, the unknown and uninvited guest. Also, because the hall was crowded and nearly every available seat occupied, she felt decidedly less conspicuous.

Last night, upon their arrival, they'd enjoyed a small but delightful offering, the bread gorgeous in both flavor and texture, the cheese having not even the smallest spot of mold on it. After they'd filled their happy gullets, there had been nothing else to do but to make their beds, and Ava had slept soundly for only the second time in weeks—the first being the previous night, in the loft of the Kenith barn with John.

This morning, and all day, she and Innes and Hamish had made themselves scarce, keeping out of doors. For a while in the late morning and early afternoon, with little else to do, they'd lent their hands to the work in the fields, the trio taking charge of one pair of oxen and the ploughshare. Ava had led the team by the rope reins, possibly repeating, "walk on" and "come along" a hundred times to the mindless beasts, while Hamish and Innes had controlled and managed the ploughshare, Innes directing their path while Hamish used his great weight and strength to force the blade of the tool deep into the ground. Thus, they'd made themselves known to that tenant farmer and his wife, Edane and Eliza they were, thereby relieving the heavily pregnant woman and her one-armed husband of some of their workload. The couple had shown their appreciation by sharing their midday meal with them, bannocks and ale and a leftover pottage—watery, having little meat, but tasty all the same—and Ava had been pleased for both the industry and the modest relief they'd been able to offer the pair.

Sitting now at a trestle table furthest from the laird's table, Ava struggled to give any attention to those in her immediate company, her regard so vigorous upon the persons seated at the head table. Truth be known, John Craig, seated at the laird of Lismore's side, only held her attention some of the time.

Instead, she was fascinated by the laird and mistress. Magnus and Lara Matheson, they were, and a more stunning pair she'd never beheld. Stunning was not only her mind's way of describing their appearance, though beautiful they both were. Nae, *stunning* as in the way they interacted, and the effect they had on each other. Of course, she'd first seen Magnus Matheson last night, when John had spoken with him, and Ava had assumed correctly at that time that he must be the laird.

"Beast of Lismore Abbey, he is," Hamish whispered to her from her right side, talking around the food in his mouth. "Heard all about it today. Beast, they say, for his prowess in battle. Made his name with Wallace, they said, and most recently lent his army and his sword to our king's cause. 'Tis said he slayed a dozen men with nae help from any other, walked away from the melee with nary a scratch."

Ava had slyly watched the laird of Lismore, as much in awe this day as she'd been the first time she'd laid eyes on him. He looked every inch the beast, in size and expression, being a fine match to John Craig for the fierceness of his countenance. And then the mistress of Lismore had entered the hall and everything about her husband that was brutal and fearsome melted all at once, his visage softening when his eyes beheld his wife. No beast could be found then, not the smallest snarl, when Magnus Matheson turned his gaze onto his wife. At that moment, his expression was filled only with love.

And that love was returned, tenfold at least, if anything should be made by the mistress' reception of her husband's gaze. Lara Matheson entered the hall gorgeous but clearly fatigued, her face drawn, with dark circles under her eyes, wearing a slight frown as she spoke to a woman possibly twice her age. The minute she realized her husband's presence, the second her eyes found his, she was transformed. All that was glum and weary dissipated, her face lighting at the sight of him, her smile quick and transcendent. She walked directly to his side, parting ways with the old woman, laying her hand on Magnus' arm and lifting her face to say something quietly, for his ears alone. Magnus Matheson never took his gaze from Lara and any trace of a beast which might have remained was surely eradicated by the slow smile that curved his mouth at whatever his wife was saying.

Lara Matheson ended her remarks to Magnus with a shrug, which easily enlivened the laird's grin. She turned to find her seat, held and offered by her husband, and when she sat, Magnus Matheson leaned low and intimately whispered something very close to her ear, which elicited the most transcendent smile, which she turned up to her adoring husband.

Ava sighed, not listening to a word that was said at her own table, so intrigued by that tender show of affection between the Beast and his divinely beautiful bride.

How remarkable, Ava thought, a wee wistfulness tightening her chest.

The intrigue and dreaminess faded as the meal progressed. After a while Ava stared with outright envy at Lara Matheson and her attentive husband, considering that she herself was young and alone and everything that was good and fine was beyond her reach. But oh, how she ached for it. She wanted a parade of good and kind things to happen to her, to come her way.

Her gaze wandered again to John Craig—not intentionally at that moment, she assured herself. He might well be good, had proven himself valiant and noble thus far. *Kind*, though, she could not attribute to him. She'd seen no evidence of that unless he was filled with spirits. Or mayhap rescuing her had been a kindness and she could only legitimately argue that tender and gentle were outside his repertoire.

While she debated his virtues or lack thereof, John lifted his brown eyes away from the man at his side, to whom he'd been speaking, and without searching about, fixed his dark gaze directly onto Ava, who could not entirely contain the small gasp that came. Had he felt her eyes upon him that he'd looked up at that moment, in the middle of a conversation, and looked straight at her? And was it her imagination, or was there actually a play of amusement around the normally hard line of his lips? As if he had indeed felt her watching him and was pleased to have it confirmed? Utterly motionless, they regarded each other for several seconds. She thought she recognized a softening there, some smoldering warmth oozing from his intense gaze—something effective, whatever his intent, that she *felt* his stare, felt it in her bones and her blood and a tell-tale heat in her cheeks.

Recovering herself, with a rapid spate of blinking and a gulp of suddenly close air, Ava let her eyes fall away first.

She wasn't sure what should be made of the way her pulse raced whenever John Craig studied her with such dedication. And certainly she had no name for that inexplicable emotion that assailed her whenever their eyes met. She didn't dislike it, but then she didn't particularly trust it, not knowing what it was, but invariably she dropped her eyes first on any occasion that they stared at each other.

"What say you, Ava?"

Recalled to her tablemates, Ava squirmed a bit and, still red of face, gave Hamish and Innes her full attention.

"Pardon me?" She asked, meeting Hamish's gaze, since he had been the one to ask something of her.

Hamish speared another morsel of the plentiful meat on his trencher, forcing that between his teeth, making no attempt to either chew or swallow before saying, "Innes says we should make ourselves gone soon. Wants to get on to somewhere—"

"You want to leave Lismore?" Ava asked, turning to Innes. But this fortress had so much to offer, not least of which was the abundant food that had already been lavished so generously upon them. They'd been here but twenty-four hours and already were enjoying their third meal. "But we only just got here."

"Aye, but what's here for us, Ava?" Innes asked, his brows drawn sharply. "Bollocks, but I've never passed so idle a day. What's there for us to do?"

Ava gasped in full now, able to retort promptly, "We spent the day laboring in the fields like true farmers, Innes. My God, but I've blisters all about my palms." She held up her hands to show proof of this. "And we did only just arrive," she reminded him. "Might we inquire about jobs or tasks available to us? Perhaps they have need of some help here in the keep. Mayhap there is a croft that we might let—"

"We're nae farmers, Ava," Innes corrected her gruffly. "And you ain't nae house servant. We're townsfolk. This here, at Lismore Abbey, tis nae place for us."

"But we have nae even—" she tried to argue.

"And what has you suddenly so keen to become a tenant farmer?" He asked. "Surely, nae the blisters or the thankless toil that will put you in the ground ere you've seen two score years. You ken nothing about it, and me nae much more than that."

Unnerved by Innes sharpness, Hamish offered tentatively, "I ken lots about farming. Spent almost four years with that couple south of Glasgow."

"Aye, and you groused about them and that sort of existence from the verra first day I met you," Innes reminded him. "Said you'd nae ever commit to such thankless industry again, said that couple was made mean by their near-fruitless efforts, year after year. Said you couldn't wait to show them your back end."

"Aye, I did," Hamish admitted reluctantly, and then chewed on the inside of his cheek for a moment. He frowned as a thought occurred to him. "But I said as well that it was mostly how miserable were those people that drove me away."

Miserable, indeed. Ava had once seen the evidence of what torment they'd shared with Hamish, in the form of crisscrossed markings, red and white, puckered and twisted, across his thick back. She slanted a sympathetic look at Hamish before returning her attention to Innes, wondering about his hurry to depart so promising a location as Lismore.

"Should we nae stay on a bit, at least a fortnight or more?" She asked, unwilling to explore all the reasons behind a desire such as this, though she knew there was truth to her arguments, that Lismore Abbey might have plenty to offer them. She surged ahead, leaning her elbows on the table to remind Innes of Lismore's greatest qualification. "I dinna ken it can be ignored, how secure this would be—must be—living here, with the garrisoned filled to the brim with men-at-arms, and behind so formidable a wall and with—"

"Aye, and what of it when the army leaves?" Innes barked at her. Catching himself then, as his voice had risen with his ire, he too leaned forward across the thick pine board. "They do that, you ken," he hissed at her. "They dinna ever stay too long. Wars to fight, kings to elevate to their consequence, the little man always left behind."

Ava knew she absolutely did not want to talk politics with Innes, and presently, she didn't even want to pursue this conversation with him, not with he being so curiously surly. Mayhap he only needed a few days inside Lismore to know some appreciation for everything it might be able to offer them. She waved her hands dismissively and returned her attention to her own meal, sadly ignored for the last few minutes.

"We need make nae decision just yet," she said airily. She noticed that Hamish's trencher was empty of all but the broth that soaked the hard bread. The helping ladled onto her trencher was more than she would ever eat in one sitting. Hoping to steer conversation into a different direction, a bit bewildered by

Innes' rigid views and wishes for them, she pushed her trencher to the middle of the table so that it sat halfway between her and Hamish. "Help me finish this, will you?"

Hamish's eyes widened with delight, and he eagerly broke off a hunk of his trencher, using that to scoop up a good portion of the meat and vegetables in the pottage filling Ava's bread plate.

Innes, however, was not yet done with their discussion, as Ava had hoped to be.

"We're nae crofters," Innes maintained, a bite to his tone, seeming only to stare blindly at the shared meal in the middle of the table. Until another frown furrowed his brow and he snapped at Ava, "And why would you refuse to consider a greater circumstance for us somewhere else? Or do I need to ask? Mayhap I should simply spin my head round and find the reason? Probably got his eye on you again, nae any different from how you canna keep yours from him."

Ah, now his hardnose stance made sense.

It was not the first time Innes had exhibited jealous tendencies, and thus it was not the first time Ava questioned why she should be made to feel guilty for bringing out this behavior in him. They were naught but friends. If ever he'd implied any wish to be anything more, it had never been more than that, an unsaid inference—hints and vague clues and sometimes imprecise expectations and nothing more. Always, Ava was glad that it had only ever been that, an insinuation of some future relationship between them. But Innes had never acted upon it, and Ava had never been forced to reject him as she would have, and thus his anger now—and every scowl specifically thrown her way since they'd met John Craig—was both uncalled for and unappreciated.

"And why," she challenged him, "would you refuse to consider a greater circumstance right here and now? Or even to entertain the possibilities? And dinna say again we're nae crofters. We're nae brewers but we did that. We're nae weavers but I spent all of last summer working beside Dottie Og. We're nae hunters but rarely has a week passed that Hamish's traps were nae engaged. We're nae bad people but we thieve. We were nae too proud to beg when we needed to, nor too desperate to leave Dumfries when that dinna agree with us anymore. Dinna say what we canna do or have nae done, Innes. I ken right now safe and warm and so charitably fed exceeds all else."

Hamish, with a full belly and a sated sigh, arms limp now upon the boards, agreed. "Ava speaks the truth. The captain said there'll be a bounty on us now, for what we did in Lanark." He wiped the sleeve of his tunic over his mouth. "I dinna like running so much. Let's rest now."

Innes' expression was grim or frustrated, his jaw set firmly.

Ava reached across the table, meaning to lay her hand over his and offer some compromise. Before she could, Innes slid his hand off the table, crossing his arms over his chest while he refused to look at her.

Her own mouth clenched at his childishness. But she said anyway, "Let's discuss this again in another few days. It's too soon to ken what might be best for us."

And then, having some notion that Innes' eagerness to leave Lismore had been instigated by her apparently unconcealed fascination with John Craig, she did not follow the Lion's departure from the hall, even as she noticed in her periphery his every movement, including when he stood and strode through the hall and out into the night.

Chapter Ten

When she lived at home, truly the only one she'd ever known such as it was, at the house in Wauchope where her father was lord, she'd often found her greatest escape at the break of dawn. She would leave the quiet keep and take the path along the lane and then east over the little beinn they called The Bard, where she would sit and greet the sun.

Having slept so warmly—if not comfortably; there was little the straw and rushes could do to alleviate the hardness of the timber floor inside the hall of Lismore—Ava didn't mind stepping out into the morning chill. Outside, just before dawn, everything around her was painted with dawn's gray light. She inhaled happily of the crisp, clean air.

The sky was only a few shades lighter than black, the stone of the keep and the wall were not pale brown but gray. Indeed the soldiers atop the wall, and two more by the well were seen in shades of gray, as if someone held a thin and gauzy gray fabric in front of her eyes. Still, despite the drabness of color, it remained Ava's favorite time of day, when all was still and mostly silent, when the true darkness of night had taken its bow, making room for a new day. She didn't quite understand why this time of day spoke so eloquently to her, how the virtue of it overwhelmed her senses, but then she did not often question her love of it, not any more than she wondered why she enjoyed the song of the wind through the pines or the sight of a perfectly cloudless blue sky.

Near the gate, she whispered to the guard atop the wall her intent to walk about, her face tilted upward.

"Use the man door, lass," said the dull-faced lad just before he gave himself over to a huge yawn, suggesting he too might soon take his bow with the changing of the guard. "I would advise you dinna stray too far, lass. The fog is creeping heavy out yonder."

Ava nodded and lowered her face, approaching the small door tucked inside the large gate, pleased for the lad's assessment. A good, rolling fog only added to the allure of a quiet gray morn. Ava liked few things better than walking in the quiet softness of a morning fog, where somehow—here more than anywhere—she was able to forget all the tangled misfortunes of her short life.

She'd already met the tiny village of Rowsay, adjacent to the castle of Lismore, and skirted about the fields south of those sleeping crofts, aiming for the hills beyond, and the higher elevation where the wispy fog should be thicker. She left a trail of disturbed dew in the hard brown grass as she climbed the hill. At the summit, not so much higher than the village itself, the fog was blown and scattered by a capricious hand, thick as soup one moment and then thin and see-through in the next, though always it moved faster than Ava did.

At the top of the hill, she sat on her skirts and her cloak, crossing her legs, facing the east and the place where the sun would rise.

Though it was early, the sun not yet risen, she'd found the kitchen already bustling, and had begged two of the freshly fired bannocks from the cook. As the plump woman, who showed a wide space between her front teeth, had looked about to refuse, Ava had been obliged to promise that she would eat only this until last meal, not wanting to appear either gluttonous or as if she expected that she might eat whatever she wanted and whenever.

They'd lost much of their warmth by now, but Ava didn't care and pulled one from the pocket of her léine, taking small and appreciative bites of the dense biscuit, savoring the oat-y flavor.

She'd eaten but half when a voice spoke to her through the shifting fog.

"I dinna intend to startle you," came the voice of John Craig, a full few seconds before he appeared out of the thick morning fog, coming from the same direction as she, from the keep. "I saw you slip out through the gate and wondered what mischief you were about so early."

Ava did not miss or misconstrue the irritability of his tone, which had her feeling as if she were being accused of something greater than any general innocent mischief. But she left off retorting first with some wonder about why her morning walk and sit should peeve him.

"Peace, I suppose," was all she could offer as her reason, pretending that she hadn't noticed his pique. "But that is unfair," she was quick to qualify, aiming for a cheery voice, if only to confound him as he did her. "Lismore is quite ripe with a peaceable nature. Solitude, I guess is the more true reason."

Innes' accusations of last night weighed heavily on her. He'd supposed that she wished to try out Lismore Abbey as their home solely because of John Craig. *Solely* made that assumption false, was all that she'd acknowledged to herself.

"You will accuse me of encroaching then," John Craig guessed, standing in front of her, close enough that she could kick out her foot and make contact with his fine brogues. "And what have you there?" He inclined his head, his brown-eyed gaze on the half-eaten bannock. "Thieving again, and from such generous hosts?"

"Nae," she answered tartly, wondering what he was about, that he seemed to *want* to pick a fight with her. "I made a deal with Cook, promised this would be my morning meal, and naught anything else. I did nae steal."

"'Tis rather dreary, the grayness," he said then, glancing around, confounding her by moving so quickly from his accusation. "Does this bleakness color your solitude?"

Ava considered his pensive query. An entire mood was created by this wistful ambiance she loved so well, and when she spoke, she revealed parts of herself usually only examined in this atmosphere, but admittedly with some attempt to steer him from thinking poorly of her. As if she'd steal from the house that had offered her succor!

"There is something about the gray dawn that...feels as if the world has stopped, or could stop, that mayhap the sun will not come over the edge today. Sometimes I wish I could live just here in the gray dawn, where everything is peaceful."

"That's a tall wish," he said, his tone hinting at thoughtfulness now, but mayhap only because his attempt to rile her had come to naught.

"Are you now considering that you might wish the same?" She asked, aiming for a light and teasing tone. "Surely your life is as eventful as mine is nae. Mayhap you would like to dwell in the stillness of the gray dawn."

He chuckled quietly, though it lacked humor. "I am now considering it, aye."

But he wasn't, she knew, not really. He was only being agreeable suddenly and for whatever reason, but he didn't understand.

He wanted the eventful life, possibly did not idle well, wanted his challenges and plenty of busyness, wanted to fix things and make right rule, she guessed.

"I've said it before," he told her, "your life of late is nae without a certain chaos."

Ava shrugged, curling her cold fingers deeper into the folds of her cloak, thus hiding what remained of her biscuit. "Small chasms in an otherwise tedious existence."

"So you wish to escape the tedium?"

"I wish..." she began readily enough but stopped just as quickly, unwilling suddenly to allow the charitable mantle of the gray dawn to see her admit that she wanted to belong. To someone. To something or some place. But not, she realized, just to anyone or anywhere.

John Craig, inexplicably curious this morn, prodded from another direction. "Did life begin for you in Lanark?"

"Nae. I was born in Wauchope. I am the daughter of Baron Cowie, William de Vaux, lord of Wauchope and Staplegorton—bastard daughter, I should say, which should answer possibly one or two of your next questions."

"Aye, it does. Save for *how*—how did you find yourself removed from Wauchopedale and living hand to mouth in Lanark?"

"I...my life was nae...I dinna care for it. So I left it behind."

"Verra bold, though nae surprising now that I've kept a bit of company with you. And what is the verdict then, having lived both lives?"

Ava tilted her head, appearing to contemplate this. There was no need for deep reflection, however; she'd asked herself the same question a hundred times by now and knew the sad answer just as well. "When I was verra young, it was cold and dreary, lonely in truth. I thought certainly it would be different when I grew up, when I was ten and six, ten and seven, and more. It did not change though, even as my circumstance did. 'Twas cold and dreary just the same, only in a different location. And lonely still. That is, until I met Innes and Hamish." She laughed briefly. "It was still cold and dreary, and aye, it was still lonely. But finally, at least I was nae *alone*."

"And you and the quarrelsome Innes are...?"

Only for a split second did she consider feigning ignorance about what he was asking. And yet, in order to answer in a timely fashion she hadn't then time to consider *why* he might have asked this.

"Innes and I are friends."

"He would like to be more."

"Aye."

"Tries to establish himself as more," he remarked.

"He does," she acknowledged.

"But you...?" he fished.

"The bond of either poverty or sympathy is nae a sweet thing." Of course, that only partly explained her lack of affection similar to Innes'. So often, she thought she *should* know or pretend a greater emotion toward her friend. It seemed to be something that might make sense, being that they were like-minded in many regards, and that they shared a parallel leaden dullness in life.

"And yet you will go where he goes, though you say you are naught but friends," he predicted, and then explained where he'd come by this knowledge. "Eachann said that Innes is already talking of quitting Lismore, though his footprint is barely known here."

"Aye."

"Why is that?"

"He feels that we might fare better—"

"Nae," he interrupted, shaking his head, his gaze heavy on her, his tone laced with that hard edge once more, "why do you cleave to him? Why would you risk yourself, striking out from security toward an unknown?"

"Innes and Hamish are all that I have. Do you nae find comfort in things that are familiar to you?"

"Do you nae find comfort in new things that are an improvement over the old—Lismore over Lanark? Or a safer wager against the odds of a good landing in any other burgh."

Ava turned a questioning eye to him. And despite her arguments to Innes on this very subject last night, she was compelled to defend her friend and his want to leave. "'Tis the same, only in a different location. I am still the bastard daughter of a baron living hand to mouth. That is unlikely to ever change, geography will nae improve that." And she'd had enough now, talking about herself and how life would always be hard, was growing decidedly uncomfortable under his increasing—or perpetual—frown. "And what of you? Why are you yet here, at Lismore Abbey, when surely a place so grandly named as Blacklaw Tower must call to you?"

"Aye, and I'll get there."

Ava noticed, but did not challenge, that he acknowledged her statement without actually answering her question.

Like her possibly, he was unwilling to be the subject of discussion. He turned and eyed the dawning sun, murky and hazy beyond the still-lingering fog. "And what of sunrise, when it comes? Your gray dawn is done. What then?"

Ava stood, a bit disenchanted by his mercurial moods. She did not brush at her bottom, sure that it was dew-dampened but not dirty. Her shoulders shrank inward, the cold seeping in. "Life goes on then," she said.

After giving him a quick bow of her head, she walked away, down the hill. She frowned now, wondering if she'd revealed too much of herself. Had she wanted to do that? Did it matter? Did she really, knowing she would likely never see him after another day or two, care what he thought of her?

The quick and resounding *yes* that answered in her brain was unsettling, in the way that regret was disconcerting.

Regret though hadn't anything to do with how much of herself she'd disclosed to him. Regret, she realized had more to do with that other part, about her leaving in a day or more, about going to some place where John Craig was not.

***

He watched her walk away but was only afforded a few seconds of that beguilement before the fog swallowed her up. He'd been strangely surly with her, he knew, but hadn't been able to stop himself. He'd been right pissed at himself for having followed her in the first place when first he'd spied her leaving the yard. He did not appreciate that he seemed to have no control over that, his incessant and gnawing curiosity about her.

Christ, but what a beast he'd been to her. 'Twas not her fault that he suffered daily—nae, hourly—from some form of torture, recalling the night he'd held her in his arms in the loft of the

Kenith barn, and then reviling himself for not having sought more at that time. How easy it would have been to excuse whatever he might have given or taken, simply by recalling how much he had in fact drank that night. He'd wakened that next morning in such a mood, angry already that dawn had come, and he knew no relief from desire, and she was yet as innocent and beguiling as ever.

These days, reminding himself of his truer and most admirable purpose in life presently, to be able and effective in defense of king and country, had less and less affect on his unruly fascination with her.

John sighed. But wasn't she just full of surprises? Daughter of the nobility, who chose to live meanly rather than in what comfort should be supposed of the house of a Scots' lord, titled and landed.

Ava Guthrie was rather a contradiction, speaking so blandly of a cold and dreary tedium but having in her history that occasion when she'd stopped a hanging with a kiss. He didn't want to think her remarkable, wanted less to be enthralled by her beauty—no less vibrant inside the gray dawn, he decided—but there it was, the truth: he thought her extraordinary and found her utterly—almost maddeningly—alluring. Maddening, which accounted for the constant teeth-gritting in her presence, he supposed; he didn't want to be captivated by her.

Still, how many times had he revisited in his mind the sight of her at almost any time of that night they'd spent at the Kenith Crannog? When she'd smiled so readily, captivating any and many, he was sure. First smiles noted on beautiful women would likely keep hold inside a man's brain for some time, but those instances on that night when he'd witnessed so many glorious and sunny smiles on Ava Guthrie, transforming her from frightened and unsure lass with enchanting green eyes to that stunning, mesmerizing goddess—and *Jesu*, so very kissable, it had seemed more on that night than all the others—was unlikely to be abandoned in his lifetime.

And mayhap now, here at Lismore, hidden from any hunting English and so well protected, she would be free to show more of those smiles, but damn, he shouldn't be hanging around just waiting on those. He was the Lion of Blacklaw Tower, owed his devotion and allegiance just now to Scotland's freedom, and to Robert Bruce more now than ever. He had no business mooning over some homeless enchantress. He didn't want to believe his fascination with Ava Guthrie was anything like the rare and true devotion that Magnus held for Lara. Ava was merely a passing fancy, not unlike any he'd known before or would know again; she was not something that should divert him from his duty and dedication to freedom. Frankly, more often than not he regretted acting on any attraction to a woman, romance and what little he allowed himself to feel being a dangerous diversion in a time of war. He had nobler objectives in mind for his life.

So, aye, he should get on to Blacklaw and she should go with Innes, wherever that besotted man led her.

Why are you yet here? She'd asked, appearing it seemed to have no idea that she kept him here, while he only pretended to Eachann and to Magnus that he waited on word of his king or of Sir James or of the war. She wouldn't like it, he thought, if she knew that truth.

Hell, he despised it himself.

***

The village of Rowsay, belonging to Lismore and its laird, was of course vastly different than the much larger and more congested Lanark. Ava noticed immediately that as an agricultural society, the people had no choice but to be out of doors as that was where the majority of their work was, even as mean weather would have kept the townsfolk of Lanark inside on such a blustery day.

She herself had little choice in the matter, since she was not of a mind to idle away her day only sitting uselessly inside the hall of the keep. While she was pleased to make her bed there, she did not want to abuse the privilege of a roof over her head by lazing indolently there all day.

Hamish and Innes had gone out of doors earlier, with some expectation of watching the training of the Matheson and Craig armies, which apparently took place regularly in a vast field outside the walled fortress, a quarter mile north, Hamish had said. Having no other calling, Ava might have joined them, but she was gainsaid by some vague premonition that she might not be able to hide any significant curiosity about John Craig, should he be in attendance, and worse, that Innes would give her grief for her inability to keep her keen attention away from that man.

Thus, she'd wandered into the village, walking along the twisting lanes, hoping to come upon some purpose, mayhap someone in need of an extra pair of hands. The cottages here were of various sizes but universally tidy. The small yards included wattle fenced, sleeping winter gardens and larger pens for small livestock, mostly game hens. Men were well-accounted for, here among the crofts, one working on a farming implement of forged iron while another made repairs to a low section of his thatched roof; many more were seen in silhouette upon the fields beyond the cluster of homes. Women and children were scattered about the village proper, and more were heard behind the thin walls of wattle and daub.

Between two crofts, two women were doing laundry, the steam from the cauldron of boiling water as white as their breaths in the air while the wind plastered their skirts against their legs and put red spots on their cheeks and nose. One woman, manning the heavy stick that stirred the pot, leaned into the steam to be closer to the woman opposite her, her face animated as she spoke quickly, nodding all the while to punctuate her words—gossip, no doubt, if Ava should judge the reception of her speech, as the other woman's brows lifted halfway up her forehead and her jaw gaped before she clapped a hand over her mouth to stifle her burst of laughter. The speaker smirked thinly and nodded once more, pleased to have imparted news that wrought such scandalized delight.

Grinning at their simple pleasures, Ava did not intrude but walked on.

She was surprised to see the mistress of Lismore, Lara Matheson, exiting one of the well-kept crofts, turning as she stepped outside but continued speaking to the old woman she'd visited, who stopped just in the doorframe.

Lara tapped her hand on the cloth covered basket over her arm. "I am grateful for this, Marion," she said.

"Give it straight to Cook," said the hag, wrapping a woolen shawl around her slim shoulders. "She'll ken what to do with the fern leaves. Sten's congestion'll be gone in nae time."

"Verra well," Lara assured her. "Will you come up to the hall later?"

"Aye, I will and who's that there?" The woman named Marion asked then, narrowing her eyes as she met Ava's gaze.

Ava waved haltingly, slowing her step, sorry to be caught staring and listening, just as Lara Matheson turned and faced her from the stoop of the croft.

"I am Ava," she introduced herself.

"Come with the Craig from Lanark, did you nae?" Asked the bonny mistress. At Ava's nod, the laird's wife said to the old woman, Marion, "Saved his neck, I've been told."

The narrow eyes widened, possibly only as much as they were able, still being small and sunken in her weathered face. "Nae a bad neck to save, if that's what yer business is."

Ava could not help but grin at this. "Nae my business, ma'am. But as it was rather my fault, I had no choice in the matter."

The old woman took one step backward, into the shadows of her home. "C'mon then. We'll sit round a fire, and I'll be wanting to hear all about it."

Ava hesitated, but only because it seemed awkward to pass on possibly walking and talking with Lismore's mistress to spend time with the hag. Lara Matheson spoke next, removing any of Ava's indecision. "Yes, let's. Sten's cough can wait another half an hour." She lifted her hand, indicating Ava should precede her into the dark interior.

Amused by this unexpected turn—the laird's wife taking on the role of a chattering hen—Ava gamely stepped forward.

Marion's croft was not quite the mean and wretched hovel as were so many on the outskirts of Lanark, though it was only one room open to the roof, blackened by smoke. A peat fire burned on a hearthstone in the center of the room, heating a cauldron and its contents, and being surrounded by two three-legged stools. A boxbed was built into the wall to the right of the door, its curtain of stained linen half open, while the left wall showed a pen where chickens clucked and pecked and a lone sheep lay, uninterested in visitors. Straight across from the door was a long counter built against the stone and clay wall, the top of which was covered with a variety of plants and herbs and roots, fresh and dried, and whole and ground.

Before Ava had considered the two chairs/three person conundrum, Marion settled herself onto the floor, proving more agile than her age suggested, lowering herself easily and steadily to the ground onto crossed legs.

"Sit, sit," she said, picking up a ladle to stir whatever boiled in the kettle.

Ava and Lara each took a stool, the mistress setting down the linen-covered basket at her feet.

Across the fire, tucked into the corner adjacent the bed box, Ava spied a large wooden tub, hanging from a peg in the wall. 'Twas newer, would be her guess, the staves not darkened with age and regular usage, but then more remarkable for being found inside a peasant's house.

"Mistress spoils this ol' woman," said Marion, drawing Ava's attention from the unexpected find. "Had the carpenter contrive that thing, and once a week she sends down three lads, those that'd rather be drawing swords and nae a bath, but there you have it, and they fill my tub and this ol' woman soaks away the years."

Ava returned her awestruck regard to the tub, truth be told a wee envious for the boon provided that *ol' woman*.

Marion mistook her gawking. "What's that puss? Dinna mean I only wash up once a week—"

"Oh, good heavens, nae!" Ava quickly corrected. "I dinna ken that at all. I was only...envious."

"Then you must partake—" Marion began to offer.

"Nae! I was nae asking or hinting."

"And yet I'm offering."

Ava considered this, the grand luxury of such a thing—a soaking bath, indoors, near the fire mayhap. At this moment, she could not recall the last time she'd been favored so. "Truly?"

"Anytime," Marion said, leaning forward once more to stir the contents of the pot.

"I'll even lug my own water," Ava vowed eagerly.

"That will nae be necessary," the mistress said then. "Will be nae hardship to ask the lads to come down one more day and fill the tub." She laid her hand over her chest, over the fine blue wool of her kirtle. "I am Lara, by the way, just to make it official."

Ava smiled readily. "Yes, of course. And thank you so much for your hospitality, for me and my friends, Innes and Hamish."

Leaving the ladle propped along the rim of the kettle, Marion asked, "Did you forget so soon what sits us around the warm fire?"

"I did nae," Ava answered promptly, somehow not at all unnerved by the older woman's impatience. And neither was she made anxious by the two sets of eyes sitting so raptly upon her, believing both women only curious. Sliding her hands along her thighs until they rested at her knees, she began with the qualifier, "'Tis nae so remarkable a tale. And I am only slightly shamed for my part in it, but would have been...inconsolable, I guess, if he'd...if he had been..."

"Aye, you'd have been right pained had he hanged," Marion cut in quickly, spinning her hand around to hurry along the telling.

"Well, yes. Of course. It was all my fault, as I said. I was stealing oats from the granary and was caught—"

"Stealing rarely ends well for the thief," Marion intoned sagely, but without rancor.

Realizing she desired their good opinion, Ava was quick to explain, "It wasn't for me but for a woman who'd—"

She paused when Marion lifted her hand and spun it around and around again.

A cursory glance at Lara Matheson showed her biting back a grin.

"All right," Ava said. "Um, I was caught—discovered—upon my exit and one of the English soldiers...um, thought he would make me pay for my obvious crimes in a most dastardly way—and that, likely before I would have been tossed in a cell. And then...he was there—John Craig, though I didn't ken his name or anything at all about him at the time. And he...saved me, but in the process, he did kill that man. And then more guards came, and he was overtaken, and my friend Innes got me out of there."

Marion removed her skinny gaze from Ava and turned it upon Lara, her brows lifting, widening her eyes. "Dinna take him for a savior, but mayhap any reason to slay the English was seized upon."

Lara Matheson only shrugged at this and urged on Ava. "But how did you then return the favor and save him from being hanged?"

"Oh, gosh," Ava said, her heartbeat increasing as she was just then overcome with that same ominous anxiety she'd wrestled with for three whole days, wondering what she might do, if anything at all. "I didn't ken what to do and I was a wretched wreck,

I can tell you that, so fearful that a man would die for me. But then," she paused and now lifted and dropped her shoulders, "I just...I don't know why, but I pretended I ken him, and begged the sheriff to let me say goodbye. And mayhap only the mob's surliness made the sheriff grant me such a boon but then while I kissed him I had my knife—"

"Kissed him?" Marion cut in, leaving her mouth open after that had been asked.

"You kissed him? John Craig?" Lara asked, her hazel eyes open wide.

"Um, yes," Ava admitted. "I dinna ken what else to do, but I needed to—"

"Aye but that explains a bit then," Lara Matheson said, a teasing smile playing about her bonny face.

Bewildered, Ava crunched the fabric of her léine in the fingers at her knees. "I'm sorry. Explains what?"

"Verra little, truth be told," said the mistress, "but something that my husband said. Magnus wondered if he at one time looked as ridiculous as John has these last few days, the way he watches you—devours you, I've since noticed, after Magnus alerted me."

Ava's mouth gaped, same as Marion's had seconds ago.

But that was simply...him looking at her. Wasn't it?

Unless it was more, unless his heart raced, and his breath caught the way hers did when she stared at him.

Nae, it did not, must not. Too often—almost on every occasion—when their eyes met, he appeared to be so angry with her. This very morning, he might well have come upon her in the fog with his sword drawn, so provoking was he.

"So that's how you did it," Marion said with several nods of her head. "Makes sense now, using one of the few weapons available to you. You dinna strike me as the earl o' hell sort, riding in hard and furious. Come soft and quiet, like the fox that you are, and good for you."

They seemed less alarmed about the entire tale—stealing, murder, the hanging that wasn't—than they were about the kiss she'd employed. But she was happy to not relive anymore of any of that which took place inside Lanark. She turned to Lara. "You...you ken John Craig well, then?"

"I do nae," she answered. "I only met him—and Magnus actually, just last year. So I ken verra little about John Craig."

"He's nae so different from your laird," Marion remarked easily.

Lara reminded her, "But then we ken him nae so well to even say that with any confidence." When Marion only shrugged at this, Lara continued. "He is...when he comes, or when he's here, I ken my husband will soon leave, or plans are being devised. I dinna...dislike him, I only ken when he comes...he will take my husband away, to war. He is a cousin to Magnus, and my husband cherishes both their kinship and their friendship. Likely, he would tell you there is nae other he'd rather have at his back, counts him as honorable and sure-footed, in mind and heart."

A worthy endorsement, in Ava's mind, she already so in awe of the laird, Magnus Matheson.

The talk moved on, Ava inquiring of Marion if she were Lismore's healer, having supposed as much for the counter of plants and herbs, and because of what she'd first heard from Lara, that she'd collected some treatment for someone's congestion.

"I am nae, but then the one who is lives a long way off," Marion said. "I've nae gift, but only a wee knowledge gathered after all these years." As if struck by inspiration then, she pointed at Ava, her eyes lighting again. "Mayhap you'll lend your strong hands, lass? Come the spring, when foraging will be so much less in vain. This one is busy with her bairn, dinna like to be gone so long, or might yet be carrying another and then the laird will nae allow her to lift so much as her own arm. Again."

Ava had no idea that Lara had a child. "Oh, but I...I dinna ken I'll be here very long. Innes and Hamish and I are likely to strike out again, for, well..." she slowed and then paused, taking in the stares aimed her way, two similar gazes possibly presuming she was daft. She shrugged, tired of explaining herself to strangers. "They're my friends."

Lara graciously offered that she was welcome to remain at Lismore. "Unless, of course, you'll be going where ever John Craig goes."

Ava's frown was instant. "I will n—why would I...? Nae, I...why would you ken that?"

Lara and Marion returned their attention to Ava, who felt rather as if a torch had just been thrust near her face, putting her into a glaring light, expecting answers.

"I am nae going anywhere with John Craig," she said more firmly.

Lara nodded. "Mayhap nae. Or, certainly nae unless you invite yourself."

Ava didn't understand this, and her puzzled expression might have said as much so that Marion clarified, "He's that sort, kens a woman will only weaken him. 'Hap as well, he's the type that dinna see what's right under his nose, nae for what it is."

Ava laughed nervously, believing both of them to be a wee fanciful. "I might suggest less inhaling of the herbs and whatever else boils so faithfully in that pot. Nae carrying a full shilling, nae either of you."

She clapped her hand over her mouth as soon as the words emerged, horrified at what she'd just uttered.

To her fantastic relief, Marion cackled almost immediately, loud and craggy the sound, slapping her crooked fingers onto her knee. Lara followed in kind, but with less zest, her laughter quieter, sweeter, though her smile was bright.

Ava knew a vast relief and soon joined them in their merriment, right after she'd apologized profusely for speaking so cynically.

Chapter Eleven

"I've met a wee thing come here in the spring," Hamish said. "'Tis broad and blue and—"

"You did the sky already," Ava reminded him. "And I said then, 'twas too easy. 'Tis the only thing of blue for miles around."

It had been a week since they'd come to Lismore Abbey, and each day that came and went only gave Ava more reasons to never want to leave. There was no denying the generosity of Lismore Abbey in regard to shelter, warmth, and sustenance. Lismore had, essentially, welcomed them with open arms. They tried daily to return the favor, to make themselves useful and constructive so that they did not only appear as indolent, ungrateful beggars. Today, while Innes kept time with Eachann—about what business Ava had not been told—she and Hamish searched the woods to the northwest of the keep, scouting the traps laid by Lismore's huntsman. They'd only been about it for a quarter hour and already three hares dangled in a jute bag from a loop in Hamish's belt.

She'd not ever heard or played so trifling a game as this one before she'd met Hamish, giving clues in rhyme to whatever thing was spied, but years ago he'd told her he recalled it from his youth. He'd seemed quite proud to introduce it to Ava, so she'd played along with him ever since.

"Och, and I forgot I named the sky already," Hamish said now, slapping his hand lightly against his forehead. "Aye, and here we go. I've met a wee thing come here in the spring. 'Tis tall and brown and sometimes comes down."

"The trees," Ava guessed. "Or rather, a tree trunk."

"Aye, but which one?" Hamish asked.

Ava laughed at this. "Hamish, we'll be all day about the game if I have to pick which one of the hundred trees in this wood you might be meaning."

"Fine then, but you dinna get a whole point," he argued. "Mayhap only half."

"Verra well. So I've eleven and a half and you have four now. My turn. I've met a wee thing come here in the spring. 'Tis soft and—"

"Do you hear that, Ava?"

"I heard myself speaking," she teased him for interrupting her. Hamish was regularly—frequently—distracted.

"Nae," he said, holding up his hands as if to quiet all the woods, the wind and the rustling of dried leaves, the critters too. "Someone is crying—or laughing, I canna tell."

Ava paused and soon heard what had given Hamish pause. 'Twas not laughing, she was sure, but she could not identify the sound, a vague wail. She did, however, believe it was coming from ahead of them, further north. "This way," she pointed, and she and Hamish hastened their step, watchful now for traps solely so that they didn't step into one.

The crying continued intermittently, guiding them to the source, which turned out to be a lone ewe, stranded upon the moor just outside the wooded vale. No sheep had any business being out here, so far removed from the herd. They were kept close to the village, alternately moved from their pens to the pasturelands, but Ava didn't believe any should have wandered this far. No sooner had she thought this than another full-grown ewe appeared, lifting its head from the tall grass of the moor, about thirty yards beyond the first.

"Good grief," said Ava. "But they must have wandered. We should get back and alert—"

"We can bring 'em in ourselves," Hamish said, approaching the closer of the sheep.

"How? We haven't a harness or rope."

"Dinna need naught but a stick," Hamish said, looking around for just that. Finding none in the grassy moor, he ambled back into the woods and emerged moments later carrying two limbs, each almost four or five feet long, one tucked under his arm, and one which he stripped of smaller offshoot branches, which also mostly debarked the thin, dried limb. He handed that one to Ava and set to work on the other, his fleshy but strong hands making quick work of the task. When he was done, he tapped the malleable topmost end on the ground and said to Ava, "Tap left or right behind them, urging them forward." He approached the closer ewe and did just that. The ewe was not startled and did not spring into motion, but she did begin to move as Hamish encouraged. "See?" He said, throwing a glance over his shoulder at Ava. "Go on with this one," he said. "I'll get the other."

Ava stepped forward and around to the far side of the ewe, meaning to direct it back from where she and Hamish had come. A few taps of the long twig successfully moved the sheep forward.

"Daft yoe," she heard muttered behind her.

Turning she saw that Hamish's trudging toward the second sheep might have sent it into a panic, as now she was running, not with any great speed but in the opposite direction.

"This way, you filthy beast," Hamish grumbled, giving chase to the lumbering ewe. "Go on, Ava!" He called backward. "I'll catch up."

Grinning, Ava focused on her own task, spurring the ewe up the incline and into the trees. Here, the task was moderately more difficult, as the *daft yoe* did not march with its uneven, bouncy gait straight through the woods but meandered left and right, weaving its way carelessly about and around the pine and birch and hazel trees. Ava realized fairly quickly that if she moved too hastily or too enthusiastically to correct its path, the ewe tended to be spooked and only went further and faster in the wrong direction.

"You are daft, you silly creature," she groused now, following and smacking the thin branch behind the ewe, trying to turn its direction as it began to move faster and too far east. "Hamish!" She called out, fearful she herself would now be lost in the woods if they strayed much further if she could not redirect the ewe's course. "Hamish!" The faster she ran, trying with dwindling success to wrangle the stupid creature, the more swiftly the ewe tried to escape her.

"Ham—" she began to call again, but the word was cut off when her foot caught in the viny tendrils of undergrowth. She went flying, her arms flapping upward in front of her, thankfully brought down with time enough to stop her from landing face first. Ava turned an angry eye onto the woody, creeping culprits, and took a moment to free her foot. Almost instantly, she was bitten by inspiration as she saw and felt how supple and sturdy were the vines.

"Here, sheepy, sheepy," she cooed to the ewe as she began to tug the vines from the earth.

***

He was not on this occasion actually following her. Having so steadfastly avoided Ava of late, John hadn't been in close proximity to her in days, in fact saw her only at meal times when she sat at the table with Innes and Hamish, at the opposite end of the great hall from where he took his meals at the high table with the larid and mistress. Thus, he was surprised to be so far removed from the keep and the village when he heard her voice.

Still, and so it was, that once more John Craig rode hellbent to the rescue of Ava Guthrie. Hellbent was overdone, since her cry—calling Hamish's name—had sounded more frustrated than frightened. And then, *hellbent* rather advised that his efforts of late to put her from his mind may have been in vain, if this brow-furrowing and gut-clenching should be his reaction to her call of distress, the very thought of her in danger.

He kneed the flanks of his destrier and followed the sound of her voice into the woodlands, but then heard nothing else after the second time she called for Hamish. Worry did gnaw at him after a moment, while he maneuvered the horse through the tightly knit trees, and while he dissected the tone she'd used. Had she been fretful? Was she in danger?

John gritted his teeth and raced on. He couldn't explain it, what she did to him, what effect she had on him, and what power she unwittingly held over him. In some way, she made him feel more alive than any woman or any battle ever had. But Christ! Didn't she drive him crazy? Shouldn't he hang onto the raw fury that had begun their relationship, because he'd nearly hanged for her? Even as this was being examined inside his head, part of him was compelled to admit the other half of the truth, that above and beyond the conviction that she was nothing more than a nuisance, there had been that fascination. Regularly when he did see her, a war waged inside himself. The need to ride or walk straight up to her and engage with her, mayhap tease a smile from her, have one of those for himself, or simply stare into those remarkable green eyes of hers fought against his certainty that she was trouble or would cause him grief, somehow or someway.

When he finally spied her inside Lismore's compact northern forest, her figure unmistakable, he yanked slightly left on the reins, angling his steed to meet her, wondering what she was doing pulling a fat sheep along with her, away from Lismore.

No sooner had he cause to wonder about her actions than the answer came to him. Any charitable thoughts he had of her, those mostly associated with that lone but stirring kiss and his fascination since with her tempting mouth, were expelled by what she appeared to be about now. John seethed anew with fury, that she would practice her thieving so blatantly here at Lismore, where they had been extended so generous a welcome.

Why, the ungrateful little brat!

"Ava!"

She whirled around, her lips parted, as shocked to find him here as he was her. His attention was momentarily arrested by the sight of her, rosy-cheeked skin and lips, the forest hue lent to her green eyes, the way her hair spilled all around her, a wild and decadent mantle of chestnut.

"What are you about?" He barked at her, wrenching his gaze away from her face to assess the situation.

She did indeed have an ewe leashed to her, oddly by way of a harness of vines, which only served to darken John's mien and mood.

"Hamish and I discovered two ewes on the other side of the forest, upon the moors," she said. "They must have escaped the pens or the pasture. Hamish is—"

"Aye, and you are what? Helping yourself to the wayward yoe? And how did you expect to get—"

"God's teeth," she frothed, her own glower swift and as dark as John's. "Are you accusing me—again!—of stealing?"

"What else should I be supposing you are doing?"

Transferring the viny rope into only one hand, she thrust the other fist onto her hip. "You might expand your wee mind and imagine that I am trying to get the bluidy beast back to Rowsay."

"I might have kent as much," he said mildly before increasing his thunder, "if you'd been heading *toward* Lismore and nae away."

"Is it only me?" She asked, her bonny face tilted up at him. "For whom that eager willingness to believe ill is reserved? Or do you suppose the worst of anyone and everyone?"

"I base my estimations of a person on what history I have known with them."

"Aye, I stole from the granary the night we met," she cried at him, "but that dinna make me a thief!"

John said nothing, only crooked his head at her, his scowl intact, waiting for the absurdity of her statement to settle.

When it did, she rolled her eyes and threw up her hands. "Fine. I am a thief. But nae in this instance. I was trying to help," she said.

"Again," he insisted, "a wee difficult to believe since Lismore is that way." He pointed with his thumb over his shoulder.

"So just because I was turned around in these stupid woods, you seriously believe that I am attempting to make off with a bluidy ewe. And what is my plan then?" She snapped at him. "What? I'm assembling an entire herd miles away from here, one by one and day by day, and I'll nae depart Lismore until I have numbers that satisfy me? Forget it," she said next, and wrestled to unknot and untangle the vines she'd wrapped around the ewe's fat neck. "I certainly dinna need your condemnation. I dinna need you snarling at me, believing the worst, every time we meet." She jerked and pulled, and the ewe bleated her upset. "I'm sorry, sheep. 'Tis nae you but him that has me peeved." Finally, she wrestled the vines over the ewe's head and tossed them aside. She faced John then while the ewe ambled away. "You can imagine what you will of me," she said. "I have just now realized I dinna crave the good opinion of a flawed man."

"I'll give you ten seconds to explain that remark," he clipped at her.

"I need only five," she shot back. "You are irrationally arrogant and unjustly mean and thus, flawed; nae worthy of *my* good opinion." With that, she turned and walked away from him.

"You are dangerously close to being labeled a shrew," he called after her.

"And you, sir, have already been branded an arse," she hollered backward and then grumbled, though he heard it still. "At least in my mind."

John spurred the destrier forward, catching up with her. "Have you nae consideration for the man who saved you from being assaulted?"

"Aye, I do," she said, not bothering to look at him. "About as much as has the man for me, the one *I* dinna abandon to his hanging. And what are you about? Always on my tail? Why do you follow me everywhere?"

His scowl was instant as he lied to her, "I assure you, at nae time do I seek out your company."

"Then off with you, you miserable man," she demanded as she went right around a cluster of pines, and he skirted them around the left side.

"And be accused of your death, when you fail to find your way and can only wander the woods until you meet your demise—felled by the cold, or by bandits or beasts, or by English mayhap?"

"The only beast causing me grief presently rides a bay destrier," she murmured.

Once more, he stopped moving, drawing on the reins to bring the horse to a stop.

Jesu, but why did he allow himself to be riled? *Flawed man* sat unwell with him, but nae, he didn't think he was improving that condition with his present behavior. Still, he couldn't seem to help himself. Or, for whatever reason, he wasn't yet ready to be parted from her, would rather keep company with her, shouting and squawking, than nae be with her at all. Or mayhap this was the safest way to be with her, when dander was up and insults and accusations were hurled, when enthrallment should nae be possible.

Bluidy hell, but he wanted to kiss her. Still? Always, since he'd met her?

A nuisance indeed. A bluidy beautiful nuisance.

"You'll have to wrangle that ewe yourself now," Ava called out, stomping through the crisp bracken of the forest.

Let her go. Stay away from her. Go get the sheep. Find a true battle in which to engage.

So much good advice, shrieked by the wiser half of his brain.

John dismounted, jaw tight, intent on collecting the roaming ewe.

Ava continued to grumble—purposefully loud enough to be overheard, he was sure. "So righteous he is, calls Innes quarrelsome. Hah. A more volatile man I'm sure I've never met."

So then he forgot about the wandering ewe and stalked after her. And either now or later, he couldn't rightly say he didn't know why he pursued her, or what his intent was. When he was almost upon her, she sensed or heard his coming, and whirled around. Ava's reaction to his suddenly close proximity made his intent to kiss her—to kiss her senseless and show to her how little she affected him on the whole—fall by the wayside.

When she turned, and upon encountering the savagery of his countenance, she shriveled and lifted her hands in front of her, ready to defend herself.

Jesu, he was indeed the arse she accused him of being, and many other despicable things, but he was no abuser of women. John stared at her while she cringed in front of him, his current scowl now attributed to what she apparently thought him capable of.

Her mouth was open, a gasp interrupted or ended. John stared at her gorgeous pink lips, worthy of so much more attention than this clumsy situation called for.

The hand he'd lifted, meaning to grab at her arm before she'd turned, fell to his side.

Ava recovered herself, her cheeks pinker than they'd been at first sight, and straightened her spine, mayhap a wee shamed by her unaccountable cowering. Nae, but not unaccountable—that response had been learned.

Through gritted teeth, angered that she would liken him to any person who had once abused her, and as thoughts of a kiss were abandoned, he informed her, "You're still going the wrong way."

A shudder racked her willowy figure as fear departed completely. "Well, bluidy hell," she cried, sounding as if actual tears were imminent, "just point, would you!"

"That way," he said, expending great effort to soften his tone, pointing forty-five degrees to the left of where she'd been going. "Or just wait for me," he suggested.

Her wide green eyes blinked rapidly and were taken away from him as she shook her head forcefully and turned, lifting her skirts to hurry away.

John exhaled a ragged breath and planted his hands on his hips, watching her run to escape him.

Flawed. Miserable. Quarrelsome. Aye, he was that. And apparently so much more, in her eyes.

An arse indeed.

But for the best, aye, that she should know all that about him.

***

She tried to convince herself that she hated John Craig. She spent the better part of the day engaged in that industry. She did that even as she threshed grain for over an hour with a woman named Beth and when she ran into Innes, still with Eachann and visiting the bladesmith. Innes had been proud to tell her a sword was being forged just for him. Unimpressed, Ava only passed by those men. After that, she was distracted from the time lent to the pursuit of developing a loathing for John Craig by recalling that she'd rather forgotten all about poor Hamish. Luckily, she happened upon him, entering Rowsay, ewe in tow, just as Ava would have gone out searching for him.

He was as red-faced as any other time he'd engaged in any physical activity but was smiling broadly for his success, walking straight and tall and with his shoulders thrown back.

"Gave me quite a run, she did," Hamish said when he saw Ava, hitching the thumb of his free hand toward the mindless sheep. "But here we are."

"Good for you, Hamish," Ava called out to him, genuinely gladdened by anything that pleased him.

After that, her endeavors to encourage dislike and disinterest, which should have been easy enough given her encounter with John Craig earlier, was yet again interrupted as she came upon folks, women actually, milling around outside Eliza and Edane's cottage.

The woman, Beth, whom Ava had only just met today, waved her over when she spied her.

"The bairn comes," Beth said excitedly, reminding Ava that Eliza had indeed been heavy with child only days ago.

Ava smiled, as she assumed was expected, but her mood was sour, and she hadn't yet any reason to coo and cry over newborns, having so rarely met any, and so she trudged on, wishing for someplace of her own to while away hours and hide her sullenness.

Summoning hatred was difficult work, exhausting actually.

She found she wasn't very good at it, certainly not where that devil, John Craig, was concerned.

She'd been so sure—after she was even more certain that he'd been about to strike her—that he'd meant to kiss her this morning. Or at least, that he'd been pondering the very idea, if anything should have been assumed by the way he'd stared with such dedication at her mouth. The thrill provoked inside her, the way her stomach had fluttered, and her heart had sung, told her she'd wanted just that.

Foolish girl, she chided herself.

You're going the wrong way, he'd said instead, which should have served as a fine warning to her wayward thoughts as well.

But sweet St. Andrew, why—how!—was she attracted to a man such as him? Aside from his monstrous good looks—oh, what those piercing brown eyes did to her!—he had little to recommend him. He was surly, he thought ill of her on every occasion, he didn't have but that one expression—anger, in many degrees—and she knew for certain, after quite a number of days in his company or close to it, that smiling was not something he practiced when he hadn't enough drink in him, nor any good humor that might accompany so fine an expression.

Her world and her life were dreary enough. She didn't need to be infatuated of someone who only practiced hostility.

Infatuated? she scoffed, picking up a thin tree branch that looked very much like the one she'd used earlier with the sheep she should have proudly returned to the village but had not. Idly, she walked along the low stone wall that circumvented one side of Rowsay, dragging the stick along the fence as she went.

She tried to imagine one thing—just one—about John Craig that intrigued her so.

She came up with quite a few, his kiss being foremost on the list. His striking appearance ranked fairly high; for the life of her she could think of nothing negative about his broad shoulders or those massive arms of his. How strong and brave he was counted as something, she was sure. The way he devoured her with a look could not be ignored, try as she might.

But mostly, the problem seemed to be that she had no control over how she reacted to any of these most disagreeable things. Apparently, she could not simply tell herself, *dinna be melted by his simmering gazes.*

Oh, and wasn't that a fine reason to disavow any benevolent thoughts about John Craig? That simmering gaze of his, the one that regularly devoured her, did not at all soften when he looked at her, not the way Magnus Matheson's eyes did when he beheld Lara.

Ava clung to this, as strenuously as she did to the knowledge that all of it might well be for naught, her troubles might only be short-lived. Either she and Hamish and Innes would soon depart Lismore, bound for wherever Innes thought they should, or John Craig would leave, called to war or back to his Blacklaw Tower.

Her mood did marginally improve as the day went on, her meeting with John Craig growing more distant.

When next she walked through the village, no persons were gathered any more outside Eliza's hut, and Ava bit her lip, wondering if that were a good sign or nae.

As she wended her way along the twisting lane, she spied Marion exiting her own cottage, pulling the door closed behind her.

Ava called out a greeting and immediately asked after the expectant mother.

Marion met her on the dirt road, a basket hanging over her arm. "Weary but smiling yet," Marion informed Ava. "Another lad to her growing herd, hale and hearty as they say."

"That's wonderful."

"Are you going up?" Marion asked. "Almost time for last meal."

Ava considered this, grimacing a bit. "I dinna ken I will tonight.

Marion folded her hands together at her middle, which thumped the narrow basket against her thighs. "Thought I'd hear you rapping at my door by now, having at that bath I recommended to you."

Ava had thought about it several times since first it had been offered. "I...I dinna like to overstep bounds."

Marion rolled her eyes. "The boundaries circle outside the bath, lass. I said as much. If you're nae going up to the keep, then sit right here. I'll send the lads down right quick, have the tub filled before an hour has passed."

Her own weariness forgotten with such a temptation, Ava said, "Marion, if you truly dinna mind, a bath sounds like absolute heaven."

"Go on, then. Wait inside, stoke the small blaze. There's towels on the pegs near my bed."

"I cannot imagine a way to thank you for such generosity," Ava said next.

"Aye, you can. Enjoy the boon, that'll be thanks enough."

"But I dinna wish to put you out of your own—"

The old woman scoffed at this, lifting a hand and waving it downward. "Just said I was nae going to be home anyhow. Go on, then, before all your whingeing turns me off the idea."

Ava grinned outright at this and nodded eagerly, moving up the walk to Marion's cottage as the old woman strode away from it.

Chapter Twelve

When she lived at the baron's house, she had many times partaken of a bath in the garderobe with other female servants. Having been consigned to the lowliest of servants, the scullery maids, she and those of her station had been allowed to use the tubs and the heated water *after* the ladies of the house—her father's wife and true daughters—and the remainder of the female household staff had taken their turns. She'd known then that it was both a blessed amenity and a bitter humiliation. But she'd understood that as a beggar, she could not afford to be choosy.

How silly she'd been at that time to grumble about the used and cool water. All her baths since she'd left Redhall House, for the past five years, had been out of doors and in fresh water, which was, even in the short-lived heat of summer, never truly warm. Thus, Ava stood motionless inside the door of Marion's cottage, hardly able to contain her excitement.

Motionless but for a moment, glancing around at the one room house she'd perused once already, before she leapt into action, adding peat from a tall basket to the fire and stoking that until it was blazing bright, brightening the dim interior. Next, she pulled the tub itself down from its hook and, unable to see any spot where it might regularly have sat, she set it down close to the fire, truly in the only spot it might fit.

As it had on her first visit to Marion's cottage, the kettle suspended over the fire was filled with a pottage of some concoction, one Ava did not want to burn. She removed that from the fire, thinking to replace it when she was done. She found another pot, this one empty, and gave it a sniff, supposing it was clean-ish since she detected no foul odor. And then, imagining that any lads come with water for her bath might be a while yet—surely they heated larger cauldrons up at the keep, did they not?—Ava dashed out of the croft and skipped down to the stream at the far side of the pasture, going along the same stone wall she had earlier. There, she filled the kettle with clear water and then was sorry she'd filled it so high since it was heavy and awkward on her return trip. But she trudged on, intent on having the most perfect bath, which should include this kettle of extra heated water to add when the original bath cooled.

She took note of the setting sun, streaking the western sky in shades of purple and orange and smiled at nature's beauty, her mood charitably inclined by the prospect of a hot bath.

Inside the small croft once more, she left the door ajar and set this kettle on the tripod over the fire.

And then she waited, undoing the braid in her hair, running her fingers through the long locks, though the interim was not as long as she would have suspected.

They were not lads that came, but four soldiers, grown men, and Ava was briefly embarrassed by this, though she couldn't say why. They worked in teams, each pair having a thick timber stretched from the shoulder of one man to that of the other, the extra large cauldron suspended by its handle from that stout branch.

"This'll be the tepid water, lass," said one of the men as he and another emptied that into the tub. "By the time we get on back, the other pots should be boiling." When he straightened, he grinned at Ava, seeming to see her truly for the first time. He did not move, even as the other two men waited for space to step further inside.

"Aye, and keep on mooning, mate," said one of the waiting men, whom she thought might be Henry, "dinna mind us and this heavy load."

The blaze that Ava had invigorated showed that the cheeks of the man directly in front of her suddenly flamed red. He smiled still at Ava, backing up awkwardly, inadvertently bumping the now empty pot against the full one wanting to be dumped into the sturdy tub.

A bit of scrambling took place, the first two men and their pot trying to get out of the way of the next two.

Ava clapped her hands together in front of her mouth, nodding her gratefulness, now a wee embarrassed for the man and his gawking and also by her overwrought emotions. She thought she should not be *this* excited over something so simple as a bath.

The man whose name she thought was Henry said to her, when that was done, "The mistress wanted that you have this." He withdrew a linen wrapped lump from inside his tunic. "Soap is my guess, and we'll both smell like roses now that it's stained me inside."

Ava smiled her gratitude, a bit in awe of this unexpected boon. She brought the wrapped linen to her nose, closing her eyes as she inhaled its scent, not roses but the sweet, tender fragrance of violets.

It was another fifteen minutes before the second load of water came, these pots blessedly steaming hot, before she closed the door behind the departing men and their twice-emptied huge kettles. When she was alone again and finally, she readied the towels near the tub, sitting them on one of the three-legged stools, and set the soap on top of them, within reach, before she quickly undressed, slipping into the divinely heated water.

She sank back against the smooth wooden staves, buried up to the top of her breasts in the steamy water, and stayed like that for a long time, unmoving, thinking of nothing but the luxury of this bath.

Perhaps she would have idled longer, late into the night, but for her concern for the fact that Marion would eventually return to her own house and would prefer, like as not, that Ava and her bath were not here when she did. Ava planned to return Marion's house to how she'd found it, so that it might be guessed but not seen that she'd actually been there and had her bath. Thus, she got on with the actual washing, this endeavor made all the more glorious by the gift of the scented soap, wondering vaguely if Lara Matheson had begged prettily of her husband for such a prize, or if the laird had sought benefits of his own by presenting her with such an extravagance. Ava wasn't sure how things of that nature might work, matters between a husband and wife, when wants came into play. Did one simply ask? Beg? Promise things in return to have what you wanted?

She got on with the business of washing her hair next, not an easy task given its thickness and length, and made more difficult because there was no one to pour water over her head, and the tub was of good size but not so large that dunking herself completely to rinse her hair was easily done.

All told, she thought three quarters of an hour might have passed since she sank herself into the bath before she gave up the splendor of it and stood to exit the tub. Before she grabbed for a towel, and though the fire had slimmed down and the air had cooled, she spent a moment wringing water from her hair, bent at the waste so that it all drained into the bath.

She had just finished this and reached for one of the towels when the door opened behind her—not with any great force and not preceded by a polite knock of warning that Marion had returned. It had been many years since she'd been naked in front of another, lastly those other scullery maids with whom she'd bathed, so that Ava whirled, a bit flustered, clutching the towel to her front, though it concealed little since she'd not wrapped it around herself.

But it was not Marion who stood at the door.

"God's bones," she squeaked, stricken by the sight of John Craig standing there, as gape jawed as she.

The seconds that passed as they stood, each shocked into paralysis, seemed as full minutes. Ava stared at him, at his eyes, horrified when he did not meet hers at all, but moved his gaze sharply over her from head to toe. His glittering gaze swept over her unabashedly, not with the derision she might have expected of him but with a startling awareness, one that ignited little fires over every inch of her bared skin.

He was ferocious at this moment, seething and branded by fire, his knuckles white upon the door handle. She felt decidedly and alarmingly like a wax candle, melting under the heat of his gaze. She was aware of her breasts in a way she'd never noticed them before, her body reacting to the unmistakable fury of his perusal; behind the towel her nipples swelled to peaks, tight and aching. Her heart raced and her mind dimmed, aware of naught but him, filling up the doorway.

Finally his eyes landed on hers but still neither she nor he moved, only continued to stare at each other. Ava's chest rose and fell erratically with some combination of thrill and acute embarrassment, the former seriously outweighing the latter.

And finally—finally!—her wits returned to her. Ava gasped and jerked her arms and hands, adjusting the towel until it at least covered the entire front of her.

"What are you—?"

"Marion said that—"

They'd spoken at the same time, with identical violent tones.

A glare was exchanged and then they did it again, spoke simultaneously.

"Marion said what?" She all but shrieked.

"What the hell are you about?" He growled over her.

"Marion said I was bathing, I presume," she defended hotly, "since she gave me leave to do so!"

"She—never mind. I..." he said but let it hang, while his gaze drifted again, down and back up.

Ava realized what her own shock and humiliation had prevented her from seeing initially, that he was not only angry, that some other thing lived and breathed inside him now. He was taut with whatever churned in him now, his nostrils flaring while a muscle ticked in his cheek.

Comprehension came slowly and not without a wee shock for what she imagined boiled in him at this moment.

He was not simply annoyed to have found her where he thought she should not be and he suffered no embarrassment for having disturbed her, finding her stark-arse naked—John Craig likely didn't *do* blushing awkwardness. He was...not unaffected by what he'd stumbled upon. He was, if she read him correctly right now, intrigued—mayhap so much more—by the sight of her.

Oh, but this changed everything. Didn't it?

Breathless now, baffled and taunted by this possible truth, Ava considered him through a different lens. Unless she read him entirely wrong, had misread what looked very much like swallowed-groan-torture, she had no choice but to fathom that he liked what he saw, although clearly he did not want to. At the very least, he was in no hurry to take himself away from her.

All her want of one more kiss from John Craig rushed to the fore. Ava suspected this, now, would be her best chance yet. Before reason and wisdom and self-preservation assumed a larger role inside her head, Ava made the bravest move of her life, straightening her spine as she slowly lowered the towel to her waist.

Surely, this type of breathing would be fatal, she thought, suddenly unable to draw in breath or exhale it fully, while she stared at him, as hopeful as she was fearful. Never in her life had she been so bold.

Why am I doing this? she wondered as she judged his reaction—he grimaced, his mouth twisting with a mounting anger, briefly meeting her gaze with his savagely gleaming brown eyes to express his fury at her for this move, before he raked those beautiful eyes once more over her body. It seemed some force stronger than him moved his eyes downward, over her breasts and their taut peaks.

But when he made no move to her, Ava cursed herself a fool. Why had she just done that? Never say that she only craved approval, acceptance, yearned for love from any unlikely source. Nae, it was not that. She was fascinated by him, smitten if truth be told, could not even be dissuaded by his frequently apparent contempt for her, it seemed.

She wanted him to want her.

He moved in the next second and Ava's heart lurched in her chest.

John Craig did not step forward but backed up, out of the doorway, pulling the door closed behind him.

Devastated, Ava's breath burst from her in an explosive exhalation while tears gathered in her eyes. Mortified, she drew the towel upward, her fingers shaking as she covered her breasts once more.

Oh, the humiliation!

Short of crying out, *Take me*, she couldn't have made her wish any more obvious.

And he, with his brutal mien and those white knuckles upon the door handle and his very departure, couldn't have rejected her any more cruelly.

***

John shut the door and leaned his back against it, a thundering, incoherent mess of thoughts racing through his brain.

What the hell had he just done? fought for supremacy in the pack. *How had he managed that feat, closing the door between them?* was not far behind.

He pulled his fingers away from the latch and lifted them in front of him, the gray shadows of evening showing how forcefully his hand shook. Clenching that fist tight, he lowered his hand and closed his eyes, allowing his head to rest against the door. Right now, having made that decision to leave—one from which he might not ever recover—he was compelled to recall every second of that encounter, knowing it would never come his way again. Compelled, nae. Directed by a ravenous greed and fright, that the images burned into his brain would too soon be forgotten, might be lost somehow—nae more than he deserved.

Try as he might, he'd simply been incapable of respectfully removing his gaze from her when first he'd opened the door. Hell, he should have closed the door a split second after he'd opened it, walking into that volatile, combustible scene.

Bluidy hell, but that was all he needed, to have every suspicion confirmed: that she was made of more curves than only those straight lines hinted at by the shapeless léine and mantle she wore; that her skin was exactly the color of rich cream; that her breasts were bountiful, provocatively round and tipped with pink perfection; that her bottom, the first thing he'd seen upon opening the door, was firm and would fit, each globe, flawlessly into each of his hands.

Made for sin, she was, every adorable and tantalizing inch of her.

Most significant, the greater question had been answered: that their kiss was not the beginning and the end, but only a preface of more to come, what surely must follow, as expressed just now by her daring invitation and his body's damnable response to it.

She'd innocently offered him just that—more—her boldness unbound at that moment, so much hope in her astonishing green gaze. Actually, her green-eyed gaze had been a contradiction, had it not? Candid and hopeful...but then tinted with so much doubt.

But doubt was not what had prevented him from striding forward and crushing her in his embrace, the idea of which had flitted temptingly across his mind for more than only one brief and magnificent moment—and well before she'd offered herself so bewitchingly. Nae, 'twas what he'd learned at supper this night, that word had been sent from Sir James, which had gone first to Blacklaw and was now distressingly old, and that had expressed faith—read as a command—that the Craigs would join the Douglas army near Ayrshire. There had been some coded inference that Magnus and John both agreed suggested Robert Bruce himself was returned from his self-imposed exile and hoped to make amends for the grievous losses at Methven and Dalrigh last year. Apparently, the Earl of Pembroke, Aymer de Valence, the man who'd routed the Scots army at Methven, was in Bruce's sights again.

That was all it had taken, the imperfect timing of that missive, to have stayed his hand.

His cock, having a will of its own, paid no heed to the call of king or country, had risen to the occasion of the promise of its own freedom, from want of Ava. That was a slap in the face against all that he'd pretended to believe about her, about what he felt about her. His body's reaction to her brilliant nakedness put to rest any pretense that she meant nothing, that he wanted nothing, that he was stronger than any ungovernable attraction to her.

Damn Sir James! And damn Ava Guthrie, for showing more of that beguiling mettle, above and beyond her beautiful body, on this of all nights!

And damn most of all that old hag, Marion! Begging so sweetly of him after the meal, "Will you nae run an errand for me, lad?" she'd asked. "Fetch my shawl from where it hangs behind my door?" Aye, he might have sent another in his stead, but truth be told, without Ava's presence in the hall to hold his attention, and since all discussion of Sir James' message had been debated and dissected to fulfillment, plans made to depart on the morrow, John had found himself without any other purpose in the great hall of Lismore once he'd finished eating.

Aye, but the crone had been up to no good—conniving is what she'd been about. No better than Morvel, and neither of them considering how quickly and effortlessly machinations could go awry. If what Ava had said was true, that Marion had given her permission to make use of her cottage and her tub, Marion had purposefully sent him down here with some hope that he might walk in on her just as he had. The why of it made no difference; it was done. Disastrously so.

He'd just pushed himself away from the door to Marion's croft when the silence of the night and the diminished cacophony of his mind allowed him to hear a new disturbance coming from inside. A revived, savage scowl contorted his face as he leaned closer to the thick portal.

Jesu, was she crying?

Indeed, she was. A cry that sounded less sad than tormented, angry mayhap. The rough keening noise hurt his head and heart, more so the latter for his part in her tears. John groaned anew and rapped softly on the door, knowing he owed her...something, knowing he couldn't leave her as he had.

He wasn't sure an apology should be expected, though he rather felt she was due one. Mostly, he just wanted to address and hence dissolve the major issue between them, what might have seemed like a rejection of her. That was the last thing he wanted her to believe, even as he still maintained—to his utter regret—that it was the right move to make, none.

At his knock, the rhythmic hum of her sobbing halted abruptly.

"It's open, Marion," she called in a fragile voice.

John cleared his throat, about to announce it was still only him, lest she not have dressed by now. Before he might have spoken, she apparently recognized the owner of the throat-clearing and a cry of, "Oh, God. What now?" came next.

Through clenched teeth, he asked at the door, "Are you covered now?"

"I am! But do nae—"

He opened the door again, this time closing it behind him.

She was garbed appropriately now, in her worn and thin kirtle and léine, though her long and damp hair remained loose, shimmering with gold strands courtesy of the flickering flames. She was no less gorgeous, only more mysterious, for how so much brilliance, visible only moments ago, could so easily, so quickly be concealed.

She might have been bent over that very fire and the kettle suspended there, but straightened at his entrance, and now she stood, stiffly erect, the visibly bulging veins in her neck announcing how tightly she clamped her mouth and jaw.

And aye, she had cried, might have only swiftly scraped her sleeve over her cheeks to remove the evidence of tears, but it was there still, in the shimmer of her wet eyes and the redness of her nose, in the moistness of her lips. And he was not unaffected by this; his heart seemed to burn to ashes inside his chest and then melt away.

He scrutinized her face closely while she stared wordlessly at him. He opened his mouth but hesitated, catching sight of the way her hands fisted at her sides in response to what he'd yet to say.

Words had rarely failed him before this moment. And then his brain stopped working entirely, so that his chances of putting out an apology worthy of her seemed frightfully slim.

While he remained unable to speak, her cool and wary stare deserted him, fixing on his shoulder and then leaving him altogether. Stiffly, she addressed the kettle again, removing one and replacing it with another. She turned then, presenting her back to him, picking up the towel that had minutes ago caressed her flesh as he'd longed to do.

"Ava," he finally began, "I...if I'd taken one step...if I'd touched you," he said, the sound of his ragged voice competing for air time with the noisy flapping of the towel before she began to fold the cloth with an austere condition to her movements. "If I'd touched you," he started again, speaking to her slim back, briefly debating the want to add, *the way I yearn to do*, before opting to forego sharing that scintillating truth, "there would have been no turning back. I would be compelled to stay, or you would be forced to leave or wait or...." He sighed, hating himself as much as he did her feigned indifference right now. "Ava? Lass, you ken as well as I neither of those things is viable at the moment."

It sounded as weak as he felt at this moment. And yet it was truth. Having just gotten word that his army was being summoned to Ayrshire, he could little afford the distraction of Ava Guthrie right now, now more than ever. And she deserved so much more than only one night.

Still, it was only part of the reason. He knew—he was absolutely certain—that Ava Guthrie was someone with whom he could not possibly be satisfied to share only one kiss or one night.

But for now, he could give no other explanation to it, not even for her, not even to himself. Any more would delve into helplessness and vulnerability, his own failings. And something stubborn in him would not give way to allow any of that. Now more than ever, he could not be weakened by her.

He would leave on the morrow, but he would not tell her this now. Another war inside himself: telling her that he was bound to leave might force speech or responses from her that surely he'd forfeited with his rejection; not telling her opened a door to her, one of guilt if she made no reply now but then never saw him again.

"Ava?" He tried one more time.

The towel long since folded and set down, she only stood with her back to him. He thought her arms might be folded across her chest. When she said nothing, remained maddeningly impassive, did not acknowledge any part of what sounded even to his own ears as dreadful reasoning, John turned and left her again.

Chapter Thirteen

Her mortification of last night was not instantly recollected when came the dawn since other goings-on first called her attention. Sleeping as she had for more than a week now upon the hard timber of the great hall of Lismore Abbey, it was impossible to ignore the early morning activity, so many people hustling and bustling ere the sun had shown its face.

Ava was woken by a large thud as something was dropped inside the hall near the door to the bailey. A subsequent, "Bollocks, mate. Use two hands," stirred her to full wakefulness, just in time to see two soldiers, either Matheson or Craig men, lugging a chest through the hall. Others scurried about, including Lismore's steward, Sten, whose long robes flew behind him as he raced from the hall, calling for someone named Andrew.

She yawned and stretched a bit and found Hamish, the closest person to her, already sitting up, staring from their darkened corner on the northeast wall of the hall toward the gray light of the morn, visible through the open door.

"What happens?" She asked, sitting up herself, aware of many figures moving around the yard, in and out of view through the doorway. Sleep-clouded yet, she scratched her fingers on her scalp, moving the tangle of hair away from her face, wishing she had thought to braid it.

Without turning toward her, keeping his gaze on that activity in the yard, Hamish answered, "Och, that's right. You were nae here at last meal. You dinna hear—the Craigs and the Beast's army are making ready to depart."

Ava stilled, her hands dropping slowly to her lap, her hair falling back down around her face.

These words, then, were what first recalled to her the humiliation she'd suffered the night before.

He was leaving.

If I had touched you, there would be no turning back. I would be compelled to stay, or you would be forced to leave or wait....

"Dinna ken what that means for us," Hamish mused.

Ava glanced left and right. "Where is Innes?"

"Out with Eachann," Hamish informed her. "Gone at first light."

"He's nae...? He's nae leaving with them, is he?" How was so much changing without her knowing!

Hamish shook his head and yawned long and vocally before he answered. "Nae, but the captain was to leave two of those English steeds for us, Innes said. A gift from the Craig for our part in his Lanark escape." Hamish's grogginess evaporated a wee bit. "Aye, you missed it, Ava—and where were you last night? Couple of lasses brought out instruments, a lute and one had a gittern—Innes said they were the devil's officers, but I ken he dinna mean these ones but those others—remember that pair came through Lanark two years back? How he doted on the red-haired one and then one day she was gone, nae hide nor hair to be found? And remember, Ava, how Innes was sorely bitten and then biting at us when she'd gone? He dinna pay them nae mind last night, and mayhap because they were nae red-haired, but I danced, Ava. You ken I love to dance."

"Aye, I do, Hamish," she said absently, vaguely recalling also Innes' obsession with that red-haired whore, who'd used him for three days and then had left, as Hamish had reminded her, without a word to Innes. He'd been crushed, and then impossible, surly and unapproachable for another whole week.

She did not dwell on that, though, or even Hamish's affinity for dancing, though she was pleased he'd been presented with another opportunity to do so, the last one at the Kenith homestead. One wouldn't know it to look at him, but he danced with a lightness of foot and a much surer grace than which he regularly moved; he was entirely a different person when moving to music, Ava had always thought.

But her mind was snared and caught on that most disturbing news Hamish had shared.

The Craigs were leaving.

He was leaving.

If I had touched you, there would be no turning back. I would be compelled to stay, or you would be forced to leave or wait....

She jumped to her feet and ran her fingers again through her hair, a bit desperately now, this time with a greater effort to tame the wild, uncombed locks, knowing there was no time for her to sit and braid it now. Mechanically, she twisted the length of it into one tail and then knotted the thick mass onto itself, a regular and useful style she'd long ago adopted since she was so rarely in possession of ribbon or string to confine it. The knot sat on the nape of her neck, the tail of that falling down her back.

"Come," she urged Hamish, "we must show ourselves outside." *Must* was overstated; certainly a fare thee well would not be expected from either she or Hamish. But she wanted one last glimpse or chance or come what may and she wanted Hamish at her side so that she didn't look as eager and frantic as she felt at that moment. The weight of uncertainty lay heavy upon her, afraid she might never see John Craig again, and that last night's encounter would tarnish what few memories she would be left with.

She took Hamish's hand when he got to his feet, mostly to keep hers from shaking, and pulled him toward the door with her. "Act natural," she said, an admonishment more self-directed than meant for Hamish.

Outside, Lismore's bailey teemed with destriers and sumpter horses, men, and carts, shrouded in a sea of Craig and Matheson plaids and a heavy morning fog, the vapor's nebulous claws reaching for the ground, only to be scattered here and there by the brusque movements of men and beasts.

"Let us find Innes," she said, thinking that a fine pretense to walk through the throng of men and horses.

Ava and Hamish were forced to sidle around and between the dozens of horses and men readying themselves in the yard. Carts were loaded with arms and food stuffs; Magnus Matheson was seen, a large but wispy figure inside the thick rolling fog, talking quietly with some man who was not John Craig; two hounds dashed about, making more than one horse skittish with their play. But John Craig was not found. Growing more anxious as men began to mount, one after another, Ava pulled Hamish along behind her, moving toward the perimeter, heading toward the gate, wondering if John Craig would be there, ready to lead his army.

"There's Innes," Hamish said, drawing back on his hand, turning toward the middle of the yard.

Ava let him go, having spied Innes there as well, but not John Craig. She continued on, ignoring Hamish's confused call of, "Ava? Where'd you go? He's here."

She skirted around the rumps of two more destriers, her left shoulder and hand brushing the outermost boards of the stable walls, her head swiveling, neck craned to find him.

And then he was there, just in front of her, the fog rolling around him as he strode purposefully toward her, his face set grimly, though his eyes burned with some new intensity.

Ava paused, laying her hand at her neck, willing herself to breathe, to not embarrass herself again.

John Craig fixed her in his brown-eyed vise and did not break stride as he met her but took the hand at her side and kept walking, turning her around, bringing her inside the stables with him, all the way to the dark recesses of the rear of that building.

Ava said nothing and did not drag her feet. She squeezed her fingers around his and followed. In the shadows of the stables, he stopped and turned, pulling at her hand until she came up against his hard body and with a tortured groan, he crashed his lips down on hers. Instantly, a jubilant cry of blessed relief erupted inside her, swiftly overcome by the heat of his kiss. He cradled her cheeks in his hands, his fingers delving into her messy hair. He molded his mouth to her and slid his tongue along her lips, absorbing the shudder of her yearning. Ava opened for him, clinging to the waistline of the leather brigandine he wore, tipping her face up to him, every inhibition gone. A deep-throated groan filled her ears as he deepened the kiss, exploring her mouth with his tongue. This would be all she would have, and she gave him everything, showed him her desire and her sorrow, moving her hands over his arms and through his hair, standing on tiptoe, joining her tongue with his. There was no sigh of contentment, no tentative invitation, no hesitancy at all; she was feverish in her desire to have so much in just these few seconds. Still, never for one second did she believe herself in control, of her own body or this kiss. John slid his hands around her back, turning them both around until her back was against the wall and he sculpted his body against her, all of him so blessedly hard, plundering her lips and mouth again and again until they were heated and breathless and Ava's heart pounded against her breast.

A minute passed, maybe five, before he broke the kiss and breathed raggedly against her face, his forehead dropped against hers.

"*That* is what I wanted to do last night," he rasped at her, this new and husky voice causing a stirring deep inside her. "That and so much more. Dinna ken otherwise. I wanted more—all of you, Ava—but I ken I was leaving today."

Ava nodded but knew not what to say. A million questions fought for space, for leave to be spoken. But what could she ask that was not only her assuming this kiss meant anything more than what it was—a desire for now that could not be assuaged? The kiss jettisoned some of last night's humiliation, though certainly not all of it. She would not chance such boldness again, would not ask him where he went and when he might return, if she should remain here at Lismore until he might return.

Instead, she waited, hopeful, that he might give her something to which she might cling.

How much might have been saved, or revealed, or known, if she'd been able to claim even an ounce of last night's courage. Because she did not and because he said nothing else, she laid her palm against his rough cheek and closed her eyes, taking stock of this exact moment, wanting to commit it to memory.

Where their foreheads touched there was heat. Her lips were wonderfully kiss-swollen, and her limbs felt deliciously like jelly.

The weight of him leaned against her, the hardness, the heat, all of it—him—was a glorious thing. The tingling of her belly and lower was another delightful sensation, even as it seemed dark and forbidden. His warm breath teased her cheeks and a lock of his hair brushed at her temple. His hand found hers, he entwined their fingers and squeezed, and rubbed his mouth softly over her parted lips.

"Be guid, Ava," he said. "Be safe."

She nodded briskly, kept her eyes closed, a bit frantic now, sensing the end was nigh, with these parting words. Tears were imminent but there wasn't anything she could do about that, tears but a tiny shame when compared to last night's larger one.

"You as well, John Craig," she said, her voice breaking. "Be safe."

And she waited. For any words that would give her hope.

One more peck of his lips to her forehead and his weight and warmth left her. Ava opened her eyes, a cry smothered, watched their arms stretch and their hands slide away until she touched no part of him, and she watched him walk away. His stride to leave her was nearly as purposeful as had been the steps that had brought him to her a moment ago.

The most compelling and vibrant person to ever walk into her dreary life just walked away.

She clamped her hand over her mouth to keep from crying aloud, her teeth clenched while her entire face trembled. She stood where she was, in the bowels of the stables, with her back against the tack room wall.

A horn sounded a moment later. Wagons creaked and harnesses jangled as the army moved out. The fog rolled with them, ushering them outside the gates of Lismore until no Craig remained within its walls.

She would have waited, here at Lismore or anywhere he asked her to, *if* it might be believed that anything would come of her rather vexing infatuation with him. *If* he'd asked her to.

Her young heart, with its first taste of love—tiny crumbs only, desire being the larger bite—went wild and in many directions in its current despair.

In the next moment, she secretly raged at him inside her head that he should have told her he was leaving, should have mentioned that last night. Part of her felt she'd earned the right to know, certainly given those words—that there would be no turning back. *If* there had been any truth to them. She feared right now that there was not.

Oh, how she tortured herself in those moments immediately following his leave-taking, until finally she was left with one true and disturbing fact: *if* he'd wanted to touch her last night, he would have. *If* he'd wanted her to wait for him, he would have asked. Mayhap today's kiss was only an act of pity, for how pathetic she must have seemed last night.

This supposition wrestled forcefully with another, one supposed in the next moment when she was feeling particularly charitable toward him: *if* he cared naught one bit for her, he would have taken her in his arms last night, would have given little thought or care to consequences or expectations. Little solace this brought her, he gone, and she believing it was done now, though barely had it begun—the *it* in question being whatever should have followed a kiss, whatever it was that seized her, what she could not stop herself from feeling whenever he was near—living more as a wistful hope than any grand reality.

If now became the most cruel word she'd ever known or thought or heard.

When all was quiet, Ava slid her back down against the wall and let the tears come, while she stared out into the gray dawn, which now would be forever tethered to the last time she saw John Craig.

***

His teeth remained clenched for miles and miles. And the oldness of Sir James' request was not the only reason he pushed his army to such a grueling pace.

They marched relentlessly and steadily south, the morning fog dissipating with greater ease than John's roiling unrest. At some point hours later, and as his head began to ache in earnest, Magnus appeared at his side, their destriers nose to nose.

"Nae easy, is it?"

"What is that?" John asked blandly, in the mood for neither riddles nor any conversation, truth be told.

"Leaving her behind, with so much undone and unsaid," Magnus answered.

John jerked a suddenly piercing gaze onto Magnus, recalling a time last year, after his cousin had first encountered Lara, and their departure then, how gruesome had been Magnus' mood at the time, for being parted from her.

"*Jesu*," John breathed, beginning to understand. "But it's different now, aye? For you? All things settled to such satisfaction." He'd known plenty of husbands and wives, plenty of pairs of lovers, but never had he considered how difficult their partings must be.

Magnus grinned knowingly, a hint of sympathy for John's new understanding coloring his own anxiety. "Leaving is nae ever easy. You would ken, aye, the more you do it, the easier it becomes. Nae true. Nae at all. Odds work against me now. How many times will I be so fortunate as to be able to return, do you ken? Have I used up all my passes?"

John rolled his eyes with this news, that possibly it only got worse. "Bluidy hell, but what's the point of it all?"

"Of loving her?" Magnus asked, which elicited a sharp scowl from John.

In love with Ava? Absolutely not! Intrigued, enthralled, besotted to some degree he could hardly deny, but no more than that!

"Has she smiled yet?" Magnus wondered, the smirk in his tone begging for a strike to the face. "I have nae seen. I dinna ken her at all to compare her to Lara, but I ken she's nae had it easy. Have nae seen so much lightness and laughter, any of that. But I ken, if *you* had—just one smile, either wrought by you or meant only for you—you'd nae be asking what the point of all of it is."

"Stop speaking to me," John warned his cousin. "Just...leave it." With that he spurred his horse on ahead, chased away by Magnus' infuriating laughter.

Aye, he might be dogged by thoughts of her now, those tainted by regret and what might have been, but he knew himself, and thus had every confidence that in short order Ava Guthrie would merely be someone that he used to know.

They rode all that day and half the next before they met up with another soul.

When next they encountered another person, they met first the arrow shot from his bow. The missile landed well in front of

Eachann and Magnus' captain in the lead, giving them pause but not quite raising an alarm. If injury or death had been the intent, likely the projectile would have met with flesh and bone.

While the Craigs and Mathesons drew up sharply on the reins, a voice called out from deeper inside the forest in which they traveled. "Claim yer business, traipsing round on the Carrick land."

Rolling his eyes, Magnus announced to the unseen person, "Magnus Matheson and John Craig, come to join forces with our king."

John mumbled at his side, impatiently speaking to the hidden scout. "And if you dinna ken that, you'd have shot more than only one arrow."

The first person to show himself through the trees was Robert Bruce himself, which alerted both John and Magnus that their marching armies had been spied and followed for some time now.

"Ah, the cousins," their king greeted them, as he sometimes did.

John bowed his head and Magnus did the same.

Magnus greeted him first with all the speculation they'd been privy to over the last six months. "Hidden in Rathlin, gone to the Isles—one of them anyway—hidden in a cave in the extreme north of the Highlands, or in the forests of this Carrick land," he said. "A ghost you were, sire, confounding nae only the English but your own loyal subjects with how you seemed to be everywhere all at once."

Robert Bruce grinned at this, glancing sideways at Sir James Douglas.

Four horses came almost nose to nose. Sir James reached forward, extending his arm to John, wearing a smirk that John had seen plenty of times before. "Your man, Eachann, assured me, there was no way you would find your end there in Lanark. Pleased I am to see he spoke truth, and you none the worse for wear."

"Aye, and here's hoping your campaigns were fruitful endeavors as well."

"Most assuredly."

"Lanark can now be ours," John advised both Douglas and the Bruce. "Assuming you've numbers to match our own, we far outweigh the sheriff's garrison in might."

"Lanark will wait," Robert Bruce said, "though you will eventually have to deal with that, with Walter de Burghdon, who it seems has made you, Sir John, his life's mission."

John scowled at this. What?

"'Tis true, lad," the king said. "He scours the country, seeking your head, or at least another opportunity to wind a noose around your neck."

John did not question how the king, having been a running fugitive for so long, might have more knowledge about this than John himself did. He only scowled at de Burghdon's tenacity—to pursue one man when all of Scotland was at war?

"We have at least one friend at Carlisle, where a letter was read saying as much." Robert Bruce lifted a brow at John. "Curiously made some mention of a green eyed lass, a collapsed gallows, and the unwitting escape of not only you, but four fugitives—and then, most gratifying, of a small unit of English in pursuit who met their end." He leaned two hands on the pommel and fixed his brown eyes onto John. "The Lion roars, as he should."

John nodded. "De Burghdon can sweep all through the Highlands, sire. Will nae take away from my commitment to you and our cause now."

"We are pleased to hear that."

A wee bit of continued small talk was made before the king and James Douglas turned and led John and Magnus and their combined armies to join the hidden forces of Robert Bruce and the Douglas, deep inside the hilltop forest.

Armies of men were not wholly unlike flocks of chattering women, set about a chore but amusing themselves with gossip and rumor, and sometimes forced to be the bearer of indelicate news. No sooner had they dismounted and settled in with the several hundred ragtag followers of Robert Bruce, than James Douglas imparted the latest horrific bulletin to Magnus and John.

They were taken aside and told of what all had befallen the king's supporters, including his own family—little of it good, most of it inconceivable.

Previously, they had been made aware of the fate of the royal women.

Last year, as winter approached, Robert Bruce had sent his wife and her ladies, and his daughter, down to Kildrummy Castle, under the care of his brother Nigel. While Robert Bruce and James Douglas had made for the western coast, escaping to Rathlin off the coast of Ireland, Kildrummy had been besieged, and though the Bruce women had escaped, Nigel Bruce and several other knights and nobles who'd aided in the defense of Kildrummy had been forced to surrender. They'd been executed at

Berwick shortly thereafter, in typical English fashion: barbarically. Shortly after that, which Robert Bruce did not learn of until his return this year, his womenfolk had been betrayed by the Earl of Ross. They'd been captured and sent to England, where the queen was imprisoned, and the Countess of Buchan—who'd laid the crown upon Robert Bruce's head—was exposed to the scorn or the pity of the public, imprisoned in a cage suspended from one of the exterior walls of Berwick.

They'd heard those unimaginable tales last fall, months after the treacherous deeds had been carried out; it was revealed now that their fates had not improved. What they didn't know, what was told to them now by a grim-faced James Douglas, was yet another punch to the gut to any man who felt in his heart of hearts that Scotland must be free and Robert Bruce, presently, was the right man to make that happen.

"Thomas and Alexander Bruce have since been caught and executed," Sir James announced, referring to the king's brothers. "Aye, tis true," he said to the aghast expressions that greeted this news. "The brothers, along with a certain Irish king and Sir Reginald Crawford, among many brave others, came with more than a dozen ships and galleys. They were attacked in Loch Ryan by the treacherous Dungal MacDouall. Some," Sir James continued through teeth that were clenched, "were beheaded on the site. Others, the brothers included, were whisked to Carlisle, where they were summarily put to death."

"*Jesu*," John breathed. A bitter, chest-tightening feeling of *what next?* rose to the fore but he said nothing.

Magnus remarked, "And yet our king seems more focused and determined than ever."

Likely he was recalling the fretful, indecisive king they'd known for several weeks last autumn when few if any of these tragedies had been known. Indeed the man who'd greeted them today seemed perturbed by little.

"Our king will ride high, carried on the wings of vengeance," Sir James predicted.

John exchanged a glance with Magnus, both considering the wretchedness of fate, one that likely could be theirs.

Later that evening, though well before the sun had set, John watched as Magnus produced a sheaf of parchment and began composing a letter.

To Lara, John assumed, chewing the inside of his cheek, wondering if that was dismay he experienced at that moment, that he hadn't anyone to write.

So much of a soldier's life was conducted by a *hurry up and wait* tradition, one to which John was well-accustomed after ten years fighting on and off, always in support of Scotland's freedom. Thus, over the many days, while this large, cojoined army waited word of the Earl of Pembroke's position—the man who had handed the most unsettling defeat to Bruce last year at Methven—John bore witness to several more of these missives Magnus crafted and sent with a messenger to Lismore.

"You run a man ragged," John finally said to Magnus, more than a week later, "off and back to Lismore—what is that? More than a hundred miles? And for what? To say we sit and wait?"

Magnus folded and sealed this current missive, giving it over to his runner for transport. He faced John and said, "He does nae ride all the way to Lismore, but to Glasgow, where Finn from the keep is waiting or will meet him and takes it from there."

John favored his cousin with a suspicious glare. "And no doubt returns with a missive from Lara."

"Usually. If I'm lucky."

John shook his head at this, refusing to acknowledge any temptation to delve further into what possibility this presented to him. Regarding Ava.

Mayhap Magnus read some insight in John's present scowl.

"Shall I make an enquiry into the lass, Ava? Ask how she fares?" Magnus offered, his lips quirked.

"Nae, I dinna need you to make an enquiry," John snapped at him.

He knew, with a battle looming somewhere on a near horizon, that cleaving Ava Guthrie from his brain was the best thing he could do right now. Knowing and doing, however, were two different things, he decided after several days of unsuccessful attempts to *not* think on her.

Chapter Fourteen

Ava spent the first truly warm day of late spring walking along with Innes inside the forest that housed that ledge where sometimes she still greeted the gray dawn. She wore an apron on this day, one lent to her by Marion, and held the ends of it gathered at her waist so that the length of it created a basket. Into this she was gathering all the nettles she could find, set to this task by the old crone, who seemed to believe it her duty to keep Ava busy from dawn to dusk—and with which Ava had yet to find any fault.

"I'm just saying you're nae yourself anymore," Innes was saying, having begun the conversation with a brusque, *And when will I see the Ava I used to ken?*

She *had* been sullen, she knew, uncharacteristically so. Possibly she hated that part of John Craig's departure the most, what it had done to her, what she'd become.

"I'm sorry, Innes," she said, not giving up any more than that, unwilling to be subjected to another of his rants about John Craig and why she was only wasting time mooning over him.

Trust me, he's nae spending his days with you in his head, he'd shouted at her three days ago.

Apparently, simply being quiet in Innes' company, even when her thoughts were not focused on John Craig, gave Innes leave to diminish what little hope remained more than a week after the Craigs had left Lismore.

Playfully, hoping to engage both herself and Innes in anything else but where this was headed, Ava lobbed a clump of forest moss at him. Loose dirt dropped from the clump as it sailed through the air and smacked Innes on the back of his shoulder. He straightened first, turning slowly toward her, one brow lifted as a rebuke.

Ava tilted her head and played coy. "Oh, good heavens. How clumsy of me. I was aiming for the basket."

"Were you now?" He asked, a wealth of disbelief heard in his tone. Innes straightened and turned fully, pointing at the basket ten feet away from where he was slicing moss from beneath a fallen log, the basket thrust into his hands by Marion, who'd said tartly to him, *Dinna ken you'll get by with only watching. This needs filling. The dryer the better.*

"That basket there?" Innes asked Ava now.

Ava smirked outright at him. "That's the one. I'll do better next time, I'm sure."

"You aim as well as you fib, Ava," he said and showed her his back again.

And just when she thought she'd not distracted him as she'd wanted to, a tuft of dirt was flung over his head, coming straight at her. Innes' aim was spot on, and Ava yelped, barely sidestepping the missile in time. She ducked behind a tree, able to use only one hand since the other held her apron still as its own basket and scrounged for another clod of earth to throw at him. She peeked out for her hiding spot and was forced to yank her face out of the way of the incoming projectile. It smacked the tree trunk behind which she hid, sending a spray of moist dirt over her.

"Left-handed demon," she accused and pivoted so that she could poke her head from the other side of the tree.

"Beats your right-handed girly pitching any day," Innes called, sounding as if he were growing closer. Ava bit back a laugh and didn't dare peek now, imagining a hand coming round the tree to smack a fistful of dirty moss in her face.

"Oh, Ava," Innes intoned in a taunting sing-song voice, very close now.

She yipped again and leapt to her feet, her apron and the nettles forgotten as she dashed through the wooded vale. Innes had always been stronger and faster, wilier, too that he was able to pluck and throw more dirt bombs at her and catch up to her. The last one smacked her on her bottom before she was tackled to the ground.

"Argh!" She cried as she went down. She wiggled and squirmed as soon as she landed and Innes straddled her middle, holding yet another clump of dripping moss above her face.

Ava managed to free her hands and hold them over up above her scrunched face, as she peered through one eye. "You have pockets full," she accused through her laughter.

"Aye, I did," Innes admitted, giving up his leverage, flopping over on to the ground at her side. "The basket was full. I was shoving more in my pockets, keep the hag from bugging me about the same busy work on the morrow."

Ava grinned, still panting from her mad dash. She and Innes stayed like that, side by side, staring at the tiny green buds decorating every limb of the birch tree under which they'd fallen.

"Why do you nae consider me, Ava?" Innes surprised her by asking after a moment. "As your mate?"

Ava stopped breathing, a frown instant. While she'd always known how he'd felt, Innes had never spoken of this before, not ever seriously. It was the first time so much was laid bare like this. She was both loath to hurt him and pleased to be able to put it to rest finally.

"I...you are like a brother to me, Innes. I...I dinna see you in any other light."

"Have you tried?" He queried with a small chuckle.

"You ken as well as any that I understand verra little about men and women, love and...all that. But Innes, should I have to try? Shouldn't it just...be there?"

"It's just there then? Your aching for John Craig?"

"Apparently," she answered on a sigh, ever disgruntled by this fact.

"Did you at least try to fight against *that*, being hopeless as it is?"

"Fight against it? Nae, I would expect nae success there. But I *am* trying to get over it."

"What is it about him?"

Ava heard, *What does he have that I do nae?*

She didn't think he'd want to hear all of it, how the shape of John Craigs' lips— the way they moved, in speech or in a kiss—enticed her so; that the strength of his arms or the prowess of his fight struck her with awe; that his walk, so powerful yet lithe, made her heart beat faster; that his brown eyes, settled upon her, no matter his mood, stirred her as no other thing ever had.

"Who can say, Innes? Why do you like cabbage but nae the kale? Why do you prefer sunsets over sunrise? Why did you spend all that time with the smithy's daughter, Helen? It's just what it is."

"I ken it might make you jealous, all that fawning over Helen," he admitted.

Ava turned her head, leaves rustling beneath her. "I believed you happy with her."

"She was nae you."

And through nae fault of your own, you are nae him.

"Dinna say it," Innes said, closing his eyes, possibly having read her mind.

"I'm sorry, Innes."

"He's nae coming back for you," Innes predicted, gently this time.

"I ken that."

"Might be time to move on, then."

"Is Lismore really nae a guid fit for us?"

"It does nae work for me, Ava. I canna breathe sometimes, too small, too quiet now."

He's nae coming back for you.

When it came down to it, to that being the only truth, when all the other ramblings of her brain cleaved to just that fact, she knew Innes was right, it was time to leave. To do so, to give up hope completely, she would have to draw on the same strength that had once sent her recklessly from her own home or employ some of that audacity that had helped her climb the steps of the gallows to save a stranger from hanging.

Lara and Marion had been wonderful, had made friendly overtures the likes of which she'd never known. However, as Innes had said, Lismore was rather sleepy these days with the armies gone. The hall at last meal was almost insufferably tomb-like, the mistress fooling no one with her stoicism, which barely concealed her fear for her husband. And much louder and inescapable, the fact that Ava felt a prisoner here, so long as memories of John Craig were tied to this place.

She already believed herself a fool, for attaching so much hope to so few reasons. Wasn't she simply ridiculous to have made so much out of so few interactions? Even as she questioned this, she knew it was only the promise of what might have been that created the biggest ache inside her.

In the end, Innes and Hamish were her family. She must go where they did.

John Craig wasn't coming back for her. And he had no reason to expect that she might wait here for him. She really did know that.

"Then we should go, Innes. Whatever you want to do."

***

As any man in the modest-but-growing army of the king, John was pleased to see those numbers swell a wee bit with the coming of more small armies. He and Magnus were especially gratified to see their old friend, William Sinclair, ride in one day at the beginning of May, followed by what remained of the Sinclair men-at-arms. Like Magnus and John, the Sinclair laird had fostered in their youth with Gilbert de Clare, the Earl of Gloucester and Hereford.

William Sinclair came from a large family that like so many others in the last decade had been devastated by war. He wore the effects of these losses on his face, etched there in the hard lines around his mouth and the icy blue of his eyes. A ferocious warrior whose strength and agility upon a battlefield were matched well by his cunning and cleverness, John was content to count him as friend and not foe.

The Sinclair rode hellbent into the king's campsite, well in advance of his own army. He approached the king straight away and went to his knee until Robert Bruce bade him rise.

"I have known you many years now, William Sinclair," Robert Bruce said upon greeting his vassal. "Never have I witnessed such self-satisfied smugness upon your face. Good news travels with you, then?"

"Aye, and plenty of it, sire," William Sinclair replied. "Pembroke does nae only ride about, his sole interest being discovering your whereabouts. Presently, he gives escort to the English treasurer—"

"The Bishop of Lichfield?" Robert Bruce questioned.

"Aye, Walter Langton himself," Sinclair confirmed. "He's making the rounds to all the English garrisons hereabouts, assuring loyalty and what have you." Sinclair raised his brow at his king, nodding as the wise man caught on.

"Assuring loyalty by way of coin, we should presume," Robert Bruce guessed and then addressed the handful of knights who surrounded him presently, which included Magnus and John. "We should not, then, wait for them to come to us, but be courteous and rush to meet them."

The universal agreement was swift and eager.

William shared all the information he had, about Pembroke's current location and the size of his current force, still too large for this ragtag and quilted-together group of loyalists.

"Ah, but chests of silver coins should not be neglected, good sirs," Robert Bruce said.

"Given the proper position," John stated, "in this land you ken so well, sire, surely we can manage a dignified stand."

"Or better yet, an ambush," countered the king, the light in his eyes piercing for its majestic purpose.

As it was late in the day, they discussed a move at first light, at which time Robert Bruce said he would have a certain idle plan in his head devised more clearly.

With the evening given freely to them, John and Magnus greeted William Sinclair more suitably, having not seen the knight since last year.

He first shook Magnus' hand and then John's, to whom he showed a rare smirk.

Clutching John's hand, not letting go, he remarked, "Just spent a guid spell in the border area, and all I hear is your name."

"Bluidy hell," John said, "You, too?"

"Murder and mayhem, they charge you with," William said, his grin unchanged. "Sounds about right, I'd say."

"Did you hear also," Magnus chimed in, "something about a green-eyed lass?"

Just as John turned a harsh glare onto his cousin, William chuckled outright—an even greater rarity.

"Dinna hear that," he replied, releasing John's hand, "but say nae more. I ken all I need to now."

William dropped his saddlebags on the ground in front of Magnus's tent and sat using that as a wedge for his back, crossing his long legs at the ankle. "What goes on here? The Bruce is in good spirits despite so much calamity having befallen his kin."

"We were only waiting on word of Pembroke's location—his advance at this time," Magnus said.

"Which will now become our advance," John added, "so your timing is close to perfect."

"And aye," Magnus furthered, "the king is a different man today than he was six months ago."

"Broken then?" William asked, a heavy frown falling over his blue eyes.

"Nae, never that," John said. "But...nae in a guid place after so many losses."

"Resolute now," said Magnus. "More than ever, and God willing, to stay as such."

John added what he'd decided was true over the last few weeks in the king's company. "He's done with being a fugitive, has come to properly claim his throne."

The next grin William Sinclair showed was a more familiar sight, a dark and nearly sinister grin of a warrior without equal. The man loved to fight. While others might wish the war done—one way or another—William Sinclair had plenty of scores to settle yet with the English. Some actually believed he had a death wish, and John was not certain there wasn't some truth in that supposition.

Will kept company with John and Magnus all that evening. There was little to do when trying to keep their presence unknown here in the hills of Ayrshire. Only once did Will give John grief over *the green-eyed lass*, having caught him lost in thought while in the midst of a dozen men.

"You're either fighting to avenge her or figure out how to put her from your mind," Will said, a bit of annoyance discerned in his curt tone. He spun his face and his gaze to include Magnus in his chastisement. "There is nae a man that fights well—fights his best—when he's got a lass on the mind."

Younger by two years, Will's scolding, such as it was, seemed a bit insolent.

Magnus growled at Will, "You worry about your own sword there, lad, and I will be accountable for mine, which will slash and strike as it ever has."

Will looked pointedly at John, as if waiting for a similar pronouncement of dedication.

"My mind sits on war and nae on one other thing," he assured him, a wee irritated that he'd been forced to make this statement.

Will nodded and walked away. A moment later, Magnus turned a ready smirk to John. "Only half a lie, I suppose, since she is a person and nae a *thing*."

"Piss off, Magnus."

But aye, it was truth. Ava Guthrie and her striking green eyes were never far away, though they shared space inside his head with that last kiss he'd stolen from her. So then he was as surprised as any might have been, when finally they were called up to fight and he was able to successfully compartmentalize, tucking thoughts of Ava out of reach as the royal Scots' army approached and took position on a level field at the base of a hillock, not more than a quarter mile wide, constrained on either side by deep and broad bogs, close to Loudoun Hill.

Immediately Robert Bruce instructed that ditches should be dug directly in front of them. The bog extended far and wide, with naught but one causeway breaking through—the only route available to Pembroke and his surely larger English force. They would be obliged to come straight at the Scots on that road, having little choice but to approach only three or four abreast at most. The hill immediately behind the Scots effectively cut off any possibility of a flanking move by Pembroke. *If* the English militia was able to race across the road that split the bog, defying the Scots' archers, they would then have to struggle across the ditches, and then they would meet with Scots' spearmen, and the rest of the men-at-arms. Idle now for so many weeks since the ambush and thrashing of the English at Glen Trool—John and Magnus and their men even longer than that—the Scots were eager for another chance to redeem all that had been lost a year ago.

It came to pass exactly as Robert Bruce had intended, the English knights coming at them along that constricted highway, the forward of that frontal charge that was easily repelled by Robert Bruce's spearmen, who efficiently massacred the English knights, trapped on such hostile ground. The king called for more men to come down the hill, and they fell onto the disordered and panicked English knights and those who had such courage to continue coming. John and Magnus answered this call, they and most of their armies daring to go out beyond those ditches, fighting with such intensity that the rear ranks of the English fled in panic and the battle was over before it had fully begun. The rear guard of this Scots' militia had not lifted their swords at all, wore not one spot of dirt or blood on their persons, though still they could rightly say they'd been at the battle of Loudoun Hill.

Sadly, both Pembroke and the treasury's chest escaped capture.

***

The very first time Ava met Lara and Magnus' bairn, Will, was only minutes before she left Lismore Abbey.

Innes and Hamish waited on their gifted coursers in Lismore's bailey as Ava accepted a jute sack filled with bread and linen-wrapped cheese from the steward, Sten. Already they'd been given flasks of ale, which had been happily secured to the saddles. And, almost as appreciated as the foodstuffs, they'd been provided with a small canvas tent.

"I canna thank you enough for your charity," Ava said to Lismore's steward, Sten. "The tent, specifically, seems a Godsend to me."

"I only wish we could have done more," Sten replied. "But with the army gone, so then are most of their supplies."

"This is more than generous of you," Ava said to Sten. "We dinna expect or—"

"But you *need*," Sten reasoned gently. "And you and Innes and Hamish have been quite helpful during your stay. We can hardly send you off without recompense."

Ava's returning smile was genuine, if not a wee bittersweet. "We might go back and forth all day, Sten. I could mention how gracious Lismore has been in its welcome and you might say that you were pleased to receive us, well entertained by Hamish's lightness of feet."

"He is surprisingly sprightly," Sten allowed. "Take care of yourself, Ava."

Marion stood beside the steward, wearing a sour puss that did not surprise Ava. She'd already given her grief when first she'd announced their intention to leave yesterday.

"Makes nae sense to me," Marion said now, "to leave this for that—what's unknown."

Fearing that even given hours and hours to explain, she would still not be able to make these kind people understand that her place truly was with her friends. "But you will wish me well all the same, will you nae, Marion?"

"Sure and I will," said the old woman, "even as I ken right here" –she tapped her fisted hand at her breast—"that this is nae the last time we will meet."

Next, Ava faced Lara, holding her infant son in her arms, his eyes as blue as his father's, his contented gaze fixed straight up at his mother.

"Your son is beautiful, Lara," Ava commented first. "How blessed you are."

"Aye, and will you nae reconsider, Ava?" Lara asked, sounding fairly desperate. "I fear he'll come here first, nae go on to Blacklaw when they're given leave. He'll be expecting to find you here."

Ava shook her head and hid her anguish behind a forced smile. "He will nae. He might well come to Lismore, but it would nae be for me. And this is the right move for me to make now."

"But shall I tell him anything from you?" Lara asked, a knowing look about her pretty face.

Ava needed only a second to consider this. "Nae. We said our fare wells."

Lara's usually placid expression turned anxious "You could stay, and wait, and—perhaps he would want—"

"I can nae, Lara. Please understand."

"I do *nae* understand," Lara cried. "Where will you go? How will he find you?"

Ava lost a bit of her composure. "He will nae want to, Lara," she snapped and then closed her eyes, silently pleading for patience, for peace. Opening her eyes, she advised her friend, "He said nothing to me, dinna ask me to wait, dinna tell me—" she stopped, catching herself, letting the rest stay in her head. Opening her eyes, she spoke calmly again. "We said goodbye and he asked nothing from me. Thus I owe him nothing." Ava set her hand on Lara's arm, quieting her growing distress. "I have to go. Thank you for everything, Lara."

A few minutes later, the two horses carrying three people rode outside the gates of Lismore and around the loch, keeping to the north of the village of Rowsay before making clear of Matheson land altogether. Ava appreciated greatly the easy pace set by Innes, with whom she rode once more. Aside from foodstuffs provided by the kind folks of the Matheson keep and the generous donation of an extra shift and gown from Lara, Ava noticed one other addition to their meager possessions.

"We are armed now?" She asked Innes, conversation easy when the horses moved at only a slow trot.

Innes glanced down at the sword now fastened to his hip, and which was wedged between her thigh and his.

"We are," He replied proudly, sitting straighter in the saddle. "From Eachann 'fore he left. Nae a bad man, that one."

"But do you ken how to use it?" She was compelled to ask, never having witnessed Innes brandish anything larger than a dagger.

"Few quick lessons by that man," Innes admitted, "enough to see us safely from here to there."

"God willing," Hamish supplied at their side.

Ava was struck by a thought. "Why did neither of you ever consider taking up the sword as your vocation?"

Hamish's response was an immediate and loud guffaw that aptly stated his thoughts on the matter, at which Ava grinned.

"Death warrant, that," Innes replied over his shoulder. "For the most part, those men train all their lives for that role. We're nae more soldiers than we are farmers."

"You keep limiting us, Innes," Ava charged.

"Truth is truth, Ava. We are what we are and there is nae sense pretending otherwise, getting lofty in our speculations." He went on, waxing poetic once more about how grand all would be once they reached Edinburgh.

Ava paid him little heed, believing his expectations to be painted with a kinder brush than what her own would have shown. They would struggle—they would always struggle—and he did them no favors by pretending they would not.

Truth be told—not that she would ever admit so much to Hamish and certainly not Innes—she felt decidedly vulnerable as they traveled. She didn't recall that any marching in the company of John Craig had left her with a similar feeling of disquiet, one that had her constantly looking over her shoulder and scanning her gaze across any horizon they approached. She was ill-at-ease in the wide open landscape of this war-torn countryside and likely would be unable to settle before they reached Edinburgh.

And yet as they marched on, she was quite proud of herself that she was able, quite often and successfully, to push from the forefront of her mind any thought of John Craig that fought for attention. At least during the day time. At night, curled up inside the tent she'd been given, her mind whirled with thoughts of him, hoping she would dream as she had that night in the loft of the Kenith barn, in John Craig's arms.

Chapter Fifteen

Almost from the moment they'd departed Lismore, Ava had been chewing either her lip or her cheek, awash in consternation. She spent the better part of the first day in the saddle with Innes, trying to talk herself into the idea that this was indeed the right move to make. She had no business wishing and hoping—such luxuries were not for the likes of her. Hope was meant for people to whom it might actually come, people with families and means, people who lived a less desperate existence.

Though she wanted to, she did not cry, but giving into tears was mostly staved off by Innes' presence—he would scold her harshly, she was sure—and Hamish's rather regular chattering.

Of the latter, mostly any speech from Hamish came in the form of questions.

Are we really going to Edinburgh?

Do you ken we might trade this horse for a pair of shoes in Edinburgh?

Will there be a market?

Innes, do you ken there'll be a monastery there?

This last one begged a question from a surprised Ava, who laughed first at this unexpected query.

"A monastery? Monks? Whyever would you wonder about that, Hamish?"

"I've been thinking on it for a while, Ava. Monks dinna ever have to raise a sword. I dinna ken they ever go hungry. Always they have a place to lay their heads." He chortled, in that familiar high-pitched Hamish fashion. "I dinna guess they've ever been chased out of town by the English."

Ava laughed as well, supposing, "They also probably did nae ever take down the gallows in Lachie fashion."

"They dinna have to," Hamish sent back. "They keep their eyes to the ground, dinna stir up trouble such as that."

"I would categorize that nae as trouble, Hamish, but as heroic," Ava said, "and you should do the same."

"Aye, but still I'd like to become a monk, I ken," Hamish said.

"I suppose there are worse reasons to take up a monk's robes," Ava allowed. "If a monk you choose to be, then so you should."

Innes rarely contributed to any conversation, as was his way. If he were not griping about something or at someone, he did not normally have too much to say.

Innes kept one eye on the sun's path, which kindly advised of their direction, and they stayed mostly hidden as they traveled, keeping to the trees or tall brush, avoiding open fields as much as they could. They bedded down overnight inside the cover of the forest, Ava pleased for the gift of the tent since it had rained two nights in a row.

On the third day, when Hamish had apparently run out of questions and conversation, they marched along primarily in silence after Innes' morning grumbling that he'd thought they have reached Edinburgh by now, that Sten's directions must have been skewed, or outright wrong. The quiet of their journey allowed Ava's mind to torture her with her continued disquiet, all of which was centered around John Craig and what might have been.

Honestly, she couldn't say that he'd given her any reason to assume there was a chance that he might be glad to find her waiting for him at Lismore, if he should go there before heading on to his home. Above and beyond that, Ava wasn't sure he'd even earned a second chance from her. But she knew she had—or more specifically, she *deserved*—the right to know one way or another, if they stood a chance, if he would possibly want her in his life.

For her own sanity, she never considered, not for one fleeting second, the possibility that he might not survive whatever war threw at him now. That was not a possible outcome, she believed. It just was not.

Briefly, she wondered if she'd read too much in what few pleasant exchanges they'd known together. *Be guid* and *Be safe* were simply too generic and did not exactly imbue her with so much confidence.

Ah, but his kiss. Shouldn't so much be read into that kiss? That devouring and hungry kiss? So much suppressed heat and desire unleashed for those few glorious moments—or had that only been her? Nae, John Craig had been a starved man, teased by sweet meats for days and days, finally able to bite.

I wanted more—all of you, Ava, he'd said, the memory of which was what finally brought her to a conclusion and thus, a decision.

Having determined that she wasn't very good at resisting hope after all, she realized she wasn't afraid to have it quashed, not when the alternative was to have no hope at all.

I will go to Lismore, and I will give him the opportunity to tell me yea or nae.

Now she simply had to tell Innes and Hamish of her intentions.

Before they moved any further away from Lismore, she begged of Innes to stop.

Innes glanced up once more at the sun. "Hold it for another hour or so," he said. "We'll take a rest closer to the noon hour."

"No, Innes. I need to stop now."

Innes mumbled some inarticulate, profane thing and stopped the horse, allowing Ava to dismount. But she did not go off into the trees for privacy as he might have expected. Instead, she untied the rolled-up bundle of garments Lara had sent her off with and took one round loaf of the bread and one flask of ale they'd been given for their journey.

She faced Innes then and the frown he now wore, which showed a dawning of understanding.

"You're daft. You're going back?"

"I am, it's just something that I—"

"Ava," Innes interrupted, seemingly with great patience, "this is a big mistake."

"Where are you going, Ava?" Hamish asked at the same time, maneuvering his mount to stand next to the horse she'd shared with Innes.

Taking a deep breath, she announced, "I'm returning to Lismore. I have to—"

"Bluidy hell, Ava," Innes snapped now. "He dinna want you! He left you!"

"But he had to—"

"Aye, he had to," Innes repeated, with enough contempt that she was made to understand he didn't believe what he'd just said. "Left you with nae promise, nae anything."

"Who left?" Hamish wondered.

Hugging the rolled up clothes to her chest, Ava implored Innes. "Please try to understand. I have to at least...ken for certain that something or nothing might have come of it."

Innes shook his head, a sneer upon his face as he glared down at her. "He might bed you, Ava, but that's all you'll get from him, mark my words."

The old supposition that maybe at some time she might have gotten with Innes, because he was here and all she had, because they were likeminded, understood each other, was never further from reality as a possibility than at this moment. They were not alike at all, and though he was her friend, she began to suspect that they were only together now and for all these years because she'd had no one else.

Indeed, Innes used their assumed like-mindedness as part of his argument.

"We're nae like them, any of them," he said. "We're dirty beggars, Ava, nae anything more. Scrappers, we are, and bound to stay that way. You dinna belong with him, a laird, or at Lismore or any other keep, any more than I do."

"I belong where my heart tells me I belong," she argued plaintively.

"Drivel, all that," Innes shot back.

"Innes, I'm going back to Lismore, and I am sorry, but I dinna need your permission to do so." She paused and watched all the anger play about his reddened face. "You are my friend, Innes. I'd like this to always be true," she said in a pleading tone.

"Go on, then," he barked at her, waving his hand angrily. "Get out of here."

Ava looked at Hamish, seeking his opinion.

"You're going back to wait for John Craig?" He asked, is mind finally catching up.

Ava nodded wearily.

Hamish rubbed his eye with his thick knuckles, looking as someone who'd just woken and wished to erase the sleep from his eyes, and stared down at her from the saddle of the horse. "Tis nae for me to tell you what to do, Ava, though I dinna want to be parted from you."

She smiled weakly at him. "But you need to get on to Edinburgh, Hamish. Find that monastery."

"Aye," he said with a smile, "and so I will."

Innes leaned forward over the pommel, his scowl intact, and snarled at her. "You go on then, and forget you ever ken the likes of us, Hamish and me. We're nae friends, you and me, nae anymore."

"Innes, please," she beseeched.

He was deaf to her pleas, kneeing the mare into a trot which took him away.

Ava's shoulders sank as she removed her gaze from Innes' swift departure and returned it to Hamish.

"Hamish, I..."

"He'll be fine, Ava," Hamish assured her. "You ken he's never riled for so long."

"But..." she didn't know what else to say, even as she felt strongly in her conviction that she needed to do this.

"God be with you, Ava," Hamish said, revealing a bittersweet smile that thankfully held no animosity.

She laid her hand on his thigh, all that she could reach, about to give a farewell when a noise came at her from the direction in which they'd come. Ava squinted into the dense trees, able to make out many figures coming at them. They were yet dozens of yards away and moving slowly, but flashes of red tabards and dull silver helms advised of the identity of the party: English militia.

Her heart leapt into her throat. She didn't know where they were exactly, if they trespassed on some land presently claimed by the greedy English king. And hanging from Hamish's saddle were the three hares he'd caught just this morning with the slingshot with which he was so proficient. They'd be charged with poaching, a hanging offense.

"Riders," she whispered to Hamish, whose face was turned as well, having heard the soldiers coming. "English. Get out of here, dinna let them find you and your poached game. Tell Innes to ride hard. Go!" She took her hand from his thigh and smacked the rump of the horse with great force, sending the befuddled Hamish quickly away.

Hindsight came but a second later, realizing she should have clambered up onto the horse with Hamish rather than scaring him off. Too late to remedy that, Hamish already swallowed up by the closely set hazel and ash trees.

She did not only stand there and await their arrival but began to run herself, though not in the same direction as Innes and now Hamish had gone. She darted away to what she thought was west, though she couldn't be sure. And mayhap this was a mistake as well, for while the English had only been walking through the forest, she could very clearly hear now the ruckus of pursuit as dozens of fleet-of-foot coursers chased her.

Her pulse sped dangerously, and her breath caught in her throat, along with the yip of fear that her mouth was suddenly too dry to put out. She dashed over small crevasses and around trees, hopped over a muddy spot left by the recent rain, but knew fairly quickly how vulnerable she was, being on foot while those men were all mounted. Certainly, she should not expect to outrun them.

And so she did not. She thought she'd not sprinted for more than a minute before they overtook her, several riding ahead of her that she was suddenly surrounded. When one mounted man appeared before her, she changed directions, only to have that path cut off as well when another appeared. She did this twice more before stopping, turning in a circle to find that every direction was protected, and thus cut off as a means of escape.

While she panted heavily and lowered her arm, which had steadfastly carried those garments lent to her, she stared at each man surrounding her, into cold and remote eyes, shrouded in the shadows of their helms. And then two of those mounted men shuffled left and right, creating space between them, from where came another Englishman, this one elevated in status if anything might be gleaned from the fineness of his garb and the heraldry decorating the shield that hung, unemployed, over his leg.

His helm was more elaborate than the simple kettle helms with nose guards worn by the others. His entire face was concealed inside the shiny metal, the lower half resembling a pig's snout for how it protruded out around his nose and mouth. When he stopped, not more than ten feet from Ava, he took his time removing one fitted glove and then lifting the face of his helm upward, this made possible by hinges soldered into the space that covered his ears.

Pushing the pig snout up and away did nothing to remove the sow as the animal of comparison. This man, whoever he was, owned a pinched and pink face, with button-black eyes and an upturned, bulbous nose that dominated his meaty features.

Ava cringed inwardly when he leveled his black eyes on her. This was not the face of a kindly game warden.

After dabbing his gloved knuckle against the tip of his pig nose, the man said, with seeming politeness, "These heathen lands are vast and so frightfully unforgiving. I will be happy never to see them again."

Ava gave no response, assuming that none was expected.

"But imagine my surprise," continued the small man upon the big horse, "having only been granted the commission and the task a week ago, to stumble upon one of the very persons I seek."

Before she might have stopped herself, Ava laid her fingers against her chest and uttered weakly, "Me?"

"Yes, you, young woman," he affirmed sharply, forgoing any pretense at civility. "You caused quite a melee with your little stunt on hanging day."

"I ken you have me confused with another, sir," she said meekly.

"Of course I do not." He rifled inside his great surcote and produced a scroll of vellum, unrolling the thing, turning it over when it must have been upside-down, and then lifting his nearly invisible brows until they disappeared completely under the partially lifted snout of his helm. "The bulletin was rather unmistakable—John Craig, self-named Lion of Blacklaw Tower, enemy to the crown, and a certain green-eyed lass. And with her should rightly be found a thick oaf of little regard but for his size, and one Innes Seàrlas, both charged with causing mayhem and damages, and with aiding and abetting fugitives." He lifted his gaze from the scroll and fixed Ava with a telling sneer. "A thick oaf of little regard," he repeated, "large but not particularly clever—and would that be the hulking man-child you so unceremoniously just sent on his way, soon as you realized we'd been following you?"

Following her? For how long? Still, she maintained her oblivion, Innes' tactic of *when questioned, play dumb* rising to assist her. "I dinna ken any of what you're saying, sir. I dinna ken those people."

"Of course not," he said, quite agreeably, that attitude shattered with his next words. "Of course you lie" –he paused and consulted the scroll again—"Ava Guthrie. As would any, I am sure, charged with murder and the sort of mayhem for which you will swing."

The blood drained from her face. And before she caught herself, panic made her disclose some of her culpability. "I dinna kill anyone. I only helped—" she stopped abruptly, realizing her error.

"Take her," commanded so gently from the pig man as he rolled the scroll tightly took a moment to settle in, so that Ava did not move until others did, horses closing in on her, meant to detain her.

She tried to flee, and actually was able to squeeze between two horses and run away from the circle of English soldiers sent to find her.

As she ran, she heard the pigman call out loudly, his strident voice carrying easily, heard even over the pounding of her heart. "For those watching, you may have your freedom presently. We will take her, but we want the Lion himself, John Craig. Show yourself, John Craig! You have a fortnight to arrive at the garrison at Lanark and take her place under the noose!"

She never got far enough away to believe that escape was possible, or that they weren't gaining steadily on her. Adeptly, they kept stride with her. Still, a scream was torn from her as one of her pursuers leapt from his horse at her, landing on her back. The weight of him sent her hard to the ground, her forehead the first thing to meet the hard earth, the last thing she recalled before all went black.

***

After the victory at Loudoun Hill Robert Bruce had decided, quite sensibly some thought, to retreat once more to the safety of the mountains. They spent the next few days hunting and—for lack of pursuit, or anyone to chase themselves—relaxing.

Always there was some suspicion that Pembroke had regrouped and was on their trail, so that they continued to move stealthily, keeping under cover during the day. And then one night their suspicions were confirmed when a vulgar beggar woman stumbled into their camp in the mountain glen. While so many were simply off-put by her manner and appearance, Robert Bruce was instantly suspicious of the woman.

"Seize her," he commanded, at which time William Sinclair, standing closest and already holding his sword at the woman for her unexpected arrival, did take control of her person.

It did not take long for information to be scared out of her, Sinclair a menacing enough interrogator that the woman was not truly harmed but by what fright did to her. She gave up fairly quickly that indeed, Pembroke had sent her, that the English earl was combing these very woods and mountains, was closing in on them even now.

Robert Bruce wasted no more time on her but strode quickly to don his armor and within a quarter hour, the entire Scots army under his command was charging down the mountain, once more stirring the English quickly into chaos, which saw them riding feverishly in many directions away from any confrontation.

After that, the Bruce decided they should split up, they were too big now to march unnoticed through this area, so close to Ayr. They parted near Cumnock, where the king declared he would lay low until he could again be made aware of Pembroke's location.

John and Magnus and their armies retreated north and then east, recruiting loyalists along the way. At the king's advice, given with a crooked grin aimed at John, they skirted well north of Lanark, and then spent two full days in a forest south of Glasgow.

John caught Magnus again with the ink and parchment, sending his love to Lara.

"Aye now, our stop here," John said with little good humor, "is explained. Close enough to Glasgow you might make the trip yourself to meet the courier."

Magnus ignored him for a full minute, attending his letter-writing instead. When finally he lifted his gaze from the parchment, he made a pretense of innocence and asked, "Shall I include some greeting to Ava for you?"

John gritted his teeth and now ignored his cousin.

Indeed, Magnus did take the ride himself into Glasgow, and because he was a bit tortured by inactivity, John accompanied him. Henry, having been idling beside John at the time, asked to join them as well and so the three of them rode out the few miles to Glasgow.

The town, consisting of only four roads laid out in the shape of a cross, was quiet at midday when they rode through. John nodded at a pair of black-robed friars, who walked along the main road, their hands hidden inside their wide sleeves. John squinted ahead, to where sat their friary, on the east side of High Street, about midway between the market cross and the town's cathedral. A half dozen horses were hitched to a rail outside the town's only inn, but the door was closed tight, denying him any notion of whether the taproom was crowded or not. At that moment the cathedral's bell tolled the hour, lifting John's gaze heavenward momentarily.

"Bluidy hell, this cannot be guid," Magnus growled next to him, effectively lowering John's gaze.

Following where Magnus stared, John caught his breath, shocked to discover Innes Seàrlas inside Glasgow.

He stood against the front wall of the cutler's house, denoted by the relief carving depicting two crossed knives, but thrust himself out of the shadows as soon as he spotted them walking their destriers down the middle of High Street.

John and Magnus exchanged quick, hard stares and sped forward, reining in sharply. Neither said a word but imagined immediately that something was afoot, something dreadful must have happened to have sent Innes and not the regular courier, and he wearing that brutal scowl, aimed particularly at John.

Ava.

His heart stopped beating in his chest and he leapt from the steed before it had stopped fully. Innes charged him, ramming his shoulder into his midsection, shouting, "You bastard! This is all your fault."

John made quick work of gaining the upper hand. It needed but one hand yanking Innes upward by the collar of his tunic while his other hand caught the fist Innes tried to swing. "Bluidy fool," he hissed at Innes marching him backward until his back was once more against the cutler's store and they stood in the shadow of the overhang. "Dinna waste time on your petty anger. Where is Ava?"

"De Burghdon has her!" Innes shouted, his face red, his eyes watery. "But he wants you, says he'll make the trade, but only for you."

"How the bluidy hell did the sheriff of Lanark get his hands on Ava?" Magnus shouted and then blanched. "*Jesu*, never say he came to Lismore."

Innes shook his head, his face haggard, child-like for its misery. "Nae. We left Lismore, more than a week ago." He shoved at John's hand on his chest, holding him in place. "But she wanted to go back."

John's face and head welled with fury. His lips shuddered for how tightly he pinched them to keep from barking out his reaction to this bit of news. So she'd left Lismore, had been foolish despite his admonition to be safe and be wise, had struck out on their own.

"Was that your idea?" He asked in a dangerously low voice. "Moving on from Lismore?"

"Does it matter? She wanted to go, said aye, it was time."

"You bluidy fool," he seethed at Innes. "And where did he catch up with you?"

Innes raged, "What the bluidy hell does it matter where? She's gone! Taken! By some manky bastard working for de Burghdon—sent to find you, he said! But happy to use her as a pawn."

John digested this, while pain gripped his chest.

"Dinna stare at me as if this is my fault!" Innes exclaimed. "She turned back—because of you! Some baffling and hideous fixation with you. She'd nae have been caught if nae for you."

"By the robes of St. Columba, you let her retreat by herself, you coward," John accused, ramming his forearm against the smaller man, smacking him against into the timber wall once more.

"Cease!" Magnus shouted, trying to wedge himself between them. "*Jesu*, John, cease!" He shoved John backward a few steps. To Innes, Magnus asked, "And how do you ken he'll trade Ava for John?"

With a snarl at John, Innes turned to Magnus and exhaled a frustrated breath. "He said as much. He ken me and Hamish were nearby, shouted out for us to hear. Show yourself in a fortnight and be hanged instead of her."

Blood drained from John's face, though he still boiled with emotions, fear presently for what answer might be received to the question he was forced to ask. "When was this?"

"Eight days ago," Innes said. "I raced back to Lismore, hoping you'd be there. Sten advised I would find at least him here eventually." He inclined his head at Magnus.

John knew only a little relief for this, that he still had time. He turned to Magnus, putting the hotheaded Innes from his mind. "Go on, I'll...I'll return when I can."

"John, you canna—"

"Yes, I can!" John roared. "I can and I will. I dinna need my whole army—likely de Burghdon will expect just that. Eachann will keep with the Craig army; he can lead them as well as I if they're called. Keep 'em close to you, Magnus."

"You have me, laird," Henry volunteered. "And my sword."

Having forgotten about the lad's presence, John nodded in his direction and said to Magnus, "And I'll see what value if any this one has," he said, throwing his thumb over his shoulder at Innes.

"John," Magnus was obliged to remind him, "we are under the command of the king presently."

There was not so much censure in his tone, so that John didn't think he needed to ask the obvious question, though to make his point he did. "If it were Lara...?"

Magnus nodded, likely having anticipated the query. "Go then," he urged, "but you'll have to return lest you be considered a defector."

Passively, Innes stepped away from the side of the building and approached Magnus, withdrawing a folded and wax sealed letter from his tunic, which he sheepishly handed to him. Magnus scowled at the man, swiping the missive irritably from his hand.

Magnus did not hold back his opinion of the man. "Bluidy half-wit, you are. Do yourself—and Ava—a favor and do as he says. When he says it."

Innes did not acknowledge the mild set-down but turned away and mumbled something about his horse left near the market cross.

John met Magnus' gaze, as dark as his own.

"God speed, my friend."

"Aye."

They embraced quickly as farewell and claimed their own steeds, Magnus going one way and John and Henry the other, following Innes, who half-ran, half-walked down the road to recover his own horse.

Henry walked his horse beside John and asked casually after a moment, "I dinna ken half of what that was about, but I take it we're off in pursuit of the lass."

"Aye," John agreed through clenched teeth, his eyes boring holes in Innes' back even as his mind churned with vivid and awful images of a captive Ava, imprisoned in that filthy gaol, treated poorly, misused and abused.

"He's going to tell us every goddamn detail of what took place as we move, since he's wasted enough time already."

"But what if we canna—" Henry started.

"We will," John cut him off. "Either she is freed, or I die trying."

Chapter Sixteen

It took all the rest of the day to reach Lanark, and that was riding swiftly over hill and glen after their slower beginning, when John was given a full accounting of what had happened and how Ava had been trapped but not Innes or Hamish.

"And where is Hamish now?" John had asked at the end of the tale.

"His horse went lame on our return to Lismore," Innes had told, "but I could nae wait on him, and I dinna want to be slowed down by riding two on this mare. I needed to get to Lismore. He continued on foot, may be there now."

Though he wasn't surprised by Innes' abandonment of Hamish and while there remained some possibility that the lad himself might be in danger, John agreed it had been the right move at the time.

If he counted up all the hours he'd spent in the saddle over the years, hundreds and hundreds by now he was sure, John knew for certain never had the ride seemed as long or as excruciating as this one. While he was adept at putting things in their place, keeping emotions at bay to be able to act and react from the head and not the heart, he simply could not this time. Not when Ava was at the mercy of those damnable English. He recalled too easily the dankness of the cell in which he'd sat for three days, the reckless abuse of the guards, so pleased to jab clubs into his gut and fists to the side of his head; he recalled the mean gruel as well served to him, infested with bugs, and the lone cup of water they'd given him, being in reality someone's piss. Being a female, Ava would be subject to other means of torture or abuse, the prospect of this weighing most heavily upon him. Trying to settle himself, knowing he would be of little use to her if he were weakened by fear, he imagined that his own name might protect her. If the sheriff, de Burghdon, had bothered to chase him down, even weeks after his dodging the noose, there had to be some reason he was so dedicated to the task. Mayhap supposing his prisoner was valuable, in that she would bring the prize of the Lion of Blacklaw Tower, might be what kept Ava untouched.

It was early evening when they neared Lanark. They rode along the ridge over the same river by which they'd escaped, on the opposite side as the cave in which they'd hid. 'Twas mostly an open area and John reined in under the canopy of a small grove of rowan trees, close enough to see the walls and castle tower of Lanark but far enough away to remain unnoticed.

"Why do you stop?" Innes snapped almost immediately. "God's teeth, but are you—"

"Innes," John warned sharply as he dismounted, "do nae try my patience at this time."

"You canna mean to go on foot," Innes persisted. "We need to hit 'em hard and—"

"We need to investigate first, you bluidy simpleton," John seethed, turning his attention to Henry.

Henry and Innes sat side by side upon their steeds. Just as Innes began to spout some other grievance or directive, Henry's hand shot out and captured Innes by the collar. He yanked him close, pulling him until he was crooked in the saddle, their faces only a foot apart.

"Say and do what you want when this is done," Henry barked at him. "Right now, you do what he says." He shoved him away, not softly, and added, "Whatever the hell this shite is between you two, you put it aside until the lass is recovered."

When Henry returned his attention to John—who managed to hide his shock over the lad's timely outburst; Henry was fierce in battle but mostly stable and good-humored outside of it—John said to him, "I ken you're the best shot we have to get in there and find out what you can. They ken me and him."

Henry nodded and asked no questions. He was a scout, would know what he was about.

Innes cleared his throat and held up his hand, almost defensively. "I'm nae arguing with that notion. But I suggest I might have a better chance finding out things. I have friends inside."

John was not so stubborn that he did not consider this. "But can you do it without being discovered? Will be hard enough to get Ava out, just us three. But if you're caught—getting out two with only two presents a far greater challenge."

"If I can wait until dark, I can get in," Innes assured him, with enough cockiness that John didn't doubt it.

"Verra well. We only need to ken where exactly she is—I assume the castle gaol, where I was. And you'll need to get an estimate of guards on duty, and if those numbers are increased from what you might regularly see." From his own time imprisoned, John had a fair idea about the workings and layout of the castle and gaol itself.

Innes nodded, finally dismounting. "You got a plan when you have those answers?"

"Nae yet," John admitted. "We have only stealth as our weapon. A quiet break and take." He stared down Innes. "But we *will* get her out of there."

"You sound fairly confident for a man who just admitted he has no plan," Innes remarked, though little rancor was heard.

"Do you ken failure is an option?" John challenged by way of explanation for his conviction.

Innes nodded, not as an answer, but as understanding.

John knew one thing that Innes likely did not. If it came to it, if it was all he had left, he would give himself up to secure her release.

When darkness came Innes went on foot. They had since removed from that grove of rowan trees, taking to a larger wooded area, where John and Henry awaited his return. John was sure no minutes of the day ticked by as slow as these ones over the next hour and a half.

He could not help but reflect upon the last time he was here, at Lanark. He pictured Ava, that initial smile he'd witnessed from her, the one given to the despicable Englishman. With little hardship he recalled his own fascination with her at that moment, because of that smile. Just as easily, the image of her boldly marching up the stairs to the gallows came to him. Not for one moment did he believe she hadn't been scared out of her mind, but how brave she'd been then, and for a person she'd not ever met. How she'd beguiled him that day, with her beauty and bravado.

His shoulder leaned against a tree, his arms crossed over his chest, he closed his eyes briefly, sending up a prayer to a god he wasn't completely certain even knew of his existence, asking that if in nothing else in his life, he might be successful now.

When finally Innes returned, he was breathless for the sprint that brought him back and then more animated than John could ever recall, his face alight with glee.

The glee was not a good match to his first words though, eliciting a ferocious frown from John.

"She's nae there," Innes said, blowing out a long breath, his brow dotted with perspiration. "She's nae inside the wall. They've put her up at Carstairs instead."

John was only vaguely familiar with the castle and couldn't yet contemplate what this might mean.

"Four miles east, as the crow flies," Innes said. "It's just near the site of an old Roman fort. De Burghdon is the sheriff of Lanark, though he is rarely seen here, but is also the constable of Carstairs Castle. Lives there, by my understanding."

"*Jesu*," John breathed with a burgeoning hope. "Like as nae, he expected I—or we—would come to Lanark, attempt a rescue. He moved her but dinna ken we had the means to find this out." He smacked Innes on the shoulder, and showed him a smile, his first in many days, which was matched by Innes' delighted grin.

"Aye, now the sad news is they actually garrison more there than the Lanark castle, normally as many as forty, knight, men-at-arms, footmen, but it's said they'd moved half of them into town, anticipating your arrival. But there's no wall around Carstairs, mayhap only a handful patrolling at night," Innes said. "For you and your sword—and Henry, too—will be child's play. I'll be there as well, do what I can but...Sweet St. Columba, this is...perfect."

John agreed but did not want to get ahead of himself, and neither did he want to be caught unawares for merely presuming, going in half-cocked, driven only by assumptions.

Henry must have thought the same. Standing next to John, he asked Innes, "What do you ken of Carstairs?"

"Verra little," Innes quickly disappointed them, but then just as swiftly, another grin widened his mouth. "But Harailt, the old stonemason—he dinna work hardly nae more but he did at Carstairs many years back, detailed a bit of the layout. Sheriff keeps chambers top floor; gaol is on the ground floor. Harailt said it once housed the Bishops of Glasgow and little has it been fortified since. The brewery and bakehouse are built into the ground floor. There's a small door, half-man size, in the wall of the brewery above a trough, was meant for disposing the spent grains."

Henry's eyes went wide. "Bollocks, almost sounds too easy."

John agreed and cautioned they would know better when they arrived at Carstairs.

"This is guid work, Innes," John praised. "Just what we needed. Well done."

They spent the next hour making plans, more than one in the event that any information they had was not found as it should before they set out to the east and Carstairs. The moon was bright, but the rolling black clouds would work in their favor, offering enough full darkness if they timed their movement properly around the angry nighttime sky.

Be brave, lass. I'm coming.

***

Ava was fairly certain that she was specifically left in pitch blackness only to add more horror to her confinement. If that be the case, these English could happily count their success as won.

Imagine for yourselves any hell that troubles you and multiply that several times, John had said of his own imprisonment, though surely that had been reflective of his time spent inside the Lanark castle.

True, she could attest now, though she had to imagine that John Craig's detention in the gaol had been more hellish, for the marks of aggression on his handsome face after three days kept in English company.

She had not been abused, not physically in any fashion, not after they'd arrived at this location, the name and site of which Ava had no idea and had not been told. Close to Lanark, she guessed since she'd been greeted upon her arrival by Walter de Burghdon himself. Of that man, her enemy and captor, she had since decided and was obliged by truth to admit, there was much of honor. A true gentlemen, even inside a devil's war, he'd been.

Ava had not recognized the three-story castle they'd ridden up on more than a week ago but had quite easily put a name to the face of the man who stepped out of the tall building to greet the coming party. Her ignoble coming—she'd wakened from her stupor draped face-down over the back of a horse, her hands and feet tied under its belly and had remained that way for many more agonizing hours until they'd finally stopped here—had produced anger on her behalf from the nobleman sheriff and she'd been quickly unbound and hastened to her feet.

Of course, he had not invited her within at that time as an awaited guest, had not produced any light fare to ease the ache in her belly or even the smallest drop of water or ale to quench her dry and scratchy throat. But he'd shown humanity, having been angered by her casually cruel treatment thus far, and had even gone so far as to tender a wee regret.

"My apologies, Miss, for the inexcusable behavior of these men," he'd said, casting a snappy frown at the man who until this moment was the highest ranking, the one who'd read her name from that bloody scroll with such derision. "I can assure you," de Burghdon continued, "it is *not* our general intention to abuse frivolously."

Having little expected such kindness, Ava had no available response but a nod.

Walter de Burghdon was possibly two score or more years, was of average height, with kindly blue eyes and close-cropped dark hair, receding eagerly from his forehead. He dressed impeccably, garbed in fine wool and linen and wearing high boots of supple leather, the black so shiny Ava was sure they must be oiled daily. He owned a belly just round enough to suggest either he indulged too little in activity or enjoyed regularly well-cooked and bountiful meals.

"I cannot guess what your relationship is to the criminal, John Craig," de Burghdon had said next, "but it remains that crimes were committed and thus reparations must be paid."

As he seemed to expect some reply from her, Ava spilled the truth, though she hadn't any hope it would do her any good. "Sir, John Craig only acted in response to an assault on me. I-I was thieving from the granary—but only to help feed my friend's bairns," she was quick to qualify, "and naught but what a family of five might need for the day, truly nae more than that. Before I could...make off, one of your men-at-arms accosted me, as I deserved to be. But...your man had intentions uglier than only detaining me for theft, sir. And...John Craig arrived, seemingly out of thin air, and—"

De Burghdon held up his gloved hand to forestall the rest of the story. He shook his head, as if to say none of it mattered. "Be that as it may, young woman, one crime begets another, do you not see? Your theft—and of greater import, your other crimes—resulted in further and more distressing criminal activity. We are, at this time, still recovering from the unrest and carnage initiated by you on the day of the hanging. The town lives in unhappy unrest."

As if chastised by a caring father—he spoke so gently, as if trying to impart a lesson to a much younger person—Ava bowed her head in shame and left off advising that the town lived frequently in *unhappy unrest*, and likely would so long as an uninvited, unwanted foreign entity ruled their lives. "I am sorry, sir. I just couldn't let a man die for me."

Walter de Burghdon sighed rather gustily. "Yes, yes. But now we must—"

"Will I hang now?" Ava lifted her eyes to him, her hands fisted at her sides, holding on tight to all the terror that consumed her.

The next look he gave her was initially sorrowful but swiftly incited into a mien less fathomable.

"We will discuss that at a later date." He lifted his brows and said pointedly, cocking his head down at her, "John Craig will hang, you understand. He must, for the murder of a king's man."

Ava was compelled to speak the truth as she believed it. "Sir, I...I'm nae sure John Craig will give himself up for...simply for me."

The sheriff pursed his lips at this. "Mayhap you should have kept better company, young woman, someone worthy of your boldness and allegiance. Perhaps a man of better honor."

Ava scowled instantly at the man. "He has great honor, Sir!" She defended. "It's just that..." she let that go, quite sure it made no difference.

With that he'd bowed his head curtly and returned to the castle, entering through the grand entrance, the arched door fitted with decorative wrought iron straps, and that enclosed under a stone entryway into which was carved a depiction of some long-ago monk or saint.

Ava was summarily taken by the arm and led around to the rear of the castle, entering through a doorway more befitting her station in life and present circumstance as prisoner, the wood splintered and discolored by wear. She was shoved through a narrow passageway, which turned and turned until she arrived at what she assumed was the castle's dungeon—a newer addition to this fortress, she presumed, the three doors staring at her all fitted with large and heavy locks, the metal clean and not blackened by age, as if what have once been storerooms had only been turned over to cells for prisoners.

The passageway here was illuminated by a lone torch, suspended on the wall between two of the doors, casting a bleak light on the dank gaol. Small windows, no bigger than Ava's face had been cut into the doors and fitted with metal bars.

The courtesy and sympathy shown by the sheriff outside obviously was not practiced by his castle guard, as one of those freshened doors was opened and she was hastily pushed inside. The door closed behind her, leaving her in near total darkness, save for what pitiful light was shared from that torch.

She had not been mistreated, though, but for being left in that eerie darkness all day and night, and for the slurs and insults lobbed at her—*heathen's whore*, she heard more than once—on those few occasions the thick door was opened. It opened twice a day only, for food to be delivered. On almost every occasion of this, the plate was only dropped from waist height, when usually more than half of its contents were bounced and spilled onto the hard dirt floor.

Thus, she sat on this her eighth night in the sinister blackness, with naught but her thoughts and what few noises she could discern to occupy her. By now, she'd almost fully convinced herself she was going to die, and yet somehow, amazingly, that dominated only half of her thoughts.

As they had almost since the very first moment she'd met him, thoughts of John Craig seized the majority of her attention, not least of which was the miserable fact that she was now doubly sorry that she'd left him, left Lismore when she'd refused hope.

She needn't close her eyes to imagine him—his handsome face, the way his brilliant brown eyes had so often studied her with such thorough and heart-skipping regard, that gloriously crooked smile he'd shown numerous times that night at the Kenith crannog—the inky shadows of her cell were a fine backdrop to the images she begged to come.

Ava folded her arms around herself and imagined they were John's. The memory of John Craig's kiss brought her peace but only for short spurts of time. Her present circumstance proved painfully adept at showing her that prior to the advent of John Craig, she had little on which to draw from her short and dreary life that might give her either peace or joy.

How tragic, she mused. *Bound to die and with so few memories to share my final days, with even fewer to mourn me, none save Innes and Hamish possibly. What a waste of a life.*

Any distant, not fully embraced hope that John Craig might come, that by some improbable means Innes and Hamish had managed to find him, that he might imperil his own freedom for her, had by now dissolved completely. She wondered if this was how he had felt, as she did now, forlorn, hopeless, afraid not of death but of the way in which it would come to her.

It was only the coward in her that cried, and only when calm was unattainable and a riot of thoughts—all associated with a rope around her neck and she dropping and dangling, neck snapping or mercilessly not—tortured her with gruesome images.

She scratched at her scalp, briefly wondering about the figure she would present when finally she was brought out in that horse-drawn cage to the gallows. It was just damp enough inside this prison that her hair hung limply around her in long snarls, and it was just cold enough that she was sure her skin was tinted blue, and mayhap her lips were bloodless. She was more than certain that her old worn and weary léine was bereft of hope, sullied and torn in many places at this point.

As she had for the last week, she sat on the cold ground and leaned her back against the earthen wall of turf block, drawing her knees up to her chest as she courted sleep, the only relief she knew. Perhaps she'd only just closed her eyes or possibly some time had passed, she could not say, when a noise startled her to groggy wakefulness.

So few disturbances did she hear in this remote part of the castle, this one now brought a gulping dread to the fore. She knew the hour of the day based solely on the arrival of what little fare she was allowed, which she'd initially figured as midmorning and late evening. Her half-eaten trencher sat a few feet away from her, near where all the carelessly spilled food lay, having been dropped hours ago. It was late at night, or should be, she thought, pressing herself further against the wall in fright for what might come through the door, and why.

What had initially roused her now was realized to be a heavy and swift thud of footsteps. Ava stared with frightened eyes at the small and useless window in the door. She saw naught but the barely flickering golden light of that single torch, the trajectory of her gaze aimed at the ceiling of that passageway. Swallowing thickly, she tried in vain to make out what was happening, nearly impossible since only sound was available as a clue and that was nearly drowned out by the sudden and thunderous hammering of her heart.

Before it even struck on her to entertain hope of a rescue, she heard what sounded precisely and beautifully like John Craig's voice.

"Christ!" He seethed with much impatience. This was followed by a scrape of steel, a sound she recognized as his sword either exiting or entering his scabbard. Next, she heard the now recognizable sound of a jangle of keys, the ones that opened these cages. "Ava! Where are you?"

'Twas a hiss and not anything greater than that, but so blessedly familiar that a joyous cry burst from her as she sprang to her feet.

"Here!" She cried. "I'm here!" She lunged at the door, banging her palms against the wood. "Here," she whimpered, relief and joy colliding, taking her voice.

A key grated in the lock, first one which did nothing but make John curse again, and then another that mercifully scraped and turned. She was forced backward when the door was pushed open.

And then he was simply there, filling the doorway, so large and unbearably beautiful in this instant, his lion-brown eyes glittering with furious purpose. And Ava was weary and afraid, and she didn't think twice about rushing at him, flinging herself at his broad chest. His strong arms swallowed her up, crushing her against him. She felt his cheek against her matted hair and oh, what glory she knew for how his fingers pinched so desperately into the flesh of her back!

Too soon, those fingers gripped her arms and pushed her away, though kept her still within his grasp, but with enough distance between them so that he could rake that beloved hardened gaze up and down her.

"Did they hurt you? Do I need to kill anyone?"

A trembling laugh fell from her lips. "Nae, nae. Oh, John." She curled her fingers into his padded brigandine and lifted her watery eyes to him.

John covered her hands with his, wrenching them off his chest, keeping hold of only one. "We have to go."

Ava nodded, still wobbly with disbelief and joy.

"I'm here, Ava," John said, entwining his fingers with hers. "I've got you now."

Chapter Seventeen

While her hand in his, coupled with the fact that she appeared on the whole tattered but otherwise unharmed, gave John a respite from fear, he knew they had still a long dash toward freedom. Hearing nothing in the passageway by which he'd come, he pulled her along behind him through the twists and turns of this part of the castle.

Earlier, when they'd come upon Carstairs, finding it was not surrounded by any great defensive wall, John had advised Innes and Henry that he alone would enter the castle. Having watched the castle for nigh on an hour, they'd determined that the guard consisted only of a dozen men and most of those were situated at the front of the castle, watching the main road and the front entryway. His speculation must have been correct, that de Burghdon had anticipated that John and his army would go to Lanark, either quietly or charging with righteous force. In his erroneous assumption, de Burghdon had left Carstairs—and himself if John chose to exact any personal revenge—entirely too vulnerable. Of those dozen men, they did make regular walks around the small perimeter, a pair at a time. He and Henry had surprised and easily dispatched two men, and John had moved on toward the shadows of the bakehouse wall while Henry and Innes had removed those not-quite-dead men before they'd retreated as ordered to the place where they were expected to wait with the horses. John had guessed and Innes and Henry had agreed that they would have no more than ten minutes before those two disabled men were missed.

He'd not expected to find any castle guard inside the brewhouse where he'd entered via that squat door Innes had learned of, but then he'd also not expected to encounter any other person in the bowels of the castle so close to midnight. And yet as he'd moved stealthily from the brewhouse and through the corridors opening to other kitchen chambers and the exterior bakehouse, he was surprised to see a young lad inside the scullery. The lad, standing upon a stool to make himself tall enough to reach the basins in which he was still scrubbing pots and pans, turned his head over his shoulder as John paused. Clearly, John would not slay a child, or even maim him simply to silence him. The lad was tiny, might not have seen ten summers, and was dressed as any local villein might be, in tattered breeches and tunic, possibly signifying his birthright as Scottish. Seconds ticked by while John met the solemn gaze of the gone-still child. When he did not immediately raise an alarm with any cry but moved his small gaze to John's breastplate and plaid, and the lion's head brooch holding the latter in place, John lifted his finger to his lips to incite secrecy. The lad barely moved his head, his lips parting as he continued to stare, but with that nod, John had moved on.

Now, though, their exit was fraught with danger. If those two incapacitated men had been discovered, the grounds would be swarming with English soldiers, and Henry and Innes would be too far to lend their aid. Also, John would have to pull open that door to the rear yard with naught but hope that any English watchmen were not presently making rounds.

He was surprised to find that same lad from the scullery standing at the end of one corridor when he and Ava approached. John drew up, his breath hitching, while Ava crashed into his back.

This time, the lad held up his hand, putting his finger to his mouth same as John had, asking for silence. A faithful and patriotic accord was extolled as well with that silent motion. He then wiggled his small fingers, waving John and Ava forward. He moved then and John followed and stopped again when the lad reached the main rear door. Slowly, as to make no noise, the lad unlatched the nighttime locks, and held his palm toward John so that he and Ava remained still once more. Standing only half behind him, and still with her hand in his, Ava clung with her other hand to John's upper arm.

The lad then pulled open the door and peered outside, showing his face seconds later to hurriedly wave them forward once more.

At the door, John paused but briefly, giving the child a clap on the shoulder for his assistance.

"God speed to the Lion of Blacklaw," the child stunned him by saying. "Go."

Stunned, John could only imagine that indeed the child was a Scots' lad and that he must have attended his hanging all those weeks ago. Mayhap he'd even cheered on his escape then.

John winked at him but needed no further urging before running out into the night, dragging Ava behind him again with a curt command of, "Run!"

Ava stumbled after only a step or two, but John's hand kept her upright. Without a cry or any noise at all, she used her free hand to hike up her skirts to her knees and they were off again. They sprinted straight across the yard, needing to get far away from the glow of the numerous torches set in regular intervals around the castle. And while the rear yard was indeed clear as they'd exited that narrow door from the kitchen buildings, sadly it did not remain so. They hadn't run more than fifty feet when a surprised shout reached them. The first call of "Ho, there!" was followed almost immediately by another cry, this time of the watchman calling for assistance as he chased after John and Ava.

"Keep running," John encouraged Ava as they went further and further into darkness, though yet were still upon open flat land, albeit dashing across uneven ground.

"Where—where is your army?" Ava asked, each word timed to her breaths.

"With Magnus," John told her. "Nae close."

The clouds parted then, and bright moonlight shone upon them. John seethed a curse, knowing they would be easily spotted now, but then was thankful for the light as he and Ava had almost run straight at a tract of bogland. He skirted around this, holding his free hand against his sword so that it did not bump at his leg so much to be a hindrance to speed.

The sounds of horses now in pursuit coincided perfectly with the moon once more being shrouded by those thick, rolling clouds. 'Twas naught but rolling pastureland from here all the way to the tree line, several hundred yards away. He'd known that going in, that they would have to make the trees to realize the greatest chance of success.

"Innes and Henry are there," John said, "in the trees."

"Innes?" She repeated, possibly all she could manage now, the wind stolen from her.

It was another half a minute before they put the first tree behind them. John slowed but not because he assumed they were safe yet, only to give respect to the severely uneven ground inside this woodland.

"Here!" Called Henry from somewhere far to their left.

"They're on me!" John called back, advising he could not stop yet. "Innes!"

A great rustling and scrambling overwhelmed all other night sounds, as John and Ava ran, he angling them toward the left now, and Henry and Innes began to move as well. They converged after another long moment had passed.

Immediately, John shoved Ava at Innes. "Take her. Keep going, as we discussed. To the horses. Dinna wait for us."

Before Ava had even acknowledged Innes' presence, she whipped her face around, her loosened hair flying around her head, and balked at John's directive. "Nae! John, come with us."

Drawing his sword with one hand, he pushed her again at Innes, unwilling to argue with her now about their chances of outrunning as many as ten riders. "Go!" He ordered again, meeting Innes' gaze and not Ava's.

Innes firmly took hold of Ava, at first wrenching her away until she followed voluntarily, though her feet did drag.

John heard Innes caution or reprimand her. "Dinna look back."

John met Henry's gaze, his placid expression barely noticeable but not unexpected. Few were the times Henry was worked up into any frenzy. "*Goirt*," John instructed in their language, letting him know they would have to use stealth to overtake five times as many as they were.

Henry nodded and faded into the black shadows of the trees. John moved a bit off the path that had brought him here, taking up a watchful position behind a tree to wait. He closed his eyes when the clamor of horses plunging into the woodland came to him, trying to count by sound how many gave chase.

At least eight, he figured, but did not discount that it might be more. And then he didn't suppose the frayed ropes they'd strung earlier between trees here and there, about neck high to a riding man, would do all the work for them.

Nothing mattered now, but that Ava got away. He'd been strict in his earlier instruction to Innes, that no matter what happened to either him or Henry, he was to keep going, all the way to the ruins of the ancient keep they'd stumbled upon late this afternoon, more than a mile away, where they'd made their plans and had hobbled their steeds.

Flipping the hilt of his sword in his hand to regrip it, John waited for the first doomed Englishman to come upon his position.

***

"Innes, wait," Ava cried pitifully. "I can't...nae more."

"'Tis but a wee distance now," Innes urged. "You can."

She allowed herself to be dragged further. It was not that her chest burned for lack of air or that her legs might give out at any second, though these concerns were indeed real, having not run like this since that fateful day and another daring escape weeks ago. Nae, Ava was sure the foreboding dread attacking her right now might be the death of her, fear for John Craig, at the thought of him facing down surely dozens and dozens of de Burghdon's men.

Her mind and heart thus terrorized, she had no idea about distance or time, save that it felt as if they'd run for miles and too many hours had passed before Innes finally slowed. She had no idea where they were. They'd run across a series of meadows and furrowed rigs, up hills and down, and through more than one grove of trees. When Innes finally stopped, they stood amid what looked to be an inhospitable land of overgrown brush and vines. Ava looked left and right, her breath caught once more when she realized they'd come to the site of an abandoned ruin. All was charcoal gray under the light from a cloaked moon, the half walls of stone that remained, the ivy and other clingers that snaked everywhere around it, the outline of a naked tree visible inside the skeleton of the primeval fortress. Innes ducked inside the crumbled wall by way of a section that was now only as high as his knees.

Still panting, Ava followed, beyond delighted to find three steeds tucked inside one corner, one of which she immediately recognized as John's. She hastened her step toward the idle horses.

"We have to go back—"

"Nae," Innes countered curtly. Standing between two horses, where he was untying the ropes that kept them stabled here, he shot a hard glare at Ava. "Nae," he said again, with less roughness. "He told me nae matter what, we were to convene here and *wait* here, you and I."

"But Innes, we can—'" she began to argue, horrified at the very idea of leaving him now.

"We canna. We will nae," Innes insisted, returned to whatever he was about with the ropes now. "He came for you—risked everything, will be at the king's mercy should Robert Bruce learn of his dereliction—and all he cares about is that you are safe. He came at *my* behest to save *your* hide. We *will* adhere to *his* plan."

"But to leave them without—"

"Damnit, Ava," Innes hissed at her. "Dinna fight me on this—nae him. Let us imagine he kens most what is best. We are to wait one hour, nae more, nae less, and then we go, whether he comes or nae. He was adamant on that point."

Ava gasped, this representation of Innes a far cry from that one that had run from Lanark with her, or any she'd known since then. Still, she could have wept at the idea of riding away from here, when John's fate was unknown. She wouldn't, she knew. She couldn't, not if it meant she would never see John again or know his fate. She'd done that once, and not under duress at that time, and had discovered it was wrong.

"Where is Hamish?" It occurred to her to ask then.

"He's safe," Innes said then, stepping away from the horses who were now untethered, ready she presumed to be mounted and raced away when needed. "Or I imagine he is. After you were taken, I made straight for Lismore. I could nae imagine another way to find John Craig." Innes stood before her and sighed heartily, telling, "Hami's horse went lame, but I could nae slow. I bade him walk, but then I departed Lismore for Glasgow before he'd made it there. Sten said he'd send a few out to collect the lad. I'm sure he's guid, Ava, safe and sound at Lismore as we speak."

"I hope so." Impulsively, she closed the distance between them and wrapped her arms around her friend. "Thank you, Innes."

His hand landed on her back but did not move. "Did you ken I would make nae effort...?"

Awkwardly, Ava removed herself from him. She told him honestly, "It never occurred to me that you would not try to find John Craig. I only did nae ken if you would be able to."

Innes narrowed his eyes at her. "You had another fear?"

Lowering her gaze from his, though little the murky night showed a person, Ava admitted, "I...I dinna ken if he would come for me."

Innes surprised her by barking out a snort of a laugh. "Sure and if you'd seen his face when I caught up with him, when he was told of your arrest, you'd have nae cause to doubt. Looked as you did just nae, at just the idea of leaving here without him, if it should come to that."

Tears she thought she might have been done with from the moment John had thrust open the door of her cell returned now, and she was besieged again with a fit or anxiety for John's current well-being.

Her mind racing with what happened and what could still happen, Ava only gave half her attention to her surroundings outside of these ruins, what little she could make out of the midnight scenery. Until something flickering in the distance caught her gaze. She squinted into the night, and stepped away from Innes, going to what remained of one wall of this ancient building. There, beyond the trees of the closest glen, upon a tall hill whose peak met with the night's eerie black clouds, she spied the golden glow of several lights, hazy and stationary, raising awareness but not concern.

"What is that?" She asked of Innes.

"Christ, Ava, how should I ken?" Innes replied, barely sparing a glance in the direction in which she faced.

His impatience remained steadfast. Or was that resoluteness, fixated on adhering only to John's instruction and not of a mind to concern himself with any other thing?

"Only rarely have I been more than a few leagues from Lanark to ken what surrounds us," he said then with less hostility, coming to stand next to her. "A keep, it seems," he acknowledged. He pointed in that direction now. "Aye, I can make out a tower. Torches on the walls, those lights," he decided.

Disregarding the unknown home as irrelevant then, Ava faced the direction from which John and Henry would come, praying to God that John did indeed come to her. Seconds and minutes played as hours then. At times, Ava held her breath, wishing for no other noise to interfere with any sound that should alert her of his coming.

Though it felt as if forever had come and gone, in truth she had only to wait another fifteen minutes before she heard them, certainly more than one, the sound of footsteps—not hoofbeats—upon the cold, hard ground. New tears welled, these of joy and hope. Reflexively, with an excitement she could barely contain, Ava grasped at Innes' sleeve as he stood next to her. Possibly though, that roused him to caution, and he dragged her backward, into the corner of those ruins, pulling her down into a squat, taking no chances.

She did not balk at this, not wishing any more than he to be confronted by an enemy coming their way rather than John or Henry. But then she heard his beloved voice again, just as the footsteps reached the crumbling old stone.

"Ava!" John called out, his voice hoarse, only loud enough to be heard by someone very close.

At the same time the clouds made way for enough moonlight to show shadows now, silhouettes moving around the grounds here, Ava sprang to her feet, all hope and joy overshadowed by what greeted her, John leaning heavily on the younger and smaller Henry, obviously injured.

A cry caught in her throat as she raced to where John buckled onto a section of wall that was only waist high. Henry peeled off him just as Ava reached him, Innes on her heels. And then she didn't recognize the sound that came from her throat as being made by her when she saw all the blood.

Ava froze, her immediate thought after recognition of so much blood being to wonder how he had run at all, how he could sit even now, how he'd not collapsed completely. His face was splattered with red droplets, she noted as she moved to within two feet of him, but she saw no torn or sliced skin there; one spot of his hair was matted and appeared wet, with more blood, she had to assume; his brigandine was intact but his arm, covered only by his woolen tunic, was bared to the elbow, the fabric rent and hanging. There, the very clear mark of a blade slashed across from the front at his bulging bicep around his previously unmarred skin to his triceps, from where a steady stream of blood appeared to continue flowing, some of it slanted along his arm, that which had flowed while he'd run. Ava saw then that while his breastplate was indeed whole, there were several places where a knife or sword had obviously stabbed or jabbed; the lightness of the quilted padding, exposed when cut into, poked out from several spots, one of which was tinted red with blood. Ava whimpered and perused him further, hardly able to do anything about the anxious crunching of her brows, only made worse when she moved her gaze lower, over his thighs, one which showed yet another slice of fabric and skin and a corresponding wet stain all around that area.

"John...?" she breathed, stepping closer, between his open thighs, lifting the skirt of her léine to use as a rag but not knowing which blood to address first. "What—" she began, pressing her skirt against his arm.

"He would nae die, that last one," he said mildly, mayhap a wee bit dazed from blood loss.

"Sweet Jesus," she whimpered. Keeping her hand and her skirt firm against his arm, she stood on tiptoe and slid her hand around his neck, pulling his head closer to peruse the gash there, on his left side, another slice which produced another moan from her.

"Looks worse than it is," John rasped, his breathing jagged.

Ava lowered herself and turned to address Henry first, finding him bloody as well but not so drenched as John, and then Innes, to whom she said, "We need to find or get some place to tend these wounds."

While Innes and Henry nodded, John downplayed his injuries. "We need simply to get gone from this area."

"John, you canna ride in this condition, nae far or fast," Ava cautioned firmly, laying her hand against his still-heaving chest to steady herself and keep pressure on his arm. "You will only lose more blood."

John lifted his uninjured arm and collected the hand laid against his bloody brigandine, turning it around in his until their fingers were interwoven once more. "It's done, Ava," he said when she met his steely midnight gaze. "That's all that matters."

"Nae, John. 'Tis nae all that matters." She stopped what she was doing and pulled to have her hand freed, backing out of the embrace of his legs. She bent, wanting to tear strips from the hem of her chemise, but her shaking hands could not manage to make a single tear. Straightening and turning, she presented the that hem to Innes, who stood closest, not caring that she revealed her hose-clad legs from the lower thigh and down. "I need strips torn," she said.

Innes reacted instantly, coming to her aid, rending the fabric with ease, once and then again when Ava asked for another. She tied one around the gash in John's arm, saying over her shoulder, "Innes, those lights we saw before, that keep. That's where we need to go. We can beg respite there."

"Aye," he surprised her by agreeing so readily. "Henry, there," he said next, behind Ava so that she imagined he was showing the lad where that place was.

"Naught to lose by approaching and inquiring," Henry surmised, allaying Ava's other fears for how strong he sounded.

Next Ava tied the second torn strip around John's large thigh. "This piece is too narrow for either your leg or the gash there. Will nae be much help," she told him. Briefly, she surveyed that sloppy handiwork and met John's gaze.

For a moment, she melted with the letdown of so many fraught emotions, trying to read his hooded gaze, believing she saw at this moment what was most true, a well of poignant sentiments there, surely mirrored in her gaze. She felt that she could not look at him without her heart in her eyes anymore, not after tonight, and she chose to believe what stared back at her was the same, intent, earnest, brimming with tender sentiments.

Boldly, as she'd only ever been since she'd met him, she laid her palms against his cheeks and kissed his lips. She closed her eyes and silently offered a prayer of gratefulness as she did so, another round of weepiness forthcoming. 'Twas but a fleeting and heartfelt kiss, though she was sure he would understand that it was painted with more than only appreciation.

"A reckoning yet needs to come, lass," he said softly to her when she pulled her mouth from his, the hand of his good arm yanking at her hair to keep her close, so that their faces were but inches apart. "For leaving Lismore."

She owed him nothing, she knew, in that regard. Though his departure had been nobler, answering the summons of his king, her withdrawal from Lismore had not been without its own merit. But she would not argue this with him now.

"Can you ride?" She asked him.

"Aye, but ride with me. You'll have to take the reins."

Ava had never controlled a horse before, but she didn't fear she could not do so now. John would be with her.

As John rose to his feet, Henry appeared with his laird's steed, advising Ava to mount first, giving her a boost with one hand, in which she put her foot. She took the reins and waited while Henry then helped his laird gain the saddle, throwing his leg over and plopping down immediately behind Ava. His arms circled her, and he collected the reins from her after all.

"I can manage, with your back here to keep me upright," he said, sounding a tad weaker now, possibly for the slight exertion of climbing onto the destrier's back.

Ava did not balk, knowing she'd have had to make up as she went along how to move and guide a horse.

But she did not give up authority completely.

"And we're walking, Henry," she instructed when he began to lead the four of them from the ruins, "nae meaning to let more blood by any slapdash galloping."

"Aye, lass," Henry concurred without argument. "Innes," he called backward, his voice not above conversational, "watch our backs."

"Aye," came his agreeable reply.

Chapter Eighteen

The lights they'd spied from the ridge which housed those ruins turned out to be a vast holding which included a large keep surrounded by a formidable curtain wall, inside of which they'd spied many more structures than only the tall keep. Outside the wall sat a row of cottages and barns and more than one two story dwellings, all neatly built in a straight line on the north side of the lane leading up to the fortress, more burgh-like than rural looking, though clearly this was not a chartered town.

Now well past midnight, but not yet close enough to dawn for even the farmers to have risen, the settlement was silent, the clop of their four steeds the only noise made or heard.

Occasionally John leaned heavily against her, until he seemed to catch himself and straighten, taking his weight off her back. She thought she might rather have ridden as she did with Innes, behind him, with her arms around his middle, holding him up.

No sentry or any other person was seen atop the wall so that Ava wondered if any had even realized their coming.

Knowing Henry's bloody visage might not be well-received, nor Innes' often surly countenance, Ava slid off the horse, hopping down to the ground, and walked toward the gate.

"Ava, *Jesu*, wait," John said, his voice bleary, she decided, which only imbued her with greater purpose.

"You canna—" Innes began.

"I can," she amended for him. "Am I nae the most unthreatening?" Ava asked.

She walked up to the gate, which was truly naught but a door, but a few feet taller than herself, and thwapped her palm several times against the smoothed-by-time wood. When nothing happened, she did it again after a moment.

After another few seconds, and just when she'd moved her hand to knock again, a tiny door inside the door, one Ava had not noticed, opened before her eyes.

Startled by this, and by the scowling eyes leering at her through that face-sized space, Ava took a step backward.

"Wat?" Was queried brusquely by the man behind the eyes.

"I-I have the laird of Blacklaw Tower, Sir John Craig, with me. We are in need of—"

"We're nae a hostel nor an abbey, lass." The miniature door was summarily closed in her face.

Frowning at his rudeness, Ava slapped again at the wood.

The wee door once more was swung open. "Wat?"

"I've just said we are in need of assistance," she snapped at him.

"And I've said, have I nae—" he began, even as he started to shut the peephole again.

Ava pushed her hand against the hinged wood. "Listen to me, you fool," she demanded. "I have a faithful knight of the king here, in dire need of care. You will cease with this—"

"Wat king?"

Ava gasped, having not considered this, that she might have found the abode of an English sympathizer. Before she considered what he might *need* to hear to see them allowed entry, the truth was spat at him. "There is only one king, Robert de Brus."

This gave the man pause. He straightened in the door's spyhole and peered starkly at her, his face filling the whole of the opening. His gaze went over her shoulder, to where no doubt the shadowy figures of her party were noticed.

"The Lion of Blacklaw Tower," she ventured bravely, "is wounded and in need of care."

His gaze returned to her, and with a harried look that hinted that he didn't care so much about their allegiance or their troubles, but more about his interrupted slumber, he harrumphed, "Needs the mistress' say so."

"Then please advise your mistress that we have come, seeking succor," Ava instructed tartly, even as she understood in no way did she look the part she played, that of imperious harridan.

A quick nod was followed by the little door once again closing in her face.

Ava returned to John's side and addressed him and the others. "He is fetching the mistress." She surveyed John's face, taking note of his pallor.

Before she made herself distraught with what the bare torchlight showed, John advised in a mild and quiet tone, "Needs but a wee ministration, and mayhap a spot of whiskey if this house deigns to offer so much, to see me right."

Ava doubted that was all, but as he sat straight and tall yet in the saddle, her concern did not intensify overmuch.

'Twas no more than a few minutes before the door opened, the large, entire door this time and not only that inhospitable peephole.

And before the four people awaiting possible charity stood a half dozen men-at-arms, standing in a straight line, three and three with a space between the men in the center. The man who'd first peeped through the door stood now just at its edge, having pulled it open all the way, still holding the heavy latch.

A woman appeared then, walking to take up the space apparently left just for her, between her sentinels. Ava's mouth hung open as she stared at the woman. Good heavens, but what a glorious creature.

She was not particularly tall but appeared somehow willowy, her hair flowing loose around her shoulders, so little of it contained in the hood of her mantle. Her eyes were large and round, which gave her an air of innocence while her bearing and her armed retinue lent her an air of great authority. Ava nearly gasped at the richness of her garb, as the mantle in which she was draped was of deep burgundy velvet, decorated with gold braiding, the entire hem of it embroidered with golden threads detailing vines and thistles.

The woman stepped forward, which prompted her castle guard to take a few steps forward as well.

Ava narrowed her eyes, taking note of the cream colored cotton hem of her gown and dainty slipper peeking out from under the hem of her long surcote. She'd have wagered ten pence, is she had it, that the woman was yet garbed in only her nightclothes, had simply wrapped herself in the outer mantle to disguise this.

"You are a knight of Robert Bruce?" She asked first, stunning them all with her very English voice.

But the man at the gate had clearly spoken in a rough Scots' accent. Ava thought, trying to convince herself this house was safe.

John dismounted, not without difficulty, and came to stand beside Ava.

"I am," he said.

The woman, certainly of no more years than as many as Ava could claim, glanced between John and Ava, and sent her wide-eyed gaze over Henry and Innes. Returning her attention to John, she raised her chin and pronounced, "I need to speak to the king on a most urgent matter. I am willing to offer you respite here at Gladstone if you will promise to convey me to your king upon your recovery."

John scoffed at this, sounding much stronger than he appeared just now. "I'll nae be bringing any stranger into the king's company."

Ava thought he meant, any *English* stranger. Reflexively, she grabbed at his arm, meaning to suggest he employ a more pleasant tone, while he yet needed help.

"Fair enough," the woman said evenly, "but then I am afraid I cannot assist you. God be with you, sir." She waved her hand and the man at the door began to push it closed.

"Wait!" Ava called, rushing forward two steps, drawn up short by more of those guardsmen moving in reaction, forward and with their hands reaching for their swords. A similar set of noises was heard behind her, and she imagined John, Henry, and Innes, standing poised as these men did. "Please," she begged, meeting the young woman's gaze. "We mean no harm. We need only one night. We're happy for anything you might offer us, a place in your stables would be fine. I just want to clean and bind his wounds."

"How did he come by those injuries?" She asked.

Ava frowned at this, her mouth opening without sound for the second time in as many minutes. She decided that nothing but the truth would serve her now. "I...I was imprisoned by the sheriff of Lanark. He freed me, and suffered...this," she said, waving her hand backward at John, "because of me. Please."

The torchlight was not great, but it spilled generously onto this woman's face. And for one fleeting moment, until the woman schooled her expression to that virtuous haughty mien again, Ava could have sworn that she saw a melting something, a wistfulness, possibly for what John had dared and risked for Ava.

"Please," Ava implored again, clasping her hands together at her chest. "But one night and we'll be on our way. Mayhap a message can be delivered to the king."

The woman moved her large eyes again to John. Her shoulders lowered ever-so-slightly, as if she'd forced them up and back until now.

"The Lion of Blacklaw Tower should not be subjected to the miserly despair of the stables," she said, "as if he were not so grand as his legend. Come."

And she turned and walked away. Two of her soldiers followed her as she retreated to the interior of her keep while the others relaxed their rigid stances.

Ava's eyes widened and she turned and showed John her delight in a gaping smile.

He nodded, but did not smile, and turned to retrieve his destrier.

"I'll get 'im," Innes said, swiftly dismounting and coming to take those reins.

With that, Ava and John strode forward to enter the keep.

Inside the wall, the yard was vast, and as previously noted there were several outbuildings, in addition to the large castle itself, which was comprised of two towers, joined by a sprawling three-story keep that was nestled against the south wall and then turned a corner and stretched to meet the tower at the east wall.

'Twas more grand than even the castle at Lanark, expansive and well-kept.

They walked up a short span of buttressed steps and through a door that put them immediately into a great hall, gloomy with shadows at this time of night. The left wall of the hall was dominated by a huge and wide staircase of gorgeously carved wood, which lifted onto the minstrels gallery and what Ava might presume were the family's quarters.

The gorgeous woman stopped in the center of the hall, beneath a broad hanging candelabra where only three of the many tapers were lit at this time.

"I will advise the kitchen staff to bring water and bandages and salves," the woman said.

"Oh, no. Please do not wake anyone," Ava said in rebuttal. "We dinna want to be a bother. I can do all that if you point the way to the kitchens."

"'Tis of little bother," said the woman. "Sir John, are you able to climb the stairs?"

He nodded. Ava thought John's color actually looked much less alarming in this soft light inside the hall and wondered if only the gray gloom of night had tinted his skin that sickly gray.

"Remain with your man then," said the woman, addressing Ava. "I will check on you after I've spoken with Marsail."

Ava did not correct her on this mischaracterization, but said, "I dinna ken your name. I dinna ken who to give my gratefulness."

"I am Catherine Dersey—" she began.

"Lady Catherine," her loyal henchman put in.

"Pray do not be pretentious, Sachairi. These people have other matters on their minds."

"I am Ava, my lady, and we do heartily give you thanks," Ava said while the old soldier threw a look of chastisement at his mistress.

With a nod, the woman departed by way of a door under that grand staircase.

"Your men will be housed in the barracks," said the man called Sachairi. He was mayhap half a century in age, of average height even as he projected an air of giant purpose in regard to his lady's security.

The next half hour passed by in a whir. Sachairi shepherded them to a chamber on the second floor, in the south wing of the keep, where a bevy of household servants soon appeared, sadly but likely roused from their beds, bustling about the room, lighting a fire in the hearth, setting up supplies on the bedside table, taking stock of their patient, one pronouncing him, "in need, but nae dire," which put Ava wonderfully at ease.

Ava, wanting to do for John herself, but finding that she was only in the way of these very efficient middle-aged women, was backed further and further away from him. She stood near the door now, able to see only snippets of John as three women stood around him while he sat on the side of the bed.

She was startled by a hand on her shoulder.

She turned to find Catherine Dersey, garbed now in a fabulous frock of midnight blue, her sandy blonde hair tied into a knot at her nape.

"Ava," she said with a bright and welcoming smile, "let us see to the insults to your person now."

Ava slapped her hand between her breasts. "Oh, no, I'm nae harmed at all, my lady."

"Perhaps not physically, but surely you would enjoy a reconstitution."

"A reconstitution?"

"A freshening." Lady Catherine clarified.

Ava's expression and shoulders softened with no small amount of delicious joy at the very idea.

"Nae, I will do it," they heard John say to those hovering women. Barked, actually. "Leave it."

Ava turned back to the interior of the chamber, just in time to see John stand, rising as a phoenix amid those three crowding women, one of whom held a pair of scissors. As he began to lift his brigandine over his head, Ava moved to help him, sure his wounded arm did not make even so simple a task easy. She was surprised to find Lady Catherine's hand on her arm, holding her back. The lady's gaze was on John, even as Ava turned to question this interference. Lady Catherine shook her head, silently advising Ava to surrender John to the management of those surely able women.

Ava pivoted again, facing John once more, at the same time he doffed his tunic.

Stricken, she stared unabashedly at his broad naked torso, at the dark mat of hair on his chest, at all the rugged beauty of sinew and flesh and bone. All else, people and damages and circumstances, faded from awareness. Ava saw naught but him. Eagerly, her eyes traced each ridge of muscular definition, over his broad shoulders and sculpted arms, down across his flat abdomen and..."Oh, my," Ava whispered.

"Indeed," Lady Catherine said on a breathy exhale.

They seemed to recover themselves at the same time. Ava blinked and Lady Catherine said, "Come."

But this crept into John's awareness. His gaze swung round to the pair at the door. "Nae," he said, "she stays with me."

"I will not take her far, Sir John—"

"Pardon, my lady," he said courteously but firmly, "but you will nae take her anywhere."

"Oh, but he is fierce," Lady Catherine uttered in a whisper at Ava's ear, thankfully not offended by John's obvious mistrust of her or her intentions.

Yes, he is. So fiercely magnificent.

Lady Catherine opened her mouth, possibly to argue further for what she wanted.

"I dinna have any need that canna wait," Ava said first. Truly, she did not want to leave John.

"She stays with me," John reiterated at the same time.

The three woman brought to tend John stared unabashedly at him while he focused his attention on Ava and the keep's mistress. One of those women, with a pale and pinched face, elbowed another and when she turned they widened their eyes at each other, barely bothering to conceal grins, and what Ava supposed might be a universal delight at John Craig's superb physique.

She could find no fault with this, her own reaction having been similar.

"Very well," Lady Catherine finally said. Ava did not know her well enough to say if a smile should have been heard in her tone.

The lady departed once more and Ava, exhausted now, assumed a chair in front of the fire, since her help was not needed. She fought to keep her eyes open, her head lolling against the tall back of the chair, facing the warm fire. At one point, she was briefly startled by John's scolding of one of those servant women.

"If you reach again for my blade, woman, you'll find yourself at the wrong end of it. It stays where it is."

For some time, here and there, noises from somewhere outside this chamber caught Ava's attention. After more than a quarter hour had passed, she was surprised to see a door on the inside wall of this chamber open and the mistress of the house return via that entry.

"I have brought the reviving to her, Sir John," Catherine Dersey said, waving her hand through the door. "Does this, then, meet with your approval?"

John stood and walked through while Ava remained in the large chair, frowning with curiosity. John was still impressively bare-chested, but his face was perfectly clean now, devoid of all that blood. His arm was bandaged in clean linen strips and his sword was not on his person but leaned against the side of the bed. When John returned he nodded at the lady of the house and offered his thanks, and then advised, "But leave the door ajar."

"Yes, sir," said Catherine Dersey, sounding once more as if laughter was hidden behind her words. "Come along, Ava. His Mightiness has granted you a boon."

Ava's curious frown was not abolished, but after a nod from John, she stood and followed Lady Catherine into the adjoining room. There, in a chamber similarly appointed as the one John occupied, sat a tall copper tub, blessedly filled with steaming water and situated directly in front of a freshly made fire.

"Oh," Ava sighed with a delicious joy. "For me?" She asked of Lady Catherine. At the woman's nod, Ava did not mind succumbing to a bit of her own fawning. "You are an angel of mercy, my lady."

This, the young woman found most amusing, said her rich laughter. How different she was already from that stiff and imperious young woman who had greeted them at the gate. "How silly you are to fuss so gratuitously over a bath," Catherine Dersey remarked. "But then, how silly is your man to fuss so needlessly over your safety. Is he always like that?"

"I-I dinna ken. I only just met him a short while ago."

This seemed to shock the woman, until she frowned and then nodded, as if coming to some conclusion. "I suppose that does make the most sense. The blush of new love and all that. Most beguiling. So you've only just met him recently, you are both grossly besotted with each other, and that is why he came to your rescue and then you stood up so fiercely for him, to have the gate opened and he admitted. And of course, the warrior in him—protector, defender, all that—he is not about to let you out of his sight. Would that every girl had such a champion."

This, Ava decided, was the difference. *Girl*.

At the gate, they'd met Lady Dersey, the young woman of stiff haughtiness, allowing strangers to imagine or know little of her. Here, inside now, and though barely more than strangers yet, Catherine Dersey was simply a girl, one who—not unlike Ava—had been enthralled by John Craig's splendid form, and now was envious of one thing she believed Ava had—a champion in John—that she did not.

Regarding everything else supposed in her statements, Ava decided she would have to evaluate those at another time. Right now, she continued to stare with longing at the steamy water of the bath.

"Oh, dear, and look at me havering on." Lady Catherine went to the door between the two chambers and moved it until it remained open but a few inches. Returning to ava, she urged, "Come, I will assist you if you do not mind."

"Mind? My lady, I—you should nae be—" she paused when the beautiful creature waved a dismissive hand at her.

"Pray do not be troublesome with any odd notions about what I should or should not do. We are of an age, are we not? Both female, with naught to distinguish us but the names of our parents?"

Ava knew this absolutely was not true. They were as different as night and day. Before she would have stated this, another bark from John erupted from the next door chamber. "God's teeth, woman! Do you wish to cleanse it or are you meaning to scrub until the slice is deeper still?"

Ava covered her gaping mouth at his outburst.

Catherine Dersey grinned anew and pulled Ava nearer to the tub.

"I fear I will befoul both the glorious water and the tub itself," Ava protested yet, but only mildly now, wanting both the bath and this woman's company more than she did not.

With a pointed look from the unexpectedly gracious lady, which Ava read to mean *chose yea or nae*, Ava nodded and began to undress.

"We are not so different," Lady Catherine asserted again, taking from Ava the léine she'd doffed, "both put into untenable circumstances that require might and well-connected...protectors. The lot of a woman, I suppose."

Ava removed her worn and torn chemise and then her old, threadbare hose and shoes. Only mildly discomfited by her nakedness, Ava slipped into the tub and considered the lady's remark, and her earlier request of an audience with the king.

"Lady Catherine, I believe this bath and your attendance brim with purpose, do they nae?" Ava asked with some suspicion, even as she wondered if she were possibly already lulled into agreeability by the splendor of the heated, rose scented water.

Lady Catherine collected a pitcher and returned tub-side and beseeched with some seriousness. "As I have extended aid to your man, will you not now give me the opportunity to plead my case? I must get to the king as quickly, as soon as possible. All may seem well and good inside this manse, my friend, but I must express to you how imperiled my life is at the moment."

Twas not only the glory of the bath that unfurled Ava's sympathy and willingness to listen. Immediately she was struck by some memory, of herself on more than one occasion over many years, wishing she had but one person to listen to her, to champion her cause when all seemed so desperate and desolate.

"Please tell me what I can do to help," she said, knowing it was the right thing to do.

Chapter Nineteen

When those women finally left, John listened carefully for sounds in the next chamber. For a long time, he heard only the murmur of voices, Ava's and the Lady Catherine's. He had no idea what two people who'd only just met could possibly have to say to each other at such length.

He'd learned his lesson once though, so that he did not consider even for one minute barging into that chamber while Ava might yet be about her bath. He'd had his own, or rather something like it, those heavy-handed women subjecting him to a good scrubbing from a basin and cloth, as if he were naught but an invalid. In truth, his arm and thigh ached annoyingly, but neither wound was so grievous that he couldn't have washed himself. He forgave them all their militant severity—treating him no better than a stained pair of breeches whose blemishes needed a harsh scouring with rocks and gravel—since he'd been offered a tray of bread and cheese and a flagon of wine when they were done.

He paced for a while and then went close to the door and called out, "Ava?" when the voices lowered even more.

"I'm here," she called back from the other side of the door. "A few more minutes, if you please."

He pictured her inside that tall copper tub he'd spied earlier, pictured her fair skin and dark hair splayed about her shoulders. This, of course, provoked the memory of that time he'd stumbled upon her at the crone's cottage, fresh from her bath. He closed his eyes and let the memories flood him, every inch of her naked flesh, as he'd seen it then, supple and silky, her breasts proud and taut, her expression wholly mesmerizing in its innocence. Even now, weeks away from that night, his hand fisted at his side for what he denied them on that occasion.

He was put in mind of that first night he'd met her, or had seen her since they had not met, had not spoken even one word to each other. And then as he'd seen her the morning of the hanging, so striking when she'd turned down her hood and revealed herself to him. Had that been the moment he'd realized her destiny and his would forevermore be entwined?

Had he known that? Is that what he'd been fighting against all this time?

He was returned to the present when other voices—decidedly male—were heard murmured next door. He did not hesitate then to push open the connecting door Lady Catherine had left ajar.

'Twas merely lads emptying and removing the tub, he was relieved to see. One of those hatchet-faced women who'd tended him was here as well, gathering up towels and linens, already having in her arms what John recognized as Ava's discarded clothing.

Ava sat upon a small stool, dressed in borrowed clothes, fine enough that he must suppose they belonged to the young lady. The lady herself stood behind her, combing out Ava's long, damp hair.

"There you are, and you look much improved," said Lady Catherine, having realized his hovering by the door.

Ava lifted her face to his, her lips parting in a warm smile, one of appreciation he thought, that he was none the worse for wear. And he was struck right then with an urgent need to say something to her, something powerful, something that would alter the course of their lives, he was sure, but he didn't yet know what those words were. Or, they were there, but scrambled in his brain and not meant for mixed company.

"Your color is so much better than earlier," Ava commented when he said nothing.

Apparently, healthy color was measured by the hue of one's chest, as that was where her green eyes rested.

"How do you feel?" Ava asked, finally dragging her gaze upward to meet his.

"Improved," he said, and then inclined his head toward the Lady Catherine, "and we have you to thank for such generosity of spirit."

The impudent young woman set down the comb and tilted her head at John, lifting her brows with expectation. "A generosity I might hope to have returned."

Aye, he might have guessed as much.

"But might we speak about all that on the morrow?" Ava asked, coming quickly to her feet. "Or, in fact, later today?"

"Of course," said the woman, who then proceeded to shoo all the busy persons out of the room. With a conspiratorial wink at Ava—which elicited a frown from John—Lady Catherine closed the door behind her, leaving Ava and John alone in this chamber, in which he supposed she would spend the night.

Ava did not move, but fidgeted with the ribbons of her nightrail, the open expression he'd first come upon gone with those people or lost to the intimacy of this situation. While she couldn't now meet his gaze, he let his wander over her, finding her feet bare and the fabric of a shift and nightrail both thin enough to show that her nipples were peaked high upon her chest.

"Amid all the turmoil of this night," she said, "I did not thank you for once again coming to my rescue. Truth be told, I hadn't..." she paused and blushed furiously, and her eyes darted off him completely, "I had no faith you would come."

"You worried Innes or Hamish would nae find me?"

She shook her head, closing her eyes.

John stared at her, understanding dawning. He said nothing aloud, but surely his face showed a man made sorrowful by this knowing, by what she'd thought.

He'd known from the moment he entered this adjoined chamber and had found her sitting so beautifully upon that small stool, her smile natural when she saw him, that he wouldn't be returning to that other chamber tonight. Without a word, he closed that door, and thought to ask something he'd wondered about for quite some time.

"Why did you risk yourself? That first day, at the gallows?"

Ava briefly bit her lip. "I told you, I could not have someone die for me."

"That's nae why you climbed those steps," he said as he closed the main door all the way, sorry that there was no latch to lock. Facing her again, he lifted a brow and waited.

"It is," she said to his dirty leather brogues and the wool of the breeches covering his knees, gorgeously flustered now. "I couldn't live with myself if something had—"

"That's nae why you kissed me."

She turned her back to him, suddenly unwilling to have him see her agitated blush, even as she must know he'd been witness to the bewitching event several times already.

"Why, Ava?" He stepped closer, close enough to take hold of the end of one long lock of her brilliant auburn hair, twirling the silken tress in his fingers.

"Because of the way you looked at me that night at the granary."

"How did I look at you?"

"I dinna...I can nae explain it. I felt it, though. And then you smiled at me—the most ridiculous response when you've just caught a thief—"

"Ava—"

She drew a breath, and answered on the exhale, rushed and agitated. "You looked stricken, but happily so, as if you ken me or...as if you wanted to. Nae one has ever looked at me like that before." Before he could have reacted to that, she whirled around, a wee startled to find him so close. "And why did you come for me tonight?" She asked, breathless now.

"Because of this," he said, dragging her against him by pulling at the ribbons at her neck.

He traced the soft fullness of her lips with his tongue before he covered her mouth with his. Their bodies reacted at once, in synchrony, sparks shooting through his blood while Ava shuddered against him and tipped her face up to him.

He deepened the kiss at once, the time for soft and sweet long gone, his need and want a fearsome combination. He molded her lips to his, as if to commit them to memory, and used his tongue to great effect, sweeping deep inside her mouth, catching her moan of surrender. He slid his hands down along her sides, biting his fingers into her hips to bring her hard against him, crushing her firm breasts against his bare chest. He strayed from her succulent lips and left a trail of kisses down the column of her throat and up to her ear, pulling gently at the lobe.

"For this alone?" She asked, her hands threaded in his hair, her voice husky with desire. "Just a kiss?"

"More than a kiss," he said, still about that business before he stopped and parted just enough to meet her hooded green eyes. "More than any of the dozens of kisses about to come this night," he answered, backing her toward the tall bed. "But allow me to speak with my kiss, for it will be far more eloquent than my words."

She did, and he claimed her lips again, feeling as much devoured as *the* devourer, for how achingly sweet was her response. But he was given pause again, feeling her small hands at his chest, pushing rather than clinging.

"Why did you leave Lismore and not ask anything of me?" She asked when their lips touched no more. "I would have stayed, I would have waited, if you'd but asked."

John stared with a certain severity at her, no more eager at this moment than any other to reveal—or remind her—of certain truths. But the time for truth was here and now.

"I went to my king, Ava. I did nae ken if I would come back. A return is nae ever guaranteed. 'Twould nae have been fair or kind of me to have asked as much from you."

"That is only half the truth, is it nae?" She asked, her chest heaving against his, still so tight in his arms.

John ground his teeth for a moment. *All* the truths, apparently, would come now. "I dinna want to be beholden to any, nae you most of all, to have my mind so befuddled by someone as to cause me mischief and mayhem upon the battlefield."

"Ah," was all she said to that.

John released her, a huge sigh escaping.

"I feel as if that should anger me," she said, her hands sliding down his arms as he backed away. She clasped his hand at the end, drawing him near. "But it does nae."

Panting a bit, John asked, "Why nae?"

"I dinna claim to understand you, John Craig, and I ken you dinna want to be...obliged to any, nae in any way, but I ken mayhap you've realized what I have: it's simply stronger than I am, this need for you."

Jesu, but is nae that the truth!

"And I'm done fighting a battle I can nae win," she said next.

There was nothing he could do about the fierce look upon his face then, not while exhilaration roared inside him. With a low growl, thankfulness married hotly with passion, he yanked her against him once more and consumed her with a brutal kiss.

"But your arm," she murmured against his lips after a moment, "and your leg."

"Hurt like the devil and I dinna care," he rasped against her flesh. "Too long has this been in my mind."

"But—"

"Hush," he persisted. "Kiss me."

***

Ava scarcely knew herself, this wanton in his arms but decided swiftly enough that she liked her. For too long, she'd accepted too readily all that was wrong in her life, trying to make it seem right. This was right, she just knew it. Being with John was right. She refused to let some warped voice in her head try to convince her now that it was wrong. Or that she was not worthy of it.

She allowed herself to be walked backward again, felt the side of the bed meet with her calves. Deftly, John bent and scooped her up and gently laid her on the massive bed, joining her and mating their mouths once more only seconds later. His hand snaked between her back and the plump feather mattress, stroking downward until one half of her rounded bottom was in his huge hand. He squeezed, drawing her against his rigid frame, until she was conscious of the hardness of his erection pressing hotly against her thigh. Ava wrapped her arms around him, pulling him closer, leaving no room between for ambiguity. And oh, how wonderful it was to be in his arms in this way, and he sculpted so perfectly that pure adoration seemed barely a skip away from her present infatuation.

Ava arched her aching breasts against him and met his tongue stroke for stroke, her mind incapable of making sense of all—every blessed thing—her body felt. He wedged one knee between her legs and covered her heavily, the weight and firmness of him a glorious thing. Resistance never entered her mind. Surrender was so easy, so satisfyingly easy.

"Take everything off," he commanded, his voice low and filled with need, shrouding her as the steam of the bath had earlier. He paused then, seeming to catch himself. He dug his elbows into the bed on either side of her, his hands on her cheeks. "This dinna come from nowhere, Ava. You ken that." His beloved brown eyes searched her face. "And I ken you feel it, too. But...but if you say nae, I will stop. Or you can say aye, and I will show you how I feel."

He waited, might even be holding his breath, his brown eyes drowning in desire.

Ava was not confused, but for *how* to say what she wanted. "I have never lain with a man, John, but I want to with you. The ache inside me...you ken how to fix it, do you nae?"

"Aye, lass, I do," he said, his eyes shining, crinkling a bit at the corners, same as his mouth did just then. He leaned forward, which shifted all of his body on her, so that she was aware of all of him at once, and said, "The ache is guid, Ava. That's half my job done right there, making you want me."

Ava couldn't help but laugh at this. "I still dinna ken what my role is."

"I will teach you." He surprised her by grinning, announcing quietly, almost reverently, "Apparently you need only to breathe in my proximity, or turn those green eyes on me, or speak so that I might watch your lips move."

Ava gasped at such a revelation. "And," she said, "mayhap you will teach me how to show you how *I* feel?"

"It will be my pleasure, love."

"Everything starts with a kiss, I have already learned," she said, lifting herself to receive his.

This would be the last bit of control she would know. Ava was not sorry and suffered no concern to turn herself over completely to him. In short order, she learned that her hunger never waned, only soared with each touch of his hand or caress of his fingers, or stroke of his tongue.

John shifted again, holding himself up on one arm so she wouldn't bear all his weight. He left her lips and trailed kisses down her neck and to her ear. Ava closed her eyes and ran her fingers over his warm flesh. She felt his fingers in the middle of her chest as he unknotted the ribbon that held her borrowed nightrail together. When it was untied, he separated the sides, urging Ava to withdraw her arms from the long sleeves. While she did this, his hand skimmed over the soft cotton of her nightrail, defining her stomach and ribs and her breasts with his touch. A small sigh escaped her, and he brought his lips back to hers. He took her mouth with greater need, cupping his hand fully over her breast, naught but the soft cotton shift separating their skin. His thumb flicked back and forth over her hardened nipple with tantalizing slowness.

A fervent thrumming fluttered in her stomach and her sex ached with need.

Too soon it stopped. John's hand left her breast and began to bunch up the chemise she wore until many folds were in his hand at her waist. He pushed it upward. Ava abetted his want to have it gone, lifting her bottom off the bed and then her shoulders and head until John had raised the entire length of the fabric over her head, carelessly tossing it aside when all of her was free, leaving her garbed now in only her bright blush and a deep well of nervousness.

The latter was alleviated almost instantly by the look of worship in his gaze as he raked his brown eyes up and down. She smiled for how fierce he looked even now, as fierce as ever until he parted his sensual lips while he stared, showing such pleasure at what he found that Ava lost that one specific worry of hers, that he was so much more magnificent than she. The arms that had initially wanted to cover her naked body now reached for him, clasping at his arms. She'd always thought herself too exotic or unusual looking to be considered even so much as plain bonny, but John Craig's slowly moving, admiring gaze said that to him, she was bonny indeed, and that was all that mattered.

"Simply perfect," was all he said to add to his gaze, and Ava's pulse pounded anew.

His arm encircled her waist, and he drew her roughly against him and they both gasped at the feel of her breasts crushed against his iron-hard chest. She didn't mind the lack of gentleness, felt an urge to have everything all at once as well. He kissed her again, attacking her with renewed fervor, and a furious heat inside her burned much hotter.

He suckled her lower lip and gave her another scorching kiss and his hand slid between their bodies, plumping her breast, finding the nipple and teasing it expertly. Soon, he pushed her deeper into the mattress and lowered himself on her. His mouth replaced his fingers at her breast, arcing his tongue across the bud, then moving onto the other breast, drawing her nipple fully into his mouth, using his teeth and his tongue so that soon she began to writhe under him. A river of molten heat ribboned through her body. It snaked all the way to her fingers and toes and pooled between her legs with an alarming and desperate intensity.

Just when she thought she could stand no more, John lifted his head and sat back on his knees, pulling her legs down on either side of him. Her skin pinkened under his gaze. He touched the fingers of his left hand to her ankle and traced a pattern up her leg, over shin and knee and thigh, his eyes hungrily following. Whisper soft, he skimmed those fingers over the triangle between her legs and up across the flat of her stomach, back to her breasts, just gliding across. Ava held her breath, tormentingly aware of the gooseflesh that followed in the wake of his touch.

He met her gaze, a slight crook of delight turning up one side of his mouth as his hands moved down again.

"I canna get enough, just looking," he rasped, "But damn, Ava, I have to have more."

Shakily, she nodded. Already, this was heaven. More was good.

And then his hand moved between her legs, already parted by his body sat between them.

Ava had never felt anything so...deliciously naughty in all her life. She saw in her lower periphery the sharp rise and fall of her own chest.

"Oh," was all she said when his fingers stroked like a feather over her womanhood, other words escaping her presently. And then, "Oh," given now lower, deeper, as his fingers moved beyond the curls between her legs to caress her. As if they had a will of their own, her legs fell open to him, and his fingers moved further, to the very center of her. Ava squirmed against his hand, her eyes closed as the blissful torment built. She whimpered softly and arched her back as John slid one finger inside her, his own growl deep and satisfying in so many ways. His finger moved in and out of her, which opened her eyes abruptly, likely showing him both her startling innocence and her growing hunger.

The only coherent thought that she could grasp at spilled from her as words. "The ache is guid."

And the threatening grin he'd teased for some time now came full force, beautifying him beyond imagining.

"Aye, love, the ache is guid."

He rose up over her, his finger leaving her but settling with great satisfaction upon that nub where so much feeling lived. Ava's moan of pleasure became one of despair when he took himself entirely away from her, leaving the bed completely.

John stood just at the side of the bed, raking his gaze and then one hand of fingers in the lightest of caresses over her flesh, from shoulder to navel, lighting all kinds of fires. Then he worked at the ties of his torn breeches, giving Ava a moment's pause, being reminded now of his injuries. The bandage around his arm had not earlier been spotted with blood but now it was. She followed the path of his breeches when they were stripped away, meaning to make a judgment about the bandage around his thigh, but her regard never quite made it that far. Instead, her avid gaze was arrested by the sight of his jutting erection. In truth, her gaze was greedy as she made an eager inspection of his manhood, it being inside the pool of firelight. Ava swallowed down a gulp, but knew no fear, only a heightened awareness of what was to come. So then she couldn't help it that she lifted her green eyes to him, allowing all her need to be seen.

"*Jesu*," he murmured and returned to her, joining her on the bed, magnificently touching so many parts of her.

But now he was featherlight in his kiss, again that reverence, of which Ava wanted no part. He nuzzled the hollow of her cheeks and skimmed his lips across her nose to the other cheek before rubbing his lips over her mouth, as if he would learn the shape and texture of them this way. All the while, Ava strained against him, inviting his full possession, her hands moving over him, from his shoulders to his back, over his arms, along his hips, until finally he shifted and settled his weight on her and between her quivering thighs. His shaft probed with unerring devotion at her center and Ava dug her nails into John's shoulders, never having known such a powerful need to be possessed.

"I'm sorry, love, but there's nae a damn thing I can do about the pain," he said, almost choking on the words as he nudged the tip of his erection inside her. He put a hand under her, lifting her hips, and slid further into her tight opening.

Ava groaned with astonishment, not having believed the ache and need and thrill could be multiplied. And just as she wondered what pain he'd spoken of, John thrust forward and made her his, provoking a cry of anguish for the unexpected discomfort. She froze, biting her lip and squeezing her eyes tight while he went still also and dropped his forehead against her.

She didn't think that was it and couldn't believe that all that splendid torture would have ended so disastrously. More than that, she was awash with guilt, afraid to say to John that she no longer liked this very much.

Except that she did. Pain aside, she was connected right now with John as intimately as two people could be, felt closer to him than ever, and his hand was brushing her hair away, his touch so heartbreaking in its tenderness, and he said, "I dinna ken who *they* are but they say it only hurts the first time," and a small laugh came unbidden from her.

John shifted, flexing his shaft inside her and Ava gasped, not unaware of a small pain but more conscious of other sensations.

"It gets better then?" She asked with some hope, able to open her eyes now, finding his tender gaze upon her.

He kissed her lingeringly and then nodded against her. "Much better."

"Move like that again," she requested.

He did so in small, leisurely increments. John levered himself upward a wee bit and grabbed her hips to show her the motion and she matched his pace. There was pain, but it was small compared to the pleasure. Her body welcomed him, tightening around him, the sensation as titillating as it was satisfying. In and out he moved, his arms and shoulders rippling with corded muscles, his face etched with need. Ava kissed him feverishly and rocked with him while blood rushed to every corner of her body.

John reached between them, his fingers finding that nub where lived so much pleasure and began to stroke skillfully. Something wild and wicked grew inside her, sharp and greedy and growing, until it burst upon her. She was inundated with tickling heat and a toe-curling storm of bliss and cried out against his hot flesh before dropping her head back upon the mattress.

While he hovered above her, his body thrumming and teeth clenched as he moved in and out, he held her astounded gaze, and Ava continued to shudder with delight, her nails digging into his skin. She brought her eyes back to his, bright with excitement, her expression wondrous, awestruck. John grunted and surged hard inside her. He pressed his lips to her, smothering his own low growl as he exploded inside her.

Filled with the feel of him, the taste of him, the scent of their coupling, she closed her eyes, still shaken. Against her lips, he murmured, "Jesus bluidy Christ."

Neither moved.

Minutes passed in the silent aftermath of warmth and intimacy. John's breath fanned against her ear as his face was buried there.

Ava closed her eyes, nearly trampled by the sentiments raging through her now. She dug into them but could find no remorse. It should be there, she thought initially. Quite easily, though they were new, she recognized the physical reactions, the still-thundering passion, the tingling in all of her limbs, the heat coursing still through her, that particular fullness and throbbing at her woman's place. But while her emotions just now were a jumble, she could barely decipher any negative. Surely that must follow what they had just done, shouldn't it?

Nae, she concluded instinctively and suddenly. This was right, as she'd guessed it would be.

John withdrew from her and collapsed at her side, drawing her up against him. He grazed his hand along her sides, skimming his fingers over the curve of her hip and the sides of her breast. Ava laid her hand against his chest, still rising and falling. She felt him press a kiss into her hair.

"I dinna ken what it is, what I feel when I'm with you," he said. He paused for quite a moment before adding, "But I ken I dinna want to be without you, lass. You belong with me, Ava."

A heartfelt smile curved her lips before she answered. "Aye, I do. I dinna ken love, nae in all my life," she told him. "But this feels like what it should be."

Ava nestled snugly against his chest. And oh, what beauty was found there, just being in his arms. She understood a person never missed what they'd never had, but she knew just then what appealed to her now, the quiet companionship, the thrill of not being alone. How remarkable, she thought as she dozed off. A tiny flower of contentment blossomed inside her.

Chapter Twenty

His arm and leg ached yet, and his head throb where he'd been knocked against the hard ground last night during the skirmish that netted their freedom. Despite this, John had gone to sleep knowing he would like to explore more of Ava, and *with* Ava. Though neither of them had long been able to keep their eyes open last night, he'd had some idea that he would have liked to wake leisurely and open her eyes with his touch and his kiss. Last night had been but a prelude, he knew. An unimaginably delicious introduction to all that was to come. He did not dwell too long on taking himself to task for denying himself what he'd discovered in this bed with Ava last night, what he was sure was comparable to true heaven, what he never wanted to be without.

His wish remained only that, however. Instead, he was wakened by a crisp knock at the door that did not wait on any call for entrance. The door was shoved open, and Lady Catherine showed herself with stacks of fabrics or garments draped over her arm.

She stood frozen, a gasp only half-realized, her pale cheeks reddening quickly, but she made no move to remove herself from the doorway.

John scowled at her, stiffening against Ava, thankful at least that they were well concealed under the heavy counterpane. He pointed abruptly at the door so that she would depart, clamping his lips over the bark that wanted to come, not wanting to rouse Ava this way. Lady Catherine stuttered something unintelligible and deposited the items of clothing onto the small stool, and after one more covert but curious glance at the still-sleeping Ava, she backed out of the room.

When the door closed, he glanced at the closely shuttered window in the room, seeing hints of gray dawn light, but not any other brightness to say that morning was well-advanced. Relaxed once more, but knowing they would have to rise now, he pulled his arm out from beneath Ava and rose up over her. Her lashes fluttered and she mumbled something, shifting onto her back. And John was quite sure that the slow and sleepy smile that evolved while her eyes were yet closed was the most beautiful thing he had ever seen.

He kissed her curved lips, letting his mouth linger over her, until he felt he should inform her, "I fear our presence is requested by the lady of the house."

"Was she just here?" She asked. At his nod against her, she said sleepily, "Thought I heard the door open."

"You are...you dinna mind that she just saw us like this?"

Finally, her eyes opened. She searched his face, as if she might be wondering if he were embarrassed to be discovered like this. "We have nae done anything wrong."

He kissed her again, proud of her resolve. "We have nae." Meaning to get out the news he must share, John said succinctly, "I canna stay. I have to return, Ava, to the king's army, to where I left Magnus."

"And where shall I go?" A hint of worry furrowed her brow.

"We're closer now to where I need to be than we are to either Lismore or Blacklaw."

"Perhaps I should..."

"You belong with me," he said firmly. "Doubly wanted now by the sheriff after last night's escape, I will nae trust your safety to anyone but me, or a larger presence of soldiers."

Ava's expression softened. She lifted her hand and laid it against his whiskered cheek.

"I said as much to Innes but a few days ago. I belong where my heart tells me I belong. That's what propelled me back to Lismore—or rather what my intent was 'fore the sheriff's men caught up with me."

He kissed her leisurely and then forced himself away from her, rolling away and then leaving the bed to dress.

"I ken the lady brought you something to wear," he said idly.

Ava sat up as well but did not leave the bed immediately. Holding the bed linens up over her chest, striking an innocently provocative pose, one he might like to recall at some later date, she worried her lip a wee bit before speaking.

"John, dinna be angry, but I told Lady Catherine you would—wait, dinna make that face—I promised her nothing but that you would listen to her plea."

He ground his teeth, as much loath to deny Ava anything as he was to get involved in affairs that were none of his concern. At the same time, he thought it regrettable that she disturbed his delight at her eager but innocent perusal of his naked body by introducing this now. He strode into the adjoined room and returned with his own clothes, first turning the torn tunic right-side-in before dragging it over his head. "I will listen, but that is all. Ava, I abandoned my position in the king's army," he explained. "Robert Bruce may yet want me in irons, nae listening to me whingeing about some spoiled lady's troubles."

"She is nae spoiled—just the opposite, about to be shackled." She came onto her knees, still holding the bedsheet, and pleaded the lady's case in earnest. "Please, John, just pretend it's me. Any or all of those times in all my life—living as the butt of every jape inside my father's house, taking the abuse heaped by my siblings, those who should have loved me. Mayhap it's me fighting for scraps at Dumfries, 'fore I met Innes, beaten black and blue by someone who thought I'd cut the alms line; it's me, inside the gaol at Carstairs and sleeping on the floor at Dottie Og's with broken ribs for being kicked by her stupid goat. Lady Catherine is me, John, without anyone she can trust, with nae even one person to speak for her."

"Apparently," he said with a hefty amount of distaste, donning his braies and breeches, "she has you now as her mouthpiece."

"And I have you," Ava replied. Her shoulders sank, and for a fleeting moment she looked disappointed in him, which cut hard and deep. "Why bother fighting for Robert Bruce and Scotland if you will nae fight for all of us?"

John sat on the side of the bed, only a foot away from Ava, and began to pull on his boots. "Did she spell out her woe to you?"

"She did."

"And you ken it's worthy, nae of my time, but of Robert Bruce's?"

"I ken you might want to hear what she has to say."

"Verra well, but I make nae promises."

His boots fastened, he turned and considered her and could not contain the wee grin that came. "Dinna be supposing you may—"

Ava laid her finger against his lips, effectively silencing him. "I would have begged your ear for Lady Catherine even had we not shared a bed last night."

Even as he suspected a long and irksome day lay ahead of him, his heart was light right now, and he allowed his grin to expand. "The bedding then was simply...for nae reason at all?"

Ava's grin was exquisitely impish. "I ken there must have been a reason at the time," she said and tapped her forefinger now against her own lips. "For the life of me, I canna recall—"

He moved swiftly, reaching around her neck to bring her to his kiss, devouring her hungrily, about three seconds away from laying her down and stripping himself of his clothes once more. "Does this bring anything to mind?"

Serious again, Ava assured him, "Aye, many wonderful things. It's all coming back to me now."

"I ken as much. Constant reminders, you'll need." He sighed, feigning a weariness at the very idea and then smacked her sweet bottom. "Get dressed. We're off in an hour."

***

Ava blanched and blushed at the telltale stain upon the sheets of the bed before flipping the linens over the evidence, thankful when a servant appeared with a basin of warm water and several cloths. Though the woman had wanted to stay and help with her toilette and dressing, Ava had politely dismissed her kindness, knowing there was evidence also on her own body she needed to erase. Her sensitive skin tingled anew while she'd washed, so many memories evoked of the night passed. Not all could be erased, she was pleased to learn.

John had gone downstairs a few minutes before Ava, meaning to speak with Henry, and might already be outside. Ava had taken a few minutes more to garb herself in the soft cotton kirtle and the very generous gift of a heavy wool léine of rich green. The kind lady had included a pair of hose, the likes of which Ava had never known, sumptuous for their silkiness. Additionally, there had been a pair of shoes, of finely tooled leather in a light fawn color, of a sturdiness and quality that Ava had never thought to touch let alone wear.

Innes was just walking in from the bailey when Ava came into the hall.

She rushed at him and threw her arms around him, kissing his cheek with great affection. "I dinna ken how you managed to find him or...or what that might have cost you, but you will forever have my gratitude."

Innes did not prolong the embrace. "Aye, you've said as much, though you dinna need to. Did you ken I would leave you to hang?"

With a wee distance put between them now, Ava shook her head. "Nae, I dinna. But bear sweetly with my appreciation, Innes. I will be showing it for some time to come."

He rolled his eyes at this, seeming none the worse for wear, either from what surely had been a harrowing week for him or for what he'd thought he'd had to sacrifice, what pride he must have expected to swallow, to be the one compelled to beg help from John. But then she considered his position last night, so firmly entrenched under John's banner that it had been he scolding Ava that they must adhere to John's plan.

"Innes, we are to stay with him for a bit now," she said haltingly, expecting to hear some announcement that he would not, would be again striking out on his own.

Instead, Innes nodded. "Aye, I ken it's safer all told." He blew out an aggrieved breath, as if reluctant to confess what came next. "I have nae business traipsing around a land I ken so little of. Inside a burgh, I am my own, but outside...I yield to my limitations. I can nae more put you at risk."

"Or yourself," Ava insisted. "Stay with me. With us," she amended.

"Aye, for now." He nodded at her and then ambled over to the high table where a small repast had been laid out.

A moment later, Ava was surprised to see John returning to the hall, coming from a doorway under those stairs, holding out his arm allowing Lady Catherine to proceed him, The lady's mouth moved at the speed of light and her man, Sachairi, was directly behind John but upon clearing the door positioned himself once more at his lady's side.

Ava did not move, but kept her distance, trying to read John's expression as he listened to the young woman's plea. As ever—save for so many of those splendid minutes of last night—his scowl was severe. But then a subtle shifting of his expression took place and Ava knew that Lady Catherine would be journeying with them to the king's company. John was clearly angered by the tale Lady Catherine wove for him, but then Ava saw that his teeth were clenched, and his face was overtaken by displeasure, when he realized that his honor would not allow him to leave the lady to the fate being thrust upon her, with naught but that dedicated Sachairi and those few castle guards they been greeted by last night to stand in her defense.

When Lady Catherine finally paused, her shoulders sagging now that her case had been made, John said something to her that had the lady covering her mouth and her spark of delight with her hands.

Ava smiled softly at this.

And then lady Catherine's voice was louder in her excitement. "But I am ready, Sir John—we are!" she hastened to exclaim. "I spent all the last few hours packing and—"

John held up his hand, showing one finger. "You get one satchel, same as any. We're nae taking wagons full, nae a wagon at all, nae retainers or a lady's maid, naught but your chosen men. We're moving fast and light."

This did not deter the woman. She nodded, eager to be compliant. "Give me but five minutes." And she dashed up that elaborately carved staircase, suddenly seeming very young for her zeal, and disappeared from view while John spoke quietly with Sachairi, who nodded his head almost continuously at whatever orders or cautions John was giving.

True to her word, Lady Catherine returned after only a very few minutes had passed, wearing that fine burgundy mantle again and carrying one woven valise. Over her forearm hung another garment, which she thrust into Ava's hands, since she'd come straight to her.

"You must wear this cloak, Ava," she said. "We cannot be meeting the king, our very own Robert Bruce, in anything but our best."

Ava grinned. "Your best, perhaps, lady Catherine."

"If you do not call me Ceit as I've asked so many times by now, we shall not be friends, I fear." She flapped her hands at the mantle she'd thrust into ava's hands. "Go on. Pray do not change your man's mind for keeping him waiting."

Knowing what Lady Cath—Ceit—had walked in on this morning, there was now no point in arguing her assumption of *your man*. "Thank you, Ceit, for...for everything."

"Ava, with Sir John's acquiescence, which I suppose might not have come without his consideration of you, I am now far deeper in your debt than you mine."

Soon, the party that would travel, the Craig party of four and now Ceit's party of three—of course that man, Sachairi, would not let her out of his sight, and he picked one other soldier to travel with them—convened in the bailey where their steeds were waiting.

As soon as Ava stepped outside, draped now in a luxurious woolen mantle of deep gold that would go far toward keeping her warm on what appeared to be a rather frigid day, Innes walked his steed over to her, expecting that she would ride with him as she had since they'd acquired a horse of their own, such as it was, and save for last night when she'd been needed to keep John steady on his.

Ava glanced with unconcealed longing at John, who was cinching something onto the back of his saddle. He lifted his gaze as she'd come into the yard and now called out casually to Innes while he stared at her. "Ava will ride with me."

"Like that now, is it?" Innes asked, aiming his retort at Ava.

But it was John who replied. "It is. Is that going to be a problem?"

Innes drew in a long breath and exhaled slowly. "Nae, sir. Been coming for a while, by my reckoning."

Ava bit her lip, concealing both her joy that Innes had not made a scene and her greater thrill at the prospect of spending all day so close to John.

Ten minutes later, the party marched out through that lone door in Gladstone's wall. Henry led the procession, followed by Lady Catherine and Sachairi, the lady riding side-saddle and adeptly managing her own gray mare. John and Ava followed them, and Innes and Lady Catherine's other man—introduced as Duffie—brought up the rear.

Ava, too, was seated sideways, and happily so, comfortably surrounded by John's strong arms. She was sure she wouldn't care how swiftly they traveled or how rough the terrain. She was more than happy with her circumstance since he used only one hand on the reins while the other was wrapped so snugly around her waistline. She laid her hand over his and wondered however she had been so lucky that night at the granary, to have been met by John Craig.

***

"I ken she would be a bit of trouble," John said in a low voice at Ava's ear when they were an hour into their trek, "so count me pleasantly surprised that she's expressed nae one complaint thus far."

"Why would you ken that about her?"

"Seems a wee high-strung, mayhap fussy and inflexible," he answered, not believing he was too far off the mark on that estimation about the Lady Catherine.

Ava turned her face more toward him so that her words did not travel far. "I ken she's only terrified and possibly at wit's end, but then verra grateful for your help."

John did not challenge this. He'd had some thought over the last hour that if he'd regularly ridden with Ava in his arms like this since first he'd met her, like as not he'd have succumbed sooner to his desire for her, would have been tempted and teased over the edge far quicker.

"Christ, but you feel guid in my arms," he whispered at her ear.

"I far prefer this mode of travel," she said, "so dinna ken you can fob me off on the back of Innes' horse ever again."

"Aye, but I dinna ken what our immediate future holds, Ava," he warned her. "You might be again assigned to Innes, simply to see you removed from the danger that comes so close to so large an army. I'll want you safe, removed to either Lismore or Blacklaw. But aye, so much depends on the king's response to my return."

"Are you worried about his reception?"

"Nae so much. He needs me, needs my army. But aye, if he wanted to, he could make my life woeful for a while for what I've done."

"Will it help if I speak up?"

"I would nae have you speak for me, Ava. 'Twas my decision to come for you—and one I'd make again and again, no matter the cost." He'd leave it at that for now, even as he knew there was much unsaid and unknown between them. Still though, he was unwilling to make promises he wasn't sure he could keep.

Robert Bruce yet had a long fight ahead of him. 'Twould not be any less chaotic as had the last ten years of fighting. And John was determined and proud to be at his side, in whatever capacity, to fight the war for freedom even as he knew his chances of survival were as any man's, unlikely for what the future held for any sword-wielding man.

At John's instruction, Henry led them to where John and his army had last assembled with Magnus, just before they'd ridden into Glasgow. The wind was brisk, but the air and ground were dry, making for a relatively easy march. And going straight west from Gladstone to that location without any derivation north or south saw them arriving well before sunset.

Henry, in the lead, vanished from sight here and there, always wanting to be aware of their surroundings. When they approached where last the Craigs and Mathesons had gathered, Henry came riding back toward the rest of the party. He stopped a hundred yards ahead and thumped his palm three times on the top of his head, his signal clear to John, who waved his hand in acknowledgment.

He was not entirely surprised to learn the king was here, that the parties had joined again. But truth be known, all would have been easier if only Magnus and his army were here, and the king had yet or hadn't any need to learn of John's brief abandonment.. However, the fact that they were yet ensconced here in this same spot in the forest advised John that while something might be brewing as an upcoming action, nothing was imminent, and thus John's short desertion might not be received as overly ruinous.

"What does that mean?" Ava wondered. "Is there trouble ahead?"

"Nae, love," he answered and then spurred his destrier into a trot to catch up with Lady Catherine and Sachairi. "My lady, be advised that it will be best if you do nae speak until or unless the king requests your voice," he cautioned. "And if requested, speak in truth and fact only. Do you ken?"

"I understand, Sir John," replied the young woman, her cheeks brightened with color, though he could not say if that were a consequence of the ride or her sudden anxiety about meeting with the king.

As was his practice, Robert Bruce did not ever show himself straightaway to an arriving party. They were therefore greeted by Magnus and Eachann and several other higher ranking lairds and knights.

One of the first things Magnus said answered what might have been one of John's first questions, since he saw neither Sir James Douglas nor any of the Douglas plaids among those soldiers who showed themselves now.

"The Bruce only arrived this morning," Magnus said, giving John a look that expressed he should feel relieved. "And Sir James has just gone in the last hour, about a wee reconnaissance east of here." With that, Magnus addressed Ava. "I am pleased to see you recovered and sound of body, lass."

Ava nodded her thanks and challenged Magnus a wee bit. "But you do nae seem *surprised* to see me."

Magnus grinned, moving his gaze onto John. "Nae, I ken only hell coming or heaven crumbling would have prevented him from getting you out of there." Next, Magnus tossed his head in Lady Catherine's direction. "What have you there?"

Before John could have answered, the small clearing in the woods where they met was crowded yet more as several others revealed themselves. William Sinclair showed himself only seconds before Robert Bruce did.

John dismounted then, unable to read the king's expression as he moved his gaze, more sharp than curious, over this unexpected party. John brought Ava down from the saddle and turned to address his king.

Without embarrassment, he strode to where the king stood and went onto his knee before Robert Bruce, lowering his head in supplication.

"Rise, John Craig," said the king. "Your worth and your fidelity have never been distrusted." He said this almost peevishly, as if he were angry that John had assumed so meek a position, expecting malice of him. "Your timing and resolution are another matter, but of lesser concern, the former surely out of your hands."

John rose to his feet, standing only an inch or two taller than the king, and met his dark and crisp gaze. "You are gracious in your mercy, sire."

"What I am," Robert Bruce said, still edgy it seemed, "is curious about those you travel with. Now several times I've heard of your green-eyed lass, and her I spy and will want to have dialogue with, and soon. But never let it be said, John Craig, that you have now been rescued by another bonny lass."

"Nae, sire," John said, relief allowing him to grin at the king's smirking supposition. "I bring to you Lady Catherine Dersey from Gladstone Manor." He turned and waved her forward, not surprised when her man made to follow. Magnus stepped in front of the soldier, shaking his head. John said to the king. "I ken your trencher is full just now, crowded with purpose, but I supposed you might want to hear what the lady has to say about her own circumstance, which rather affects our cause."

Robert Bruce lifted a brow at this and turned his gaze to receive Lady Catherine.

She dropped into a slow and deep curtsy, lowering her head respectfully, not rising until the king bade her do so.

"Lady Catherine Dersey," the king repeated. "My lady, forgive me, but I do not know you, or of this Gladstone."

"You do not, my liege," Catherine spoke in a sure voice, "but you will, eventually, if nothing is done to protect it. If my uncles have their way, it will be another forward center in the vast supply chain of the English, arming a war and feeding the men who bring it."

"Explain, if you please," the king requested.

"I am the daughter of Muireach Dersey and Elaina de Clare, sire. My mother, now gone, was the daughter of the Earl of Gloucester. My father passed a few months ago, leaving the Gladstone estate to me." From somewhere within her voluminous mantle she produced a ribbon-tied scroll, which she presented to the king, and continued as he opened and perused that. "My three uncles—brothers to my mother—have informed me that as I have not yet come of age, that they mean not to adhere to my father's wishes, but to petition the English king for his ruling on the matter. They have plans to install me in a convent and split the land between themselves."

Without lifting his knitted-brow gaze from the scroll, the king remarked, "Apologies, my lady, but I fail to see how this can be of consequence to me *at this moment*." He now did lift his dark eyes, laying them on John with some admonition for bringing this case and this woman to him at this time.

John allowed Catherine Dersey to speak for herself, recalling how effectively she'd done so earlier with him.

"Sire, the wealth and importance of Gladstone cannot be understated," she said. "Nor should it be taken for granted, its location and usage. Presently, it serves as a prominent leg in the English supply chain from Carlisle. While my father ailed, my uncles had already turned their allegiance without his knowing, promising much to the English king in the hopes of being in receipt of future favors, most specifically the title to Gladstone and its thousands of acres. As we speak, and which I have shown to Sir John, the crypts of Gladstone are filled to the brim with swords and arms, and casks of wine and whisky, and enough barrels of grains to feed a sizeable army for many months. All of this belongs to the English, and which my uncles voluntarily transport for them."

Robert Bruce again removed his frown from the parchment and transferred it onto the woman. "Your father made you a ward of the crown."

"The Scottish crown, sire. He had some suspicions about the steadfastness of my mother's brothers, expecting duplicity of them."

Robert Bruce grinned at the woman. "And did your father suppose of you this bravery?"

"He knew I was raised by a fearless woman."

"So she must have been, and God willing, such fine creatures are peppered all about my kingdom." He turned and favored Ava with the sudden warmth of his gaze. "And all somehow flocking to John Craig at the moment." Returning his attention to Catherine Dersey, he lifted his brows and rolled the scroll tight again. "Your uncles currently reside at Gladstone? And keep an army there, I presume, to guide and guard these transports?"

"They come and go from Gladstone, sire, but aye, the army in total should be counted in the hundreds, all Scotsmen, most pressed in service to...England and its dead king. Vassals of his son now, I daresay, or soon to be. But I only need to hold Gladstone, to keep—."

The king held up his gloved hand, silencing the young woman.

"Pray, my lady, one more time. Did you say *the dead king*?"

Lady Catherine gasped. "My liege, have you not heard? The Hammer of the Scots, if not already dead, is soon to be."

"How have you been made aware of this, young woman?" Robert Bruce asked in a steely voice. "How can you know something so fantastic when my own spies and messengers do not?"

She lifted her chin, obviously didn't like her integrity being called into question. "'Twas the reason that I implored so strenuously to Sir John now—my uncles had been called to Carlisle, they and their armies, requested to escort either the dying king or his body. My captain, Sachairi, was privy to all this by way of his position. I needed to act now, sire. Will you honor my claim to my own home, my father's wishes? Will you go further, sire," she boldly begged, "and provide me a champion, one who can fend off the armies contracted to my uncles, upon their return to Gladstone? I will have failed both my father and my country if his beloved Gladstone, here in the heart of Scotland, the wealth amassed by my loyalist father, should be confiscated by any greedy English hands."

While all those who watched waited, eyes moving between Lady Catherine and Robert Bruce with quiet alarm and mayhap even kernels of joy for what news she'd shared about the expected demise of the English king, Robert Bruce made up his mind fairly quickly.

"You may keep your Gladstone, my lady," he said, returning the scroll to her. "Here are many witnesses to my decree. And you may have your champion to make sure it stays in your devoted hands. With me now are my most trusted knights, the finest warriors and fiercest hearts in all the realm. Choose your champion."

Lady Catherine Dersey moved her gaze around the closely gathered knights, Magnus and John and Will Sinclair among quite a few others. John nearly rolled his eyes when he saw Simon Stewart actually take a step forward and thrust out his chest, attempting to project an air of worthiness. Either he supposed an easier time defending a keep rather than traveling in the king's company, or visions of luxury and wealth floated before him in the form of Lady Catherine. John had always thought him unexceptional in battle, knowing twenty knights of greater valor and cunning.

John had some suspicion that Catherine Dersey was not any simpleton to choose Stewart. Nae, this one was clever, was as brave as Ava, as cunning as Morvel, as resolute as Lara. John caught sight of the furious twisting of William Sinclair's mouth, while he snarled at Lady Catherine, possibly hoping his malevolent mien might dissuade her from selecting him.

"You vouch for their faithfulness to my cause, sire," Catherine Dersey asked, "which I have vowed I will pledge to your campaign?"

"I do, my lady," assured the now-amused king, that his own cleverness and assurances should be accounted as suspect.

William Sinclair, likewise, standing directly across from John, bristled at her query, that his honor should be called into question.

"I choose him," decided Lady Catherine, pointing her slim finger at Will Sinclair.

"Ah, excellent," said the king. "William Sinclair, he is, my lady. Sir William, will you accept this task in my stead, you and your formidable army? To secure this keep and hold it fast for Lady Catherine, and thus upset that bothersome supply chain of the English?"

John bit back the smirk that threatened to overtake him, when he spied the vein throbbing in Will's temple.

"As you wish, sire," Will Sinclair gave his assent through gritted teeth, sending a feral glare to the woman, who met his hostile gaze and never blinked.

God love her, John thought, because Will Sinclair certainly would not.

***

"She was remarkable, was she nae?" Ava asked sometime later, when they were alone and walking amid the forest, close to camp but far enough away to ensure privacy. "So bold, so daring—just plainly spoke what she wanted, but nay with arrogance or even woefulness, only with a certain surety that right would come her way."

John had to imagine that Will Sinclair might disagree.

"Dinna wish for more boldness, lass," he replied to Ava. "You have your own brand of courage."

"When pressed, aye, I can be courageous," Ava acknowledged. She paused then, in words and motion, compelling John to stop and face her. "But I have not said what I want, not to you," she stated, her green eyes nearly incomprehensible in the darkness. "I want you, John Craig. And I want...to ken something tangible from you. Dinna pacify me with half-truths and promises too lazy to be believed, spouting something so vague as *I belong with you* before you send me away or march off to war."

Charmed by this version of Ava, he suggested, "Then say what it is you want."

"I want to be yours, and you mine. Nae only for now or until some uncertain time, and nae only if or when we are together, but for always."

He did not believe he needed to remind her that his *always* might be but weeks or months.

Give her nothing but whatever her blind trust in you deserves, Morvel had said to him. *Or give her everything.*

He pretended an indifference to Ava's assertion. It had been his intention to seek out her promise before they parted company as they would be forced to do come the morrow, when a small party escorted she and Innes back to Lismore, which was yet so much closer than Blacklaw, where his future bride *should* await him. Robert Bruce would not allow that John take her, he'd already been informed. "Less interested parties should see to the transport," the king had said, "so that a certain faithful knight is not unaccounted for twice in the same week."

"You want that I should appreciate so bold and beautiful a woman," John said to Ava now, "speaking up for herself, claiming what she wants—"

"I dinna only want it, I demand it," Ava said with some force, possibly sensing his submission—indeed, his want— in his words and tone. "All or nothing, John Craig."

"Fair enough," he said, pulling her into his arms. He covered her mouth with his, once more allowing his hungry kiss to inform her of his ravenous yearning for her. "All, love," he said against her lips. "All of me for all of you."

Ava sagged with joy against him, her arms tightening around her waist.

"All our lives, Ava," he added, lest she accuse him again of giving *promises too lazy to be believed*. He lifted his hand between them, settling his palm and fingers over her breast. "And starting now, unless you might worry someone might hear you cry out with pleasure."

Ava tilted her face up to him, smiling her beautiful smile, even as she began to unknot the ribbon of her mantle. "Can you nae simply cover my cries with your kiss?"

John's answering smile was instant and profound, felt deep in his chest. "Aye, I can do that, love."

Epilogue

Blacklaw Tower
Three years later

Blacklaw Tower was built on a promontory that jutted over Loch Breryhill, the expansive castle forming two sides of a quadrangle, boasting three towers, the northernmost being the original tower of Blacklaw, constructed more than a century ago, its walls more than six feet thick. A strongly fortified entrance with two flanking gate towers met any person coming over the range of hills, which shielded the castle from any southerly view. The castle and grounds were particularly intended to impress, with iron-grated doors, ancient tapestries said to have been woven by the first female Craigs, secret doors and passageways, and its loudly creaking drawbridge, which usually roused the entire house and village at dawn each day.

The land surrounding Blacklaw was most favorable, fertile and thickly populated with trees, sturdy pines and downy birch; having not one but two rivers, with clear and rapid currents that flowed across the demesne; in the hills and forests grew wild fruits and onions, and an abundance of heather and curative mosses.

Ava loved every inch of her home, but she particularly liked a notable spot upon one of the north-easterly hills, a small ledge that stuck out from the braeside, where few trees grew, and her gray dawn might be met amiably any morning she wished. It was not so easy to slip out and greet the dawn as she once might have and did. The advent of two bairns in two years allowed her little solitude. She did not mind at all those ties that bound her close to the keep now but certainly looked forward to the day her son and daughter might run along beside her to meet the day on that ledge.

Presently, she sat inside the nursery, upon a large chair made comfortable by the addition of a down-stuffed cushion, feeding her infant daughter at her breast. She'd deposited her toddler son, wakeful and whiny, in bed with his father before she'd scooped up this darling and sought out their privacy. Ava stared lovingly at the wee bonny face of her beloved Juliane, her months' old features already so like her fathers, wearing John's scowl so much better than her brother, James, did—he was truly Ava's son—and being in possession of a magnificent pair of perfect brown eyes. If not for the dozens of people and things that would require her attention today, she'd be happy to sit with her sweet Juliane just like this, all day long.

She heard the approach of her husband and son, James' sleepy little voice asking his father where his mother was.

"She's just here, I'd wager," said John, pushing open the door, padding barefoot and bare-chested into the nursery. "Aha, and so I was right." John winked at her, holding two year old James at his chest. Playfully, he lowered James so that his mother could kiss him again this morn but drew him back when the toddler stretched out his arms for her. "Stuck with me, lad, until your sister is fed."

"Mama," pleaded James, staring enviously at his sister.

"Soon, love," she said, leaning her head against the back of the chair, letting her gaze wander admiringly over John's naked chest before meeting his gaze. "Innes was looking for you already," she advised.

Lightly, he chided, "Dinna be ruining my morn and this sumptuous view by putting images of Innes in my head." He let his gaze fall happily onto her exposed breast, where their daughter suckled.

Ava teased him. "You didn't see or have enough of that last night?" She was amazed that after several years as his wife and with two bairns between them now, she could still blush at the thought of those glorious things he did to and with her in the wee hours of the night.

When James fussed a bit more, John sat on the floor with him, pulling the crate of toys closer to where he'd settled James between his legs. While he watched his son dig through the quilted fabric animals and wooden horses, John said, regarding Innes, "We've got the court today. He's anxious, naturally, his first outing as bailiff. Still, I would nae have pegged him as the fretful sort, but *Jesu*, he's been after me for days—should he say this or do that; what's expected of him; does he have the right to rule on boundary disputes; does he need my approval for determining compensation for damages." John tipped his face toward Ava and rolled his eyes.

"He'll find his place," Ava predicted gently. It had not been her idea nor at her urging that John had considered Innes for the role when Blacklaw's longtime bailiff had died at the end of last year. Her husband had come to her, had asked her opinion on the matter. She'd been thrilled, of course, but then not truly surprised. Innes had evolved over the years, had settled himself with a fine young lass, one of Blacklaw's own, Alison, who might have been the reason Innes had remained at Blacklaw when first they'd come, when John had yet been gone in service to the king.

"I dinna doubt it," John allowed now. He grinned at Ava. "I told him to settle, told him to take Alison to bed early, and spend the night relieving tension."

"You did nae!" Ava gasped, a giggle escaping.

"I did, and why nae? Told him better that than me forgoing all patience with his whimpering."

"You are incorrigible," she chastised with little heat.

"I'm too auld to be incorrigible, love," he retorted. "Stubborn, mayhap. I'll give you impatient even, always. But I ken he needs sometimes that abruptness, to steer him."

Possibly. She wasn't sure, but then she trusted John's judgment on the matter since he dealt more often with Innes these last few years than Ava did. "He'll work out though," she presumed confidently.

"Aye, he will, I have nae doubt." He lifted and bounced his leg as his son ran a wooden horse up and down his breeches. "I ken having someone I can trust is most important, and I do trust Innes."

Ava's heart was warmed by this. "I love you, John," she said, feeling that sharply at the moment.

Her husband turned one of his most handsome smiles on her, melting her as it never failed to do. "And I you, Ava."

She would have oozed further, would have expounded upon her love and how happy she was in this life, with him, at Blacklaw, and with their growing family, but that a loud knock sounded at the door, which had not been closed after John's entrance so that Hamish simply walked into the chamber.

THE LION OF BLACKLAW TOWER 339

James and Hamish's eyes lit up at the same time. Hamish was possibly James' favorite playmate, and Hamish sometimes found greater delight in her son's playthings that James himself did.

"What are you aboot?" He asked of James, his smile wide, sitting across from John so that their feet almost touched.

James did not answer but crawled away from his father, plodding the delicately carved figure over to Hamish.

When Hamish lifted his gaze covetously to the filled crate, John obligingly shoved it across the floor to him, grinning when both James and Hamish now rifled through the toys.

Nonchalantly, though Hamish didn't seem to notice things like breasts hanging out or bairns feeding, Ava pulled the plaid from the back of the chair over her shoulder, draping a portion of it over her breast and Juliane while she continued to nurse.

"Hamish, will you come with me to the kirk today?" Ava asked. "I said to Father Francis that I would help with the garden. But I will need help with James."

"Aye, Father Francis already asked," said the overgrown lad. "That's why I've come. When?"

"Shortly. After we break our fast."

Hamish continued to nod, withdrawing a goat and an ewe from the box and running them about the floor, pausing to inspect the carving of the goat.

John and Ava exchanged amused grins. Three children, she sometimes felt they had. And she loved them all.

The door was pushed open again and Innes showed himself, making a face when he saw what Ava was about.

"*Jesu*, Ava," he groused.

Unmoved by his manly discomfort, knowing nothing showed that should cause her concern, Ava took note of John's strangled expression, which clearly asked when their bairn's nursery had become a public hall.

Like Hamish, Innes didn't seem to mind that he might be interrupting quiet family time.

He flapped a sheaf of parchments, ignoring everyone else. "I'm just nae that guid yet, with the letters and numbers," he squawked at John, referring to the reading and writing lessons he'd been having for weeks now with Blacklaw's steward. "Nae for all this—and Christ, laird, there's thirty-three offenses to judge today. How are so many misdeeds and violations allowed inside one jurisdiction? This cannot stand."

"That'll be your job to figure out and correct, Innes," John advised and then reflected, "Some of those are simply carried over, held off since Mungo's passing, waiting on adjudication."

Innes frowned and nodded smartly. "Aye, and I *will* correct this. We canna have this kind of lawlessness."

Ava smiled at this, at John's lifted brows, at Innes' earnestness. Her grinned widened when Innes turned to leave, and then shot a look back at John, wondering curtly, "Are you coming?"

"I'll be down," John assured him, slanting a smirk at Ava when Innes departed. "I'm going to put a lock on this door," he threatened.

Ava knew he didn't mind at all how comfortable her friends were within the keep.

Knowing that James was happily entertained by and with Hamish, John rose to his feet. He approached Ava, leaning over her with a hand on each arm of the wide chair. He pushed aside the plaid and this time stared affectionately at his daughter. "She's just so damn perfect," he commented proudly.

Ava smiled her joy at this.

John kissed her forehead and then asked. "Have I ever told you how happy I am to bear witness to your smiles, love?"

"You may have."

"It is—they are—everything, Ava. All I need. But *Jesu*, say that I've played some part in them."

"Oh, love. You are the reason behind all my smiles, in part or in whole."

Ava sighed contentedly into the next kiss he gave her.

The End

Other Books By Rebecca Ruger

Highlander: The Legends
The Beast of Lismore Abbey
The Lion of Blacklaw Tower
The Scoundrel of Beauly Glen
The Wolf of Carnoch Cross
The Blackguard of Windless Woods
The Devil of Helburn by the Sea
The Knave of Elmwood Keep
The Dragon of Lochlan Hall
The Maverick of Leslie House
The Brute of Mearley Hold
The Rebel of Lochaber Forest
The Avenger of Castle Wick

Heart of a Highlander Series
Heart of Shadows
Heart of Stone
Heart of Fire
Heart of Iron
Heart of Winter
Heart of Ice
Heart of a Highlander Collection: Books 1,2,3
Heart of a Highlander Collection II: Book 4,5,6

Far From Home: A Scottish Time-Travel Romance
And Be My Love
Eternal Summer
Crazy In Love
Beyond Dreams
Only The Brave
When & Where

The Highlander Heroes Series
The Touch of Her Hand
The Memory of Her Kiss
The Shadow of Her Smile
The Depths of Her Soul
The Truth of Her Heart
The Love of Her Life
Highlander Heroes Collection, Books 1-3
Highlander Heroes Collection, Books 4-6
And Then He Loved Me (A Highlander Novella, Book 1)

www.rebeccaruger.com

Made in the USA
Middletown, DE
27 December 2022